DROPPING THE BALL

FROM USA TODAY BESTSELLING AUTHOR
MELANIE JACOBSON

*To Ranée Clark,
for all the cheerleading*

Chapter One

Kaitlyn

I AM STARING AT the pecs that broke my nose eight years ago.

Micah Croft's pecs.

Micah Freaking Croft.

It was inevitable that I would have ended up face-to-face with Micah Croft at some point. Austin is big, but it's not *that* big.

I had no idea it would be for work, no idea that he was the architect Madison had referred to a couple of times. That it was his store she meant we would visit. That he's the brains and vision behind her grand gala plans.

Why would I? We hadn't gotten into venue specifics yet, and whenever my sister mentioned the name "Micah" in tones ranging from excited to awestruck, it never crossed my mind that she meant the only person I've ever truly loathed.

He was the last person I would have expected to literally run into when Madison dragged me to Austin's Design District to look for ideas to "upgrade" my house.

How can this be happening? How can I be standing in a hipster heaven of repurposed furniture, face to pec with *him*?

I have theories, but truly, there's only one answer.

The universe hates me.

It is a hate so vigorous and specific that part of me respects it.

I draw a calming breath and step back, schooling my face into bland detachment as I drag my gaze up to meet the stare of Micah Croft.

Half of his mouth curves into a lazy smile. "If it isn't Kaitlyn Armstrong in the flesh."

Micah Croft makes the word "flesh" sound dirty, like I'm not standing in his merchant space wearing business slacks and my first turtleneck of September.

I would pay anything to rewind time by an hour, back to the point where Madison suggested we pop in at Remix Aesthetic to window-shop. Back to the point where I could have said no. I'd-rather-streak-the-next-board-meeting no. Pluck-me-bald no.

Would it cost me a pound of flesh? A year of my life? My ridiculous trust fund?

I'd give it all for that rewind feature.

Anything not to be standing here, right now, in front of Micah Croft.

Chapter Two

Kaitlyn

An hour ago . . .

Actually, no. To understand the problem, I have to go back at least a week. Or eight years, depending.

A week ago . . .

Daisy Buchanan kneads my pregnant sister's belly, and Madison lets her.

"Down, Daisy," I tell my gray-striped cat. It's a fitting name for a cat rescued from a club called Gatsby's. She's taken over Madison's lap while my sister sits on my linen sofa, one of the few pieces of furniture I've ordered. Daisy pays me no mind. "Madison, push her off. You're the boss."

"She's not bothering me." Madison looks right past Daisy, as if my cat isn't three inches from her face.

"I'm not worried about Daisy bothering you. I'm worried about her bothering . . ." I frown at Madison. "Does that baby have a name yet?"

She lifts her hand, a lazy gesture, as if naming her child is a minor matter. "I still have four weeks. You can call her Harper today, if you want."

They've been trying names a few weeks at a time. Last month, it was Mae, and before that, Ivy.

Daisy deigns to give me a glance over her shoulder before she goes back to kneading.

"Doesn't that hurt?" I ask.

"She's keeping her claws in," Madison says.

"Do your cats do that at home?"

"You know Tabitha won't mess with anyone but Oliver. Smudge, on the other hand, won't leave me alone. The second I sit down, he's on his back with his ear on my belly. The theory is that he can hear Harper's heartbeat." She scratches Daisy's head and offers me a tired smile. "You ready to do this?"

This being "take over Madison's massive job" of being the interim director of our nonprofit, Threadwork, for seven months so she can have a long maternity leave. We're meeting to go through her project binder. "I could have come over to you to review all this. I'm sure I have more energy than you do."

She grins. "Can't argue, but I wanted to see the progress on your new place." Her smile fades as she glances around the bare walls of the house I closed on two months ago.

"An Armstrong with ulterior motives? Weird." My tone is drier than the white paint she's frowning at. "I'll tell Mom to hire someone to decorate it. I don't have time, and I won't have time. Definitely not while I'm running Threadwork and studying for the bar exam. Maybe ever again, as long as I live. And I like it like that."

She tsks. "Mom is too busy with the gala, and you will be too starting next week. But lucky for you, I'm about to have a month off before my life changes forever, and I can thank you for stepping in for me by spending this month on this nekkid house."

Madison and I have been rebuilding our relationship over the last four years, and I'm used to her theatrics.

"Counteroffer: You've already said thank you four thousand times, so how about you worry about Christmas?" I say. "You have to make it extra special since it will be Harper's first one." I give her an angelic smile. "Doesn't that sound like more fun? Establishing all your own Christmas traditions? Picking out her perfect stocking? Oh, and her Christmas dress? You should do that."

"What am I, an amateur? Look at this!" She spends the next ten minutes showing me pictures of the stocking and dress she already ordered, plus an adorable tiny pink Santa hat and a small, flocked Christmas tree for the nursery already decorated with gold and pink ornaments for the baby. "I even have ones that say Harper, Mae, and Ivy so we're ready to go as soon as we decide on the name."

"I can't. It's so cute!"

"I know. Now about your house—"

"Yeah, but Halloween." Still trying to divert her. "She'll be a month old. You'll need a costume."

She shows me a picture of a baby in a hedgehog costume.

"Stop it." It really is so cute, I can't stand it.

"No, you stop," she says. "Stop avoiding this. We're talking about your house."

"I don't want to talk about wall paint. I want to talk about New Year's and the gala. I want you to bring me up to speed, so I can tackle it *now*." I clap my hands on *now* to match her theatrics, and Daisy flinches and glares at me.

"Get off Harper's head, and I won't do it again," I tell the cat.

"I think that's her bum, not her head," Madison says. "But believe it or not, because I'm brilliant even as this fetus drains my energy like an adorable baby vampire, your drab house and the gala are about to intersect in a way that can only be described as fate."

See? Dramatic. "Is this a trick to make me talk about paint color?"

"Nope. In fact, let's start with the New Year's gala, and you'll see."

I flip open my portfolio—a ridiculous Tom Ford design, the leather embossed to look like crocodile—and pull out the Montblanc pen my parents had included when they gifted me the set after my law school graduation in May.

I settle into my chair and nod, ready to take copious notes. "Go." I've been working part-time at Threadwork since the beginning of the year, but my focus has been on operations. Madison started Threadwork two years ago to rectify the wrongs done in the past by our family's ready-made garment factories in Bangladesh, and that's where I spent the summer, getting up to speed on what we fund, like microloans for entrepreneurs. But the biggest thing was learning the ropes at the Marigold Institute, our job retraining center for factory workers who want to advance or change careers.

"Mom is a beast," Madison begins. It's a compliment, something I wouldn't have thought possible a few years ago. "She's pulled in her best people from the symphony and museum boards. They're busy making it the prestige event of the holiday season and selling out their hundred-thousand-dollar tables. Sami and Pixie Luna will do an acoustic set." That's her best friend whose band is wrapping up their first summer stadium tour. "You'll never guess who we got to emcee."

"Give me a hint."

She puts on an announcer voice and says, "The star of stage and screen, she's broken your heart performing her bluegrass-infused songs of love gone wrong on *Austin City Limits* and made you laugh from the soundstage of her smash sitcom, 'Country Comes to Town.' It's—"

"Sara Elizabeth is doing it?" This is huge. Madison nods, and I cheer. "That's amazing!"

"She said she owed us a favor for signing her as the spokesperson for Copperhead Boots." That was the first and most iconic Armstrong brand, started over a hundred years ago.

"We probably shouldn't tell her that she's the one who did us a favor," I say.

"Exactly. Let's see . . . what else. Oh, do you remember the gala theme?"

"Discovery," I say. It's supposed to be Met Gala meets Austin, but Madison wants it to focus on a different area of fashion industry reform each year. Except make it glam. This year, guests' gowns must be by designers from underrepresented markets.

"Yes, and you already picked your designer, right? Wouldn't want you stuck in something off the rack," she says, smirking.

We buy off the rack, of course. They're just very expensive racks. Is it pretentious? Maybe. But it's mostly the consequence of growing up in fashion.

"I went with Maheen too," I say. Maheen Sultana is the Bangladeshi designer Madison and Mom had chosen. "Keep it in the family and all. She took my measurements when I was in Dhaka, and we did a pattern fitting before I left. She'll come up a month early to do fittings for you and Mom."

"Good, because I have no idea what size I'll be in three months for the gala." She rubs her belly again. "All our other spotlight designers are booked for couture dresses too."

"Love it." It means so much income and exposure for them. Couture dresses are handcrafted, taking anywhere from a hundred hours for simpler pieces to thousands of hours for a royal wedding gown. (When we went to Givenchy for one of my sorority formals, the designer who did Meghan Markle's dress told us the train alone took five hundred hours.) Maheen had a small team of tailors and seamstresses working on my dress, all of them being paid from the ten thousand dollars I would have spent on a couture gown in Paris. "You mainly want me to focus on the silent auction?"

Madison nods. "And this is where your house enters the picture. The architect for the gala also makes upcycled custom furniture, and—"

"Madison, I don't want to live in an arts-and-crafts project."

"Baby sister, I am *offended*," she says. "As if I would ever suggest that for your fancy-pants sensibilities. It's not what you're picturing. This guy's thing is reducing construction waste, so he reclaims things like wood and tile from construction demolitions to repurpose them into new pieces. You'll understand when you see it, but his aesthetic is exactly right for your house. So congratulations on having a date with me to check out his showroom on Saturday."

"I don't have time—"

"You never do," she says. "Yet when have I lost one of these arguments?"

I look at her like she's grown a second head.

She is currently growing a second head, technically.

"You lose at least half the time," I say. We're equally stubborn.

"Let me rephrase. When have I lost one of these arguments since I've been pregnant?" As if she can sense another objection coming, she changes strategy. "I want to spend time with you while I still can. Let me do your house."

I snort. "You're having a kid, not defecting to North Korea."

"My dearly beloved only sister, I am nesting. I have done everything I can in our house, and Oliver might short-circuit if I make one more change. Your place is the perfect project for me before I push this watermelon out of my—"

"Fine!" I shake my head, unable to fight a smile. If I'm going to carve out free time for anyone, it's Madison. "Yes, you transparent puppeteer, you can do my house. I'll go with you on Saturday."

And that's how I end up in Micah Croft's showroom, staring at the pecs. The Pecs. *The Pecs.*

Chapter Three

Kaitlyn

I STRUGGLE TO FIND my composure as I stand here in front of Micah Croft. No luck, so I fake it by offering him a smile.

Had Madison sneezed when we walked out of her house today? I learned about a Bengali superstition in Bangladesh this summer that sneezing when someone walks out of the house brings bad luck. Running into Micah, unprepared, is the worst luck I've had in ages.

"Hello, Micah." I can't fake my emotions, but I'm a pro at hiding them. I'm sure my face shows about as much life as my bare walls do. Curse those bare walls and this moment they've led me to.

"You know each other." Madison acts like I've just won a jackpot, not run into a former classmate after several years.

"Micah was the class valedictorian," I say. "We go way back."

Madison's eyes widen for a split second. She'd been out of the house for three years by the time I graduated, but even she had heard my furious rants about having to settle for salutatorian at the last minute. She keeps her smile in place. "I didn't realize you went to Hillview, Micah."

She's saying this for me, letting me know that she's aware of the situation—*now*.

"High school doesn't usually come up when people are looking to hire an architect." Micah's tone is relaxed. Of course it's relaxed. It's always relaxed. It was one of the most irritating things about him. The *most* irritating was that gleam in his light brown eyes, like he was laughing at me but I didn't know why, and it's happening now. Again.

"Guess not. So lucky we ran into you today," Madison says. "You would have met next week anyway, but now we've got a jump on introductions."

Did Micah know I was involved with Threadwork when Madison hired him? Would knowing he'd eventually work with me have made him more or less likely to take the job?

"Yeah, lucky," Micah repeats. The trace of humor in his tone makes me realize that I have been standing here barely two feet from his muscles, almost frozen, for at least a full minute.

Crap, it's high school all over again.

I take a step back so fast that the heel of my boot catches on the edge of the jute rug we're standing on and I stumble. I probably would have landed on my butt except Micah grabs my elbow and holds me until I'm steady.

High school. All. Over. Again.

"You good?" he says, and even though his expression is concerned, I have no doubt there's another laugh lurking in there.

"I'm great." I smooth my hands down the tweed of my slacks and force my mind to focus. I'm an adult now. With an important job. And nothing to prove. And he's standing here in jeans and a beat-up-looking gray T-shirt. In fact, I am Micah's client, which means for right now I'm essentially his boss.

This helps me locate my spine, which I straighten the tiniest bit, as if it will close the height gap between us. I'm five feet six, but even in three-inch heels, Micah towers over me. I hate noticing all these things when I don't want to. How he's filled into that height, shoulders and chest broad, jeans skimming over muscled thighs. Dark hair tidier now, but still on the verge of being too long. He's Jacob Elordi minus three inches and make his jaw normal. His reedy emo teen self might have appealed to adolescent tortured poets, but his grown self?

His grown self is so much worse. Not reedy. Not emo. Very, very grown.

Boss, I remind myself. I can handle this.

"You're an architect," I say. "I didn't know that's what you were interested in."

"You didn't know much about me at all." He says it without any bite.

Madison's eyes dart between us. She can read a room better than anyone I know, but there's more history here than she realizes, so I need to steer the conversation.

"My sister suggested we come check out Remix for some interior work I need done." I glance around his showroom. Even though it's a galling sort of irony that Madison thinks Micah Croft's aesthetic would fit me best, I'm satisfied to see she's wrong. It's a smaller showroom, but it's still filled with conflicting styles, a hodgepodge of pieces a more generous person might call "eclectic."

Design Row is basically an upscale mall except they call the spaces "showrooms," and it's only for home interiors. The showroom next door is nothing but kitchen faucets, and the showroom across from Remix Aesthetic is all ceiling fans.

"Is it hard to compete with Only Fans over there?" Madison asks.

I refrain from rolling my eyes. Sure, I *thought* the joke, but of course she has no problem *making* it.

Micah laughs, a low, rich rumble, and the hairs at the nape of my neck stand up.

I can't believe my body is having unauthorized reactions to him after all this time. I have got to get out of here. "You have some interesting work, but I need a different direction. Good to see you."

I turn to leave, but Madison snags my wrist and gives it a gentle tug. "Since we've lucked into running into the owner himself, why don't you show us some of your favorite pieces? I'm thinking statement pieces, like a dining table to start. Once we have that, I can pick colors and accents to complement it."

"Always a good move." Micah fixes me with a thoughtful look.

I want to twitch. Scratch suddenly itchy spots. Shift from foot to foot. Instead, I slide my hands into my pockets like the spotlight of his light brown eyes isn't pinning me in place.

As if he's reached a conclusion, he gives a brief nod and switches his gaze to Madison. "Scandinavian, natural textures, muted tones?"

Madison's eyes dart from his to mine to his again, a small smile curving her lips. "Got it in one," she says in a tone of approval.

What? No. No approval. I do not approve of my sister and my high school archnemesis summing up my style in a single guess. I do not approve of Micah's tone when he says "muted." It feels like an insult.

I curl my hands into fists in my pockets where they can't see me do it. "I'd prefer something besides fancy IKEA."

Micah smiles. "I offer literally the opposite of disposable furniture. Why don't we go take a look?"

Without waiting for an answer, he turns and heads toward the other side of the showroom while Madison mouths, *Be nice*.

Easy for her to say. Her past did not just come back to haunt her.

Freshman Year

In which Micah appears . . .

I SHOULDN'T BE NERVOUS. It's the first day of school on the campus I've attended for three years. But that was the middle school. Today I start at the upper school. It's on a completely different part of the grounds, and since many kids don't start at Hillview until high school, there will be at least one new face for every face I know.

One more step puts me officially on the upper school grounds, other students streaming past me from the parking lot and into the school like that last step—first step?—isn't a big deal.

How many of them will know about the scandal surrounding our family? How many of my classmates will rush to tell the ones who don't know?

A flash of purple catches my eye as Madison—finally done touching up her makeup in the car—passes me. She's wearing metallic leggings and a black corset top, crappy quality that I know she hates. When she came downstairs to drive us to school, Mom said, "This is not who we are."

Madison had shrugged. "It was made in one of our factories. It's exactly who we are."

The outfit is a protest, and Mom doesn't say anything else because we both know the next line out of Madison's mouth if Mom keeps pushing. *You're lucky I'm going to school at all.* She tried to drop out of Hillview for public school over the summer to make a point that she wasn't going to take our parents' "dirty" money. They had to threaten to pull the Armstrong endowment that funded scholarship students at Hillview to make her stay.

It's been like this since the factory collapse last year. If she and Dad aren't in a shouting match about it, her silent treatments are just as deafening.

As she disappears into the building, I glance down at myself to make sure I've done everything I can to deflect the attention Madison goes looking for. Khakis. Polo shirt. Hair in a ponytail. Nothing to see here.

I head straight into the bathroom and find a stall to hide in. As soon as I lock the door, my bestie chat lights up.

MEGAN

Grrrrls. We have cute new boyzzzzz.

LULU

I've seen 3

MEGAN

Where are you Kaitlyn

I'm supposed to meet them by the lockers we were assigned last week during upper school orientation, but walking the halls right now feels like volunteering for a public shaming, and I can't.

Stomachache. See you at lunch.

MEGAN

First day nerves. Sorry about Chinese!

That's my first class. The hardest language ever, but Dad thinks it'll be good for me to learn it so I can communicate with our Chinese suppliers when I start working for the company. Lulu was going to take it with me, but she can't because she's Chinese and already fluent in Mandarin, so the school said no. Bad enough I have to take it by myself, but having it first period? Not how I want to start my first day of high school: in a subject I don't know except for what I tried to practice on Duolingo this summer.

I stay in the stall until the bell rings, and then I slip out, eyes on the ground, and head to class.

The teacher asks our names and seats us alphabetically. I slide into mine and watch the other kids file in. I watch the new kids especially, most of them coming in with smiles, some real, some hiding nerves. Except one kid. One kid who comes in wearing a hoodie and jeans despite the late summer heat. And Vans fraying at the toe. Strong "I don't care about impressing you" energy. Is it real or an act?

He tells the teacher his name is Micah Croft. Ah. He's probably related to that Croft girl in Madison's class. Their family owns a NASCAR team or something. He gives me a tiny nod as he walks down the row next to me to his desk, and for a split second . . .

The universe glitches.

Meeting his eyes creates the tiniest friction, enough for my brain to capture and imprint his face. Thin with high cheekbones, dark hair, light brown eyes in a thick fringe of eyelashes, and his mouth? It doesn't look like it smiles much.

I drop my gaze without returning the nod. I'm not stepping out of my safety bubble until I'm very sure who I'm dealing with.

As if starting with Chinese by myself on the first day isn't bad enough, Drake Braverman walks in.

I slouch, hoping there's a new kid coming between A-r-m and B-r-a, but the teacher points him to the seat behind me.

"It's Chinese, not death row," Drake says as he passes me. "Smile, Kaitlyn."

I do not smile.

I survive the day. If people are gossiping about me, they keep it low-key.

Only a hundred seventy-nine days to go.

Chapter Four

Kaitlyn

I TRAIL AFTER MADISON and Micah, annoyed with myself for doing it, like they're equals and I'm the tagalong. Micah is my age, *my* former classmate. Why do I feel like a little kid?

He stops at a table for eight and says, "What do you think about this one?"

Madison's happy gasp is her answer as she trails a finger over its edge, but I take a minute to walk the table's perimeter as Micah describes it.

"It's made from a conference table from an office building teardown, but I upgraded the top."

"What is it?" Madison asks, running her hand over the shiny surface. It's a creamy tone with a swirling design of amber bits running through it, but the pattern feels controlled and organic all at once, and I'm trying to think of what it reminds me of.

"This is recycled glass tile in resin," he says. "The tile is from an executive washroom in the same building. I had it in my workshop for a few months until I saw a murmuration of starlings, and then I figured out what to do with it."

That's it. All of a sudden, I see it, how each piece of amber glass is like an individual bird in a flock, but as a whole, they're moving as one in the hypnotic, fluid curves of a murmuration when hundreds, even thousands, of starlings swoop and swirl through the sky.

In a word, it's gorgeous, and I want it.

But I don't want it to be from Micah Croft.

"Glorious." That's Madison's word for it. "I didn't see this last time I was here."

"I turn over a lot of pieces now that I have the showroom," he says. "As soon as one sells, I move in the next one."

I survey the surrounding pieces more carefully. A mid-century style credenza. A rustic farmhouse coffee table. An ultramodern accent cabinet. "You made all of this?"

"Yeah. Started as a side hustle in college and turned into therapy." He shrugs. "I only work with recovered construction material, which is why the styles differ. I'm not in control of what I'll be able to salvage. Each piece has to make its own sense, so they're not cohesive. But when someone has the eye . . ."

He doesn't have to finish that sentence with the words *unlike you*. I can hear them as if he yelled them, and I try not to flush.

He's calling me out for my dig about a "different direction" and "fancy IKEA," but I've learned a survival tactic to fight a blush: turn the embarrassment into anger. That's one of Dad's lessons. *Never stay on defense.*

Except I like to keep my emotions in a specific range, so I default to irritation over anger. Anger is messy, and I am never messy.

I pull one of my hands out of my pockets and tap the tabletop, like I'm checking its soundness, the click of my red fingernail satisfying in the relative quiet of the store. "Not bad for scavenging."

"Salvaging," Micah says, like I don't know the right term.

I chose "scavenge" on purpose. "Right, salvage. Like junk cars people can donate."

"I don't think those cars are worth twelve thousand dollars," Madison says, examining the price tag hanging near her corner.

She knows cost isn't an issue, and I'm sure that would cover the price of a single chair at my parents' dining table, but it does tell me that Micah's pieces are in demand. Not a surprise since I wanted this piece desperately the second I saw it. But he won't get the satisfaction of knowing it. I steal Micah Croft's most defining gesture and shrug. "I'll take it."

Madison does a shimmy. I think it's supposed to be a happy dance, but she probably can't get her midsection in motion without knocking herself over like an unbalanced washing machine. "Good choice, Katie-Kat. I'll be able to pull together such a pretty dining room around this."

"I don't want pretty," I tell her. The word conjures delicate floral wallpaper and scrolled furniture. "I want—"

"Serene," she says. "I know. I *know* you." Our eyes meet, and a collection of contentment molecules in my chest organizes into a murmuration of its own, because even though it's taken time, we've grown as tight as sisters should be.

"Do you want to look at any other pieces?" Micah asks.

The answer is yes, I want to look at more pieces. Now that I understand how he works, I want to see and study every single piece in this place. I want to guess its inspiration, see if I can figure out how his brain was working when he made it.

Which makes me sound like I'm reviving a high school crush. It was never like that. Except for most of my senior year. But that crush lasted exactly as long as it took to break my nose.

"No time to look right now," I answer him, a half second after the silence gets awkward. I am Cool Kaitlyn, and I am not excited about his eclectic wonderland.

"Then I'll have my assistant handle your purchase and schedule delivery for you," Micah says. He waves down at his casual outfit. "I only stopped in to grab something from the back room, so I need to get back to my workshop."

Oh no he isn't. He is not going to one-up me on who ends this interaction. *I* am ending this interaction, and he's trying to beat me to it.

"I have somewhere to be too, unfortunately," I say. "I'll send my own assistant over to handle this purchase next week."

"I can't hold it past Monday night," he says.

"I'll let her know. We better get going, Madison." I turn to walk past my sister, who is trying to hide her confusion.

Micah falls into step beside me. "Sounds good."

I reach back to snag Madison's wrist and pull her along, not slowing down even a tiny bit. I *will* beat Micah out of this store.

"Do you have a website with all your available pieces?" Madison asks, hustling to keep up.

"I do."

"Great. Katie's doing a minimalist thing right now, by which I mean she has exactly one room furnished, so I'll set up operations in her moonscape of a house and look at your stuff online to figure out what else to put in there."

Micah's designs moving into my home . . . It gives me that exposed feeling again. I'm shivering in my emotional SKIMS while Madison plots to spend thousands of my dollars on making my house a shrine to Sir Pectoralis Nosebreaker.

I pick up my pace, feeling guilty for forcing Madison to keep up, but I'll make it up to her. We'll stop for a half gallon of her new obsession, Blue Bell gooey butter cake ice cream. I don't want to live in a world where they discontinue it before her pregnancy is over.

When we reach the entrance, I sense Micah veering left, which is the way we need to go, but I guide Madison toward the right.

"Good to see you," Micah says. "It's been too long."

I glance at him over my shoulder, like I'd already forgotten he was there. "Oh, yes. You too. See you around."

But what I mean is *It's been too soon.*

Way, way too soon.

I walk as fast—but casually—as I can in the opposite direction until we round a corner, then I stop. *I literally ran into Micah Croft.*

"Why are you speedwalking your waddling sister like we're running from the mob?"

Madi's breathing is labored—uh, make that a bit heavy—and yes, she's waddling, but it's cute. Even pregnant, Madison's the hotter version of me. Imagine a bombshell blonde—Margot Robbie—glammed up on the cover of *Vogue*, full lips pouty, blue eyes sparkling. That's Madison. By contrast, I'm . . . like a serious Elle Fanning. Imagine someone painting Madison as a subdued Victorian-style portrait, the blue of her eyes muted, thinner lips, flatter hair. You'd see it and think, *She's probably pretty when she smiles.*

I am. And I do smile. When I have a good reason to.

"You aren't waddling," I tell her.

"Liar. Did we just run away from Micah?"

I scoff. "Pfft. No."

Her eyebrows go up.

"Fine, yes."

Her face loses some of its laughter. "Are you going to be okay working with him?"

"Of course." Not. Of course not. "Don't even worry about it. Let's go to the car." I slip my arm through hers to turn us in the right direction.

"Katie, you're going to make this weird with him, aren't you?"

"Oh my gosh. Settle down. I will not make it weird."

I will. No question about it. It's never on purpose, and that's the whole problem.

Freshman Year

In which it gets worse . . .

I'M ONE PERCENT LESS nervous on the second day of school. I kind of know what to expect, at least from teachers. I don't have to force myself to walk onto campus. I might have succeeded in becoming a beige shadow of myself to my classmates, but just in case, after I walk in with Megan and Lulu, I hide in the bathroom again before first period.

I'm first in my seat. The new Croft kid comes in a minute later, still in his ratty Vans and dark hoodie, although this time he's swapped jeans for basketball shorts. Guess he's done dressing up. His long legs are thin but muscled beneath tanned skin.

Why do I notice? *Stop*.

His eyes flicker to mine, but there's no nod today. I hope he didn't notice me staring at his shins. He goes to his desk and slouches, hands in his hoodie pocket.

Drake comes in a minute before the bell. He says, "Smile, Kaitlyn," again, but this time he brushes against me. He's looking for a reaction. I lean slightly away. I don't smile.

This is going to become the low point of each morning. Maybe other kids would think hiding to eat their lunch or reviewing book-length class syllabi is the low point, but no. It's Drake in Chinese class.

The third day, the new kid doesn't even look at me before he slouches into his chair. How many days in a row can he wear that hoodie? I do catch a faint whiff of Acqua di Gio as he passes because Hillview is more Armani than Axe. Either way, he smells like he cares at least a little.

Drake walks in seconds before the tardy bell and stops beside my desk. "Hey, Kaitlyn." I look up at him because it's the least amount of encouragement I can give him. "You should smile more."

I answer by leaning the other way to pull my class notebook out as the bell rings. I do not smile. This time his friends laugh, and my body goes too hot with a dump of adrenaline, urging me to go hide in the bathroom. I stay put, but this "smile, Kaitlyn" is becoming a thing, and I don't want it to be a thing.

By Thursday, I'm dreading first period. Not only do I keep catching myself staring at some new detail on that Micah kid every morning when he walks in, I am in the dumbest power struggle ever with Drake. Now that his friends are paying attention, he's going to step it up. All I have to do to make it stop is smile, even sarcastically.

I sit down. The new kid comes in a minute later in his hoodie and shorts. A thin leather bracelet peeks from under his cuff. Drake shows up right before the final bell again. He pauses to say, "Smile, Kaitlyn."

I do not. I keep my eyes straight ahead, watching the second hand on the clock, but while Drake stands there waiting for a reaction, I scratch my eyebrow with my middle finger.

Two of Drake's friends sit ahead of Micah. One snorts and says, "You got cooked, Drake." The other one makes a kissing sound.

After roughly a century, the bell rings. I let out a quiet breath. I made it.

Except Drake isn't letting it go today. As Mrs. Meyers—uh, Meyers-laoshi—takes us through our pronunciation drill, Drake leans over and says, "Your outfit is fire." His friend next to us gives a muffled snort.

Right. My white polo and gray chinos. So fire. I ignore him.

But he keeps up his stupid freshman boy crap. The next time the teacher isn't looking, he sniffs and says, "Mmm. Is that perfume or your skin?" From the corner of my eye, I catch his friend giving him a fist bump.

Halfway through class, Meyers-laoshi gives us the option of working quietly or alone with a partner to practice the three sentences we've learned so far. I choose alone.

Drake uses the cover of the low chatter to lean all the way into my space and say, "You're so hot." His friends laugh and bump knuckles.

I hate this. I ask permission to get water and leave to fill my almost-full water bottle. When I get back, I'm in my seat less than a minute when I hear a different voice.

"I like your hair." It's low. Quiet. I glance back. It's the new kid.

My hair is the color of . . . nothing. Of dust. Of the grit that blows across West Texas during the winter. Of oatmeal and burlap and old stucco. I don't do anything with my nothing-colored hair except wear it in a ponytail to keep it neat.

The new guy saying I have good hair is like telling a Kardashian that no one notices the Botox.

So he's one of them.

Great. Got it.

Chapter Five
Micah

KAITLYN FREAKING ARMSTRONG.

It finally happened.

I'd realized a month after she hired me that Madison Locke was Madison Armstrong Locke, and I'd probably cross paths with Kaitlyn again. I've known since late spring when Madison announced her pregnancy that I would finish this project with Kaitlyn.

I've known for two weeks that I had a meeting coming up with her. I've looked forward to it, even.

But that did not prepare me to see her standing in my showroom today, her eyes running over my furniture, assessing it, no hints of her opinion on her face.

I open the door to my truck and toss a folder on the passenger seat, buckling up. It had been exactly like high school in the worst ways. But also in the best one.

Crack a joke that makes her mad? Check.

Play it cool while I get a read on her? Check.

Wish I could sketch her, even as she frowns at me? Check.

But also . . .

Want her to respect my work? Check. And then she does? Check.

She bought Starling.

I've debated pulling that table from the showroom to save for my own home, but although I live comfortably, I'm not comfortable enough to walk away from a twelve-thousand-dollar sale. I'd half banked on it being too unconventional for anyone to want it.

Kaitlyn Armstrong wants it. She tried to play it off like she was picking up a card table from Target, but I'd become an expert in reading Kaitlyn during our four years at Hillview, and I'm still fluent. Wonder had flickered across her expression when I'd mentioned starlings.

That's how well I know her face. Not sure how I feel about being able to read it like no time has passed.

I pull out of the parking lot and head toward home, replaying our showroom interaction in my mind. She still has a classic vibe, but with new details.

Kaitlyn hadn't been the kind of girl a guy would catcall. She was buttoned-up and serious. Even though Hillview is the most elite private school in Austin, they don't require uniforms, but that had almost been Kaitlyn's aesthetic. She'd been a jeans-and-Oxford-shirt kind of girl.

She's still slender, but with subtle curves. Her hair is shorter, falling to her chin in a sleek, shiny curtain, like varnished beech.

She'd been wearing a thin black turtleneck and slacks. And yet-cI've seen women in little black dresses—very little black dresses—that weren't as sexy as Kaitlyn had just been, covered almost head to toe.

Her posture is different too, poised but not at all tense. I might not have recognized her if it weren't for one big tell: the familiar disdain in her eyes.

Pure Kaitlyn, vintage grades nine through twelve. Also vintage: the strong suspicion she tried to make leaving the store into a race.

I'm sorry she feels like I ruined her chance at valedictorian, but the incident she blames me for? I didn't cause it. In fact, I was the first one to her side to make sure she got help. And as for beating her GPA, it was a fair fight all the way down the line.

Which means even with the disdain, our run-in is a good thing. It's given me a chance to see for myself that she's doing well, and maybe I'll be able to set the record straight as we keep meeting.

Maybe I'll even be able to get us on a different footing. Wish my footing today wasn't my beat-up Vans and woodshop clothes, but I can't sweat that now.

I pull into my driveway and park. The garage could hold two cars—if it weren't my main workspace. I hit the opener and climb out, grabbing the folder I needed and head inside the garage. It's full but organized, walkable aisles between my workbenches, tools lined up against one wall, odds and ends sorted against the other.

This had been plenty of room when I started upcycling furniture during college, and by the time I graduated four years ago, I was selling things as fast as I could make them. But I could only make things when I had salvage to work with, so I'd put out the word to my boys, and they started bringing me so much scrap that I had to put up sheds in the backyard to hold it.

The garage itself is the workshop. It always smells like woodworking chemicals and sawdust in here, and if I had to describe the scent of happiness, that's it. The faint acrid odor of the paint stripper might make other people's noses wrinkle, but for me, it triggers something in my body that tells it to relax.

I set the folder on the table where I do most of my mosaic work and pull out the pictures. They're from an elderly client, Mrs. Davenport, who prefers giving me reference photos the old-fashioned way—neatly clipped from magazines at the library when the librarians aren't watching. I'd suggested she could tell me the magazine issue and I could look it up online, no clipping required. She'd reassured me that she only chose issues that were about to expire anyway.

Never mind that she lives in a mansion her departed husband bought forty years ago. Never mind that she has a full-time gardener who also serves as her handyman and the driver of her beautiful old Mercedes. Never mind that she's commissioned me to make a mosaic water feature for her backyard that will cost her five thousand dollars. Mrs. Davenport still only buys groceries on double-coupon day, stores all her leftovers in old Country Crock tubs, and steals her expensive design ideas from magazines at the public library.

The door leading from the house opens.

"Hey, Ma," I say as she stands on the threshold. She's wearing the same sweatpants and Pepsi T-shirt she had on yesterday. "You good?"

Her gaze skitters around the garage before landing on me, and I stifle a sigh. She'll say she's fine, but it's not one of her good days.

"Fine, I'm fine." Her tone is irritated, like I'm prying. "It's a mess in here."

It's not. Full of stuff, yes. But everything has its place. Even things that might look like junk won't be for long. But this is a losing argument, and it's not why she wandered out here.

"Do you need help with something?" I ask.

"No." It's sharp. "Can't I come out here to see you?"

"Of course." I proceed carefully here, because she will look for every reason to turn this into a fight. "How are your orders going?"

"Why? You want to tell me how much more stuff you're selling?"

"Nah, I'll never get as many orders as you do." She sells wooden peg dolls online, customized for different families or teams. In early fall, she switches to doing nativity characters only, and she's four times busier than the rest of the year.

"Don't have a boss, don't need a boss." She jabs her thumb at her chest. "I'm an untrained genius. I built a business without all the extra college and training. If I'd gone to college like you, *I* would be the one making all the money. Don't forget that. One day, the right set of eyes will see my work, and then you'll see that I'm the real deal."

"I know you're the real deal—" I say but she steps back into the house, shutting the door harder than she needs to.

I rub my head, feeling a tension headache starting. I've noticed a couple of other signs that her meds might need adjusting, but a call to Dr. Karumbaya can probably wait until Monday morning.

I pull my phone from my pocket and turn the ringer on before I set it on the workbench. I'll be tiling the basin of Mrs. Davenport's water feature, and it's the kind of work that will absorb me as I ponder the placement of each mosaic piece, making minute tweaks.

I doubt Mom will leave the house today, but if she does, I don't want to miss a call from a neighbor letting me know.

The broken pieces of glass from a corporate office call to me, begging to be rearranged from senseless shards into an Impressionist-style basin for the water to splash into before it's reclaimed and sent back through the pump to spill over again. And again.

A thump reverberates from inside the house, probably a chair getting knocked over. Again.

And again.

Freshman Year

In which Micah does not make it better . . .

ON MONDAY, NO ONE talks to me. *Yes.*

Drake seems to have lost interest in his game over the weekend. With no one to impress, Micah leaves me alone too.

It already means the second week of school is starting better, and it only improves when the morning announcements advise that the school media center is now open. They say "media center," other students say "library," and I say "place to eat lunch without being bothered."

Megan and Lulu make me eat lunch with them at least once a week, but we compromise by eating out on the grounds beneath a cedar tree. The other days, I have my own lunch retreat in the library to study and reset. Every now and then, other students will come in, but always solo, always finding their way to their own table/life preserver/Formica oasis.

It's a perfect plan for two whole weeks—until a new scandal breaks about my dad, accusing him and the company of stealing wages. Big news outlets follow the story, but it's a scroll-way-down type thing. Not in Austin. Here it's a front-page headline and top of the evening news. There is no scandal tastier than a homegrown scandal, so they make sure to air it on Monday and flog it for the rest of the week. Austin is a very anti-capitalist city for a town that runs on capital. Hypocrites.

The coverage is more slanted than the angles we've been solving for in geometry all week. Dad came home the day the story broke and told us that it was a major distortion of the facts and explained what really happened.

Madison turned it into an argument, of course, using sound bites from the news to convict him. I tuned her out because she's jumping to the conclusions the media wants her to draw, but she should know better.

Between the fights at home and the definite side-eye from people in the hall between classes, this library goes from retreat to fortress.

A fortress that Micah Croft breaches, ambling in like the twenty square feet of empty tables and carpet around me aren't a moat of metaphorical lava meant to discourage random ambling.

No, he ambles up in his Vans, the right toe starting to fray now.

He stops at the other side of the table. "Kaitlyn?"

I glance around like I'm checking for other people before meeting his eyes. "I guess so."

"Right. I know you're Kaitlyn. Kaitlyn Armstrong, right?"

I raise my eyebrows and wait. So help me, if he tells me to smile, I'm shoving this table into his scrawny chicken thighs.

"I'm Micah."

"I know."

"That day, um." He taps the table with his knuckle a few times. "I meant it when I said I like your hair. In Chinese class."

Like I'm not going to remember. Does he really think I'm going to trust that this isn't another trick? He was volunteering at the table for the World Without Exploitation Youth Coalition earlier this week during campus club rush. What are the chances he's suddenly bringing up the hair comment two weeks later, exactly when our company is once again being falsely accused of exploitation?

None. The chances are none.

I roll my eyes and push back my chair.

"Wait, I mean it," he says.

I stand and hitch my backpack over my shoulder. "You said that. I believe you."

He pauses. "You don't."

"I don't." I push in my chair hard enough for it to make a soft clatter when it hits the table. I wish I had something besides sarcasm to rely on. A snappy insult. A way to make him the butt of a joke like Drake made me. But all I've got is silence and retreat, so I use them both.

He calls, "Bye?" as I walk out.

I don't look back.

Chapter Six

Kaitlyn

I'VE LEARNED NOT TO doubt my sister. Her first wedding is urban lore in Austin, and her second wedding—to the same guy—is still spoken of reverently by the good people of Cleveland County, Oklahoma, where they held it at her in-laws' horse ranch.

But my faith in her stretches to the breaking point as she pulls into the nondescript parking lot of a commercial warehouse off Highway 183 where she plans to stage the gala. Besides a Tacoma pickup with a matte blue-gray finish, there's no other sign of life. No trucks waiting to be loaded with freight. No vehicles of other workers.

"Scared yet, Katie-Kat?" Madison asks, grinning.

"Of what? Mafia guys waiting to kidnap me for ransom? No. Pulling off an event to raise a million dollars? Yes." It is blander than I could have imagined. This place doesn't have spooky vibes, which is almost a shame, because at least that would be *atmosphere*. It's just an empty warehouse with a boring off-white stucco exterior, no romance to it. Not even graffiti to keep it interesting. It is the instant rice of buildings.

"Micah is here," she says, cutting the engine. "You'll see."

"This is not the type of building I'd expect an architect to be into."

She climbs out of the car, and I follow suit. Micah gets out of his truck at the same time.

It's a much different Micah today than jeans-and-ratty T-shirt Micah from Saturday. Madison warned me that the A/C wouldn't be on in the warehouse, so to dress comfortably. Early September temperatures in Austin are approximately the same as my gym's sauna, so I chose a tailored sleeveless sheath. Micah is in black pants and a short-sleeved buttoned shirt with a black vintage map print on it. They're not tailored, but he's chosen the right size and cut for his athletic build. He's on the lean side but well muscled.

Pecs, remember?

I don't know if he's feeling the ninety-degree heat like I am, but he appears cool and collected, offering a smile as we meet up at the warehouse door.

"Good to see you, ladies," he says. "Has Madison told you what to expect?"

I nod. "I've seen the plans."

He laughs as I cast a skeptical look at the industrial gray paint on the windowless door. "Not a visualizer? Isn't that what you said, Madison?"

"Yeah," Madison agrees. "Don't take it personally if she's not catching the vision yet."

Micah's easy smile doesn't waver at all as he punches in a code on the door's electric key pad, then swings it open and waves us ahead of him. "We'll jump right into the event space."

We walk into a big, concrete box. It takes me two seconds to take it all in. Concrete floor. Aluminum walls. No shelves. Nothing to break up the grayness but support poles painted in safety orange.

Madison and Micah watch me, expectant looks on their faces.

"Madi, I know we're saving on hotel costs, but . . ." I trail off, glancing around again. It's an empty Armstrong Industries warehouse. I knew it had been leased for a few years by a company that manufactured roofing shingles, but it's been vacant since the spring. Open industrial ceiling, exposed beams, rows and rows of fluorescent lights. "Free might be too expensive for this place."

Madison throws one arm around my shoulder and stretches the other one wide. "It helps if you think of it as a blank canvas, not an empty warehouse. Micah will explain."

"I've been dying to know how an architect gets pulled into decorating for a gala," I say.

"Because your sister is a genius," he says, laidback as ever.

"And what are Armstrongs good at if not exploiting people's talents for cheap labor," she adds.

"Madison!" We can both have a dark sense of humor, but it seems incredibly insensitive to joke about exploiting Micah—especially *in front of him*.

But Micah laughs. "Let's look at this from the center of the room, and I'll paint a picture for you."

I'd dressed for battle today, wearing four-inch heels so I could chip away at his height advantage, and my shoes tap-tap-tap with a slight echo in the cavernous space as I follow him across the concrete floor.

"Did Madison show you her inspiration?" he asks, sliding his phone from his pocket.

"Church gym glow ups," I say.

"Basically," Madison says. "You know how wedding planners can make them over with tulle and lighting? I was pricing out hotel ballrooms, and every time I found myself getting furious that hotels will force you to use all their vendors and charge five times as much as things cost, I would think about those church receptions. I knew we had a big square space, so I started asking around."

I smile, knowing how Madison gets once she's set on a course of action. "What exactly were you asking around for? How did we get from wedding planner to architect?"

"People won't cough up money for church gym tickets. Definitely not warehouse tickets. We needed something buzzworthy. I watched a documentary about art installations, and it all clicked," she says. "I contacted the city arts council about locals who specialize in large-scale art installations. Then I emailed them and requested proposals, and Micah submitted his."

"Art installations?" I tilt my head, studying him. I can't decide if this fits with my high school image of him. "You didn't take art at Hillview." We weren't in every class together, but the Hillview upper school wasn't that big. Most of us knew each other's schedules without trying.

"My uncle chose my electives," Micah said. "He didn't want to pay for art, so I learned from this guy at my community center and took classes in college."

I'd known two of his cousins at Hillview, but Micah hadn't lived with them, so what did his uncle paying have to do with anything? Micah was a Croft. The Crofts had money.

As if sensing my confusion, he meets my eyes, and his hold a challenge. "I told you, Katie. There's a lot you didn't know about me in high school."

"Kaitlyn," I correct him. In college, friends had started calling me Katie, and now Madison does too sometimes. But at work, I'm Kaitlyn.

"Right." His smile fades. "Kaitlyn."

"When did you do art installations?" I press. Is Madison sure he has the experience to do something on the scale it will take to impress Austin's wealthiest residents?

My phone vibrates, and I ignore it, but Madison says, "I sent you a text so you can see it."

It's a picture of an outdoor tunnel running the length of a city block. It's formed by brightly colored arches in painted shades of blue, yellow, and orange. Origami birds hang from wires across the top and down the sides, forming the tunnel. They're arranged in a wave of color, a full rainbow gradient that makes the whole thing look like it's undulating.

"It's wild, isn't it?" Madison asks. "How they look like they're flying?"

It is. It's both epic and beautiful.

"You really like birds, huh?" That's what I say. That is what I say to this man whose work has once again moved me. I hear how snotty I sound, but it's not what I intended.

Madison shoots me a warning glance, and I clear my throat, adding, "It's cool."

"Thanks." Micah's tone is polite.

"I mean it. I didn't say that well. I'm not always the best with words." At least, not when I'm outside of a work environment. "Would you tell me about it?"

"That was my senior year at UT," he says. "The city wanted to do an art installation that reflected the diversity in Austin, so I submitted this design."

"More pictures," Madison says as my phone buzzes again.

These are closeups of the birds, and I realize now that they're made with all different kinds of paper, mostly from newspapers and magazines.

"Are these doves?" I ask Micah.

"Yes. On the nose, maybe, but it's a symbol everyone understands, and it's a simple fold to teach."

"This must have taken lots of birds to fill in," I say. There are thousands.

"Swipe," Madison says.

I do, and now it's a picture of the structure before the birds were added.

"First day it opened," he says. "I only made one dove." He leans over my shoulder to point at the screen. "If you enlarge it, you'll see mine. It's the green one right there."

I see it, a single origami bird, midway down the tunnel. His chest touches my shoulder, barely the brush of a dove feather, and he straightens and shifts away.

"People could only fold one," he explains. "We asked them to choose a piece of paper that represented something about who they are. We had newspapers and magazines from all over the world, old books, cookbooks, office memos." He gives a small, tired laugh. "I collected every paper I could find from construction demolition sites for months. Then we let people choose a piece and showed them how to fold a dove."

He's close. Close enough to smell. It's not Acqua di Gio anymore. It's better. Fresh and musky at the same time. Whatever it is, the scent is hijacking my concentration.

I focus on my phone and swipe again. The tunnel is about a quarter filled in, birds hung by color, the idea taking shape.

"More people came every day," he says. "Volunteers helped them make their bird and then chose where to hang it. It was pretty cool."

"That's my favorite part," Madison says. "Passersby made the art, and you ended up with this one massive thing built a person at a time. Do you get it now? Why Micah is the artist for this?"

I let my screen go dark and look at Micah as I slide my phone back into the pocket of my dress. "I do."

He gives me a slight nod, and I wonder what it means. Was it curt because my "you really like birds" comment annoyed him? Efficient because Micah isn't a wordy guy? Was that a "cool guy" nod?

"I solicited proposals for a gala-worthy installation for a soulless industrial space." She gestures to Micah. "His won. Easily."

"I was the cheapest," he says.

Madison narrows her eyes at him. "Don't even. Micah dug so far into the theme that his design came alive, even as a digital drawing. When I realized he wanted to use only reclaimed materials, I couldn't offer him the contract fast enough."

Micah shifts, and I swear if he'd been wearing a tie, he would have reached up to loosen his collar. "But she's not telling you that a big part of my appeal is that the architecture firm where I work is allowing me to use twenty hours a week to focus on this, starting in October."

"It's a generous subsidy, and we'll recognize them as gold sponsors," Madison tells me. "But it's not why I picked him."

Had it always been this hard for him to accept praise? I'd always thought of him as disengaged, but that's not what I'm seeing now. I'm already reinterpreting the "cool guy" head nod.

"Paint the picture, Micah." Madison's eyes are bright as she waits for Micah to do his thing.

"Think a canopy of marigolds, like you had a whole field of them but then lifted it to the ceiling." He walks us to different areas of the cavernous warehouse, showing us the illustrations for what he has in mind in each section.

Every few minutes, he stops to check with Madison, asking her the first time if she's good in the hot warehouse, checking in on her with a glance after that.

She insists she's fine, and after twenty minutes, we've covered every section of the open space, Micah explaining which materials he already has, which ones he's still sourcing, and when the installation itself will begin.

"First of October," he says.

I give him a knowing look. "Is that so Madison can't come bother you because she'll have her baby?"

"Hey," Madison protests, but Micah's eyebrows go up.

"Wait," he says, staring at her form-fitting cream knit dress. It looks like it's going to split and eject a pumpkin any second. "You're *pregnant*?"

His delivery is so deadpan that it takes Madi and me a beat to realize he's joking, and then her laugh echoes through the empty warehouse. I couldn't keep a straight face if I wanted to, but I try, giving him back his "cool guy" nod. That's what makes him break, a laugh rumbling out. It's almost more of a feeling than a sound.

"I better not still be pregnant by October first," Madison says. She looks at me. "You got this gala, right? Because I don't want to come back until this thing is a freaking Met-level wonder ready to make us a couple million dollars."

She's not really asking. Her faith in me is as complete as mine is in her, but I tell her anyway. "I got this."

"Good, because I've had to spend so much time with Micah lately that we almost put his name into the baby name rotation."

"It *is* unisex," he says.

"So is Merle," I tell him. "Doesn't make it a great choice. Kaitlyn, on the other hand . . ."

Micah frowns. "You have an unfair advantage if we're competing for who your sister should name her baby after."

The word "competing" reminds me who I'm dealing with, and my humor fades. I wouldn't have put it past old Micah to try to win that competition for real. I know he's joking now, but I'd be an idiot not to watch for the ways in which he will try to one-up me.

I'm the boss, I remind myself. I make my tone brisk and professional. "Will we need to meet again this month?"

"Depends on how hands-on you want to be," he says.

Evil glints in Madison's eyes, and I cut her off before she can make a "hands-on" joke. I say, "I manage people only as much as they need to be managed. How often have you and Madison been meeting?"

"As needed," she says. "Depends on which phase of the project we're in."

"I'll supervise as much as I need to." I choose the word *supervise* to remind him of our roles here. I expect him to bristle and tell me he doesn't require supervision like he's a kid on a playground, but he doesn't say anything. "If it looks like you have everything running smoothly, I'll leave you to it so I can focus on the fundraising side."

He nods. "I'll be in touch."

Does he have to keep using words like hands and touch? Is he doing it on purpose? Keeping me off-balance was the only hobby he'd seemed to have in school.

"You can let me know if we need to adjust the communication," he continues. "I'm sure we will."

My gaze sharpens at the last words. Something in his tone I can't quite name tells me this is a subtle dig. It's polite but also . . . not? I'm used to him laughing at me. This is not that. There's almost a weariness? boredom? irritation? in his tone. It's like the way less-seasoned sales associates in department stores sometimes handle my demanding mother. They think she won't notice their disdain—until she demands a different salesperson who will suck up to her, and they lose a massive commission. But whatever the undercurrent in his tone is, it's subtle enough that I can't call him on it either.

"Great," I say, already turning toward the exit. "I'll look forward to your updates." See? It's not that hard to avoid words about hands or touching.

"You're a genius, Micah," Madison calls behind her as she follows me to the exit.

I don't look back, walking out of the warehouse and over to the passenger side of her car, a Porsche Cayenne she upgraded to from her smaller Mercedes because she needs a "mom car" now.

The heavy steel door clangs shut on the warehouse, but she doesn't disarm the car. I glance over at her and sigh. She's standing with her arms crossed, her eyebrow raised.

"It's hot. Open the car," I say. Austin women might break out our sweaters and boots when August ends, but only because we'd have to wait until November to dress seasonally if we went by the temperature. It's almost ninety degrees right now. Rude.

"You aren't getting in this car unless you promise to tell me exactly what your problem with Micah is."

I tug at the door handle. "You already know it."

"No. This goes beyond him beating you for valedictorian."

"He's annoying. He's always been annoying. It's not that deep." I tug on the door again.

"You lying liar who lies," she says, her tone pleasant. "He's adorable and funny."

"To you, sure. And how nice for you. Can we go?"

Madison says nothing, only twirls her key ring on her finger and watches me. I glance past her to the door. Micah will walk out any second now, and I don't trust her not to ask him about our friction. Who knows what version of events he'd give her?

I drop my head. "Fine. I'll tell you."

Click click. The door unlocks as Madison walks to her side.

We get in, and after starting the car and turning on the air, she gets us on the road, then flicks a glance at me.

"Now talk."

I shake my head but give in. "It was his first week at Hillview, freshman year . . ."

Chapter Seven
Kaitlyn

"Micah was a punk back then," I say as I finish laying out the story of how we got off on the wrong foot and stayed there. Maybe that will be enough, and I can avoid the most embarrassing part of the story. "Basically, the first time Micah Croft decides to talk to me, it's to jump in and paddle with the douche canoes."

"It's hard to imagine Micah that way," Madison says. "He's so laidback, and he's one of those people who works hard because *he* needs to be happy with it, you know? He doesn't seem like he'd ever try to impress other people."

Tension creeps into my lower back, and I force myself not to stiffen in my seat. "I'm sure he's fine now. I'm telling you how he was then."

"Katie." Madison darts a look at me. "I believe you. In a lot of ways, you and I are different from how we were then too." She shakes her head, smiling. "Those boys are very lucky you weren't the Kaitlyn you are now."

"If I'd been the Kaitlyn I am now, they wouldn't have been making fun of me in the first place." Eventually I got around to a glow up. And a backbone.

"That was a hard year," she says. "And I was so wrapped up in why it was hard for me that I abandoned you, huh?"

"You did what you could with what you had," I say. "We both did. We had to."

"You're giving me too much grace, but thank you." She watches the road, but I get the feeling her attention is only half on her driving. Finally, she sighs. "Maybe if I'd been less wrapped up in my own martyr act, I could have set Drake straight, kept Micah from ruining your life, and things could have gone differently for you."

"I've never blamed you for any of that." I don't want her pregnancy hormones burying her in unnecessary regret. "We both made it out of the mean streets of Hillview alive."

Madison frowns. "But if I'd stepped in back then you could have graduated with honors, gone to college, and gotten into an elite sorority. Maybe you could have gone on to law school, inherited millions, bought your own house, and then run a super amazing nonprofit organization."

Her lips are twitching, and I snort at her list of things I've actually done. "You're right. This is on you."

"Your amazing life is on me? Fine, I'll take the credit," she says. "So how did Micah ruin your life again? Because if that *is* the whole story, my next question is how much longer until we can forgive Micah for saying you have nice hair?"

Oh, this is rich. "Is the queen of holding grudges asking me when I want to let my grudge go?"

She shifts in her seat as much as her pregnant belly and the steering wheel allow her to. "That's fair. But knowing you, there's more to the Micah story. Let's hear it."

"Or we could *not* talk about it?" I say in a voice empty of hope.

"So you're saying this part is as juicy as a Fredericksburg peach. Yesss."

I drop my head against the headrest with a muffled thump.

"Oh, I'm living for this now," Madison crows. "Spill."

I groan but straighten. Might as well get the stupidest part over with. "I mostly ignored him and that whole group for the rest of the year. Sophomore year, I only had two classes with Micah, and it was easy to avoid being in a group with him. By junior year, the company wasn't in the news as much, and I was building up my resume for college, so I tried being more . . . social, I guess?"

To get strong letters of recommendation, I'd had to step it up. I was going to apply to a few Ivies. I didn't want to *go*. Dad had loved the idea of me telling Yale "no" so I could dump them for his beloved UT. Grades weren't enough. I'd needed to be in clubs, get elected to a couple of things.

"By that point, I was indifferent to Micah." It had started out true that year, anyway. "He had this annoying habit of acting like he was above it all—but he'd quit trying to talk to me, so I didn't care. We ended up getting grouped together for a project in our econ class in the spring, and he was all right. Did his part. Had good ideas. Didn't say anything mean."

"But you still don't want to forgive him?"

"I did," I say. "Way back in our freshman year. I was over it."

"But you didn't want to be friends?"

"We almost were. Right around then, I found out that he was ranked second in our class. It turned into a semi-friendly rivalry. My day could be made or broken depending on whether I outscored him on a test, even if it was by a point."

"Can we look at it like the competition was a good thing? Maybe it helped each of you be better than you would have been without the other."

"You really want me to like Micah, don't you?"

"It's selfish, but yes." She glances at me. "I don't want to worry that I'm forcing you to work with someone who causes you massive stress while I'm cooing at my baby."

A pang of guilt ripples through my chest. "Definitely don't worry. Our competition was healthy. It did push me to do better. I already knew that back then."

"I don't believe you. You wouldn't still be mad."

"I wouldn't be if he hadn't ruined everything with two weeks left to go until graduation. You know how I said we were almost friends by then? We'd choose each other for group projects, and sometimes we ate lunch together in the library."

"Stop. You're embarrassing me with the spicy details."

"It wasn't like that, dummy."

"But why not?" she demands. "Was he not hot yet?"

I squirm. "He was cute. But I didn't have the bandwidth for that. I was focused on school."

"No heart-poundy feelings for Micah. Got it." I hesitate so long that she reaches over and pinches my arm. "Katie-Kat, *yes* to heart-poundy feelings?"

"Kind of," I mumble. Around the last two months of school, I'd realized that it meant something to me when Micah complimented a score I got or gave me a nod when he agreed with a point I'd made in a class discussion. Maybe it was realizing that Micah knew better than anyone how hard I worked, and I liked being seen by him. "I had a crush on him our last semester."

It's such a weak word to describe how consumed I was with him. Completely, utterly obsessed. When we were in the same room, every single one of my senses was tuned to him. I knew where he was at every point of the day on campus. I studied everything he wore, looking for silent clues or messages about his feelings in the details. Did he switch from his checkered Vans to his black ones because they were nicer and he wanted to impress me? I caught a whiff of his cologne one day in our Chinese 4 class and wondered if he'd worn it because he knew we would work in pairs that day.

As soon as I'd realized that was my hope, I'd also started worrying that he'd see how much I liked his attention. How much I watched him. What that said about how I . . . felt.

I'd spend calculus staring at the back of his head, daydreaming about how he might ask me to prom. Then I'd feel giddy and avoid my friends at lunch—where they would talk about prom as obsessively as I daydreamed about going with Micah. If the subject of dates came up, my face would have given me away and they would try to pry out of me who my blush was all about. If they succeeded, they'd do something well-intentioned but humiliating to get him to ask me, so I'd hidden in the library instead, but sometimes Micah found me there and settled in beside me to eat and study. Then I'd end up with my heart pounding too hard and out of rhythm. I'd last as long as I could with my cheeks flaming. When I couldn't take it—sure he'd hear my loud heartbeat—I'd mumble an excuse about checking in with a teacher and leave.

That was a rough two months. I touch my cheek, remembering. It's a miracle I don't have burn scars from the pining. All that pining that never mattered. He hadn't asked me to prom. I'd gone with Megan and Lulu. Micah didn't go at all.

"You had a crush, but now you hate him." Madison's tone makes it sound like she's studying the medical file of a mysterious case. She pauses for a moment, then gasps. "Oh, Kaitlyn, did he reject you?"

"No! Settle down. I don't think he knew. Not at first. I didn't get the feeling he thought of me that way at all."

"Why? Did he say something?"

I make a noncommittal sound. "I experienced electrical shorts anytime he was near me, but he always acted the same, so . . ."

"It wasn't mutual," she says.

"I don't think so. Avoiding him worked pretty well until about a week before finals. But then I stayed late after school one afternoon, and I had to walk by the soccer pitch to get to my car. I wasn't paying attention, thinking about the chapter test in calculus the next day, and this kid shouts, 'Hey, Micah, isn't that the Kaitlyn chick who's super into you?'"

Madison boos. "We hate that kid."

I smile even as I remember the flood of humiliation as soon as the kid had said it. "I haven't stayed in touch."

"Did Micah act like a complete tool?"

"He didn't do anything, but when I looked over, he was shirtless." I remember the hitch in my breath and how my palms broke out in a sweat, which had never happened before.

"Ohhh. Shirtless boys are devastating when you're seventeen," she says.

"This was catastrophic. I think I went blind for a few seconds? It was partially panic, like *How did this kid know? Is it because Micah knew and told him?* Then add in the devastating shirtlessness, and yeah. He had a really nice chest."

Madison gives a soft laugh of understanding. "Don't know why you said that in the past tense."

"But my blackout or whatever . . ." I squeeze my eyes shut for a split second, helpless against the worst part of the memory. "I walked right into a pole."

"Oh no. Is this when—?"

"I broke my nose," I confirm. "I broke it walking into a pole while looking at a shirtless boy I had a crush on—in front of him. And no, that isn't why I was mad at him."

I've read that the human brain can't recreate the sensation of a pain you remember in the body. But right now, I'd argue with science. I remember the excruciating jolt as I slammed into the pole and my vision went white. That's the color of pain. Searing white. My nose hurt right away, but my brain wasn't far behind, throbbing within seconds from the impact.

"I remember dropping straight to the ground, hunched over because I thought I was going to puke. Micah and his friend ran over, yelling my name, and I wanted them to stop. It was the loudest thing I'd ever heard, but it also sounded like they were in a tunnel. Micah was trying to get me to look up, and I did but only to tell him to go away because I wanted him to be quiet. His friend started yelling about blood, and I looked down to see it all over my shirt and my hands." The memory is becoming more vivid as I relive it.

"Micah told him to calm down, that it was only a bloody nose, and to go to the locker room and get paper towels. He told me it was fine, he'd had a bloody nose before, and said to tip back my head and pinch the bridge of my nose. Meanwhile, I wanted to die, and not even from embarrassment. It hurt *so* bad." I give a faint sniff. "My eyes are stinging just thinking about it."

"It sounds horrible," Madison says.

"It was. And I hated the fuss." I don't like being the center of attention. I can hold my own if I have to do public speaking, but Madison is very much a dance-on-the-tables kind of girl, and I'm very much a don't-even-go-to-the-club kind of girl. "I told him I would go home and ice it, but he was worried that it wasn't clotting. Then he asked me if I had any tampons."

She gasps. "No. No, he didn't do the . . ."

"*She's the Man* thing and shove it up my nose? Yeah."

She clears her throat. "Okay. Well." Another throat clearing. "It was a bonding experience that should have made you closer."

She's trying to keep a straight face, and it wins a small laugh from me. "It's true I've never shared that same level of intimacy with another guy since."

She breaks down and laughs too. "I'm sorry. That's pretty bad."

"I know. Then he made it worse by forcing me to go to the infirmary." About half of Hillview's students were residential. Boarding school, basically. The campus had a small clinic with a full-time nurse practitioner. "I absolutely didn't want to go because they would call Mom."

Madison sucks air through her teeth and nods but says nothing.

"I explained it would worry her and she would overreact, that I'd just drive home and take it easy, but he wouldn't listen. He was already calling the front office to tell them we were on the way for a bloody nose."

"He didn't know," Madison says.

"I *told* him," I repeat. "I told him Mom would make a bigger deal out of it than it needed to be. I told him I needed time to go home and study for calculus, but it didn't matter. Once the infirmary called Mom, it was all over." Mom is a hypochondriac, and sometimes, growing up, it almost felt like it spilled into Munchausen's-by-proxy. She obsessed over every sniffle or bruise we got, and we learned never to show it if we felt even a little bit gross or it would become a production.

"How high did she go?" Madison asks.

"The nurse told her to give me ibuprofen and wait for the swelling to go down before worrying about x-rays—"

"Whoops."

"Exactly." Suggesting I had something worth an x-ray had unleashed Cynthia Armstrong's neuroticism, and there was no damming the flow. "By the time Mom was done, she had me at St. David's and made them call in the chief of surgery—who wasn't even on call—then she made *him* call in the chief of plastics. And every single one of them said the same thing. It probably was broken but not severely enough that it would need to be reset, and they wouldn't be able to do much until the swelling went down. I didn't get home until almost midnight. Mom gave me ibuprofen, except she didn't tell me it had sleepy stuff in it. I couldn't study. I still had to take the calculus test the next day. Want to guess what subject Micah was better at than I was?"

"Calculus."

"I got a C on that test. It dropped my grade in that class to a ninety-two, and he got a ninety-seven for the semester. When they did the final calculations for the year, he won valedictorian by an eighth of a point. *An eighth.* All because of our calculus grades, and all because he wouldn't listen to me when I told him to back off."

By now, we've reached my neighborhood, and Madison is quiet as she turns into it and then into my driveway two blocks later. She puts the car in park and turns toward me. Or tries to. It's about a three-degree turn because of her belly. Her eyes are soft when she meets mine.

"Kaitlyn," she says, reaching over to take my hand. "That's really stupid."

I stare at her in shock for a full five seconds. And then we both burst out laughing.

When we finally stop, I smile. "It didn't sound stupid until I said it out loud."

"It's not really the kind of thing epic feuds are built on."

"You can't take this away from me," I say. "I feel lost without a nemesis."

"Oh, you still have one. But it's that pole, not Micah."

"The pole," I repeat, like I'm taking this seriously. "Hmm. Less interesting nemesis."

"It's a very worthy nemesis," she says. "Iron will."

"Well, steel, probably."

"Fair point. Will of steel. Unchanging. Unbending. Relentless."

"In that case, I'm a badass. Thanks, Madi. I feel better."

"Good. Permission to practice more therapy without a license?"

I raise my eyebrows. "You'll do it either way."

"Correct," she says happily. "I want to make sure you understand you were never mad at Micah about the grades. Not even about the valedictorian thing. You were mad because when you walked into the pole, he saw how you felt when you didn't mean for him to."

I don't love this take, maybe because when a statement like that makes me uncomfortable, it has a nasty habit of being true. "Is there a medium ground between your unlicensed therapy and never suggesting I'm wrong about anything?"

She grins. "Get out and go make a plan for being nice to Micah."

I roll my eyes and climb out of her car but circle around to tap on her window. When she lowers it I say, "I'm only going in to choose a new nemesis."

"Good, because it was never Micah."

When she reverses out of my driveway like a Formula One driver, I swear she's cackling.

Chapter Eight
Kaitlyn

WE HURTLE THROUGH SEPTEMBER at breakneck speed. Madison throws her formidable energy at getting my house up to standard. I leave her to it, coming home after long days at Threadwork to find new changes every time I walk through the door. An area rug. Curtains. A room in an entirely new color and reeking of paint. She runs it all past me first, but honestly, my boring house is the least of my concerns. I say yes to all of it, knowing if I hate it, I can change it later when I have time.

Time. Ha.

I work forty hours a week, which isn't terrible. But I come home and hole up in my office to study for the bar exam. Most of my classmates started studying for it full-time the second we graduated in May so they could take it in July. But I already knew I'd be in Bangladesh until August, prepping to take over for Madison, so I'm studying for the February date. Those are the only two times it's offered, so if I don't pass in February, I'll be a year behind everyone in my law school class.

This office is the only room I've forbidden Madison to touch. White walls. A glass desk. A single chair, no rollers. Plain curtains on the window. A lamp with a curved black arm dangling the shade above my study sofa. The only color comes from an art piece on the wall, a green ombre rug on the thickest carpet money can buy, and my back lawn through the picture window, unlandscaped, another carpet of green across my half-acre backyard. Even the love seat against the wall is pale gray with a single large throw pillow, cream with one green stripe the color of the rug.

She calls it sparse. I prefer Zen. Everything else, she can do with as she likes. And mostly I like it too. Maybe I like that she's doing it for me. My big sister, big sistering in a way I'd craved through high school and college. Maybe she could turn my house into a neon EDM club, and I'd still like it because Madison did it.

She has excellent taste, of course. She's brought in some items that I'm not sure about at first, but as each room fills in, those become the items I like best because I can see how thoughtfully she's staging each space. She hired someone to construct built-in shelves, and she's filling them in with classic books, clothbound in neutral tones. There's an ottoman with a top woven of a twill the color of seagrass. A mirror with a mosaic frame in my entry.

She put the starling table in the formal dining area with a new set of chairs. It's the only thing in that part of the open floor plan, and it gives the space a sense of calm movement, like watching someone move through a vinyasa in yoga. Gentle, controlled, but a distinct sense of flow. Over the last two weeks a ritual has evolved: every morning, I walk all the way around it, tracing the edge with my finger, following the pattern as it swoops and curls. I feel centered each time I finish the circuit, ready to head into my day.

I shake my head, bringing myself back to the here and now, which is sitting at my desk in my Threadwork office, staring at the calendar, clicking from October to November to December on a loop. *Click click click. Click click click.*

It's like doomscrolling, only worse, because all it shows me is my failures so far in September, chances I can't afford to blow in October and November, and the truly small number of squares before the gala is here.

What I haven't told Madison is how badly I'm already screwing up even though she barely gave me full rein.

The day-to-day operational stuff is going fine. Shayak, our administrator in Dhaka, can run Marigold far better than I could, so mainly I meet with him weekly for progress reports. Here, there are only three other people, and they all know their stuff, so my job is to approve expenditures, basically. I don't even have to do the hard director tasks like coming up with a fundraising plan for the next fiscal year or hiring new staff. Madison might hate to admit it, but she inherited Dad's CEO brain, and she's used it brilliantly, putting everything on cruise control before turning it all over to me.

All that's left to do is solicit luxury auction items for the gala.

That's it. I don't have to find fancy guests or entertainment. I don't have to figure out the menu or book catering. I just need to line up the auction items for our wealthy guests.

In terms of theme and ambiance, Madison may talk about competing with the Met Gala, but in reality, the best comparison is the Black and White Ball, the only other truly black-tie gala in Austin. My parents have gone in years past for the same reason our gala tickets sold out: it's an opportunity to see and be seen in their couture evening wear by the Austin elite and a chance to publicly flex by bidding in the auction.

High-ticket items have to fall into one of two categories: first is experiences they don't have to arrange for themselves. A South African safari with stays at wellness retreats. A food tour of Spain with cooking lessons in each region. The second is material goods that are one of a kind. A Louis Vuitton luggage set in a rare colorway. A diamond tennis bracelet once owned by Venus Williams.

My mom wears that last item to brunch at the country club where she never plays tennis. They won it one year at the Black and White Ball. But donating to the charity is secondary for them. I'm not sure they could name what the Texas Advocacy Project—the host of the ball—does. I do though. They advocate for survivors in power-based abuse cases. The irony could choke a Texas longhorn, yes? Yes.

Irony or not, we don't have anything like that in our auction items. No celebrity jewelry touched by greatness. We do have one luxury cruise around Nova Scotia, including a day on Prince Edward Island. That will sell for sure because I'm bidding on it. I may even try to win it. There's also a Napa Valley getaway that will sell okay, but Texas likes to compete with California as much as I like competing with Micah, and we have our own wine country right next door in Fredericksburg. It'll feel almost un-Texan to bid for the Napa Valley package.

At best, I can call that one-and-a-half bid items. That isn't going to fund a year of Threadwork or the Marigold Institute.

I pinch the bridge of my nose and reach for the phone to place my next call to the executive assistant for Anne Harvey. The idea is to go down the gala guest list and squeeze some of those peaches for auction donations. It's yet another level of status and generosity when your name is associated with donating a big-ticket auction item.

"Hey, Leo," I say when I get Anne's admin on the line. "This is Kaitlyn Armstrong with Threadwork. Did you see the email I sent to Anne regarding an auction item for the Threadwork Discovery Gala by Armstrong Industries?"

"Yes, hello, Kaitlyn," Leo says, his voice brisk. "I believe we let a"—he pauses—"ah, yes, a Madison Locke know that Anne will be attending with her plus-one."

"We're so pleased to have her," I say. "We were hoping we can give her more time in the spotlight by highlighting her as a donor to our charity auction. This is a crowd that's very interested in curated experiences in places or on properties they wouldn't normally have access to. Private yacht excursions, for example." The Harveys are well-known for spending a month on their yacht in the Mediterranean in the summer. That leaves their fully crewed yacht docked for the rest of the year. "It's not even necessary for her to play host. Simply making it available for five days or so would be more than generous."

"I imagine it would be." His voice is very dry.

I want to cringe. I manage to find the most awkward way to say things. I'm not meant for sales. Or begging. But I'll do anything to keep Threadwork healthy and doing its work. "Is that something she'd be willing to consider donating to our auction?"

"I can ask." His tone is doubtful, and my heart sinks. "But I believe all of our charitable giving funds are earmarked through the end of the year already."

"That would be wonderful if you would run it past her," I say. It's normal for an assistant to start with a no. They would never commit funds on behalf of their boss. But that doesn't cheer me up, because I have only made it past one executive assistant so far, and that netted the Napa Valley trip. Every other follow-up has resulted in a no. If I'm lucky, the assistant emails to let me know. Most of the time, I have to call and nag, and that means a rejection every time.

I hang up with Leo, already sensing the way this is going to go.

"It's okay," I inform my empty office. "I've only been at this two weeks, and I've already improved my pitch."

I've been watching YouTube videos and reading articles every day about how to be more effective in soliciting donations. That helped me pivot from "Would your boss like to donate anything?" to researching each guest on the list and determining something specific to suggest they donate.

Maybe I should start listening to podcasts on the subject, something with a cheesy title like "How to Turn Every No into a Yes."

I'm an expert on saying no. I don't have room for much yes in my life, so I'm no help to my cause.

That's a bad sign.

I'd probably offer everything I own or will ever own to someone who could figure out how to make time for me. A clock where I can add time to it when I start running out. A cosmic hourglass where I dump more sand in the top when it's getting too low. Oh, but also, with no bad consequences like in every story ever where people mess with time.

I sigh and stand so I can stretch because I'm getting loopy. Time to reoxygenate my brain. A few reaches toward the ceiling and deep breaths later, I sit down again to tackle the tasks I can nail.

Except when I wake up my computer, I have an email waiting from Micah.

I am not nailing Micah.

Uh . . . I am so glad only my brain heard me say that, but a faint heat sweeps up my neck.

I mean to say that I'm not doing the best job of managing Micah or the facilities part of the project, mainly because he is so on top of it. He's been updating me via email for the last three weeks since the tour, ending each short email by letting me know construction will start as planned at the beginning of October.

That's next week. We're scheduled to meet at the warehouse, something that will happen at least weekly because laying out the event space will be a collaborative process.

I stand, still restless and needing to move. It's probably because Madison is due any day now, and it feels like everyone who knows her has been holding their collective breath, jumping every time our phones buzz.

I walk out to our small reception area. "Suz, I'm going to take a short walk. I need a brain break. Back in fifteen."

"It's nice out. Maybe I'll take a turn when you come back."

"I'm making it an official order. You're going for a walk when I get back."

She smiles and waves me off.

Our small suite of offices is on the ground floor of Armstrong headquarters, a six-story building in North Austin. It's part of Dad's restitution efforts. The company has already paid the settlement the courts ordered, but he's been trying to show Madison especially that he's willing to do more. That includes subsidizing Threadwork's office space.

Of course, this, like all of Dad's generosity to Threadwork, helps rehabilitate the Armstrong corporate image. Housing the nonprofit that works on making restitution to the victims of his corporate negligence? *How big of him*, he wants people to say. *He's changing*.

He is. Slowly. Even if there's a PR upside to his support of Threadwork, it's still a big concession for Gordon Armstrong. We try to meet him where he's at. It's been easier for me since I can read him like a book, given that we function the same way. He's the genetic culprit behind my perfectionism. But even Madi has softened since seeing his genuine pleasure at the imminent arrival of his first grandchild.

I walk out to the corporate reception area, a grand glass-and-marble lobby, wave to security at the desk, and exit into the parking lot. The weather has started cooling, the midseventies temperature perfect for a brisk walk. It will continue to cool over the next month until I'll need a light coat by early November.

Armstrong Industries is housed in an unobjectionable business park with bland landscaping, but there are enough islands of grass and flowerbeds between the office buildings to make it a pleasant walk. As usual, I start by thinking through the tasks ahead for the day or week, which leads me to my meeting with Micah, which sends me straight into mulling over Madison's unlicensed therapy. After almost a month to think about it, I've reached some conclusions.

In hindsight, I can see my intense perfectionism would have made me furious at anyone who swept in to take valedictorian at the last minute. I'd been so determined that despite the periodic media reports on the Armstrong Industries scandal, despite the constant speculation among the wealthy families who sent their kids to Hillview, being an Armstrong still stood for excellence and hard work. Being second best didn't feel like it made the same point, not to me or my parents.

To be beaten by Micah specifically . . . Madison nailed why it stung more. I never showed anyone vulnerability, not even my friends. We might joke and laugh, but I didn't let them in. So when Micah had caught me gawping at his bare chest, he'd seen the truth: I was into him enough to break my face and tank my shot at valedictorian. That had made me very vulnerable to him. We might have grown friendly through our senior year, but what would Too Cool Micah Croft say to the mousy nerd who suddenly revealed heart eyes for him when he'd only noticed her because of her brain?

It had been safer to be angry. Chilly, blaming him for overruling me and getting my mother involved, giving him an unfair advantage.

What does holding on to that eight years later say about me? At best, it says I hold petty grudges.

Not this one. Not anymore. I've let it go. And rather than deal with stressing and overthinking our meeting next week, maybe I'll go the Band-Aid route and see if Micah is available sooner. Tomorrow. This afternoon, even. There's a loosening in my chest, the stress I always carry there shrinking at this plan.

I open my email on my phone and dictate a short message.

To: Micah_Croft@astergervis.com
From: Kaitlyn.Armstrong@threadwork.org
Subject: Meeting availability?

Hi, Micah.

I appreciate the updates you've been sending. I know we're scheduled for an onsite meeting next week, but I have some time this afternoon. Would you be available to swing by my office to discuss how the construction phase will go? I'd like to know how to best support your team.

Kind regards,

Kaitlyn Armstrong
Interim Director, Threadwork

I read it over and frown at the automatic signature. Kind regards? Stuffy. But also unobjectionable in ninety-nine percent of business communications. It'll do. I hit send and turn back toward the office.

He answers me as I'm walking into the Threadwork suite, confirming he can make it this afternoon.

Good job, Katie. I can always be counted on to do the responsible thing, but this is leadership. Bonafide interim director leadership.

"Tag, you're it," I tell Suz as I pass her. "Go get that fresh air."

At my desk, I text Madison before I tackle the next round of phone calls I need to make about silent auction items.

Do you have a baby yet?

Fun pregnancy facts from Oliver: only 5% of babies arrive on their due date. 11% arrive early. The rest come late. Went to doc yesterday. Harper hasn't dropped since last week.

IS THAT BAD?

NO

It's normal. She'll drop when she's ready to be born. She's hanging out in Club Womb for a while.

You only have two days until your due date. It could happen.

Doubtful. Going to have a watermelon sitting on my bladder for another week. Distract me.

Decided to grow up and made a mature CEO decision. Bringing Micah in for a meeting this afternoon. Grudge? What grudge?

(Confetti emojis) Good job!

What time?

I'm coming

What no

Yes. Going crazy waiting. My back hurts. I NEED A DISTRACTION.

No. I don't know how to deliver a baby.

ONE WEEK. What time?

Will call Suz to tell me your schedule

4:00. Don't come.

She sends me a string of kissy lip emojis.

Chapter Nine

Micah

MADISON AND I ARRIVE at the Threadwork office at the same time. Madison smiles and says, "Follow me."

I do, and she pokes her head through the door of an office that's been empty in the handful of times I've come here before.

"Knock, knock," she says. "I found a stray in the parking lot and brought him with me."

She walks in, and I follow, giving Kaitlyn a quick nod because I'm distracted watching Madison try to settle herself into her chair. It's kind of like watching a flamingo with a basketball strapped to its stomach try to situate itself on a tricycle while wearing a long skirt. I hover beside her as she grasps the chair arms and slowly lowers herself, not sure how I can help, but everything in my training about force, mass, and momentum says this can't possibly work. But a few seconds later, she's in the chair, and I take the other seat and hide a sigh of relief.

"Love what you've done with the place," Madison says.

She's teasing Kaitlyn, who hasn't done anything in here yet. It's a standard office suite. The reception area has framed photos of the Marigold Institute building and students at work, alternating with woven mats and bowls in orange, turquoise, and red. Madison's touch for sure. Kaitlyn's office is a blank slate, a few frames leaning against one wall, faced in so I'm not sure what's on them.

"I kept waiting for you to start nesting over here," she tells Madison. "I conned you into doing my house. I thought for sure I could sucker you into doing my office."

Madison sniffs, and Kaitlyn smiles at me. "I mean to hang things up, but there are always at least five things on my list ahead of decorating."

I'm so surprised by her smile and friendly conversation, that I can only look back in silence.

"They're *right there*," Madison protests, waving toward the stacked frames.

Kaitlyn shrugs and switches her attention to me, still smiling. It's not big, but it looks sincere. "Thanks for coming, Micah. This meeting will go better if we pretend she's not here."

I laugh. "Oh, cool. Usually you pretend *I'm* not here." I don't know what's changed, but I can't resist teasing her.

Madison beams at me, but instead of getting flustered, Kaitlyn nods. "Right, sorry about that. I checked, and it turns out the statute of limitations on stupid grudges expired last year, so congratulations on making valedictorian, and thanks for coming in today."

I lean back, relaxing around her for the first time since our run-in at Remix. "Glad we're straight. I was trying to figure out the etiquette of letting a client know about that expiration."

Recognition dawns on Madison's face. "I remember now. At Katie's graduation. You gave a good speech."

I shrug, startled anyone would remember it. "Thanks."

Kaitlyn watches me with the trace of a smile. "We leave here as experts in nothing, but that won't matter if we stay students of everything."

My eyebrows go up as she quotes it. "You remember it too?"

She shrugs, and I suspect she does it to tease me. "Like Madison said, it was a good speech."

Her smile fades and I wonder what she's thinking. Is it about that speech? Or how I ended up giving it? Or is she thinking about the present?

"So this pause is more pregnant than I am," Madison says.

"Pointing it out definitely helps," Kaitlyn says.

Madison looks not at all sorry.

Kaitlyn shifts her attention back to me. "Sorry, Micah. I got lost remembering that speech. I appreciate it more now. You had some things figured out already that I only started understanding in law school. Mainly, the more I learn, the less I know."

"But it's a good thing?" I ask.

"Yes. It makes the world bigger."

"Awww," Madison says, "that's so cu—"

"Madison decided to crash this meeting," Kaitlyn interrupts, "because—"

"Because Oliver is at his office, daytime TV sucks, and I'm more bored than I thought I would be on maternity leave." She tries to lean forward. When it's impossible, she scoots up a couple of inches to make room so she can rub her back. "I can't even take Advil, and I want to use my prodigious brain to distract me. That's why."

"Anyway," Kaitlyn says to me, "I wanted to check in on what the construction phase looks like and figure out how often I should plan to be on-site."

I pull out my iPad case tucked beside me. "I'll be able to start two days earlier than I expected, so I'm glad we're meeting today. I have an idea I want to run past you. Originally we'd talked about hiding the supervisor loft at the end of the warehouse behind the false ceiling, but what would you think . . ." And I'm off and running, tapping on the screen and showing them a few rough sketches turning the loft into a deejay booth.

When I'm done, I turn to Madison. She's been particular about every nut and bolt of this build. "What do you think?"

Madison surprises me by deferring to Kaitlyn with a nod.

Kaitlyn looks surprised too but draws the iPad closer, studying the sketch. "I agree with you. I like the idea of moving the deejay here. Being intentional with the placement makes it seem less like we threw a bunch of stuff in a giant square."

Madison straightens and her eyebrows fly up.

"You disagree?" Kaitlyn asks, surprised.

"No, it's a good idea. Excuse me a minute, please."

She hoists herself out of her chair and disappears into the hallway.

Kaitlyn blinks at the empty doorway and turns back to me. "Itty-bitty bladder committee."

"Sounds uncomfortable."

"Let's move the deejay. But since we didn't go up to the loft before, I'd like to come check it out."

"Monday afternoon work?"

We choose a time before moving on to an overview of the construction next week.

"We need to build the frame," I explain, "and since we're working with reclaimed rebar, it's going to take welding. That will take most of the week because the scale of this thing . . ." I trail off as the tickle of an idea has me staring into the distance, trying to visualize if it could work.

"Are you okay?" Kaitlyn asks. "Because if the architect is overwhelmed by the scope of this project, that makes me nervous."

I focus on her. "Yeah, fine. Just wondering if we should take this thing even bigger. I was trying to run the time and costs in my head, but I'll do that later and send it over to you tomorrow if the numbers add up."

She shakes her head. "I'm not a risk taker. I prefer taking shots I know I'll make, but it's obvious why you and Madison work so well together. You both think big."

"Katie, Oliver wants to talk to you." Madison stands in the doorway, holding out her phone.

"Your face is weird," Kaitlyn says. "Everything okay?"

Madison's only answer is to wave the phone.

Kaitlyn hops up to take it. "Oliver?"

Her eyes widen as she studies her sister. "You're in labor?" Her voice ends two octaves higher than usual.

I jump up at the word "labor," then freeze. My instinct is to help, but I've never been in this situation before.

Madison grimaces. "No contractions, but I think my water broke? Is breaking? I swear I took notes in pregnant lady class, but I'm forgetting all of them. I've got a slow leak happening."

I scan her, not sure what I'm supposed to be looking for. A baby poking its head out from beneath her hem?

"I can drive her," Kaitlyn is telling her brother-in-law, "but shouldn't we call an ambulance?" She listens for a few seconds. "Okay, right, yes, we'll meet you at the hospital."

She hangs up without remembering to say goodbye and thrusts the phone at Madison, who bobbles it, but Kaitlyn is in action mode and already pulling her purse from a desk drawer.

"Sorry to cut this short," she says as she digs inside it.

"Go," I say. "Do what you need to do."

She curses, smacking her purse onto the desk. "Stupid keys."

"We're not taking your car," Madison objects.

Kaitlyn looks over at her. "You can't drive yourself through rush hour to have a baby."

Madison rests her hand on her stomach—which, wait, did it double in size?—and glares. "I am not wrestling myself into your stupid Audi."

"It is low," Kaitlyn concedes.

"And my car has the baby seat," Madison adds.

"Your car," Kaitlyn says, already moving toward the door with shooing motions. "Let's go."

"Calm down, we have time," Madison protests.

"Don't tell me to calm down. You're having a baby!"

Madison gives her a second to let that sink in, and I press my lips tight to hide a smile. I understand why Kaitlyn isn't thinking straight.

"Fine, I'll keep the freaking out on the inside," Kaitlyn says. "But we need to go."

We head down the hall, and Madison is moving fast enough to waddle, the first time I've seen her do that. I keep an eye on her even thought I'm still not sure what I'm watching for. I think the baby waving from under her hem.

When we get to reception, Kaitlyn orders the receptionist, "Do not tell my dad," as we head out the door.

In the parking lot, Madison hands Kaitlyn her keys and points to where she parked her SUV.

I stay right behind them. "I'll follow you."

"Good idea," Kaitlyn calls over her shoulder. Then she and Madison both turn to look at me. "Why?"

I stop too, stumped. "I don't know. Maybe for backup?"

"Works for me," Madison says, waddling ahead. When she reaches her car, she opens the passenger door but then hesitates.

"What's wrong?" Kaitlyn asks, climbing into the driver's seat.

"Leather seats," she says. "And I'm leaking."

"Uh . . ." Kaitlyn glances around wildly, like she'll see a solution hanging from the low hedge in front of us or hiding in the SUV. "It's okay. Baby matters more."

"No, hold on." I jog over to my truck a few spots down. I yank open the door to the extra cab and duck behind the driver's seat. A few seconds later, I straighten and call, "Head's up."

Kaitlyn catches the sweatshirt I toss and holds it up. It's a new UT one, crisp orange logo on an ivory background. "I'm not sure about pregnant, uh, water or whatever we're dealing with here, but this is probably too nice for Madison to sit on."

I grin. "I would be honored. Keep it. I'm going to back out so I can follow you."

Kaitlyn nods, trying not to look worried, but faint lines around her eyes and the tightness around her mouth give her away. Still, she turns toward Madison and manages to sound excited as she announces, "All right, Mama. It's show time."

Chapter Ten
Kaitlyn

I HURRY AROUND THE front of the car with Micah's sweatshirt. Oliver said the baby won't come for a while because Madison isn't having contractions, but I don't care. I'm hurrying anyway since this is the woman who told me thirty minutes before her water broke that this baby wouldn't come for at least a week.

I spread the UT sweatshirt over her seat. "We're good."

"Turn it front down. That longhorn doesn't need to see this."

"Good thinking." I flip it over and watch her get in. There is hoisting and grunting, and the grab handle is called upon to do more work than it was ever designed for. I don't think even with Micah and me helping her she would have made it into my Audi. She definitely would never have made it back out again.

Once she's buckled in, we get on the road, Micah pulling out behind us in his pickup.

I glance over at her. It's rush hour, but her hospital isn't far. That doesn't stop me from thinking of search phrases like "how to deliver baby in car" and "delivering baby in traffic."

"How's it going over there?" I ask.

She scrunches her face. "Okay? I don't feel contractions. If this is labor, it's just leaky so far."

"We'll be there in less than fifteen minutes."

She nods. "I want someone in scrubs to wave a stethoscope at me and confirm that this is fine, and I'll feel better."

"Do not let that baby do anything for the next fifteen minutes until we get to that stethoscope."

She gives an uncomfortable-sounding grunt. "My back is killing me. I really, really want the stethoscope. Distract me."

"For me to feel better, I need to list every vegetable I can think of in alphabetical order. Asparagus, bean, caul—"

"Why do you need to do that?"

"Keeps me from running search terms for delivering a baby in a car through my head."

"Oh. Cauliflower . . ."

D? What's a vegetable with D? We trade a quick panicked look.

"Daikon!" she shouts.

"Durian!" I shout at the same time.

"That's a fruit!" she shouts.

"Okay, daikon," I shout back.

She lets out a sigh. "Okay, escarole, fennel . . ."

She's on turnip when I take the hospital exit. I am more relieved that I don't have to figure out what to say for U, V, or X than I am about delivering my niece, so it worked. (I had wasabi ready to go for W.)

Signs point us to a covered portico for labor and delivery check-ins, and I stop the car, throw it in park, and run around to help Madison out, but Micah beats me to it, his truck idling behind mine.

When she's on her feet with Micah's help, he says, "Why don't you take her in to get checked or whatever, and I'll park the cars?"

"Yes, thanks," I say, already herding Madison into the hospital with an arm around her waist.

After that, the staff takes over efficiently, and it's calming.

"She's preregistered, so we can take her right back to an exam room," the charge nurse tells me. "Go ahead and make yourself comfortable."

I'm so keyed up it's almost a nonsense command. Make myself comfortable? Sit on the barely cushioned chairs and pretend as if something life-changing isn't happening beyond the double doors?

But I wander into the waiting area and perch at the edge of a chair, too nervous to settle into it.

Micah finds me there a few minutes later. "How's it going? Is Madison okay?"

"Seems like it. Maybe freaked out that she'll have a kid, possibly today? But calm, considering."

"That's good." He stands there, glancing around the room, but there isn't much to see beyond the beige walls and abstract watercolor prints. There's a large window overlooking the adjacent medical center and afair number of trees behind it, but that's it. His gaze returns to me, taking in my position at the edge of my seat. "What about you? Are you doing all right?"

"I'm fine," I say. "I've been researching when I take breaks from studying for the bar, so I'll be okay."

He cocks his head. "Researching?"

I wave my hand, but I have no idea what I'm trying to indicate. "Articles about how to be a good aunt. Stuff like that."

"Find any good information?"

"It's pretty subjective. Personality specific, I guess? It seems to boil down to showing up."

"Showing up is big," he says.

I focus on him more closely. "Do you have uncle experience?"

He shakes his head. "Only child. But lots of my friends I grew up with are having kids now, and I get some practice."

"Hillview friends?" I only knew of a few former classmates who had gotten married in the last couple of years.

The question makes him smile. "No. Neighborhood friends."

"Oh."

"Listen, I'm weirdly invested in this baby because I've been meeting with Madison the whole time she's been pregnant. I'll get out of your hair, but when you get a free minute, would you text me and let me know how it went?"

"Sure." It's on the tip of my tongue to invite him to stay, but he's right. It's probably weird. "Thanks for helping today."

He slides Madison's keys from his pocket. "I did park it neatly between the lines, so I'm the real MVP. It's over in the visitor lot."

"Right. Thanks again."

"Will your car be okay at your office after hours?"

"I'll figure it out." No doubt Madison would soon send up a bat signal to her besties, and once they descended, I'd be able to get a ride back to my car.

"Are you sure? I can call a buddy, and we can pick it up for you."

I eye him, impressed by his desire to help. It reminds me of how adamant he was about sticking with me until my mom came after I broke my nose. Then it had felt intrusive. Today it feels thoughtful.

"Are you looking for an excuse to drive my Audi?"

He presses his hand to his chest and gives me a *Who, me?* look.

"Too bad."

He gives me a very sad face.

"Seriously, though, I'm not worried about getting my car," I tell him. "The posse's coming. We'll handle it." Or I'd grab a Lyft.

"Good, good." He shifts his weight, glancing toward the sign over the double doors that reads "Birthing Suites." "I'll get out of your way then. Congratulations."

I give him a confused look. Congratulations?

"On being an aunt," he clarifies.

"Right," I say, a small smile slipping out. It *is* a big deal. Auntie Katie? I'll work on it. "I'll keep you posted."

He leaves, and I get up to pace, ready to jump into action. I don't know what kind of action. Anything. All the things.

Whatever my big sister needs.

Chapter Eleven

Kaitlyn

I'VE ONLY BEEN PACING for ten minutes when Oliver rushes in, a diaper bag slung over one shoulder, a duffel bag in his other hand. I help him get checked in and soon he disappears through the double doors. He's back in minutes, sans bags, looking slightly frantic.

"Turns out her back pain is actually called back labor and she's been having contractions all along. Better call Sami."

I do. Like the best friend she is, Sami is there within the hour.

Once it became clear Madison was in labor, she'd been moved and settled into her private room, and Sami and I are able to go in and hang out. Sami laughs when Madison rejects her "Birth Playlist" in favor of watching *Real Housewives* reruns on the room's TV, and we take turns walking with Madi or rubbing her back until she's so uncomfortable that she requests an epidural.

By midnight, the baby isn't here yet. The midwife on call checks Madison and informs us that the epidural has slowed her labor, which isn't unusual. She's only five centimeters dilated, and Michaela, the midwife, tells us all to try and get some sleep.

"The baby will let you know when to wake up," she tells us.

Oliver folds out the sofa bed next to Madison's hospital bed and insists that Sami and I take it because he wants to sit beside Madison.

I doze, waking often, but nothing changes. Around breakfast time, I step out to stretch my legs, feeling kind of gross after being in my work clothes all night. Sami and I have taken turns updating the group chat with their old roommates, but I shoot Micah a quick text now.

No baby yet. Been here all night. They're giving her something to move it along.

Wow. Thanks for the update. Good luck to Madison.

An hour later, Madison's nurse pops her head in. "Kaitlyn? You have a delivery at the front desk."

Madison and Sami both turn to look at me, but I shake my head. "No idea. I'll be back."

Two minutes later, I'm staring at a paper carryout bag from Tacodeli—famous for their breakfast tacos, a stack of folded sweats, and a drink carrier with four cups of coffee and a pile of creamers and sugar packets. The nurse at the desk smiles and hands me a note. "A guy dropped them off for you a few minutes ago. He was a doll."

The short note is on hospital stationery.

Hey, Kaitlyn.

Brought some breakfast in case the hospital food is as bad as people always say. Saw these sweats in the lobby gift shop and thought you might need them since you've been here all night. You got this, auntie.

—Micah

I hold up the gray sweatshirt with the hospital logo on it. Then I peek into the bag and laugh when I see at least a dozen breakfast tacos. I pull the sweatshirt over my head and have the nurse take a picture with my phone of me holding all the tacos and text it to Micah.

How much do you think I eat for breakfast?

Two tacos. But I got every kind because I don't know what you like.

This was so sweet. Thank you.

Np

"A little advice," the nurse says.

"Yes, please."

"Don't take those to your sister's room. Had to walk a husband over to the ER for stitches last week when he took a bite of a donut in front of his wife."

Madison hasn't been allowed to eat anything but the ice chips Oliver hand-fed her all night. "Good tip."

I slip into the bathroom and change into the sweats. It does feel good to change out of my rumpled work clothes. Micah even included a pair of hospital fuzzy socks with grippy bottoms. They go better with my sweatsuit than my brown snakeskin stilettos do.

An hour later, we've each snuck out to eat tacos and drink coffee, and Madison pretends not to notice when we come back in ten-minute increments looking not hungry and more awake.

"Who is this Micah guy?" Sami asks when we're all back in Madi's room. "He's a keeper."

"I got this," Madison says, and launches into a theatrical recounting of my nemesis gained, my broken nose, academic intrigue, our paths converging, and my nemesis lost.

Sami is an excellent audience, and when Madi finishes, Sami turns to me. "Great story. How much of it was true?"

Madison gives an indignant huff, but I ignore her. "Turn down the drama about sixty percent, and it's pretty accurate."

We settle in to watch a game show, and the morning stretches on. After the midday news, Madi shifts uncomfortably in the bed. "My tailbone hurts. I think my epidural is wearing off."

"I'll page the nurse."

She comes in a few minutes later and lifts Madi's blanket. "Oh, it's go time."

Oliver is on his feet. "Go time?"

"Her tailbone hurts because your baby's head is already crowning. Madi, hold tight, do not push, and I'll be back in less than two minutes."

Sami and I clear out, promising to cheer from the waiting room, passing Michaela the midwife coming into the room as we leave.

Sami and I take turns pacing and scrolling on our phones to pass the time. After almost an hour, Oliver walks out, a huge smile on his face.

"Is Madison okay? Is the baby here?" I ask.

"Mads has never been better. Come meet your new niece, ladies."

Chapter Twelve

Micah

"Too busy swiping right to join us?"

I glance up to meet my boss's amused eyes. "Sorry, what?"

Dan turns to his admin assistant. "That's what it's called when you're on a dating app, isn't it? Swiping right?"

"Yes, it is, boss," she says, grinning at me. "But Micah doesn't date. He's in his tortured artist phase."

I turn my phone over. "Sorry, Dan. Madison Locke is in labor, and I'm waiting for an update."

"Oh, are you the dad?" Dan asks. "I'm impressed. That's really taking care of the client."

I smile until the laughter dies down. "I was in a meeting with her and the interim director yesterday about construction next week when she went into labor."

"Fair enough," Dan says. "Why don't you give us an update on that project, and then we'll wrap up for the day."

I do, overviewing the October timeline and where we are with the materials acquisition and budget.

"Sounds good," Dan says when I finish. "We'll look forward to you writing the name of Aster, Gervis, and Associates in the annals of history."

"No problem," I say. "Is it okay if it goes down in history for being a disaster?"

Dan laughs and gets to his feet, signaling the meeting is truly over. I immediately check my phone as everyone drifts out of the office. Other than the picture of her tired-but-adorable self hugging the tacos I left, there's been nothing from Kaitlyn.

I'm itching to ask, but it's definitely not my place, so I go back to my desk and try to focus on the plan I'm supposed to draft for an ADU in a neighborhood that was developed in the eighties. These are my bread and butter right now, easy plans I could do half asleep, but these aging housing tracts aren't exactly inspiring. Dan has me on these because they don't require a lot of imagination or follow-through and they're easy to knock out while I work around the gala project. It means this floor plan also isn't enough to distract me from my phone.

Finally, an hour later, a text from Kaitlyn lights up my screen.

> Harper Ivy Mae Locke, born at 1:52 this afternoon, almost nine pounds. Madison and Harper are doing great.

> Congrats, auntie. Hope you got her that tattoo she wanted while her mom was napping.

> Madison won't let her go but I did give Harper a high five when she pooped on her mom.

> See? You're nailing this cool aunt thing.

> Maybe. She's not good at high fives.

> Probably a later milestone. Try again in six weeks.

> *Puts reminder on calendar*

Tell Madison I said congratulations.

I set the phone down, smiling. I wish Kaitlyn had sent a picture, but again, it's none of my business. I'm glad I got an update at all. I pack up for the day, and Kaitlyn texts as I reach my truck.

Madison says come visit.

The hospital?

Yes.

Now?

Yes. I think she's high from smelling Harper's head, but she says she owes you for the sweatshirt sacrifice.

On my way. You need anything?

Not unless you found the six hours of sleep I lost last night.

So, more coffee. Got it. Be there soon.

I make it to St. David's in less than an hour, even counting the coffee stop, and a few minutes later, I'm standing on the threshold of a patient room with a card beside the door stating it's currently occupied by Locke, Madison and Harper.

Oliver spots me first. "Hey, Micah. Come on in. Thanks for the tacos, man."

"Sure."

"Come meet our kid."

Kaitlyn, wearing the socks and sweats I left for her, shuffles out of the way, and I get my first look at Madison, snuggling a small bundle against her chest.

"I was going to offer to pick up some dinner, but it looks like you already got a burrito," I joke.

"It's taking everything in me not to gobble her up," Madison says. "Come tell me this isn't the most beautiful baby you've ever seen."

I walk to the bed railing and look down at a tiny face in the bundle Madison cradles.

"Gorgeous, isn't she?" Madison says.

She's . . . a baby? Pink. Kind of puffy eyes, closed, no eyelashes or eyebrows. I smile at Madison. "You said it. Are your parents excited?"

"They don't know yet," Kaitlyn says.

"I'll tell them tomorrow, when we're home," Madison says.

I'm pretty sure this isn't normal, but I don't say anything. Oliver explains anyway. "My mother-in-law can be a lot in medical settings. We're going to delay the fussing until we're on home turf."

I remember Kaitlyn being adamant about not going to the infirmary that day when she hurt her nose. I'd thought it was because she hated being fussed over, but later I'd heard her mom had made a huge scene and kept her at the hospital for hours.

As if she's reading my mind, Kaitlyn chimes in. "She's a hypochondriac. She'll be here all of five minutes before she's convinced she has a hysterical pregnancy. And my dad will feel awkward and cover it up by ordering the nurses and staff around."

"Boundary issues," Madison says. "If we tell them now, even if we tell them not to come over, they'll do it anyway."

A quiet rattling sounds at the door, and we all glance over to see an orderly coming in with a cart. "Dinner is here," he says.

"I'll get out of your hair," I say, turning to go.

"No, don't," Madison says. "Oliver and I both need to eat, so why don't you hold Harper for us?"

A pang of alarm ripples dully through my chest. "No, that's okay. I'm sure Kaitlyn wants more time."

Madison snorts. "She won't hold her. Are you saying you're scared too?"

I look at Kaitlyn, who is standing at the foot of the bed. She shrugs. "I don't want to drop her."

"I don't want to drop her either."

Madison sighs. "You're both idiots."

"I'll take her," Oliver says, pushing up from his chair.

"Wait, no, I'll do it," I say. "She says you need to eat."

"Thank you," Madison says, already lifting the baby toward me. "Just support her head."

Somehow I survive the handoff, settling the baby into my arm like Madison had. I hold my breath, and she gives a baby grunt, but she doesn't wake up. I stare down at the tiny burrito in awe. This morning, she didn't even exist in this world, and now here she is, a whole, actual human. It really is kind of beautiful.

"Can I go sit on the sofa with her?" I don't think I'll drop her, but just in case, it would be a much shorter fall.

"Of course, man." Oliver is busy removing the covers from their hospital trays, and I'm glad now that I said I'd hold the baby. The man clearly needs to eat if he's anxious to dive into the anemic-looking pork chops he reveals.

I walk carefully to the sofa, which means I have to go around the end of the bed and past Oliver, trying to keep my eye equally on the baby and the floor ahead of me. Kaitlyn scuttles out of my way, but when I settle onto the couch with a sigh of relief, she comes to sit beside me, leaning over to drop a kiss on her niece's head. I'd bet she hasn't been home since yesterday morning, but she still smells nice. I catch a whiff of something kind of herbal when she leans down, her hair close to tickling my nose.

"Thought you were scared of her," I say.

She straightens, her soft eyes still on her niece. "I'm afraid of *dropping* her."

"She was like this when she got her first kitten too," Madison says around a bite of pork chop, "but she got over it fast."

"I love Daisy Buchanan, but she is a *cat*," Kaitlyn protests. "Of course I'm even more nervous about a baby."

"You named your cat Daisy Buchanan?" I ask, amused. We'd studied *The Great Gatsby* in ninth grade, which is an interesting experience in a class full of filthy rich kids. I'm not sure any of them ever believed that it was a book of only villains. "Is she materialistic and amoral?"

"She was born at Gatsby's when Madison worked there."

"Ah." I look down at Harper's little face. "You're missing out. This is the coolest thing ever." Kaitlyn makes a grumpy sound, and I glance over at her. "I'm winning at baby holding." If that doesn't push her buttons, nothing will.

She squirms, frowning at me.

I look down at the baby and pretend to ignore her, until Kaitlyn grumbles, "Give me her."

"Excuse me?" I say.

She leans back against the sofa and extends her arms like I'm about to plop a cord of kindling in it. "I want to hold her."

I give her arms a narrow-eyed look. "She's not firewood."

Kaitlyn scowls. "She's *my* niece."

"But this is *my* job right now, and I don't like your form." I hear a smothered laugh from Oliver.

"Give me that baby," Kaitlyn says, and this time I know I better obey. I've heard that same determination in her tone before when we worked on group projects in school. It means she's tired of someone's nonsense, and now we're doing it her way.

I sigh. "Fine, but fix your arms. Make them like a cradle." She hesitates, and I add, "Pretend you're a Renaissance Madonna."

She rearranges them to be more cradlelike, then tilts her head at a stiff angle and makes her eyes go blank. She speaks without moving her lips. "Am I giving Sistine Chapel?"

I roll my eyes and carefully shift toward her and complete a not-terrible transfer of the baby. This time, Harper doesn't even grunt.

I sit back when the handoff is complete. The room has gone silent. Madison and Oliver are watching Kaitlyn. Madison's eyes are welling slightly, and Oliver flicks a glance my way and gives me a smile and a nod. Kaitlyn is transfixed, staring down into her niece's face like she's proof that magic exists.

Madison clears her throat. "I think she loves her even more than the cat."

"It's a tie," Kaitlyn says, not looking up.

"You're not supposed to say that," I tell her.

"Daisy is a pretty great cat," Oliver says. "We get it."

The new parents eat their dinners in record time, but Harper starts making small sounds of distress before they finish.

Kaitlyn looks at me, and I get the feeling she's trying to stay calm. "What do I do?" she asks in a low voice.

I want to have the answer, but I have no idea. "Maybe like . . ." I make an up-and-down motion with my hands.

"Weigh her like a melon?" Kaitlyn asks.

"Bounce her?" I say.

"She wants to eat," Madison says, pushing away the hospital table with her tray on it.

I surge to my feet. That's my cue to exit. "I'll leave you to it. Kaitlyn, let me know when you want to reschedule our meeting."

"Why would we reschedule?" she asks. "I didn't have a baby."

"Right." I feel kind of dumb. "So Tuesday then?"

Oliver is coming over to take the baby from her. "You *didn't* have a baby, and you don't have to stay here. Go home and get some sleep."

Kaitlyn yawns and stands. "You're right. I will. Except . . ."

"Your car is at work," Madison finishes.

Kaitlyn is reaching into the pocket of her sweat pants for her phone. "I'll get a Lyft."

"I can take you to your car."

She yawns again and shakes her head. "No, too tired for that."

"I can take you home if that's easier," I say.

"You don't know where I live."

"Doesn't matter. I don't have to be anywhere right now."

"Go with Micah," Oliver says. "That way you don't fall asleep in a random rideshare."

"Barton Hills," she says, naming a wealthy part of town. "That's where I live."

Interesting. That's more family homes, not young professionals. "No problem. I'll go pull my truck around to the entrance."

A few minutes later, we're on the road, Kaitlyn's address punched into my navigation system, but it's dead quiet in the car because she's out like a light. I'm not sure I'd even made it out of the parking lot before she slumped against the window, sound asleep.

I smile and focus on the road. It's a twenty-minute drive, and she doesn't stir once. When I turn into her neighborhood, I'm glad she's not awake because she can't see my surprise. I've been around wealthy people my whole life, but these homes have to be at least three thousand square feet each, on quarter- to half-acre lots. Even for rich people, it's unusual for someone our age to live in a house like these. But sure enough, the GPS prompts me to turn into the driveway of a house that could comfortably fit three families.

I park and cut the engine. "Kaitlyn."

She still doesn't stir.

I try again, louder. "Hey, Kaitlyn."

Nothing. She's so out of it, I'd worry except she lets out a muted snore. She'd be furious if she knew I heard it, but it's pretty cute.

How do I wake her without startling her? I decide to rock her awake, which means rocking in my seat to shake the truck. Given the number of times in high school I would have loved to be guilty of scandalous behavior in a car with Kaitlyn, it's ironic *this* is why we've finally set one to rocking.

It works. Her forehead scrunches in her sleep as she shifts to find a new position.

"Kaitlyn? You're home. It's time to wake up."

More forehead wrinkles, then a sleepy eye opens. "Mphmfh?"

"You're home," I repeat.

She nestles against the door again, eyes closed. "Mphmmmmfh."

I stifle a laugh and try my next plan, climbing from the truck to walk around to her side. I brace myself to open her door and catch her if she falls out.

She doesn't, only moves away from the door with an annoyed grunt.

"Kaitlyn," I say, giving her forearm a soft squeeze. "If you come out of the truck, you get to go sleep in your own bed."

Nothing.

I squeeze her shoulder. "Kaitlyn? Don't you want to sleep in your own bed? I bet you have a big, fluffy blanket and soft pillows."

She lolls her head to face me, her eyelids at half-mast. "Pillow?"

"Yes. Your own pillows in your own house. So nice, right?"

She closes her eyes, but her thinking wrinkles are back. "Home?"

"Home. Bed. Pillows. Blanket."

She moves her feet toward the door, and I step back to give her room, but instead of her getting out, I suddenly have an armful of Kaitlyn as she leans her head against my chest, her butt still in her seat but the rest of her trying to fall asleep on me.

"Whoa, Kaitlyn. You're almost there. I'm going to lean in and unbuckle your seat belt, then I'll help you to your door, okay?"

She turns her head to nod. "Loud heart. Mmmkay."

I suppress another laugh. If this is sleepy Kaitlyn, drunk Kaitlyn must be an entire event. I reach in to remove her seat belt, and she snuggles into me harder. Somewhere inside me, seventeen-year-old Micah celebrates.

"You're free," I tell her when I guide the seat belt to retract without giving her neck burn. "Can you walk?"

She slides her arms up my chest to clasp them behind my neck. "Nope."

My heart gives a single extra hard thump. That felt way too good.

"I'm going to carry you to your door, okay? Do you have your keys?" She mumbles our birth year, and I realize she probably has a keypad lock with a less-than-genius passcode. "Hold on tight, okay?

I'm going to pick you up." I slide my arm beneath her knees, and she keeps her grip around my neck.

I carry her toward the front path. She says nothing, only rubs her cheek against my chest, and I don't rush. She feels right in my arms. Warm. Pliant in a way that's too tempting to dwell on. Maybe it's better that we've reached the door . . .

Our birth year does, in fact, work on the keypad. I turn the handle and nudge it open with my foot.

"You made it," I tell her. "Time to put you down. You're home."

She lifts her head, stares at her open door, and burrows into me again. "Too tired. Carry me."

I obey, stepping inside, not able to resist satisfying my curiosity. She gives a vague wave and mumbles "living room." I follow the almost-point of her finger. The house is dim, only a light shining down from the stairs and another from the kitchen, but it's indirect. I can't see much detail, but Kaitlyn has gotten us to the living room.

"Sofa."

I carry her to it and set her down. She promptly curls into a ball, her hands tucked beneath her cheek.

"You sure you don't want to go up to your bed?" I ask.

"Sleepy," she says. "And if you ask me about this, I'll deny it happened. Night-night."

I stare at her, my jaw slightly dropped, but her eyes are still closed. I shake my head and smile, see myself out, and make sure the door is locked behind me.

Tuesday can't come soon enough.

Chapter Thirteen

Kaitlyn

HERE ARE THINGS THAT make me sad: I do not have red hair.

That's it, really.

It is the one ongoing tragedy in my life, because ever since I read *Anne of Green Gables* when I was ten, I've wanted to be Anne Shirley. We don't have many things in common, and red hair is the least of it. I'm not an orphan. I don't have writing chops. I'm not prone to naming the puddles and sidewalks around me things like the Lake of Shining Waters or Dryad's Bubble. And I've been so well-behaved that I was the favorite of adults my entire life.

On the other hand, Anne and I are both clever girls. Neither of us is conventionally pretty. Maybe that's why I wished to be like her so badly. Her intelligence and stubbornness made her beloved by all the best people. But her openness won her friends easily, and I've only learned to open up more recently. Still, I've found a few of those "bosom friends," and Madison is the best of them.

I don't think there's a more famous quote in that whole series than Anne's fervent declaration on Octobers. "I'm so glad I live in a world where there are Octobers," she said.

And as I walk out of my house on this October first morning in an orange suit to welcome it, I decide Anne and I are the same in this way too. It's not so much the weather; we'll be in the low seventies again today, and it's still green everywhere. But the air is crisp with possibility the way it used to feel before school started every fall.

I get into my car and rev the engine, my parents having driven it over after church yesterday.

When I hurried out of my office last Thursday, I was plain old Kaitlyn. Today I return to work as an auntie.

And as the boss, not the boss-in-waiting.

And as the woman who has been carried in the arms of Micah Croft.

The auntie thing is the most important, of course. So why have I thought about the carrying thing just as much?

Maybe I *am* as prone to romanticizing as Anne Shirley was.

I slide on my sunglasses and give my reflection a cool once over in the visor mirror. "You were tired. Mistakes were made. Not big mistakes. Now go be the boss." I flip up the visor, pull out of my garage, and head toward the warehouse.

I moved my meeting with Micah from tomorrow to first thing this Monday morning so I could retake control of the situation. We'll have a good working relationship now, but boundaries were crossed, and they need resetting. Boundaries like Madison having our architect visit her newborn in the hospital.

Boundaries like me having our architect carry me into my house to sleep.

Boundaries like how much I liked having Micah Croft there for all of it.

Mainly the baby thing though.

Micah's truck is already in the parking lot along with a white work van with "Herbert Metalworks" painted on the sides. The welders.

I walk in through the warehouse door and pause, taken aback by the change since I was last here. It's full of stuff, so much, and so many kinds that I can't process it at first. I spot Micah on the far side of the warehouse in a hard hat, consulting with a woman over some papers. They both look up when the door closes behind me.

Micah holds up a hand in greeting, and I return the hello before winding my way over. The stacks and piles begin to make visual sense. Stacks of metal bars. Folded piles of black fabric, chest high. Five-gallon buckets of paint. Piles of scrap metal.

There is *so* much here, and yet . . . it's hard to imagine it turning into the marigold canopy Micah presented in his sketches, but I remember his dove installation and decide not to doubt him.

"Good morning," he says when I reach them. "How's the baby? I'm willing to be taken hostage by any baby photo content."

"Funny, I happen to have some." I pull out my phone and open the album that already has three dozen pictures from Harper's first three days of life. "Don't think I didn't see you trying to figure out what to say when Madison asked if this baby is beautiful, but I'm here with the photo evidence that she is, and you better look at this like you're witnessing beauty incarnate."

The woman standing with him chuckles, and Micah introduces her. "This is Eva Herbert, a master welder and the best person in Texas for this job. Eva, this is Kaitlyn Armstrong, the boss."

"Your baby is beautiful," Eva says.

"My niece, and yes. Learn from her," I tell Micah. "She didn't even have to see the pictures."

"It was a weird angle the first time I saw her," Micah protests. "I was smitten the second I held her."

He coos over the pictures for a couple of minutes, and it makes me want to coo over him, but instead, I take my phone back and nod to the pile of rebar nearest us. "Let's get into it. Talk me through the week."

"Sure, but I'll turn Eva loose first."

I give the welder a professional smile. "Are you ready for this?"

Eva smiles. "Not sure this is the kind of thing you can get ready for. But I'm willing, so that counts for something."

I tilt my head, shifting to business mode. "Let me rephrase the question. Can you do this, Ms. Herbert?"

Her smile fades, and she gives me a crisp nod. "Yes, ma'am."

"Good. I can't wait to see it."

With another polite nod, she excuses herself.

Micah keeps his eyes on me instead of watching after Eva. "How are you doing?"

"Great. Excited to dive into this."

"Feeling . . . rested?"

Ah, there it is. He's not smiling, but his eyes dance.

I don't take the bait. "More than Madison. Harper Ivy Mae sleeps all the time, but not all the time at once, and she's waking her parents up every two hours to eat. She's fat and happy. Madison is delirious. But also deliriously happy. Now, how about showing me where you're going to start?"

Micah gives a small smile now, one that feels like it's more for himself, but he takes the hint and reaches over to pick up a hard hat resting on a nearby stack of empty pallets. "Safety first, then we'll walk the floor."

I settle the blue hard hat on my head and refuse to picture how much I look like a Broncos fan wearing it with my orange suit. I also forgot I match the safety poles. This suit will not be making a return visit to the warehouse.

"The point of installation art is to change the perception of a space," Micah says, leading me to a corner where we can survey the floor. "Technically, that's the warehouse. A utilitarian commercial building meant for the specific purpose of storage. This will be a multilayered change. Madison's decision to use it is the first shift in perception."

I nod. "By changing its function to an event venue."

"Yes, but it's more than that. Think about Halloween costumes. Ever see someone you know well in a Halloween costume and think, wow, this whole time I thought he was a law student, but it turns out he's really a zombie."

"Definitely."

The corner of his mouth kicks up. "Is that a lawyer joke?"

"Absolutely."

"I'll try again. If I threw on a Wizard of Oz costume right now, would you think, wow, all this time I thought this was Micah, but he was Dorothy all along."

"Dorothy, hm? I'm not here to judge your choices, but you really just jumped right to Dorothy. Not the Tin Man? Talk to me about your shoe collection. Do you have sparkly red shoes?"

"Kaitlyn . . ." he says, a note of long-suffering in his voice.

"Fine, no. I would not assume you were Dorothy, even if you pet me and call me Toto." Oh, whoops. I've conjured an image of him running his hand over my hair, gentling me.

Micah doesn't seem to suffer the same intrusive thought, because he moves on. "When you watched *Harry Potter*, did you think, 'That's Gary Oldman dressed up like Sirius Black,' or were you just watching Sirius kick butt and take names?"

"The second one."

"And did you watch *Batman* and stop and think, 'Oh, there's Gary Oldman again as the commissioner'?"

"I haven't seen *Batman*."

"That's exactly—wait, what?" He looks at me, totally baffled. "Any of them?"

I shake my head. "Superhero movies aren't my thing."

"Superhero movies are not your . . ." He stares at me for a couple of seconds. "All right. What is your thing?"

You, I almost say. *Ummm . . .* That thought jumped way too easily out of nowhere. And we're talking about movies, not unhealthy impulses. "You know how there are ten Best Picture nominees for the Oscar every year, but everyone has seen five of them and no one has seen the other five? I like the other five."

He opens and closes his mouth twice, but nothing comes out.

"Don't act like I'm being a snob while we're sitting by a highbrow sculpture you're making to the tune of one billion dollars."

"Still not returning the fee," he says, and I grin. "And you're off by several zeros."

"Anyway, I get it. Can we get back to Sirius Black and your highbrow art?"

He opens his phone. "Siri, is it inappropriate to call my client a brat?"

I lean toward his phone. "Yes, it is inappropriate to call your client a brat."

He smiles and sets the phone down again. "All right, so the actor versus role thing isn't a perfect analogy. But Tom Cruise is

Tom Cruise no matter what costume you put on him, while you're halfway through a Gary Oldman movie before you realize it's him. That's the difference between decorating for an event versus changing the perception of a space. It's not enough to put a cool sculpture in here. It has to interact with all this negative space and turn it into something."

"How do you start building Gary Oldman?"

"Always with the foundation." He walks me over to the nearest orange pole. I could not feel dumber standing beside it.

"We'll start by painting all these black and enclosing them in fluted rebar sheaths. We'll use full twenty-foot lengths but bend them to curve outward at the top." His face is so expressive as he literally walks me through the beginning phase, his hands tracing forms and shapes in the air.

This is a Micah I don't know. This is not a guy who is playing it cool and allowing himself to express emotions only in the cool-to-medium-warm range. This is what passion looks like. For a job, I mean. It's how Madison looks when she's talking about her next idea for Threadwork. It's how I feel about studying the law, and the way it imposes order on chaos. Makes wrongs right.

After he's explained the work they'll be tackling over the next week, I stop beside a pile of rebar and sweep my eyes over the space. I can't make the full connection between where I'm standing now and the concept he showed us, but . . . he's going to do it. And it fires me up to make sure that I meet that effort.

"This feels like the old days," I say before I think it through.

Micah gives me a quizzical smile. "How do you mean?"

"Watching everything you're putting into this, it's . . . motivating." It's a familiar stirring to push myself harder, to match his pace, his intensity.

His face grows serious. "Kaitlyn, I don't want you to set yourself up for disappointment." He sets a hand on my shoulder. "You're never going to be better than me at architecture."

I can't keep a straight face. "But if I start now . . ."

He shakes his head. "I'm sorry, Kaitlyn. No."

"Boo, fine. I'll have to step it up somewhere else. Like making sure I leverage this piece to make as much money for the people it represents as I can."

He drops his hand and I wish he hadn't. I want the weight of it back, and that's when I realize my stomach has been fluttering. This isn't good. Even though it's been ten years, I recognize this now. These are specific to a Micah Crush.

Micah doesn't seem to sense a change in the current between us—also familiar—and keeps the joke going. "But if we're not working on the same thing, how will we know who won?"

The flutters grow stronger as he smiles, and I shift to gaze toward the center of the warehouse. "This is one of those obnoxious cooperative games where we can only win if everyone wins. I prefer to smoosh you like a bug, but if I can't do that, I choose to feel happy about what this will do for the people Threadwork supports."

"Tell me about it," he says.

I turn to face him. "You don't know what Threadwork does?"

"I do. I want to hear it from you."

I consider that. I want to turn the temperature down, and I'd been about to do it by leaving. But talking business might be okay.

I point to my head. "Can I do story time without the silly hat?"

He glances around, then up to the supervisor's loft. "You can if you move out of the construction zone, which we can do if you want to go up and see the layout I'm suggesting for the deejay."

"Deal."

He leads us toward a corner but pauses to look down at my shoes. I'm in heels again.

"Stairs or elevator?" he asks, eyeing them.

They're only three-inch heels today. "Stairs."

There are no levels in the warehouse. It's open from floor to ceiling, but it's the equivalent of two flights of stairs to get to the loft. He lets us in and dusts off an office chair, a piece that has seen better days, the faux leather peeling and the chrome arms cloudy.

"Please, have a seat." He waves me toward it, and when I sit, he lifts the hard hat off my head like he's carefully removing a crown. "Now tell me about Threadwork."

I will. As soon as the brush of his fingers against my temples stops shorting out my brain circuits. As soon as his eyes, bright with attention, release mine as prisoner. As soon as I truly fight the need to sway toward him and melt into him like I did when he carried me into my house.

This is not like my high school Micah Crush at all.

This is much worse.

Chapter Fourteen

Kaitlyn

"Kaitlyn?" Micah's voice is puzzled. "Threadwork? I'd love to hear why you decided to work with Madison?"

Madison.

I blink and glance around the supervisor loft, gathering my bearings.

Madison and the gala. I won't be distracted from making this gala everything Madison dreamed, and that means not getting caught up in Micah again. That crush became all-consuming, and I don't have the time or bandwidth for that.

We're hitting on the right topic to channel my energy elsewhere.

I clear my throat so the first part—the worst part—won't stick in it. "Were you aware of the scandal surrounding our family company when we were at Hillview?"

He takes a seat on a short stepladder. "Yes."

"You know what caused it and how it . . . resolved?" That's not the right word. The damage will never resolve completely. But the case itself did reach a conclusion.

"The company's factories in Bangladesh were found guilty of negligence," he says. "I remember that from high school. I looked it up again before I submitted my proposal. Wiki says the plaintiffs won the largest settlement from a company in the history of the ready-made garment manufacturing industry."

I could leave it at that. I don't *have* to lay out the ugly facts for Micah. But I *need* to. I want him to see . . . me.

"In a way, it indirectly affected you because it was why I was not great to you in high school."

"Katie, you're acting like you bullied me. There's nothing to explain."

"I know I didn't bully you. But I still have regrets."

He props his elbows on his knees and leans forward, raising an eyebrow to indicate he's listening.

"This all started when I was in eighth grade. I believed my dad when he said the company was innocent. Madi never believed him, and that's why we fought. She rebelled to punish him, I obeyed to . . . I don't know. Neutralize her? It felt like we were under attack constantly, and she was disloyal, trying to separate herself from the scandal. That's how I thought of it. As a scandal. Not a tragedy. As something that was happening to us, not because of us. That's what I'm most ashamed of now."

"Fighting with Madison?"

"Believing we were victims. Because people were dead, and I felt sorry for myself." It is the ugliest thing to ever be true about me.

I meet his eyes, waiting for him to interject, to reassure me that I was a kid, and I should cut myself some slack. He doesn't say anything, only nods, and it makes me want to be more honest.

"We were never victims. My father overrode his onsite supervisor's warnings about a major construction flaw in the factory. He wouldn't allow a work stoppage. Two days later, the building collapsed, two hundred people were dead, and more than four hundred injured, but he denied liability for years."

"When did you change your mind?"

"My last year of college. A professor used Armstrong Industries for a case study in my business ethics class. Halfway through, it was pretty clear: My dad lied."

He flinches. "That must have been a hard class to take."

That was an understatement. I look out of the supervisor window, scanning the space Micah will transform over the next two months. "It was like having someone do an art installation inside me where they ripped out my worldview and told me to build on a completely different foundation. I had to deconstruct everything I believed about my dad and the company and find a way to view the world through a different lens."

"Is that when you and Madison became a team?"

I wince. "Not exactly. This is messy family drama. You sure you want to hear about this?"

"Yeah." His voice is soft. "If you're okay telling me, I do."

I take a deep breath. "Before law school, before Madison and I made up, we got in a fight and I went off on her. Her plan since high school was to get her inheritance and match every payout from the legal settlement, doubling each victim's benefit. I thought my way was better. I chose law school because I wanted to become the compliance officer at Armstrong. I wanted to make sure our corporate ethics were unimpeachable. I told her she was throwing money at a problem so she could take the moral high ground with my dad, not because she really cared."

His eyes widen slightly.

"I know it sounds bad, but at the time, I was mad about her shutting me out of her life for ten years, so maybe I was harsh." I give him a small smile.

"I wouldn't have guessed that you and Madison weren't always close. Watching you, it's like you two are as much friends as you are sisters."

"It took time," I say. "Once she realized I wasn't defending our father anymore, we figured out how to talk to each other. But since Madison's smart and good to the bones, she started looking at what would *really* help. She decided to get an MBA focused on entrepreneurial activism. Her thesis was Threadwork. It started with microfinance, but she figured out pretty quickly that not everyone wants to be an entrepreneur. Some want job security with good wages, so she opened the Marigold Institute. It offers four different management training courses. We started with garment manufacturing, but we realized that true opportunity meant giving them access to careers they chose, not fell into. We added hospitality, retail, and information technology."

"When did it go from 'she' to 'we'?"

"I started volunteering at Threadwork when I could during law school." I run my finger over my eyebrow. How do you explain something you're not proud of or ashamed of, just something that needed to be done? "We combined superpowers and bent Gordon Armstrong, scion and CEO of Armstrong Industries, to our will. He comps the office space and donates. A lot. When she asked me to act as director while she's out with the baby, it was an easy yes, and I started full-time in May."

This pulls the biggest smile of the morning from him.

"Is that funny?"

"That two twenty-something women took down a corporate ti-tan?" He shrugs. "I knew you in high school. Doesn't surprise me."

Flutters. All the flutters. Back. All back.

I pivot to work. It's safe. Structured. I know the rules. "That's why Madison is so driven to make this gala a success. She needs the first one to announce itself in the Austin consciousness with the splash of a Super Bowl halftime show. It needs to be iconic from the start."

"But you're not as invested?"

"Of course I am, but my ideas are more helpful on the Institute side, coming up with course expansions, handling the operational details she doesn't love. We collaborate to plan growth. I figure out how to implement it, but her genius is figuring out how to fund it. How to make other people see the vision."

He stands and walks over to gaze down through the window. "Nothing less than iconic, huh?"

"Yes."

He turns and meets my eyes. "Challenge accepted."

I can't say anything for two full seconds, mesmerized by his eyes, by everything they promise to deliver.

For the *gala*.

This is not safe. This isn't safe at all.

I blink and snap out of it, standing to survey the rest of the supervisor loft. "Thanks for taking the time to show me all this. I better get over to the office and find more reasons for our gala guests to spend money when they're inspired by your art." I say the last part as I head for the door, and Micah follows me out.

Before I reach the stairs, he plucks at my sleeve, and I turn.

"The grudge is still expired, right?"

"Right," I say, trying to give him a normal smile. So normal. Super normal. An everything-is-great smile. He starts to look worried. "We're good."

He hesitates. "Okay. You seem . . ."

"Remember high school? I like to work. And work is work. And I work better when it stays that way." None of this emotional connection detour.

As if someone has swiped a filter over his face, the warmth turns cool. "Understood."

He follows me down the stairs without comment, and when we reach the warehouse floor, I pause near yet another pile of rebar. "Keep me posted. Madison chose the right person for this job."

"Thanks." He reaches over and slides a rod from the top, holding it in his upturned palms. One of his thumbs traces the ribs spiraling around it. "Did I tell you where this rebar is from?"

"No."

"The teardown of the Marble Falls bridge." He scrapes a ridge. "I've had it for years."

"Weren't we still in college when that bridge came down?"

He nods. "I was on the construction crew that cleared the debris. They never care what I keep from a demo, so I held on to it, waiting for the right project. All the pink granite for the capitol back in the day came from Marble Falls." He taps it. "Rebar from a bridge leading to a quarry that helped build a legacy. Fits Threadwork."

I swallow. This man . . . he makes me want to abandon my role in all this, pull up a chair, and watch him work all day. Watch him make and sculpt and build. "I love that."

He sets the rebar back on its stack. "Drop in as often as it takes to feel comfortable with the progress."

I don't quite meet his eyes as I look over to Eva setting up sawhorses. "You won't see me much. This is clearly in capable hands, so I won't be underfoot."

"I'll walk you out."

"Don't worry about it."

He doesn't argue, only nods and slides his hands into his pockets.

"I'll let Madison know it's all coming together," I say before heading to the door.

"See you around," he says, and it's almost lost in the clanking of Eva's setup.

In the parking lot, I climb into my Audi. I replay the whole scene with Micah several times as I drive to the office, trying to understand what I'm feeling.

I like Micah. As a person.

I am attracted to Micah. That body. That brain. That sweet look on his face when he held Harper. The intensity in his eyes when he talks about the installation. The quiet way he listens.

But he also brings out old instincts that I don't love. Like the urge to compete, even over stupid things. Or the self-consciousness I worked on overcoming all through college. It's like he sees through my highlights and the high heels, the perfect neutral lipstick with a rosy tint and the tailored suits. He sees quiet, mousy high school Kaitlyn.

He sees the girl who was so quietly, madly in love with him her senior year that she couldn't hide it and broke her nose.

The shame of being transparent had burned so intensely that even in college, I'd changed direction the handful of times I'd seen him on campus. *No burning feelings here, Micah Croft.*

As I pull onto the highway, I acknowledge there's a difference now that I can't overlook: Micah seems like he likes me as a person too.

What if that went somewhere? What if that turned into mutual attraction and then more?

The flutters explode in my chest even considering it.

And that is the problem.

This wouldn't turn into another crush. There's a good chance Micah would . . . reciprocate. I've had a serious relationship. I know the signs.

I also know that for the next six months, I don't have the time. Literally. Where would I fit a relationship while I'm working and studying sixty hours a week?

I won't disappoint Madison by losing focus, and I won't delay the bar exam again to make time to possibly date someone that I only have a hunch might be interested in dating me.

You know who puts their career on a one-year pause after three grueling years of law school for a sister? A good sister. You know who puts it on pause for another six months for a guy? A weak woman.

That's not me.

I pull into work five minutes later, blaring Ciara's "Level Up," and walk into the office, boss energy on blast.

Suz jumps up from the desk when I walk in, Big Director energy in place. "Please tell me you have more pictures of that yummy baby besides the announcement Madison emailed."

I grin, happy to share the picture loot. Khôi, the accountant, and Aisha, our communications director, rush over to see, and after everyone has had their fill of the boss's baby, I walk into my office.

And stop cold.

All the framed photos that were leaning against the wall are now hanging on them instead, and if I'd had any doubt who did it, a small plant stand now sits behind my desk with a lucky bamboo on it. The stand is a striking brass-toned geometric structure of soldered wire I'm sure came from a demolished building.

Micah.

Maybe I'm not as strong as I thought.

Chapter Fifteen

Micah

I'm NOT SURE I get Kaitlyn.

Maybe I get her as much as anyone ever does. Like in high school, when seeing her instead of looking past her like so many people did made me feel like I knew a secret: She was an undercover stunner, and the otherwise-smart boys at our school were big-time blind.

It's no secret now. She's polished to a shine, and the way she carries herself draws the attention of everyone in a room before she even says a word.

It could just be me. I don't think so.

I lean against the door of the warehouse, the last one to leave. It's been over a week since we started construction, and it's been that long since Kaitlyn has stopped in. She texted to thank me for sprucing up her office, and I've sent her two progress updates so far, photos of the work, hoping it would prompt her to say she was coming for a site visit.

She hasn't.

She hasn't, and this is definitely the first time I've ever wished that a client had a habit of popping in.

I turn off the overhead lights and set the lock, wondering what I should do about Kaitlyn.

I'm into her. Again. I've got better dating skills than I did in high school. We're already on better footing than we were then with our friendship truce.

Option: Do nothing and take my lead from Kaitlyn.

No. I'm not a passive guy.

Option: Wait until this project is done, then ask her out.

Possibly. I'm a patient guy.

Option: Ask her out now.

Yes. This is what I want.

Risks don't scare me, and this isn't a big one. Either she says yes or she says no. But never asking her versus getting rejected have the same outcome: no Kaitlyn. Never asking? That only leaves regrets. What ifs? Nah. Not my thing.

Now I need to figure out when and how to ask her in a way that makes her want to say yes.

I PUT MY PLAN in place the following Monday: Give her great reasons to come to the warehouse.

Trust me, I can't believe what a genius I am either.

Normally, Austin is still hot in October. Low-eighties temperatures are normal, but the weather gods smile down in this, the second week of October, and we get some rain, which cools things down, and we're in the high sixties two weeks earlier than usual.

> Cool weather today. Warehouse isn't an oven. Good day to stop in and see the progress.

> Slammed with meetings. Progress looks great in the photos.

I try a variation of this every day until Thursday, when I get much more pointed.

> Any chance you can stop in today? Would love to show you in person.

> ...

> ...

> Unfortunately, my only open slot is lunch.

> Great, see you then.

I put my phone away, smiling. I know that's not what she meant, but I'll make sure it's worth her time. Today will be about reading her. I'm certain she isn't annoyed by me anymore, but I want to see if I'm imagining that she feels a pull toward me.

Could I take her avoidance of the warehouse as a neon sign blinking NO? Yes. But there's more to it. I'm sure of it. I don't know if Kaitlyn keeping her distance is a her thing or a me thing, but that's today's mission: figuring it out.

That and getting her stoked about how this installation is coming together.

But mostly getting a read on her.

When she walks in at 12:30, Eva is on break in her truck, having cleared out when she saw me setting up for Kaitlyn. Specifically, after she saw me create a makeshift table with stacked paint buckets and plywood, covered with an unused paint tarp, and set with Styrofoam takeout containers from a food truck that comes through every day. The clincher was when I said, "Go eat in your truck so I can see if my client is into me," and she'd walked out laughing ten minutes ago.

"Hey," I say, as Kaitlyn walks over to meet me. She's in a suit the color of pink lemonade, a fitted white top beneath, and pointy black shoes. "Wasn't sure if stopping by meant you'd have to skip lunch, so I thought I'd better have some for you in case."

Her smile is warm, like she's never dreamed of dodging me. Maybe I misread the situation?

"That's thoughtful of you. I wouldn't mind a bite to eat, but why don't you show me around first?"

"Or," I say, sliding out one of the few folding chairs we keep onsite, "I can point it out to you as we eat because that's the beauty of this open floor plan."

Her smile widens, and she takes the seat. "What's on the menu today?"

"Pork adobo nachos or chicken enchiladas in green sauce," I offer, pointing to each container. "I bought it from a truck, so you can't go wrong."

"Is that the rule?" she asks, reaching for the nachos.

"Sure. You don't eat from food trucks much?"

"I haven't, no. What?" she demands when she catches me trying to hide a smile.

"That's very Hillview of you, that's all."

"What does that mean? You're as Hillview as I am."

I shake my head. "I'm definitely not."

"Okay, Micah *Croft*. I knew at least two of your cousins. Smells like family tradition to me."

There's no bite to her tone, and I'm glad for multiple reasons that I convinced her to come today. One is that I can see we've definitely left behind our antagonistic dynamic. But the second is that I can show her things about me that she doesn't know.

"Not the way you think. You were honest about how hard high school was because of nonschool things, so I'm going to tell you some stuff you don't know about me. Couldn't know, because I made a point of not telling anyone my business at Hillview." I shake my head, remembering how much I cared about this back then when I don't care at all now. "I did go there on family money, but I was a charity case."

Her forehead wrinkles, and she pauses in the act of lifting her fork. "Don't those two things cancel each other out?"

I reach over and pluck a loaded nacho. "It's like this nacho. I eat it like normal-to-poor people do: with my fingers. You eat it with a fork."

She glances from my nacho to her fork and takes the bite from her fork anyway, eyeing me like she's waiting for me to continue.

"My mom is a Croft, so she grew up with lots of money. But for a lot of reasons, she was a hard person. She made choices that made her life harder. Got disinherited, but didn't want much to do with her family anyway. Not until I was getting close to high school age. My grandparents had passed by then, so she went to my uncle and made a deal with him that meant he would pay for me to go to Hillview." I take a bite of my enchilada, thinking about how hard that must have been for her given how much she hates accepting help. "She was fine never seeing a dime of her parents' money, but she didn't want me to have less advantages than she did. So I went to Hillview."

Kaitlyn hasn't taken another bite through this. "Wow. I had no idea. So you were a loser poor kid?"

She says it with such a straight face that I laugh and choke slightly on a piece of shredded chicken. When I wash it down with a gulp of water, I grin. "Yes. The trashiest of trash."

A small smile peeks out at me. "There's a lot of gaps in that story. I have a feeling that's where some of the hardest stuff is?"

I nod. "Perceptive."

"I've been getting a lot of unlicensed therapy," she says.

"You—what?"

"Madison. She's been working off and on with a therapist for the last two years, and she likes to try it out on me. Maybe I'm getting infected."

I tilt my head to study her. "Nah. You've always been perceptive, seeing things other people don't." I wonder if she'll ask how I know this, but the tops of her cheeks flush pink, and she lets it pass.

"I didn't see that you weren't a regular Hillview student." She shakes her head. "No, that's not right. You went out of your way to be different than the other students. I didn't realize you weren't one of us trust fund kids."

"I went out of my way to fly under the radar, that's all. I only cared about getting the grades that would get me a full ride to college."

She starts to take another bite—with her fork—then pauses and sits back, stares at me, understanding dawning on her face only to be chased by a flicker of guilt. "And I was so mad at you for taking valedictorian."

"*Winning* valedictorian," I say. "It's not my fault you bombed that calculus test like a dummy rich kid."

"Isn't it though? How do I know you didn't go out to the field that day specifically to distract me when I was walking out of school?" she asks in a teasing cross-examination.

Interesting. She's going to go there. "You mean when I was out there shirtless, showing off my sorry biceps?"

"The pecs were the problem." Then her eyes widen slightly, like she hadn't meant to make the joke aloud. "Anyway, I'm sorry I wasn't gracious about it. I had no idea."

"Sorry," I say, rubbing my chest. "Did you say something? I got distracted by my problematic pecs."

"You'll be okay. You can't break your nose on them."

I switch to my most pedantic voice. "Well, actually, you didn't break your nose on them. You broke it on a post."

Kaitlyn blinks at me, then her mouth twitches. "Micah, did you just 'well, actually' my post?"

That makes us both laugh, and I want to high-five or fist-bump her in appreciation, but while it's a shade more than professional, it veers into friend zone territory, and that's not where I'm trying to steer.

I offer her a handshake, and when she takes it, still smiling, I make sure to brush my thumb over her knuckles, up then down, leaving no question that I mean to do it. "Well done, Kaitlyn."

She slides her hand from mine and shifts in her seat. "Thanks. And Katie is fine."

I lean forward and prop my chin on my hand. "Are you saying our truce is real, Katie?"

"Didn't I tell you that in my office before you spiffed it up like a good friend does? Thank you again for that."

Her mouth says *friend*, but she's guarding her glances. Friends don't do that. People who don't want to let on that they're into you do that.

I can't push. My instincts say blurting "Hey, I'm into you, let's go out" will shut her down. I want to make myself a safe place instead.

"You're welcome again," I say. "And as your good friend, I'm going to make sure you get fed, so why don't you eat while I give you the seated tour of the progress?" When she nods, I point out what we've done so far, from the bolted perimeter to the supports Eva has welded in to start the canopy.

She asks a few questions as I "guide" us, and when I'm done, I reach for my enchiladas.

"It looks really good," she says.

"You're probably wondering why I wanted you to come out here, since I've been sending you updates."

"It crossed my mind."

"I want to get your feedback on a possible change to the next phase."

She gives me a neutral look. "Sure. Let's hear it."

"First, can I ask how much you guys want to raise with the gala?"

"Two million."

She doesn't even blink. I know the Armstrongs are one of the wealthiest families in Austin, but how rich do you have to be for that number to not even faze you?

"That doesn't stress you out?" I ask.

"We've sold all the gala tickets, so the costs are covered—including this installation—and we're already operating at a profit for the event. But hitting that total amount will depend on how well our guests respond to the silent auction items."

"What happens if they don't cough up the donations?"

"Micah, you better not try to do something noble like return your fee for this work."

I snort. "Not a chance. I never undervalue my work."

She smiles. "Good. I have a table that proves it. As for the auction and donations, that part mostly depends on me. I'll make it happen, but yes, it's stressing me out."

A big dumb grin takes over my face. I can feel it, and I don't care.

"What now?" She sounds exasperated.

"You've got the weight of two million dollars trying to bury you, raising the funds falls mostly to you, you're stressed, and yet you're sitting there, a nacho-eating queen like it's nothing. Like we're talking about organizing a barbecue. Wait, no. Not a barbecue. A potluck." I give her a fake concerned expression. "Do you know what a potluck is?"

"Micah." She plucks a plain chip from her nachos. "Are you making rich people jokes?"

"A hundred percent."

"I know what a potluck is. Believe it or not, I even organized a barbecue once."

"Slumming it, were you?"

"Don't think we're going to skip over how my nacho-eating queen act has nothing on your too-cool-to-care act you've been putting on since high school." She leans forward and taps an ivory-painted nail on my side of the table. "We. Will. Get. To. It."

"Confessing I was the loser poor kid wasn't enough?" I joke.

"Felt like an appetizer. But let's move on to your possible change to the next phase."

"It doesn't sound as awesome now that I know the goal is two million, but I thought if we built a bar in here, you could rack up even more cash. The more I think about it, the less—"

"No, tell me. What do you mean by bar? We're planning to have waiters circulate with wine and champagne."

I point to the south end. "Stage, big screen, live entertainment." I indicate the rest of the floor. "Tables. Name cards. Cater waiters."

I point to the rolling bay door. "Grand entrance. Did I cover everything?"

"Yes."

"What if instead of creating a small space near the stage for anyone who wants to dance, you clear a big space by giving people somewhere else they want to go. Specifically, over there." I point to the corner across from the entrance. "Build a bar, but make it more than a walk-up where people order and wander away. Make it a lounge space with club chairs and low tables, so it would draw people from the dining tables to come over and stay. Then you can move those out and clear even more of the center for dancing and mingling. My thinking was that a bar would entice people to spend more money, but this crowd doesn't do cash bars, does it?"

"Generally, no. But we should do an open bar with the intimate lounge feeling you described. It makes the experience feel more luxe, and our generosity prompts more of their generosity."

"Virtuous giving cycle?"

"A strategic one. Let's do it." She stands. "Thanks for lunch and the update. I need to tell the event planner she has to hire a bar staff."

I get up and gather our trash. "I'll walk you out."

At the warehouse door, I drop our garbage in the bin but pause before I hold the door for her. "Here's a confession: When we had classes together, I never said any of my ideas out loud unless I knew they were good because I wanted you to think I was a genius."

I push the door open, standing against it to give her room to pass. She stops in front of me, close enough that she has to tilt her head more than usual to meet my eyes.

"Here's a confession: I started wearing lipstick senior year because I wanted you to think about my lips."

Then she slips through the door, and she's gone.

Senior Year
Micah

I LOOK AROUND THE art room, not really seeing it. Mr. Lew, the art teacher, lets me spend lunches in here even though I've never taken studio art. He seems to get that I need to be in here anyway. Art teachers are like that.

Normally, I like to look for new work on the walls or any pieces that are in process. But I spent lunch in here yesterday, and there's nothing new.

"You okay, Micah?" Mr. Lew asks, stopping by the table I have to myself.

"Fine. Letting my brain rest." That's a lie, but he nods and moves on. My brain is speeding like it always does, currently calculating whether I can get away with hanging out with Kaitlyn in the library. If I do it too often, she'll avoid me for a few days. If I space it out enough, we'll pull out our lunches and our work but end up chatting instead of studying.

Three days seems to be the sweet spot where she won't retreat. I should wait until tomorrow. But we didn't end up doing partner work in Chinese today, so we haven't talked since lunch two days ago.

Whatever. This is stupid. Lunch barely started, and I'll have talked myself into going to the library by the end anyway, so might as well go now.

She's at her usual table, one that keeps her out of the main flow of traffic but gives her a good view of the door. I know that feeling. Not wanting to be in the mix. Always needing to see what's coming.

"Hey," I say as I set down my backpack. I always take the spot across from her but one seat down so we never have to make accidental eye contact. I want to know that every time I feel her eyes on me, it's because she chose to look my way.

She blinks up at me. "Hey."

She doesn't smile. She never does when she says hi. It makes it even better when she does smile because it's opposite of her eye contact. It's unintentional, like she's surprised to find herself doing it. I like when I'm the reason it happens. I've learned over the last three years what kinds of things will do it, saving each instance like a crow with a shiny thing, waiting to trot it out and use it again.

If she's not okay with me being here, in about five minutes she'll remember somewhere else she has to go. If she's okay with it, we'll eat our lunches and end up in a conversation. I never know what it will be about. I never try to think of things because something always comes up, sometimes from her, sometimes me.

She pulls a bento box from her backpack, opens it, and sighs.

"Tuna fish?" I guess. She hates tuna, even the fancy sushi-grade kind their housekeeper uses.

"Worse." She tilts the box my way to show me the contents.

I squint. "You got a botany project for lunch?"

She takes her chopsticks and picks up different items, naming them and dropping them. "Bean sprouts. Pickled beets. Cabbage. Snap peas. Cauliflower. My mom has decided we're all eating plant-based diets now. Raw plants." She wrinkles her nose at the box. "I like meat. And there's not even any dips. I'd sell my soul for hummus right now. But at least I've got these." She brandishes a baby carrot. "You are my only joy." Then she chomps it.

My uncle's tuition check doesn't cover the fresh meals served in the Hillview dining hall. My mother's paycheck doesn't cover a housekeeper. Or even groceries, sometimes. But cutting lawns on the weekends covers a crap-ton of frozen burritos, and I pull one out of my backpack, nuked and double wrapped in foil before I left for school this morning.

"Trade you for the cabbage and beets." I can put them in my other burrito and make it more filling. Hopefully the oversalted ground beef (allegedly) will cover the taste of the beets.

"Done."

We trade and eat, and halfway through my burrito, Kaitlyn pauses and points her chopsticks at it, then clicks them together. "So, why use forks, even?"

We have found our topic for the day. It wanders from there to a conversation about Vikings and how much we both hate Beowulf, which leads us to someone's dog named Beowulf and on to dogs in general to parks and near the end of lunch, we're somehow on the subject of what tattoo each Disney princess would get.

Kaitlyn is arguing that Cinderella is the one princess who would never, under any circumstance, get a tattoo while I'm pointing to proof of her rebellious streak as counterevidence when the slight crackle from the PA system signals an announcement coming.

"A reminder that tomorrow is the last day to buy prom tickets. They will be available before and after school and during lunch. If you are bringing a non-Hillview student, they will need a signed faculty endorsement from their own school to be submitted to a junior class officer before prom."

My stomach tightens with every word of the announcement. I'm not a school activity guy. Maybe I would be into a few of them if I could afford them. But prom is different. Iconic even if school social stuff isn't your thing. And Kaitlyn is very much a school activity girl. She'll be there. With someone who can afford to take her.

I don't care about the pictures or dinner or any of that stuff, but I think about her out there, dancing to the one slow song they'll play at the end of the night, and I always see her dancing with me.

Your boy doesn't have three hundred dollars for a pair of prom tickets. Hillview is a prom-at-the-Four-Seasons school. I don't even have prom-in-the-school-gym money.

"Do you have tickets yet?" Kaitlyn asks.

I'm trying to read her tone. It's heavy on irony, like *Haha, Micah Croft at prom, what a joke.* But there's an undercurrent there, like maybe she's . . . is she fishing? She's not quite pulling off the casual conversation vibe. Is she trying to figure out if I'm going? If she's not asking straight-out, is it because she wants to work the conversation around to me asking her?

It might not even be what she's getting at. Library time and debates about Disney princess tattoos is as social as we've ever gotten. Is she hinting she wants to go as friends? Because that's not what I would want. Are solid couples or friend dates the only options for prom? Is prom a thing where it can be a first date that turns into a more-dates situation?

I wish I had the option of pulling on this thread and finding out. Maybe for the first time ever, it truly sucks that I don't have the money for this. Even if I scraped together enough for the tickets, there's dinner, pictures, corsages . . . I'm not even sure what else would crop up.

My nasty beet-and-"beef" burrito settles in my stomach like a rock, and Kaitlyn is waiting for her answer, looking like she wishes she hadn't asked after my stupidly long pause.

I start gathering my burrito trash as I answer. "Not doing prom."

"Right. Probably not your thing."

Couldn't be my thing if I wanted it to be, which for her, I do. "I have plans that night."

"Doing something cool?"

Babysitting the two neighbor kids for the single dad next door who works swing shifts at a shipping warehouse. I watch them most Saturday nights. The pay isn't enough for me, and it's too much for him, but he's a good dude, and he helped me build shelves in our garage.

Instead of telling her that, I say, "My only plans are not to be at prom."

"Right." She stares down at her bento box.

"Gotta go grab a thing from Ms. Neely," I say. She's the college counselor, and seniors have to grab so many things from her throughout the year that it's an excuse to leave any situation.

She doesn't look up, only nods and chases a snap pea around with her chopsticks like she'll get a trophy if she gets it.

I don't want to leave her feeling like crap, but I don't know what else to say. So I turn and walk out on Kaitlyn without looking back.

We don't talk about it when I find her in the library the next week or ever. When prom photos start showing up on Instagram two weeks later, I don't know if I feel better or worse after scrolling through enough to figure out that she went with friends, not a date.

When a picture pops up with her and one of her friends instead of the whole group, I get a good view of her dress and answer my own question. She picked a strapless sparkly dress about as light as pink can go before it becomes white, and she looks . . .

She looks beautiful. I feel worse. It confirms what I've known since ninth grade. The only girl I've ever wanted at Hillview is the one furthest out of my league.

Chapter Sixteen

Kaitlyn

I'm not sure I get Micah.

If I didn't know better, I'd swear he keeps making up reasons to see me.

I liked having lunch with him last week. A lot.

I liked sitting and hearing about his work as he pointed out the progress with low-key pride. I liked the way he listened when I told him about Marigold, leaning forward, his eyes focused on me, as if he was filing away every detail some place important in his brain.

It's been over a week, and he invites me every day to come check on the progress. I want to see him. Badly. And that's the problem. I need two extra hours a day right now to make my life work, but time disappears when I'm with Micah. Slips by and I don't notice. Feelings are waiting to pounce. *Big* ones. Giving myself more time for that to happen would be totally irresponsible.

I'm going over today anyway, which has my common sense sounding the alarm. I don't care. I've run out of excuses for why I can't stop by. I want to see the progress in person. I like progress.

Progress in this case being Micah. But also the installation.

I stand in front of the full-length mirror in my walk-in closet, eyeing my outfit. It's late October, and I can go Full Sweater now if I want to, regardless of what the thermometer says, which is seventy. Good enough reason for me to tuck a whisper-thin ivory cashmere

V-neck sweater into wide-leg coral trousers and finish it off with a pair of nude pumps.

My gloss is perfect, the flick on my eyeliner is lethal, and my nerves are . . . electric.

When I park at the warehouse, only Micah's truck is there. I frown as I climb out of my car. We're two months out from the gala. Shouldn't I see a hive of activity, all swarmy with construction workers while Micah supervises, wearing a tool belt low on his hips, worn jeans fitting exactly . . .

I sigh. I have not previously thought much about tool belts. I've never seen Micah in one. Why am I suddenly imagining it? The man is definitely not standing around guessing what I'll be wearing when I walk in today. I stare down, frowning. I could have bought half a boob job for the price of these pants and paid for the other one with the rest of this outfit. But then I wouldn't have this sweater to fill out with my new boobs.

It's fine. Why am I obsessed with my boobs right now? I'm *elegant*, as Mom likes to say. Designers create with my build in mind, she'll assure me. "I am Charlize Theron," I say as I reach for the warehouse door. "And she's made it on talent." And a similar haircut.

I walk in and stop short, my breath catching as I take in the work in front of me. I've been seeing the pictures, but it's a totally different experience to stand here at the feet of this rebar skeleton and *feel* it. It soars, the frame in place, the ugly rebar bending and twisting in a ballet up to the center point. I step closer, brushing my finger over the nearest strut, making sure it's still the same rusted rebar that sat in a pile a few weeks ago. It is. My finger picks up iron dust as I run it down the ribbing.

"Hey," Micah says. I spot him on the far side of the floor. He didn't have to call loudly with only the two of us in here.

"Hey," I answer. "Harper Mae is fat and sassy, and like you"—I pat the strut—"growing bones. This looks great."

"Picturing it yet?" he asks.

I slide my hands into my pockets and skirt the perimeter to reach him, keeping my shoulders back. *Charlize Theron, Charlize Theron, Charlize Theron.* Small boobs, big sex appeal. "Charlize Theron."

"What?"

What the crap? I clear my throat. "This reminds me of Charlize Theron because you know how it looks like she should be a dancer but then she does the hardcore action movies?" What am I even saying? If I had to defend this answer in an essay, I probably could, but it would take at least two pages to untangle my thinking. So I bite my tongue on the urge to babble anymore to Micah.

"Like tough but graceful?"

I'm close enough to see his forehead wrinkles as he tries to follow my logic. See, that wasn't so hard. "Yes, like that."

"Thank you," he says.

I glance around the quiet warehouse. "Tell me the truth. Did you lose your crew? Was it mutiny? Plague? Blizzard?"

"Alien abduction," he says.

I scoff. "I don't believe in aliens."

"But a blizzard in Austin has no internal logic flaws?"

"None."

"The crew is on a supply run," he says.

"Are we talking Slurpees? Or across the border to Mexico?"

His face grows serious. "Drug running jokes aren't funny."

My stomach tightens. "Sorry, that was insensi—"

"Word gets out and my cover is blown, then the feds are here, and you've ruined the gala."

I curl my lips in to deny him a smile. "So just construction stuff?"

He nods. "And Slurpees. That sounds good." He pulls out his phone and speaks as he taps. "Get Slurpees on way back from shed. Get me red." He glances up. "What flavor do you want?"

"Nothing for me, thanks." I have major love for Slurpees, but mostly as a memory from Madison's wedding, not for the brain freeze experience.

He slides his phone into his back pocket, and I notice that while he has no tool belt, he's in jeans that give his thighs the love and respect quads like that deserve. They're old Levis, I'm pretty sure, the only denim that looks better the older it gets, and his jeans look very touchable. I mean soft. They look soft.

"Any questions?" he asks. "I know it's still pretty bare bones."

I run my eyes over the expanse of the frame. "I'm getting the dimension. Is it my imagination that the warehouse feels bigger with something in it, not smaller?"

He shakes his head. "No. Most rooms are like that until you start adding things and seeing how much really fits inside. Makes you perceive the space differently."

"A really smart guy told me that's what an art installation does. Makes you notice your relationship with a space."

He gives me a small smile. "He didn't say it that way because he's not that smart, but you said it perfectly because you are."

"Thank you." It's a compliment I've heard a lot coming from him, but it almost makes me blush. I'm ridiculous.

"I had a backup plan if you weren't catching the vision yet," he says.

"Oh? Tell me."

"Multisensory experience. Put on an evening gown, pass you a plate of crab puffs, talk about our golf handicaps and cattle futures."

"That's what you think happens at rich people parties?"

His eyes glint. "Tell me it isn't."

"Okay, it is. I didn't bring an evening gown with me. Sorry."

"I meant *I* would put it on. To sell the story."

That does make me grin. "Please tell me you have a gown here ready to go."

"Sadly, I lied about that. But I did set up the deejay booth." He slides his phone out again. "Ready?"

I cock my head at him, curious about where this is going. "Ready."

The chorus to "Can't Feel My Face" by The Weeknd pours out, and Micah bites his lip dramatically like he's doing telenovela sexy face and hits a middle school shuffle. His eyebrows go up, a challenge to dance. Madi would probably already be four steps into some choreography for it, but I only shake my head, smiling. I don't do silly. I'm missing whatever gene lets you cut loose like that.

Micah presses another button on his phone. "Not going to lie, I had a feeling you wouldn't go for that."

"Not going to lie, I'm surprised you did. What happened to Mr. Too Cool for Everything from high school?"

"I left him in high school. That guy did his job until I could get out of there."

"Did you really hate it?" I ask him.

"Not all of it." His smile now is slight, but his eyes are steady on mine. "Let's try this instead."

The opening notes of "Thinking Out Loud" come out. A slow dance. He holds his hand out. "May I have this dance?"

This is still silly, but my stomach flips anyway, like he's asking for real. I can't say no after refusing the fast dance. I accept his hand. "For gala research."

He pulls me into a classic close hold, the kind that would be appropriate for any two people dancing at a social event. "For gala research."

We dance a few steps. I know how to dance. Madison *loves* to dance, as in she was on the Hillview dance team. I wasn't into it that way, but I do have a sense of rhythm, and Mom made us both go to cotillion and learn how to partner dance. Micah's firm hold and easy movement means he probably did too.

"It looks like your uncle's money extended to cotillion," I say.

He draws back enough to smile down at me. "No, but I'll take the compliment. I'm a natural."

Natural. A good way to describe how this feels. Dancing with Micah in the middle of an industrial warehouse beneath a rebar skeleton . . . This is exactly the kind of spontaneous thing that makes me self-conscious, worried about who might walk in to see this weirdness, or hoping I smell okay, or anxious that I'm being too stiff.

Each time one of those concerns tries to materialize, it dissolves instead, like it can't penetrate the bubble Micah and I have slow-danced into. All that exists here is the multisensory experience he promised. The warmth of his hand against my waist through my thin sweater. The light rasp of the calluses in the hand holding mine. The scent of his cologne. It's different from high school and so light I can only smell it because we're this close. Grapefruit, maybe? But then it also reminds me of skiing in the Alps last Christmas.

The music fills the space around us. How did he get it to sound so full? It's pressing in on us, and somehow, by the chorus, we've drifted closer, our thighs brushing against each other as he moves us through gentle quarter turns every few beats.

I want to lean into it, rest my head against his chest, let my eyes close and all my other senses open more. I catch myself swaying toward him, the tiniest movement, too small for him to have noticed, but it's a warning to my system. Time to bring my brain back online.

"This song is such a throwback," I say. "It's been a minute since I heard it."

Micah meets my eyes. "You don't remember?"

"Remember what?"

"This was the theme for the senior prom?"

"Oh, that's right." I remember now sitting with my friends at a table, goofing off while the people who came with dates danced to it. "I'm surprised you remember." I don't add anything about how he hadn't gone.

"Here's something else I remember." He lets go of my waist to slide his phone out, and I miss the warmth as soon as he does. The hand resting on his shoulder tightens, a spasm registering a protest of him letting go. I tense, hoping he doesn't notice, but he does, giving my other hand, the one still wrapped in his, a light press.

The song stops but he doesn't, keeping the gentle rhythm of our steps through a few silent seconds until a new song starts.

I recognize it after a few measures. "'All of Me'?"

He only nods and keeps us dancing, and I listen to the lyrics. Why did he choose this one?

"Maybe don't overthink it," he says as it plays through the first chorus. "It's a good song."

I *am* overthinking. What does he mean, it's something else he remembers? I force a slow breath in through my nose and loosen my shoulders. *Let it go. Enjoy this.*

I should be telling myself to step away, make a joke, and move us onto business. But no. *Enjoy this.* That's what my brain and about ninety-seven percent of all my atoms say, so I obey.

Somewhere around the third verse, Micah's hand on my waist moves, sliding toward my lower back, drawing me closer. I should overthink this too, but I can't. My thoughts are a quiet hum, and if I had to give them words, all I could offer would be a soft sigh and *yes*. Just that. *Yes.*

"I couldn't afford prom," Micah says, "but if I'd been able to, I would have asked you."

I take that in, not saying anything for a moment before I confess, "I would have said yes."

He draws me even closer, and his breath stirs my hair, sending a shiver down my spine when he says, "This is the song I would have wanted to dance to with you."

Unhnhnhn . . .

My brain makes that and several more wordless noises. Then I lean my head against his chest like I've been wanting to, and we dance through the final verse and chorus.

What are we doing? What am I doing? Why am I doing this?

Scratch that. I know the answer to that one. I'm doing this for seventeen-year-old Kaitlyn, who wanted this so badly.

Why does current me feel the same way? This makes no sense. I should step away, laugh it off, ask a question about the sculpture. Instead, I stay where I am, head resting against Micah, noticing every minute change of pressure in his fingertips against my back, tracking the rhythm of his heart, which I feel more than hear.

When the song ends, we both step back, my hand slowly trailing out of his. Our eyes catch, and neither of us says anything. I don't know what he can read in my face, but in his, I see a smile in the crinkle at the corner of his eyes that doesn't reach his lips, an ease in his body as he taps his phone to turn off the music before he puts it in his pocket, a watchfulness in his eyes as he tries to read me.

I'm not one to rush into silences and fill them with chatter. If anything, I double down on the quiet. But this silence doesn't feel awkward; it feels fraught, like it's already full, but I'm not sure with what. It makes me uncomfortable, so I pivot to what I know.

"I see the vision," I say, successfully suppressing a wince when the words are more meaningful than I mean them to be. "Probably the crab puffs would have helped, but I get it enough."

"Thanks for dancing with me," Micah says. He's not going to let me laugh this off.

I need to change the subject though. The mood of those few minutes still clings to me like the finest spun silk, and I want to gather it around me and revel in it. I can't do that right now. Everything coming at me is feelings, and I need time to sift through them. Instead, I pluck the mood Micah spun around us away from me like it's a spider web, brushing it off as fast as I can.

"You're welcome. Good moves. You putting them to use at any Halloween parties this weekend?" I keep my tone light, an interested boss making polite conversation with her contractor.

"No, I'm low-key on Halloween. Saturday, right?"

I count in my head. "Yes, Saturday."

"I'll hang out with my buddies, have some beers, and watch a horror movie after they're done trick-or-treating."

"Your friends go trick-or-treating? As what? Overgrown frat boys?"

He smiles. "As dads with toddlers. We hang out when the toddlers are done. What about you? Do your people observe Halloween?"

I laugh at him phrasing it like it's a religious holiday. "No plans." I'd gotten some invitations, but I'll either be studying or exhausted from working and studying all week.

"Not even a beer and a scary movie?"

"I'd have to remember to stop and get beer to stock it in my fridge. Chances are that I'll spend Halloween night studying for the bar until I fall asleep at nine." I don't care if it verges on pitiful.

I'm not playing a game where I try to make Micah think I'm a hot social commodity. I want him to understand exactly how packed but boring my life is, in case he wants to . . . I don't complete the thought. Just in case.

"At home? What about all the trick-or-treaters? You know your neighborhood is one of the top five trick-or-treating destinations in Austin, right?"

I did *not* know that. "Some things are making sense now. I wondered why my street looked like a Hollywood horror set vomited on it."

"It's all decked out, isn't it?"

I narrow my eyes at him. "Yeah . . ."

"I only know that from driving past your house late at night, every night." He frowns. "Wait, are stalker jokes in bad taste?"

"Yes."

"Okay, then that was a teenage crush joke."

"Not better."

"Then I know because it's been like that for years, and I used to trick-or-treat over there as a kid. The street two blocks over from you is legendary. Every house gives out full-size candy."

"My real estate agent mentioned that the neighborhood does a lot of community spirit stuff, but I wasn't paying that much attention. I just wanted a place close to my sister's house, and I didn't want any neighbors close enough for me to hear all their noise." When Madi had lived with Sami and her other roommates at the Grove, I'd had fun going over to visit, but I prefer having space and quiet.

"You're going to get spillover trick-or-treaters from full-size-candy-bar street," he says.

"I'll keep my porch light off."

"And risk tricks when you don't give out treats?" He crosses his arms and shakes his head at me. "Looks like I'm going to have to save you from yourself. I will be at your house Saturday at dusk with candy."

I should protest. He is inviting himself into my space, both literally and figuratively, as he makes a claim on my time. But I don't want to. "Fine. I like candy."

He gives me a stern look. "The candy is not for you. The candy is for the children, Kaitlyn. You must give it to the kids."

"Ugh. If I have to."

"You do have to. This is your first Halloween on this street, right?"

I nod.

"Then definitely," he continues. "You have to set the tone correctly the first year."

I must still look grumpy about it because he adds, "Be the auntie Harper Ivy Mae needs you to be."

"Harper needs me to be a full-size-candy-bar auntie?"

He nods, his face solemn.

"Then I'll be a full-size-candy-bar auntie." Another thought occurs to me, and I don't want to bring it up, but I need to be the good boss Madison expects me to be. I swallow a nervous tickle in my throat and say, "So we're clear, this is a hangout, right? Not a date?"

Micah . . . smirks? Is that a *smirk*? I want to snatch back the question, or reword it, but it's too late.

"I'm shocked you would even ask, Katie," he says. "Are you saying you want it to be a date?"

"No! I'm just—need it to—boundaries and . . ." I trail off when Micah's smirk doesn't budge. I take a steadying breath. "Never mind. It's not a date. See you on Saturday."

"It's a date," he says. I glare at him, and he adds, "Meaning like you would say to anyone about a firm plan that is not a date. That kind of a date."

I don't know what to say to that, so I settle on a brisk nod and a "See you then" as I turn to leave. It's only as the warehouse door closes behind me that I remember I didn't ask Micah any of the questions I'd meant to about his progress, questions to show I'm monitoring the project closely.

Dang. There is no way I'm going back in to ask him now. I saw most of what I needed to with my own eyes, and I can email him any other questions I have later. There. Solved it.

When I realize I'm humming "All of Me" as I start my car—and probably will for the rest of the day—I don't know how to solve that. But I tune the radio to an oldies station and let it try.

Send help.

Chapter Seventeen
Micah

THE COOLER WEATHER HOLDS through the weekend, and when I pull into Katie's driveway on Saturday, even though it's still light out, there is a nip in the air, and I suspect many of the kids out tonight will be complaining about the jackets their parents make them wear.

I'm ready for my not-a-date with Kaitlyn, and when I ring her doorbell a minute later, she opens it and her jaw drops.

"Micah?"

"Were you expecting someone else at your door with twenty pounds of candy?" I growl in my best Batman impersonation.

"What is that voice? Are you sick?"

"You're hopeless," I say in my normal voice. "That's how Batman talks. Please tell me you at least recognize the costume."

"I don't live under a rock," she says. "I recognize the costume. I just didn't know that Batman has chronic emphysema."

"Where's your costume?" I ask.

She looks down at her outfit. "No costume. I decided to go festive instead."

I push my mask back on my head. "How is that festive?" She's wearing a pink sweater that hugs her body before ending in long sleeves that fall to her fingertips in a bell shape. It's the kind of cut and fit that screams designer. Probably costs more than my truck payment. She's paired it with black pants. "Not that you don't look nice," I add when she frowns.

"It's orange and black. Pumpkin colors."

"You think your sweater is orange?" I'm happy to check it out again, but it's not any more orange than the first time I looked.

"I don't *think* it is. It's orange. That's why I bought it."

I point to the pink sky behind me, the crest of the setting sun barely visible behind the house across the street. "Your sweater is the same color as the sky over there. What color would you call that?"

"Orange."

"That's the pinkest orange I've ever seen."

"I don't look good in pumpkin orange."

Yeah, right. She would look good in anything. "Can I come in and put this candy down?"

She steps aside and waves me in. I set the flats of candy bars on the accent table in her entryway, which is easily the size of the office in my house.

I turn to look at her again. "Unless you want to be a Real Housewife of Austin, you need to get less trendy and more cringey."

"Just because you went with foam muscles—" She reaches out to poke one, but her finger meets actual muscle, and she stops talking.

"You were saying?"

She makes a miffed noise. "I guess I'm going to be a Real Housewife because I don't have any costumes."

"I'm kidding. Your hair isn't high enough for Real Housewife. But we can pull together a costume. You have a pair of cowboy boots, don't you?" Her family owns Copperhead Boots. She may not wear them, but I bet she has some.

"Yes."

I open the door and pop my head out, scanning the street. "The trick-or-treaters aren't out yet, but we don't have long." I shut the door and turn to her. "This will go faster if I can look at your closet, see what we have to work with. I might have an idea."

She opens her mouth like she wants to object then pauses and sighs. "Let's go."

I follow her upstairs to the end of a hall, trying not to gape at the idea of one person living here by herself, let alone one person my age. I don't even work on houses like this for clients yet. The most ambitious project Dan has given me has been a freestanding pool house behind a wealthy client's mansion.

She leads me to the main suite, and I pause to admire the vaulted ceiling, a series of three mission-style wooden beams cross-sectioning it to meet a perpendicular support beam running down the center.

"You'll have to come through my bathroom," she says. "Promise not to judge."

I promise and she leads me through it. I want to take in every detail, but mostly what I notice is that Madison confined most of her work to the first floor. Upstairs, everything still has a model home feel with the builders' choices in gray and white, and if Kaitlyn ordered her own linens, she went with even more gray and white.

She's classic, yes. But her outfits always have some small detail that gives away more about her if you're paying attention, like the sleeves of her sweater tonight. I expected her house to contain subtle-but-revealing details too, but that all stopped the second we climbed the stairs.

Her bathroom counters are bare, no clutter to hint about her beauty routine. Only a potted white orchid tries to soften the space, but I'd bet the hundred dollars in my wallet that it's silk, not real.

It's hard not to go slack-jawed when we step into her closet (twice the size of my office). It's immaculate, but the sheer volume of clothes overwhelms me. It makes sense for someone whose fortune comes from the fashion industry, but I didn't expect to walk in and find the equivalent of an exclusive boutique in her house. There's so much color and texture that I can't take it all in.

"You said you weren't going to judge." Kaitlyn sounds defensive.

"I'm not. I'm strategizing." There are shelves full of shoes. Shelves. Many shelves. Of only shoes. It's like being in a movie. "You said you have boots?" There's a whole bay of nothing *but* boots, and she walks over to grab a pair from the bottom shelf.

"These are Western." She holds up a pair of intricately stitched and patterned suede boots in a fawn color.

"Are those Copperheads?"

She shrugs, like that's answer enough. Of course they are. I glance around the closet, seeking and not finding denim.

"Jeans?" I ask.

"What kind of costume are we talking here?"

"Cowgirl. Easy, fast, and you probably have everything you need."

She goes to a long drawer and slides it out to reveal at least a dozen pairs of jeans, all folded like an origami expert did it. Did she do that? Or does she hire help? She reaches for a pair near the back and shakes it out.

"Wranglers, if you can believe it," she says. "My brother-in-law made me get them when I visited his family's horse ranch."

"Did he happen to make you get a cowboy shirt too?" I ask. "Plaid? Do you have plaid?"

She turns to survey the closet before she walks over to a section and pulls a shirt off the rack. "This is my only plaid shirt."

"Uh . . ." I have to fight not to laugh. It is shiny, maybe satin, although I don't know much about fabrics. It's also a green-on-green plaid but kind of . . . avant garde? I squint, trying to figure out how I'd even describe this interpretation of plaid. "If you have a plain T-shirt you could throw on and meet me downstairs, I have something that could work."

"I can do that."

"Meet you by the candy bars."

A couple minutes later, I'm back in her foyer with a flannel shirt retrieved from my truck, staring down at a cat who has decided to sit on my foot.

Kaitlyn comes around the corner. "Oh. Daisy Buchanan. Now you show up?" She says it with mild consternation.

I look up. "Oh, Katie Armstrong." I say it with a strong thirst. I can't help it. I don't care. What is it about a woman in a white cotton T-shirt and jeans? Is it *this* woman? I've seen her in a dress sewn to fit like it was made for her, but this, *this* is what has actual drool pooling in my mouth?

"Daisy, please don't sit on the company."

"She's fine." I lean down to scratch the back of her neck. "Nice to meet you, Daisy." Her tail twitches and she stays put. I straighten and hold out my flannel to Kaitlyn, hoping my face is saying *Please enjoy this offer of a shirt to borrow* and not *Please put this on before I back you up against that wall and show you how hot you look right now.*

She takes it and slips it on, buttoning it from the bottom. "This doesn't feel like much of a costume."

"For you it is. It's like watching you pull out an alter ego from your closet. But for most people, no. Do you have makeup that would make dots?"

She looks up and wrinkles her nose. "Dots? What are you talking about?"

I wave at my face. "Freckles. Those kinds of dots."

"You want me to draw freckles on my face?"

"Yes. Freckles. Do that. Be right back."

I run back to my truck, noticing a group of trick-or-treaters about five houses away. I grab the rest of my supplies and pick a spot halfway down her driveway, setting everything up. When I go back to the house to get the candy, Kaitlyn is holding a pencil in her hand.

"Like this?" She tilts her head so I can inspect her freckles.

"Very mindful. Very demure. So no, not exactly." I hold out my hand for the brown pencil. "May I?"

She hands it to me, and I look at it closely then make a mark on my palm so I can get a sense of its resistance.

"Okay, ready. Chin up, please."

"Are you going to make me look ridiculous?"

In my Batman voice, I say, "Ma'am, I'm a trained artist."

She lifts her chin. What a canvas.

I rest my drawing hand carefully against her cheek, my thumb brushing against her lip as I go over each of her demure freckles and give them the cartoon treatment, making them big enough to show even when the light dims. I could do this quickly. I should do this quickly with trick-or-treaters incoming. But I work slowly, appreciating the softness of her skin against my fingers as I fill in her spots.

She's very still, which is very Kaitlyn. She's not a fidgeter, not a perpetual tornado like Madison, who whirls through a space. Kaitlyn, no matter what speed she's moving, or even now when she's motionless, is a soft breeze. No one ever gets tired of a soft breeze.

I reach the last freckle as I hear the sound of voices near the sidewalk, moving our way. I lift my hand and step back.

She blinks and swallows. I affected her. Being that close, it wobbled her balance. Good. I give her a slow smile as I hand back her pencil. I understand the feeling.

"Am I done?" she asks. Her voice comes out husky.

"Almost, but we can do the last part out there." I pull down my mask and open the front door as the doorbell rings. Two ladybugs, a princess, and a pirate stand on the porch, all small girls.

"Trick or treat!" they yell, but I think only two of them can say their Rs. I'm not good at guessing ages, but I'd bet they're probably not in school yet, the parents doing the early shift on candy collection like my buddies are, knowing their kids will want to go home after only a few houses.

There's a gasp beside me, and I look over to see Katie staring down at them with wide eyes, as delighted as if a pack of puppies just frolicked up to the door.

"You're adorable," she says.

She gets a chorus of thank yous from three of the girls, but the pirate scowls. "I am scary."

Kaitlyn jumps behind me. "There's a pirate, Batman," she says in a loud whisper as she cowers.

Three small voices giggle, but the pirate only gives a pleased nod.

"Aye, therrrre is," I say as Batman. "I'll give them their loot and she'll go away."

I drop a candy bar into each of their bags while Katie periodically peeks around me and ducks back every time she sees the pirate.

"Thank you," three little voices say when I've dropped in the final candy bar. The pirate leans forward, looks me dead in the eye and says, "POOP DECK." She makes every consonant count. The princess gasps, the ladybugs giggle again, and an exasperated adult in the entourage behind them calls, "Gentry Lynn! Apologize."

Gentry Lynn's eyes form slits. "Dead men tell no tales."

It takes everything I've got to keep my stern Batman face, especially when I can feel quivering against my back that tells me Katie isn't even trying.

The pirate leads her boarding party back to their parents while a mom calls an apology to me, and I give a single grim nod to let them know I will not be visiting vengeance on them for Gentry Lynn's threats to Batman.

When they reach the sidewalk, I finally let my laugh out, and Katie emerges, grinning and unrepentant.

"I understand now why I couldn't opt out. You were right. Imagine if I'd left the porch light off but they'd seen another light on in my house?" She shivers. "Thank you, Batman."

"You're welcome," I rasp, but it makes me cough, and she grins at me again. "You're a natural, by the way. You're going to ace Halloween."

She plucks a candy bar from the box I'm holding and flips it in her hand a couple of times. "I'm going to *win* Halloween."

"Not with that stupid costume, you won't."

She frowns and glances down. "Oh, yeah. What was your big plan? Because I might be giving just-came-in-from-my-fancy-stable vibes, but I am definitely not giving cowgirl."

I pick up the rest of the candy and lead her to the driveway, where I set up two camp chairs with a cooler between them. I divide the candy boxes into even stacks in front of the chairs and pick up the trucker hat resting on the cooler. I show her the front with the Herbert Metalworks logo on it. "Hat from the job site," I explain before I settle it on her head. Hmmm. "Nope. That's not it." I turn it around. "That's not cowboy either. That's not even country boy. That's just hot girl at the sports bar."

Her lips part but she just stares at me. I pretend not to notice and step back to study her, thinking.

"What?" She reaches up to touch the cap. "What do I need to fix?"

"Shhh. I'm getting inspiration."

She snorts, forgetting to be self-conscious. "I cannot take you seriously while you're in costume."

"In *character*," I tell her. I loop my thumbs through my Batman utility belt, cop style, while I consider the possibilities. Her eyes drop to my belt and there's that hard swallow again before she pulls her gaze up, right as I figure out a solution. I break character to grin. "Got it."

Cradling her face, I smear the pencil I drew on. Her eyes go wide. "Trust me," I tell her, smudging until I'm satisfied. "You need a couple more accessories."

I go back to my truck and grab a wrench from my toolbox and the chamois I use to dry my windows at the car wash. I hand her the wrench. "Front shirt pocket." And the chamois. "Back jeans pocket."

She tucks them each where I tell her. "What am I now?"

I pull her over to look in the truck's side mirror. "Batman's mechanic."

She stoops and laughs at her reflection. "Grease monkey. I get it. All right, Croft. Points for improvising."

"Am I winning Halloween so far?"

"You got cussed out in three-year-old pirate, so let's call it a tie."

"Come on and I'll finish your Halloween orientation." We walk back to the chairs. "Pick a seat. A neighborhood like this, you want to sit out and enjoy the show. Otherwise, you're running to the door every two minutes."

She claims the left chair, and I take the other one, setting a battery-operated lantern on the ground between us and turning it on. "You need enough light to enjoy the costume parade." I set the open box of candy bars on her lap and open another box for mine. "Have your candy ready to go. You'll have to choose your handout philosophy."

"My handout philosophy? As the interim head of a nonprofit, I'm pro-handout."

I love that she's so quick. I'd always sensed that she held back far more than she shared in class discussions. Sometimes I'd catch a glint in her eye or a twitch at the corner of her mouth as she listened and watched, and I'd wished I was in on her private jokes. I'd had no doubt they were funny. For those couple of months where we'd almost hung out, every now and then she'd crack one for me, and I learned another secret almost no one at Hillview knew: Kaitlyn Armstrong was the funniest kid in school.

"Settle down, grease monkey. Are you going to drop each candy bar into each bag yourself? Or will you hold out the box and let them choose?"

"Well, Batman, this sounds like psychological profiling."

"I can tell you what you're going to choose. I'm texting you. Don't look until I tell you." I tap out a message and send it. In Batman's voice I say, "I *am* the world's greatest detective."

A gaggle of boys who look like they would absolutely be smashing pumpkins if their parents weren't right behind them come up the driveway. They're at the pillowcase age where they'd rather be caught dead than carrying a Halloween tote, and they're all in NFL jerseys and eye black.

"Watch this," I tell her. "They're wearing the fifth grade special, the minimum costume you can wear and still expect candy. They will mumble, not make eye contact, talk only to each other until their parents make them say thank you, which they will yell over their shoulder while they race each other to the sidewalk."

They reach us in a jostling squad of crew socks and skinny elbows. "Trick or treat," a couple of them mumble, eyes on the candy bars. Kaitlyn pauses before extending the box. There are a few exultant calls of "Bro!" or "Yes!" as they reach over and around each other, hands scrabbling. Within a few seconds, they spin and split for the sidewalk, yelling "Thanks" over their shoulders when one of the adults reminds them, and I turn to look at Kaitlyn.

She looks from them to her box and starts trying to reorganize it. "It looks like it was attacked by badgers."

"Check your phone."

"Oh, yeah." She pulls her phone from the cupholder and reads her text. "'You want to drop the candy bars yourself. You don't want me to guess right so you let them pick their own. You regret it.'"

She sets her phone down and relaxes into her chair. "Good to know we've reached the disrespect-your-boss phase of this project."

I can't answer until I hand out candy bars to a brother and sister dressed as Spiderman and Black Widow.

"You're not my boss," I say as they leave. "You're my client."

"Which means I can fire you."

"You won't."

She sighs. "I won't."

"In fact, if I quit you would be—"

"Sunk faster than that preschool pirate could yell 'poop deck'?"

"Well said."

"Let's not fire each other," she says.

"Deal. But only because I already deposited the check."

"Works for me."

We greet more and more trick-or-treaters. At first, I have enough time to finish explaining the rules for Halloween, including the selection of beverages in the cooler ranging from apple cider to hard cider, the foam jack-o-lantern I brought as an emergency measure because "you should always have real ones unless you waited too long before they sold out," and a spray can of black hair color, which I hand to her.

She flinches away from it like it's a hot coal. "I can't put that in my hair. It won't wash out."

"It's for your cat. So we can have a black cat. It'll give us some ambiance since you don't have a full setup."

Kaitlyn shoots up in her chair but has to drop candy bars into the bags of a ghost, a fairy, a strawberry, and a Jedi before she can object. "Daisy Buchanan would *never*," she says. "Are you crazy?"

I take the cap off and press the nozzle. She squeaks and ducks before she realizes it's only hissing air.

She resettles herself like a boardroom CEO, which looks hilarious with her grease monkey costume. "You will pay." Her voice is low and deadly calm, scaring the two NFL players holding out their bags into skittering away with nervous glances over their shoulders.

"Can't wait." It comes out silky even though I meant to do my Batman voice.

Soon the foot traffic is so heavy, every driveway on the street has a small traffic jam, and I've never had so much fun on Halloween. Not even the handful of times in college that I went to a party or club where pretty girls wore tiny costumes and my buddies made sure my cup was never empty.

Sitting here and laughing with her, watching her chirp over the smallest trick-or-treaters, handing out candy and trading good-natured insults about our distribution technique, keeping fake score of who's winning Halloween . . . I can't remember the last time I felt this relaxed. Relaxed but also . . . on high alert. It's the paradox of Kaitlyn. Every sense is tuned to her, capturing every laugh, each rustle of movement, the way the light catches her eyes as she turns to tease me or lean forward to compliment a costume.

There are a handful of people in my life I'm this comfortable with, and all of them grew up on my block. But I want to whip her cap off and explore her lips with mine to confirm whether they're as soft as they felt against my thumbs. No one on my block has ever inspired that impulse.

The thought won't let me go. When she'd literally bumped into me at Remix, it shook all that loose inside me, like those feelings had been sitting unsecured on a shelf where I'd stuck them since high school, unsure what to do with them.

I know now.

The stream of kids slows to a trickle, and my anticipation builds as the candy bars dwindle.

When the candy is gone and my mask comes off, I'm finally going to do what I should have done ten years ago.

Chapter Eighteen

Kaitlyn

"THAT WAS THE LAST candy bar." I hold up my empty carton to show Micah. "Does that mean I get tricks now?"

He glances at his phone. "It's almost nine. You're safe."

"What if some hungry NFLers come by and get mad that my porch light is off?" I'm not at all worried about it. A few other lights have gone off on the street over the last fifteen minutes, and only a few kid-sized stragglers in the distance seem bent on chasing down the last of the sugar.

"Won't happen. Halloween law."

I smile at this. "So weird I've never heard these laws until tonight."

He slides his mask back on his head, and it's good to see his full face, even though the top half is damp with sweat and red lines trace where the mask dug into his skin. It's good skin. It's a good face.

"You doubt me?" he says. "What kind of proof do you need?"

"I don't doubt you. You're my go-to Halloween expert." I stand and stretch before holding out my hand to pull him to his feet too.

He ignores it and rises the way I imagine Batman must in the movies, a fluid upward motion that ends with him in Batman stance in front of me, arms folded across his chest. His chest, which bulges without the help of any foam. I like Batman stance *so* much—even when he's so close I have to lean my head back to see him. Maybe especially because he's that close.

I'd chosen a hard cider from his cooler, and I feel the effects now that I'm on my feet. My cheeks flush and my scalp tingles. I sway toward him and step back even as he reaches out to hold my elbows and keep me steady.

"You good?"

I slip away from his touch under the guise of gathering up empty candy boxes. "Yep, stood up too fast." I've been standing long enough that this doesn't actually make sense, so I hurry past it before he notices. "I'll go stick these in the trash and come back to help with the rest of this."

I go around the garage and shove the boxes in my recycling bin. When I get back to the driveway, everything is put away except the chairs, which he's already folding. I grab the other one and fold it, then hand it to him. He shifts it to his other arm and keeps his hand outstretched.

"Uhhh . . ." I look around, not sure what he's waiting for.

"I need my tool back. It would really put a—"

"Don't," I warn him.

"—wrench in things if I left without it," he says over my groan. "Don't make me come and take it."

I glance down to where it protrudes from the chest pocket of his borrowed shirt. For a reckless split second, I almost say *Why don't you try*. Instead, I hand it over. "Going to take it with you to watch scary movies in case of monsters?"

He puts it away and locks his toolbox. "Scary movie night is cancelled. My buddy with the best setup has a kid home puking, and just in case it's not from candy, no one else wants to go over and bring it back to their kids. Puke viruses set off chain reactions, apparently."

"Disappointed?" I ask. I don't know why. Maybe because I want to keep the conversation going. Maybe because I hoard every detail he shares about himself.

"Kinda," he says. "We were going to watch *Zombie Lake*, and I haven't seen it."

I need to study. I need to be in bed by 10:00 so I can get enough sleep before I hit the gym at 6:30 tomorrow morning and start another long day of work and more studying. I need to do anything but what I'm about to do. I know this.

"We can watch it here if you want," I say anyway. His surprised look makes me regret it immediately. "Never mind. I feel bad that you have to miss it after you spent all night saving me from suburban street thugs."

He pushed his mask on top of his head a while ago, but now he pulls off the hood altogether and runs his hand through his messy strands. I curl my fingers when they twitch in jealousy.

"Now that you mention it, I definitely saved you from at least five different things tonight. I deserve to watch that movie. Let's do it."

"Good. Okay." I lead us into the house in a perfect example of not remotely resetting our boundaries. "I should offer you a tour, but you've seen it already."

"Just parts. Let me change out of this costume and then I'd love a tour." He holds up a gym bag.

"Sure. I guess we'll start with the main bathroom."

I lead him to it, and he emerges a few minutes later in jeans and a chocolate brown thermal that makes my mouth water. Um, because of chocolate. Because I love chocolate, and this shirt makes me think of it.

"This is a Cardston build, isn't it?" Micah asks, surveying the great room and saving me from my thoughts. "They do good work."

"Yeah. The previous owner only lived here for two years and didn't change much, so that's why Madison was being so pushy about it."

I let him take it in, from the opposite wall of windows reflecting us in the archway to the fireplace and conversation area at one end to the dining room and serving nook at the other.

"How do you feel about her choices?" he asks.

"Are you asking if she nailed Scandinavian, natural textures, muted tones?" I repeat his words from that day in his store. "She did."

"But do you like it?"

There is so much wood, rock, and natural fiber that it should feel like a mountain cabin, but I'm nothing you would associate with cozy cottage style, and neither is this. It feels simple, modern, and warm. Sophisticated, but not in Mom's stuffy brocade settee way.

"I love it." Maybe twenty-six is too young to embrace sophistication as an aesthetic, but it's me. "I'm happy here."

"She did an amazing job," he agrees.

"You should see it in the morning." Does that imply staying through the night? "Or any kind of daylight, honestly. Madison didn't use a lot of color, but when the sun comes through the windows, it pulls out the colors she did use and it feels like a different space."

"What are some of your favorite touches?" he asks.

Madison bought so many things that I regularly notice new ones, but I do have favorites.

"I have this pretty cool table." I lead him over to the dining area.

He gives a soundless whistle. "Whoever made this is a master. I must know more."

I roll my eyes. "It's okay. One of those cocky artist types, but if you can get past that, his stuff is pretty good."

He grins. "What else you got?"

"Threadwork partners with Teak Heart a lot. Do you know it?"

"Fair trade home goods?"

I nod. "Madison worked there during college. It inspired her to start Threadwork. Anyway, she tries to get most of the decor type stuff from there, like these lamps." I turn on the cylinder lamp on the nearest side table. "Made from cocoa leaves."

"Very cool." This is not a man who will bore of interior design discussions.

"I'll show you my office. It's my favorite space." He follows me down the hall. I flip the switch to turn on the floor lamp and point to it. "Everything in here is my favorite, like that." It's simple, a black arch with a drum shade in neutral fabric. "I don't know how to explain it, but she bought that lamp and put it in the living room. But it has such a perfect arch, I moved it in here because it makes me feel peaceful. That's rope glued all over the lamp shade, but it doesn't feel busy. It feels intentional, like the rope chose its natural course and the lamp maker was smart enough to let it."

He doesn't say anything, so I point to the love seat. "I study there pretty much every night, and the lamp makes it better. I smile every time I turn it on."

I cross to the desk beneath the picture window. "And this. I never thought I'd want a glass desk. Fingerprints and all that stuff. But I love it. It makes me feel like I'm out in my yard, in the grass and fresh air because it's here and not here."

"Madison really knows you, huh?" he asks softly.

"Yes, but this is the only room I didn't let her do. It's my retreat more than even my bedroom. Some of this I moved in here after she ordered it for the living room. Other stuff, she'd send me options and I'd pick. She must have sent me twelve pictures of desks, but I knew as soon as I saw this one."

"You have a good eye. The base matches your lamp."

"Right? That perfect curve feeling again." The glass desktop sits on two black arches forming its four legs. They run parallel to the long edges, not the short ones, so it's unexpected and soothingly symmetrical at the same time. The longer arches give it the same curve as the lamp. "Do I sound like a lunatic or does that make sense to a furniture maker?"

"Makes sense." He glances down to the green rug and over to the only art in the house that I chose myself. "And that piece?"

When I lie on the sofa, my head on the lamp end, my feet propped on the armrest, this is what I see on the facing wall. It's a wood mosaic made of chips from light ash to walnut. At first it looks like gentle rolling hills against a sunrise. But look longer and you realize it's the silhouette of a woman's body viewed from the back.

"Do you see hills or a nude woman lying on her side?" I ask him.

"Both."

"Does it feel provocative?"

He meets my eyes. "No."

I agree. The artist didn't include any of the provocative parts, catching the curve at the rise of hip and following the lines to her head, the hair made from wood so light it must be birch, pooled gently behind her, no curls or tendrils to suggest motion. "She's resting. She found a place where she feels safe enough to lie down and . . ."

"And what?" It's a quiet prompt.

I shake my head. "I don't know. Maybe that's why I like it. The second I saw it, I wanted to be her, like it matters to be her, like being there is the most important thing she can do." I know why I love this picture, but do I want to explain it to Micah? Micah will understand. Am I okay with that?

"She's enough," I say, studying the relaxed curve of her shoulder. "In that moment. Probably in all her moments. But you can only rest like that and belong to everything around you if you know you're enough."

When I look over at Micah, he straightens from the wall and looks down the hall in the direction of the kitchen. "Could I get a drink? Just water."

His tone is distracted. It's like running into a light pole in front of the boy you like.

"Sure." I turn off the light, glad to hide my stinging cheeks. In the kitchen, I pull out a glass and show him the door for the built-in fridge. "I don't do bottled water, but the fridge dispenser water tastes good."

He nods and takes the glass, watching it fill while I wet a paper towel and use my reflection in the faucet to swipe at the smudges on my cheeks. At least then there's a reason for them to be red.

When he's done, I shut off the faucet and turn to face him.

"Did I get it all?" I ask.

He eyes me over the rim of his glass and nods as he drinks, and I look away from the mesmerizing rhythm of his throat muscles as he pulls at that water.

I busy myself with throwing away the dirty paper towels, and when I look up and he's still drinking, I go to work on the bottom button of my borrowed shirt, trying to figure out how to politely kick him out of the house. Probably the trusty *Actually, do you mind if we skip the movie? I just realized how long my day is tomorrow.*

"What are you doing?"

I freeze on the next button and look up. "Giving your shirt back."

"Don't worry about it. You can bring it next time you stop by the warehouse."

"No, it's okay. I realized it's pretty late to start a movie, so if you don't mind—"

"Kaitlyn."

I move to the next button. "What?"

"Katie." It's an order, but a gentle one. "Look at me."

"Hang on, I'm almost done."

His glass clinks on the counter, and he walks over as I'm moving to the middle button. He puts a hand over mine and gives it a light squeeze.

I stop unbuttoning, but I don't let go. I do put on a neutral face before I look up to meet his eyes.

"Katie, I need to tell you something."

The words everyone wants to hear, especially from a guy they keep suffering humiliations in front of. At least I'm the only one who knows my explanation of the art in my office was another light pole moment.

"I'm listening." My voice is calm and cool. Boss mode. Good job faking it, me.

He sighs and draws me into his arms, holding me until I relax against him enough for him to rest his chin on my head. I can't help it. I'm wound tight as a ballerina bun when I'm around this man until he touches me. Then I'm something offensively basic and malleable, like putty. I hate being a cliche.

"I need to tell you something," he repeats, and the words rumble in his chest against my ear. "But for reasons that I promise to explain later, right now I need to watch a movie. A loud movie. A movie with a very, very simple plot. Can we do that?"

My pride is trying very hard to step away, fake a yawn, and tell him sorry but I'll try to find time to drop by the warehouse sometime next week. But my curiosity will choke me if I let pride win. What does he need to tell me? Why does he need a two-hour distraction first?

I do step back. Micah doesn't fight me, but he also lets his hands slide alllll the way down my arms to close around my wrists, and his stupid shirt is no protection at all from the heat of that touch.

"*Zombie Lake* is that movie?"

He gives a choked-sounding laugh. "I really hope so."

"Fine." I slip my wrists free, pull his shirt over my head, leaving me in my trusty white Calvin Klein cotton tee, and shove it into his chest. "But keep your shirt."

He squeezes his eyes shut like he's in pain. "Thank you."

"You are being weird," I inform him.

"No argument." He goes back for more water, and I walk into the living room and fish the remote from a basket. The big "painting" over the fireplace is actually the TV, but the screen resolution is so high that when you use the art screensaver option, it looks like actual canvas. When I turn it on, the painting dissolves to reveal the screen. I've only used it a couple times, and it's always like a magic trick.

This time, I barely notice because I'm much more focused on what will happen when it goes off again.

What exactly is Micah planning to reveal?

Chapter Nineteen

Kaitlyn

I FIND THE MOVIE and the "Play" prompt appears as Micah joins me, but instead of sitting down, he pauses and studies me, my booted feet propped up on an ottoman.

"That's one of my pieces," he says.

It's more of a stool with an upholstered cushion sitting on top of curved iron legs. "It's cool. What's it made from?"

"Frame is from a restaurant renovation. They tore out the Western kitchen vibe, so lots of decorative iron. Eva welded that for me. And the top is woven from the curtains in a conference room from a business park demo."

I drop my feet so I can tug the stool to the couch to study it closer. I can definitely see that the muted seagrass upholstered top is made from an already-woven fabric. Like a rag rug, but far more intricate. "This used to be a curtain?"

"This lady who lives at the end of my street does handweaving stuff. Baskets. Things like that. I asked her if she could turn it into a cushion cover, and this is what she gave back."

I run a finger over it. I can't begin to guess how she did it. It all lies flat, but the closer I look, the more the pattern emerges. "It's beautiful."

"Yes."

His tone makes me look up. He's studying me, not the stool.

He wants me. He's looking at me the way I wished he would have in high school. No, that's not it. If he'd looked at me then like he's looking at me now, I would have had no idea what to do with that kind of heat. That he's in no way trying to hide it makes it clear how capable he is of masking when he chooses. It's also clear that this draw I feel toward him is mutual. Intensely mutual.

The tension isn't the kind that you cut with a knife. Or crack like glass. Or deflate like a balloon. It's the kind like a dam: high risk of flooding. Flooding of senses. Flooding by hormones. I need to take a breath before I drown in this, so I set my feet on the stool again, using it as an excuse to break eye contact.

"Want help with your boots?"

There are so many ways to take off boots. A couple of them might reduce me to a soundless blob on my sofa. It might lead him to conclude that I'm interested in way more than a truce. It might confirm his suspicions that I'm obsessed with his pecs. And encourage my constant impulse to reach out and feel how soft his hair is.

"Kaitlyn?" There's no hint of a smile around his mouth, like he guesses what I'm thinking. He knows. That straight-up knowledge is dangerous.

On the other hand, these boots really are hard to remove by myself. It's why I rarely wear them.

"Help would be great." My voice is even. It's a miracle.

Then this guy, this *man,* this piece of freaking work, he—

In a move as graceful as a dancer, he steps over my crossed legs, cups the back of my ankle to lift the boot, and he—oof.

He presses his thighs to either side of my calf and jellies my entire right leg. I draw a deep breath through my nose, making it as silent as possible, while his other hand curves over my foot and he begins to tug. Gently.

The view is—

Another deep breath. I have not spent enough time appreciating this man's backside.

As an Armstrong, I have worn many, many pairs of boots in my life. No matter how a boot is removed, there's a distinct sense of relief when it slides off, like a Victorian lady loosening her corset.

I do not get that moment. Because when he lowers my foot back to the stool, his touch radiates straight up through my legs and curls low in my abdomen, moving through my chest and warming my cheeks.

"Feel better?" Micah asks, glancing over his shoulder.

I don't think I school my expression fast enough, because the corner of his mouth twitches.

"Sure." There. Make something of that boring syllable, Micah Croft.

He pulls off the other boot, and everywhere he touches decides to burn.

This man is messing with me.

I slide one of my feet back toward me, then set it on that prize-worthy backside, and—

Push.

He tips forward and drops my boot, and his other hand shoots out to catch himself on the rug. He twists and lands on his butt, turning to look up at me with a glint in his eye that suggests payback.

"Ready to start the movie?" I ask.

He sucks his teeth, eyes on me, for several seconds before he gets up. "Sounds good."

I nestle into my corner, free to curl my feet beneath me now. What's he going to do? Take the cushion next to me and cage me in? *Bring it.* I'm not backing down.

He takes the opposite corner.

Huh. I never realized how long this sofa is. Well, whatever. It's for the best.

Daisy appears and wanders in front of me before hopping up onto the sofa and curling up next to Micah. She's a traitor even if I understand her choice.

I can't say I watch the first ten minutes of the movie. My eyes are on it, but I'm distracted by trying to guess what Micah wants to tell me, my thoughts running in a hamster wheel with "he wants to father your children" at the top to "he's quitting the gala job" at the bottom.

But then I accidentally get interested in the movie when the plot takes a group of five college friends to their old, abandoned summer camp to find out what happened to their sixth friend who disappeared there the summer they turned fifteen. She was never found, and the camp closed after her family sued it for negligence.

Chrissy—strong freshman class secretary vibes—demands the camp director's single suite for herself because she's secretly been hooking up with Tuck. Tuck who was the missing girl's boyfriend. Tuck who sneaks into Chrissy's room, because Tuck is down to—

Anyway. Tuck refers to the missing girl as Dead Jules while Chrissy giggles. Tuck quickly loses his shirt, and Chrissy is making all kinds of breathy noises.

Exactly what kind of movie has Micah picked for us? If I see Prissy Chrissy's "pecs," I'm kicking him out.

Thirty seconds later Tuck does a seductive shirtless crawl up the bed to turn the heat up. No way. I'm not watching a spicy scene with Micah. Prissy Chrissy might only have lost her socks so far, but there is a logical progression here. I straighten to look for the remote.

"Micah, I'm not—aaaaaaahhhHHH!" I scream as clawed human hands erupt from Chrissy's stomach and drive straight into Tuck's shirtless torso to yank out his heart.

Daisy leaps into the air when I yell and lands on the floor with her back arched and tail flared. She hisses. Micah jumps too then laughs until Daisy launches herself into my lap and crouches, ready to attack whatever made me scream.

Micah's laugh trails off. "Whoa, Kaitlyn. Are you okay?"

I point at Chrissy's face contorted in terror as she watches the hand—gray and decaying except for a perfect shell-pink manicure—protruding from her abdomen squeeze the beati—never mind. Ew. Ew, ew, ew.

I clap my hands over my eyes.

Micah hops up. "I got it, I got it." The sounds stop.

I lower my hands. The movie is paused, and the title card is filling the screen.

He sits on the cushion beside me. "You didn't know that was coming?"

"You did?" I ask, my voice shrill and not remotely cool.

He gets a concerned look on his face. "You don't like horror movies, do you?"

"Apparently not," I say, only half as shrill.

"Why did you agree to watch it?" he asks. "I wouldn't make you watch something you hate."

"I thought I didn't like horror movies the same way I don't like car chase movies," I said. "They sound dumb, so I've never bothered. I would have passed if you'd said ghosts or something because that might freak me out for real, but when you said it was zombies, I thought it was going to be corny, not scary."

"Oh, man. I'm sorry I laughed. I thought you were messing around when you screamed."

"How did you know it was coming if you haven't seen it yet?"

"You watch enough horror movies, you know what to expect."

"Then it's not scary," I said. "What's the point?"

"In the zombie genre, the fun is watching how gross the director can make each infection."

I press my hand to my heart like the pressure will make it stop beating so hard. I pet Daisy's back with the other one until she relaxes, stepping off my lap to sit beside me. She doesn't lie down, but she does curl her tail around her.

"We'll find something else to watch. A comedy. How does that sound?"

I shake my head before he's done asking. "No. I want to finish this one."

"It's fine, I promise. I wasn't that invested. I can watch it some other time if I feel like it."

This is a point of pride now. "If you can watch this without being scared, I can too."

"It's not a competition, Katie. Seriously."

"Sit back, press play, and tell me every single thing that's going to happen before it happens." I will not be defeated by a movie that only made him laugh.

"I—"

"Push play."

He shakes his head but reaches for the remote. "Just so you know, Tuck is definitely dead, but she's going to be a zombie. That's the trope. If the brain or heart stops, the zombie stops."

"Okay, go."

It plays out exactly like he tells me, and for the next hour, he predicts everything that will happen. My anxiety drops, but I still hate the grossness.

"Oh, pacing shift," he says. We're down to a nerd named Jasper and a likable girl named Penny, who Micah has already told me is the Final Girl, who has never done anything mean or wrong to anyone, ever, so that means she'll survive.

He pauses the movie as Jasper and Penny reach the edge of the dark woods. "Forest of doom, so there will be zombie jump scares, and I can't predict them. I can watch the rest later."

I think about it. "Penny will kill all of them and face Zombie Chrissy?"

"Of course."

"I would like Zombie Chrissy to die."

He smiles and hits play.

After two or three scares that don't make either of us jump, we're getting to the other edge of the woods, and I, very stupidly, relax. Jasper and Penny step out of the forest near the lake, victorious, and they stop to catch their breath and do that relieved, hysteria-tinged laugh of what-the-crap-just-happened. The more they laugh, the more it makes them laugh, and even I'm smiling as they—

WHOOSH and—

"AaaaaaaahhhHHH!" A blur of zombie evil yanks Jasper backward and scares me so thoroughly that I dive for Micah. He catches me with a muffled grunt but recovers quickly, settling me on his lap and tucking my head under his chin, hands shielding my eyes from the screen.

"You're okay," he murmurs, not loudly enough to drown out the wet ripping and tearing sounds as Penny also screams in terror and Jasper screams in pain. "I should have seen that one coming. I'm sorry, boss."

More nasty horror movie sounds.

I cover my ears and burrow my head into his chest. "Tell me when this part is over."

"You got it." His arms are firm around me as he narrates what's happening. The rhythm of his voice is calming, and I focus on it. This is the third time I've been in a position to absorb the vibrations in his chest against my cheek, and it has become a favorite sensation. My own heart rate is slowing.

Slowing, but pounding harder.

A minute later, Micah lifts my hand from my ear. "We're safe. They're setting up for the final battle."

That's too bad. I don't have a reason to be in his lap anymore. I start to push up, but Micah flexes enough to keep me there. A wordless request for me to stay.

I answer by relaxing. It doesn't feel like a thing that needs to be fought.

He slides an arm beneath my legs and stands, lifting me before claiming my corner. He stretches out, back against the armrest, one leg resting on the floor, situating me in the vee of his legs, my back pressed to his front.

I have to turn my head and rest it against his chest to watch the movie, but I'm not mad about that either.

We watch Penny promise Jasper to get help and leave him with a flare gun they found. Over the final half hour, she discovers that Dead Jules disappeared because she was abducted by Prissy Chrissy and the former camp director after catching them in an affair. They knocked her out and threw her in a lake. She survived and collapsed in the woods, where a fungus infected her, and she became a zombie. She is the biggest, baddest, wiliest zombie, and she's about to go for Penny when Zombie Chrissy appears. They fight. Zombie Jules wins and takes out Zombie Chrissy. Penny feels sorry for Zombie Jules but knows what she must do. Surprise! She pulls out a *second* flare gun! Skipping the squelchy details, Zombie Jules is now Dead Jules for real.

But I can't swear to these plot points, even though it's not a complicated story. I'm too distracted by Micah.

His jeans rasp lightly against my forearms as his thighs become my armrests, contracting and rolling when he tenses or shifts.

He toys with my hair, sifting tendrils through his fingers. Every strand he grazes pings a corresponding nerve in my spine, shooting pleasure bolts out to my fingers and the soles of my feet, up to my cheeks, and all through my core. I swallow my breathy Chrissy sounds. I don't want to distract him into stopping.

What am I doing? There isn't a single part of me that isn't touching some part of Micah. Of the guy who could hijack my train of thought without trying when he was only seventeen. I'm older and wiser, but so is he. And he's seasoned now.

His finger brushes my ear while he gathers another lock of my hair, and a shiver runs down my back.

"Cold?" he asks, his voice low and lazy.

I give a single headshake, not trusting my voice. I keep my eyes on the screen, and he drops it. I'd rather die than get up, but it's possible I'll spontaneously combust if I don't.

I stay.

Micah occasionally stops playing with my hair to draw me tighter and warn me another jump scare might be coming.

I think he makes up a few of them.

Somehow, by the time the credits scroll, I am both utterly boneless and nothing but pins and needles.

Neither of us reaches for the remote. The credits keep rolling.

It would be so simple to turn my head ever so slightly, and Micah's mouth would be *right* there by mine.

A quarter turn.

I want to do it. But I also want him to do it. I want him to initiate this so that if this goes wrong, it's on him. *He* took us this direction. *He* chose this.

It's hard to think over my deafening pulse, but the truth is still louder.

I want this too.

Chapter Twenty

Kaitlyn

"I wasn't lying, you know." Micah's voice is mellow. Quiet.

"Lying about what?"

He doesn't answer at first, instead combing several strands of my hair through his fingers at once, causing another shiver, sending more heat down my spine.

"This. Your hair. I always thought it was pretty." He winds a lock of it around his finger.

"Thanks to two hours in a salon chair every eight weeks." I try to sound dry. I sound breathless instead.

"It was pretty before. I had a lot of time in ninth grade to notice, since I sat behind you in Chinese the whole year. It was shiny. Like polished sugar pine."

I make sure my voice is steadier this time. "That's the nicest way anyone has ever said dishwater blonde."

His arm tightens around me, like he's putting me in check. "Who is the artist here? I know what I meant. I always thought it looked so soft." He twirls a different strand around his finger. "It is."

I take the compliment, relaxing even more against him, something I didn't think possible when I was already boneless.

We fall quiet, and it's a loaded silence. It's the kind of silence before the tension bubble at the top of an overfull cup breaks. I could live in it forever. I will die if it doesn't end *now*.

I make the quarter turn.

Micah's hand freezes. "Kaitlyn?"

I understand the question. "Yes."

He understands the answer.

His lips brush mine, featherlight, and a sigh escapes me. As if that's the final sign he needs, he kisses me again, his lips firm this time, his hand sliding from my hair as he moves it to my side and turns me so we are face-to-face.

If that first touch of our lips was another question, this kiss is an exploration with an edge of urgency, like this has been building since the day I bumped into him in his store.

His heart beats faster, matching mine. I affect him. This is not just me. His hands frame my ribcage, shifting me up, his lips dragging against mine to press a kiss against their corner, trailing more kisses to my jawline.

My sighs become more thready with each touch of his mouth, heat blazing along the path it takes, but I'm greedy and drag his lips back to mine, our breath mingling. He makes a soft sound in his throat and kisses me harder. When his tongue brushes mine, the dopamine rush is so intense, I push against his chest on reflex.

He immediately releases me, and I leverage myself to stare down at him, trying to sort through my racing thoughts.

That was amazing.

And stupid.

And better than I ever imagined it could be back when I didn't know what kissing was.

It's also the worst timing.

That's the thought that wins out as I back away.

"This isn't what I want." Zero chance I can hold my voice steady. All the breathlessness is back, and I sound dazed.

His answer is a lifted eyebrow.

"This isn't what I want right now," I clarify.

He pushes himself up, drawing in the leg that had been keeping mine company against the sofa back and tucking it beneath him, situating himself for this talk.

Because it's going to be a talk. I can feel it. The weight of things that need to be said.

"I don't believe you," he says. "Try again."

The words should make me angry, but his tone is mild. Almost curious. Still, I can't let him get away with that.

"Did you just kiss-splain me?" I demand.

"Yeah. I did."

"You're supposed to be concerned and ask if I'm okay."

He crosses his arms. "Are you woman-splaining me?"

"No, that's called *communicating*." Ha. Hillview didn't have a debate team, but I would have won, obviously.

"You could have said anything except 'I don't want this right now' and I would say it was communicating. But that was fire, Katie. Are you trying to communicate something different?"

I draw my legs up crisscross style, subtly adjusting my posture to give wise woman vibes. "I didn't say I didn't like it."

"Then say you did." His face is calm, but his eyes snap.

"Are you *daring* me?" I ask. "This isn't high school."

He leans forward, stopping short of where I would feel the need to scoot back. "Maybe that's the problem. Maybe this is exactly what we would have done back then if I'd had the guts."

Whoa. My eyes widen.

"Don't act like you didn't know," he says. "You and your stupid soft-looking hair." His mouth twitches, and I can't fight a smile entirely.

"I did use good conditioner," I concede. The tension is ratcheting down. This is okay. He's not mad that I broke off our kiss. He's got an issue with the way I explained it.

"Katie with the good hair," he murmurs, more of his smile escaping.

"That Beyoncé album was the soundtrack of senior year."

"It was the best of years, it was the worst of years."

I tilt my head. "Are you going to quote every book we read or song we heard in high school?"

"No, because that would let you wiggle out of this conversation." His smile fades and his watchful expression returns. "Tell me what just happened."

But he's opened the door, as we say in cross-examinations, and I'm not walking away. "I will if you tell me why it didn't happen in high school."

He rubs his lips together, and my pulse ticks up because now I know how they feel.

"Deal," he says. "But you first."

I should have an answer for this given how many talks I've given myself about why I can't get distracted right now. But I'd never planned for a conversation about it, and I don't have the words neatly organized.

"We kissed," I start. Then I falter because I don't know how to explain why I stopped the kiss. I take a deep breath. "I feel like every answer I give here makes a lot of assumptions."

"I won't hold it against you."

I rub my hands over my face. "It wasn't the kiss, because that was . . ."

"Fire," he supplies.

"Fire," I agree. "It's what's after the kiss. Here come the assumptions. I'm not looking for a relationship right now. I'm not saying you are. Or that if you were, it would be with me. But the way I'm wired, I don't do casual. And I don't do complicated. I've had one long-term relationship, and it made sense."

Something flickers through his eyes. Something that says he doesn't love this answer, but I don't know how to decode it.

"You think we don't make sense?" he asks.

"We'd be complicated," I say. "My last relationship was in law school. Similar schedules, similar goals. Same workload. We didn't have a problem making time when we could, didn't have issues when we couldn't."

"Sounds hot."

"Micah . . ."

He shrugs. "I've got a relationship in my past too. College. It was opposite of yours. It was intense and made no sense at all."

Another burst of hot prickles surges in my chest, but it has an acidic edge. Note to self: Google emotional acid reflux.

"It's a strange feeling to be hungry for someone all the time," he continues, his tone almost distracted, like he's gone inside a memory. "To lose sleep or an entire day because you're so wrapped up in them."

I hate her. I give him my politely interested face. "Why aren't you with her?"

He blinks and focuses on me. "Figured some stuff out. Story for another time. Maybe you and I both got it wrong, but if I had to pick, I'd still take wild over 'making sense.'"

Me too, and that's the problem. That is what the energy feels like between Micah and me. Despite his gentle teasing and low-key invitations to dance or trick-or-treat, despite his ability to read and meet a need with breakfast burritos and gift shop sweats, the truth came roaring out in that kiss.

"Fire," I say aloud. "It shouldn't mean good when it's almost always a bad thing. I don't have time to burn my life down right now. I'm barely holding it together"—failing utterly—"getting this gala delivered for Madison. And when I'm not there, I'm in my study, falling asleep on that sofa every night. And as soon as I pass the Texas bar, I have to study for the California bar because we do so much business out there."

Micah rubs his hand over his hair, mussing it as he studies me. I feel see-through again, like the day his friend shouted at me from the soccer pitch about how I liked Micah. Except this time, I told on myself.

I shift on the sofa cushion, trying to get more comfortable. "I'm not saying you want a—"

"Don't." He says it quietly. "You assumed right about what I want. But you're wrong that we don't make sense."

"We don't."

"Kaitlyn." He looks me dead in the eye. "I can prove you're wrong."

I have never felt such an equal and opposite internal reaction. Roller coaster covers it, only it's the giddy stomach drop feeling of the plunge and the terrified head feeling of the climb *at the same time*. I spent my entire senior year fighting this feeling.

Failing to fight this feeling.

Being older and wiser now doesn't mean anything when the feeling is even stronger. When I *want* to believe that Micah can make a case for us. And I can't stop myself from reaching for the chance.

Chapter Twenty-One
Micah

"You can prove we make sense? How, Micah?" Kaitlyn asks.

Kaitlyn keeps her voice neutral, but I wonder if she realizes how much she gives away by trying so hard. "In building design, I research a project, brainstorm, then sketch. Next I work on schematics with floor plans and building elevations. I figure out the math and materials and physics so I know it can withstand all stressors. I present the proposal to the client. They approve, and then we begin to build something. I can break down how that's all played out between us, but we are there, at the last stage. We're ready to build."

"There's no way to predict 'all stressors,'" she argues, "and when buildings fall, the stakes are too high."

"Kaitlyn." I move forward until my knee almost touches hers.

She doesn't move away, not even when I reach out to settle my hands on her shoulders and rest my forehead against hers. "Didn't you fall eight years ago?" When she starts to draw away, I don't let her. "And didn't I fall ten?" I sweep my thumbs over her cheeks, soothing her.

I watch her eyes as something behind them crumbles. Common sense, hard reality, time constraints, deadlines . . . they disappear.

She lifts her chin, and there's no mistaking the invitation, but I move my thumb down to rest against her lips, holding her still.

"Something else, Katie." I take a breath, and it hitches on the way out. "I need to tell you something else."

She nips at the pad of my thumb, and my breath catches again. "Tell me."

"It's the real proof."

She nips again, and I move it out of reach without letting her go. I'm barely holding it together without her teeth against my skin.

"All those things in your office? Your favorite ones? They're mine. I made them. The space you feel is most yours in this house? I'm an important part of it."

It makes sense. That's what I thought, standing in her office, seeing my work in her most personal space. It makes more sense than anything has ever made to me, and there isn't a single part of me that has the discipline to let her figure that out with time.

"You . . . the perfect curves? On the lamp and the . . . ? The woman who belongs, that was your . . ."

I nod.

A look of wonder crosses her face, and she reaches for me.

No, that's not even close. She launches herself, and I catch her, my mouth finding hers even as I fall back on the sofa, cushioning her body with mine. She picks up where she broke off the last kiss, opening her mouth to me, inviting me in, and whatever I thought was happening in my system before is nothing compared to the detonation now.

Hunger licks through my veins as we tangle. Kaitlyn tastes more addictive than she smells, her skin is even softer than her hair, and the pads of my fingers crave more texture. I explore her planes and contrasts the way I would one of my pieces as I learn it, the strong line of her jaw, the gentle curve of her waist. I'm drunk on the geometry of her.

I pull her tighter and she flows against me, like if she could figure out a way to melt into me, she would. But the temperature burns past that. This is incineration. I love knowing, as always, we are evenly matched. I've never experienced feeling so out-of-body while being so connected to it at the same time.

I reverse our positions and dip down, taking control of the kiss, and when her hands slip from my hair down to my chest to bunch the fabric of my shirt and anchor me more tightly, I break the kiss to growl a wordless warning. I pull her hands away to pin them on either side of her head, our fingers laced as I scrape my teeth over her earlobe, paying back the nip she gave me. She sighs and angles her head so I can pay back the second nip on her other ear.

To make the point about who is the boss in this moment, I bite harder, and—

Ow. I hiss and jerk my head up as evil strikes, meeting Kaitlyn's startled eyes before I freeze.

"Kaitlyn." My voice is strangled. "Daisy has her claws in my back." Daisy. Daisy is the boss.

She rolls from under me to hit the floor on her knees, eye to extremely angry eye with Daisy Buchanan.

"Daisy," she says, "good girl. It's okay."

"What? No, bad girl," I say. "Also, help."

"I am." She keeps her voice soothing. "Daisy, I'm safe. You can let him go." She lifts a hand to pet her. Daisy doesn't move, but I grunt as she retracts her claws.

"Be still, Micah," Kaitlyn says in the exact same tone she used on Daisy. "I'll have her off you in a second. Won't I, sweet girl? Katie is fine. See that I'm fine? I'm scratching her. Her tail is down. I've almost got her," she narrates in that soothing tone.

I lower from the plank I've been holding, Daisy staying put, until after offering a few more scritches, Kaitlyn scoops up the cat and nuzzles her, reassuring her she's the best watchcat ever.

I sit up and eye Daisy.

"You okay?" Kaitlyn asks.

"Yeah. You?"

She buries her face in Daisy's neck to stall on an answer, but Daisy decides she's done being worshipped and wiggles to get down. Kaitlyn lets her go, but instead of coming back to the sofa, she sits on the stool instead. Her temples are damp, the color in her cheeks high, and her hair is wrecked. I do good work.

"So," I say.

"So," she agrees. "What happens next?"

"Neither of us has to work tomorrow, so let's make out all day."

She rolls her eyes but smiles. "Be serious."

"I'm dead serious."

She sucks her teeth. "Not your worst idea."

"That's why I was valedictorian."

She dives for me and I catch her, deflecting blows from the throw pillow she snatches up, laughing as I try to situate her in my lap.

She twists so she's on my lap but facing me, sitting on my knees, hers pinning my legs together so I lose leverage.

"Keep still while I beat you around your head and neck," she orders.

"I'll settle *you* down." I yank her by the hips until she's wedged against me before I loosen my hold and smile up at her. She drops the pillow and lets her hands fall to my shoulders, looking right back.

"What am I going to do with you?" I ask.

"That's exactly the reason I called this couch meeting."

I snort. "Glad most of my meetings aren't like this, or I'd never get anything done."

Our smiles fade as our eyes connect.

"Your eyes have gold flecks," she says, her voice soft. "I feel like I've found a new secret about you."

I watch her back, wondering what she's seeing in me besides the flecks. She curls to rest her forehead on my shoulder.

"I don't know what to do next," she says. It's barely a murmur.

"Does there need to be a plan?"

"The only plan that will work is doing nothing. I can't date you."

I go still for several seconds, hating the way those words hollow out my insides. Finally, I sigh. "Is this because I am the poor son of an unmarried village woman with no prospects and I'm still making payments on my truck?"

She gives my abs a light pinch. "There's not much to grab here." She pats the spot, interested in this discovery, but when the pat turns to a light stroke, she balls her fists and rolls off me to sit beside me instead.

I drop my head back against the cushions, waiting for the inevitable.

She copies me, and we both stare at the vaulted ceiling, not that I'm seeing it. I'm lost in thought. I don't have any genius arguments here.

"Katie." I nudge her leg with mine. "You can date me. It'll work."

She presses the heels of her hands against her eyes. "Does it help if I say I wish I could?"

"It's already working. This is our fourth date."

"What are you talking about? Are you high on sugar? Zombies get your brain?"

"Lunch at the warehouse. That was our first date."

She drops her hands and turns to look at me.

I keep my eyes on the ceiling. "We went dancing for our second. Trick-or-treating was our third. Watching the movie was number four. To be honest, I usually like a kiss after the third date, but you made up tardy points by blowing my mind with technique."

She elbows me. "How is it possible you beat me in math? Or *anything*? That's bad logic and worse counting."

"Is it though? I planned for us to get to this point."

"You did not."

"I did. I knew as soon as I realized who Madison was when she hired me for the project that this was a possibility." I straighten and turn so she does too, and we form a perfect reflection, each of us with one foot tucked under us, our knees touching, heads propped on hands braced against the sofa as we study each other.

"You thought you and I would date even though we hadn't spoken since high school?"

"I said I knew this was a possibility." I gesture between the two of us. "If any of that old chemistry was there and you were single, this was a probability. There is and you are. And here we are." I squeeze her knee lightly.

"I wanted to punch you, not kiss you, when I ran into you."

I let go of her knee to rub my chest, remembering the impact. "Maybe you wanted to do both."

When she starts to object, I press a hard, fast kiss to her mouth. "I wasn't sure until you invited me to the hospital."

"*Madison* invited you to the hospital."

"She wouldn't have done it if you didn't want me there."

She can't deny that.

"Even though you seemed cool with me by then, it was still next to impossible to even get you down to the warehouse to be sure. To see if the probability would become a reality."

"Because I'm so busy. That's the whole problem."

"I had a feeling you were avoiding me more than you needed to. But I could also see your schedule is pretty tight for real, so I came up with a plan to show you that you didn't need to worry."

"Your plan was to date me without telling me?"

I'm trying to decide if she's tipped from being incredulous to getting mad. "Did you feel like you wasted any of those trips to the warehouse? Or did you leave feeling like you had a good understanding of how the installation is going?"

She frowns.

Not mad yet. "Did you also leave each time feeling like you understood me better? Learned something new about me, maybe?"

Her face says yes, but her mouth says, "You can't trick people like that."

"I didn't. I brought you down for business. We conducted business. You deciding to stay for anything else was always up to you."

"But it's not a date if we don't agree it's a date."

"Okay. Strong argument. You want to say they weren't dates, they weren't dates."

"They weren't dates!"

"Okay." I'm unbothered since I expected this reaction.

"The whole point of a date is to get to know someone and see if you're the right fit. We haven't done that. Like, we haven't specifically decided that's what we're both trying to figure out. When I think about you—" She breaks off, and I sense a confession in the unfinished sentence.

I lean forward. "When you think about me, you . . . what?"

"I think 'interesting' and then 'wish I had time.' If this was meant to be, neither of us would have to work so hard to talk me into it. If you'd asked me out for real, you'd know I can't say yes." She crosses her arms over her chest, daring me to contradict her.

"Because you're busy? Busy isn't forever."

"Busy is for the next year, minimum." She gets up and wanders toward the windows, not that there's anything to see but our reflections. "Everything I do costs me something else. Something important. I barely make my life work as it is. I should have been studying tonight, Micah. And I didn't, and that is the problem."

"Are you sorry I came over?"

"No." She turns to me again. "But what happens when I take the bar in February, and I screw up something and then I realize the four hours I lost tonight are the four hours I needed to study?"

"Lost." My voice is flat. I can't help it. That's a hell of a way to describe spending time together.

"And it's not just that. With our family name on the gala, I *have* to make sure it comes off without a hitch. When those donations are totaled at the end of the night, if it's anything less than two million dollars, it will be a failure. Failing means screwing up Madison's goals. Failing all the people in Dhaka I met this summer who are waiting for a chance they need because Armstrong Industries ruined everything ten years ago."

I turn toward her, both feet on the ground, and rest my arms on my knees as I study the floor. "It's been okay. The last couple of months. How often we've been able to see each other. It doesn't have to be more than that until things calm down." I look up to meet her eyes. Hers are guarded again.

"That's not how I work. I'm all in or all out."

"You had a whole two-year relationship with someone because it was convenient. That doesn't sound all in." Frustration clips my words.

"I was second to school for him. He was third to school and Threadwork for me." She copies my gesture, pointing between the two of us. "Is that what this is? You want to play a distant third?"

I rub my forehead. "No."

"For what it's worth, you wouldn't be a distant third." Her voice is tired. Regretful. "You would become the main thing, which means I would ultimately fail at what *should* be the main things, and that will make me blame getting caught up in you, and then . . . you. I would blame you."

"You're making some leaps there."

A shrug. "Maybe before tonight I was. But after . . ." She waves at the sofa. "Now I'm sure. Can you honestly say that tonight won't change the way we interact professionally?"

Instead of answering, I stand, gaze back on the floor, thinking, trying to decide if I should argue her out of this. But I don't want to. She's right. Anything that went wrong, she'd blame me. I dig my keys from my pocket and meet her eyes.

"That's the one thing I *can* promise you. Because you're right, you shouldn't have to be talked into this. And that's not even about pride. I don't want to wonder when I'll have to do it again." I flick a glance at the door. "Look, I should go. But don't worry about the installation. I don't want to let down Madison either."

Her lips part like she's about to say something else. But she doesn't. She turns toward the door too. "I'll walk you out."

I feel her eyes on me as I head down the walkway outside and pause. "Seriously, don't stress about the warehouse. You don't understand how good I really am. Put your energy toward the rest of it. I got this."

Then she disappears as I round the corner toward my truck.

Chapter Twenty-Two
Kaitlyn

MICAH MAY HAVE "GOT this," but I don't.

He is on my mind the whole next week, but he's as good as his word, sending me an email any time there's progress to show in the warehouse. Beyond that, there's nothing. No schemes to get me down to the warehouse. Every night I go home to study without a text convincing me I need to go "check" something is a disappointment and a relief.

I only have six weeks to find enough auction items for us to get them processed in time, properly displayed or packaged, and integrated into the flashy video presentation Madison hired a media company to produce. They keep asking me for more material, warning me they need time to film and edit and do whatever other technical wizardry has to happen so it looks as slick as a video package at the Oscars or something. They shouldn't worry. I have exactly four items so far. They can probably pull it all together in an afternoon.

One of the donations is cool. Angeline Bourque agrees to offer up two seats on the front row of her show during Paris Fashion Week with a VIP experience at her atelier two days later. Those tickets are a nearly impossible coup, but her creative director has been dressing Mom for major events for over ten years. Additionally, her ready-to-wear line is manufactured in Dhaka. She understands the need.

Other than that, Sara Elizabeth isn't going to have much emcee work to do that night.

I normally visit Harper most days when I leave work, but now I avoid it. Madison always wants to ask about the gala, and I can't stop by with nothing new to report.

By Friday, I'm desperate. Five weeks to go, and even if our guests are at their most generous, the current auction offerings will bring in a quarter million at best. I google even more articles on how to procure high-value donations, and I get the sense that only one writer researched it and the rest of them are written by AI regurgitating the same information.

I know all this stuff. I know all of it, and I've been trying, and it isn't working. But I spend the morning doing all the brainstorming the article suggests, listing out even more unusual experiences or pieces that guests might open their wallets for, as well as who might be willing to donate them.

After a lunch of a limp spinach salad at my desk, I start emailing and calling.

By midafternoon, I get somewhere.

I'm so surprised, I blink at the phone for a couple of seconds until the voice on the other end says, "Hello? You still there?"

Last month, one of Mom's friends on the symphony board, Deborah Fisk, was raving about an installation of glass bluebonnets a local artist had done on the grounds of the Blanton Museum of Art. Even I had heard of the glass artist, who shot to fame a few years ago after winning a reality show about glassblowers, then got tapped to do a chandelier in the home of the woman who owns the San Antonio Stingers.

There are eleven known billionaires living in Austin, and Deborah Fisk is one of them, so I called her, and now I'm speechless that she's agreed to donate a commissioned piece by the artist.

"Hello?" Deborah repeats.

"Hey, yes, sorry, Miss Deborah. That's so generous of you." I can't believe this worked.

"Don't say thank you yet. Gabriela is hard to book. I can put in a word for you, and I'll donate a commission worth fifty thousand, but she can pick and choose her projects now. You'll still have to talk her into saying yes."

I thank her a dozen more times, and thirty seconds after we hang up, I'm on the phone with the glass artist, who agrees to a meeting the following Tuesday. I take what feels like my first deep breath in days. Of the four major auction items I've procured, three have come through face-to-face meetings. This is good.

So good that I stop by to see Harper on my way home because I can actually tell Madison we've got a nearly done deal. That's one more day before I have to worry her with otherwise catastrophic auction shortages.

Saturday morning, I even spend the day studying when I get home from the gym. I only have to refrain from making up an excuse to text Micah five times. I wish it was him every time a text comes in, but it'll take practice to smother that reflex. If I can avoid seeing him as much as possible until this whole thing is over, then maybe I have a shot.

Gabriela Juarez ruins that shot.

I leave her glass studio in the Arts District after our meeting on Tuesday without a commitment. I didn't think it would be a slam dunk, but I also didn't think it would be the reason I'd have to call Micah.

I start my car, hands curled around the wheel, bracing myself to make that call. We've only emailed in the last ten days. His emails are professional but friendly, and I try hard to respond that way. It only takes me about an hour of overthinking to send a reply that amounts to "Looks amazing over there. Keep up the good work!" And yes, every reply sounds that forced.

Today, I have no choice but to call him, because I've made a deal with Gabriela Juarez, but I can't deliver on it without Micah's cooperation.

This is going to require a large dose of calming tea before I do this. I hit the Starbucks drive-thru for a chamomile mint blossom tea and sip enough of it to soothe my nerves before I swallow hard and order my phone to call Micah.

"Kaitlyn? Hey." The only thing I hear in his voice is surprise.

"Hey, Micah. Would you happen to be at the warehouse today?"

"I'm at the office," he says. "But Eva has a couple of her guys in there if you need something."

Sometimes I forget that everyone else has a life outside of this project except for me.

"This is something I'll need to run past you. For the gala," I add, so it's clear this is business.

A beat of silence follows. "I'd like to say I'm intrigued, but if you're running it past me, it means you need me to incorporate a design change."

"I wouldn't go as far as design change," I hedge.

"Not reassuring." He's kept his tone courteous without being overly familiar. I hate it.

"I'm not going to *require* you to do anything," I say. "But I want to run a request past you and see if it's possible."

"You're the client." There's a hint of dryness. I welcome it, relieved to get a flash of the real Micah. "I'll be at the site tomorrow after lunch."

"Great, I'll text before I swing by."

We hang up, and watching his name wink out on my dash display when the call ends gives me a melancholy pang. It's probably due to the weather. It's been in the sixties for a week, the surest sign that Austin is finally entering fall, weeks after the calendar did.

I'm going to see Micah tomorrow.

I sit with that for a minute or two while I drive. That's fine. Good, even. Best-case scenario, seeing him after almost two weeks could show me that I've been exaggerating that Halloween make out, making it a bigger deal than it was because my brain plays it on a loop like it's the script of a Disneyland ride running every minute the park is open. Worst-case scenario, I realize I'm not exaggerating at all.

At least it will be a good reminder to keep on keeping on with this boundary.

•♥•♥•♥•♥•♥•

It's a worst-case scenario.

I know as soon as I spot Micah's truck in the parking lot and my stomach flutters.

"You have got to be kidding me." I park and cut my engine. Butterflies over his truck. But I'm not surprised. Not after I spent an hour last night choosing a "drop by the jobsite to see the architect" outfit. I'm letting this matter more than it should. "Compose yourself, Kaitlyn. You will focus, lead, and delegate."

I repeat that a few times before I decide I'm grounded enough to get out of the car and go in.

As soon as I do, I pause, taking in the changes. Despite watching this develop through email updates, it's something else entirely to experience it in person. The knot of worry that has grown tighter inside my chest as we hurtle toward New Year's loosens for the first time. It's slight but distinct as it comes out as a faint gasp of awe.

There are no more orange poles. They're either black or encircled in a column or "stalk" of vertical rebar, round as the trunk of an oak, rising to curve outward at its top. The interior stalks are connected at their tops by iron marigolds four feet in diameter, touching edges welded to each other, several marigolds extending from each stalk to the next stalk in every direction, not linearly but like a honeycomb, almost. Even though Micah and Eva have only covered a fraction of the total venue area so far, the effect is alien and beautiful. It doesn't seem possible for this to exist inside a commercial warehouse, a space so functional it's the antithesis of creativity.

Whatever else may happen at this gala, no one will question the venue now. It will be the talk of the town and all over social media.

I don't notice the high mechanical whine filling the warehouse until it stops. I glance over to see Micah across the floor, hard hat and safety goggles on, holding a power tool the size of . . . I don't know anything about power tools. I can't draw a helpful comparison.

He's the most dressed down I've ever seen him in black joggers and a sage green T-shirt. He lifts a hand in greeting, then rubs his face against his sleeve, like he's sweating. But the temperature is perfect thanks to the cool weather.

There are two other workers as well, guys around my age, who each give me a nod. Micah pulls the goggles down around his neck but leaves on the hard hat as he hands his tool to the other guy and walks over to meet me.

The guy calls, "Micah?"

"Gimme a second, Ty," Micah calls back.

It's so strange to have other workers in here. I haven't seen anyone on-site besides Micah since the day I met Eva. It feels like having buyers coming through your house while you're home. Like, sure, they're allowed to be here, even supposed to be here, but it still feels off somehow.

"Hey," Micah says, stopping a few feet away so we can speak at a normal volume.

"It's good to see you." It's not what I mean to say, but it is what I mean. Maybe he'll take it as one of those things people say out of habit and not a confession.

He doesn't return the sentiment. Instead, he runs a glance over me, but I don't know how to take it. It's not a leer. I'm not sure Micah would even know how to leer. It's not cold or warm, dismissive or . . . anything. It's like he's taking inventory. *Yes, this is still Kaitlyn.*

"Welcome back to the hive," he says.

"I'm blown away."

"Thanks."

That neutrality again. I can't read his tone. "So the reason I wanted to talk to you—"

He holds up a finger. "Hold on, let me put Ty back to work. It'll be loud, but we can go up to the booth if that's okay?" I nod, and he hollers for Ty and gives him a thumbs up.

The loud whine is back. Micah hands me a hard hat from the table beside the door and leads me on the shortest route to the stairs, a diagonal path through the world he's created. I don't understand it. He's only reframed an empty space, but crossing this section of the warehouse floor beneath it feels like a different lifetime from standing on the bare slab it was in September.

We climb up to the supervisor loft, and he shuts the door, muffling the screech of the work below us. "Hit me with it," he says. "Band-Aid treatment. Tell me how much you're about to complicate this job."

"Do you know who Gabriela Juarez is?"

"Glassblower," he says. "Incredible work."

"Yeah. This is about her. A donor is willing to put up a custom chandelier commission for the auction if Gabriela agrees to it. A big piece, something you would see in the entry of a corporate building. She said 'more than a conversation piece, a showstopper.'"

"That's a generous offer. She could charge a ton for something on that scale."

"We'll easily be able to auction it for low six figures," I say. "The right to commission a piece from her is exactly the kind of thing these gala guests will go to battle for. It's exclusive, so it will matter more for bragging rights than it will for actual cost."

"Where do I come in?"

I sigh. "She's heard Rylan Hurley will be there, and she wants to catch his attention. He builds—"

"Hotels in Vegas," Micah finishes, a small smile on his lips. "I pay attention to those kinds of projects."

"Right." Of course an architect would pay attention to massive luxury buildings. "It would be an amazing get for the auction, but she has a condition."

Micah closes his eyes long enough for it not to be a blink before he meets mine. "She wants to collaborate?"

I give him that yes-and-no head shake, the one that says *Kind of but not really*. "Probably not on the scale you're thinking. She does want some of her work to be incorporated. Something already existing. She had me take pictures of the pieces she'd like us to consider. She doesn't expect us to take it all, but she'd like us to choose something—or things—substantial enough to make a statement. Whet their appetites, I guess. Or at least Rylan Hurley's."

He rubs his hands over his face then sighs. "I get it. Can't blame her for trying to get her work into his hotels. May I see?"

I hand him my phone. Our fingers brush. Neither of us react, but inside, I feel that spark. It reminds me that resistance is futile but necessary.

He studies each picture for several long seconds. I can't read his face. After a few minutes, he nods and goes back to one, standing to look out through the booth window. He rubs his finger across his lips several times. I'm very jealous of that finger.

"There's a possibility here," he says. "Do you mind if I text this to myself?"

"Go ahead."

He does and gives back my phone. "That vase in the picture. How tall is it?"

"About four feet." I hold my hand chest high.

He nods and chews at his bottom lip. "I have an idea. We'll need to go to my workshop so I can show you. Is that okay?"

I don't have time for this. I have no idea where his workshop is. I should ask him to send me a picture or tell him whatever he's planning is fine. But I want to go to his workshop. This feels like an "inner sanctum" moment.

"Sure. Is it far?"

"No. It's in my garage. I better drive."

His garage. In his house?

Better and better, but worse and worse.

Chapter Twenty-Three

Kaitlyn

I FOLLOW MICAH DOWN the stairs, pause while he lets Eva know that we're running to his workshop, and then he's opening his truck door for me. I'm buckled in by the time he settles behind the wheel. His truck is clean, like its "new car smell" days weren't too long ago. No scuffs in the gray interior.

He starts the engine, shifts, and ignores the backup camera to put his hand on my seat so he can look over his shoulder to reverse.

I didn't know I had a thing for guys doing this, but it turns out I do. It's sexy. Which is ridiculous. What is sexy about an arm resting on the back of my seat while he's looking past me, not at me? Maybe because it opens up his body frame and creates a perfect nook for nestling, like I could curl up beside him and he'd let that arm drop to settle around me instead.

Instead of backing up, Micah pauses, removes his hand from my seat, and puts the truck back in park.

"Do you hate this idea that much?" I ask, when he's silent. "Maybe I can solve this another way, like turning one of the front offices into a 'gallery space' and put several of her pieces out there."

"It's not that. It's . . ." A head shake. "Never mind."

A few seconds later, we're on Highway 183, and I wonder how long of a drive we're in for. Or really, how long this awkward silence is going to be. But barely a minute later, we're turning into a neighborhood right across from a self-storage facility.

"Welcome to Montopolis," Micah says, his voice dry. Dry like it gets when he's pretending something doesn't matter, like he's flipping the joke on someone. *You think I care that I live in Montopolis? It's funny that you think I would.*

Montopolis is what polite people call "a working-class neighborhood" and most people call "poor." Probably the poorest in Austin.

We drive down a street with a used tire store and Dollar General on one side, houses surrounded by chain-link fences on the other. The homes are small, smaller than my parents' pool house, but with generous yards. That would give away their age even if the rundown exteriors of some of the houses didn't. These were built fifty years ago or more, I would bet.

We turn another corner, and it's more of the same. Chain-link fences around cottage-sized houses. Some look as if they've never been repainted. Most are tidy if plain. A couple have been modernized with trendy dark paint and white trim. After two more blocks, brand new duplexes pop up, tall with angular roof lines. They're sprinkled among the original homes, a dissonant contrast to the single-level bungalows.

"That's . . . a choice," I say, eyeing a duplex that couldn't look more out of place between the older homes flanking it than if someone plopped a spaceship down in a used parking lot.

"Gentrification," he mumbles. He leaves it at that.

We turn down one more street, and he slows the truck. This one doesn't have chain-link fences. Most of the yards aren't fenced at all, but the two I see are decorative iron and a wood fence laid horizontally. He pulls into a driveway and parks.

The house is gray-green with a black vinyl roof, black shutters and door, and white trim. Everything looks new and fresh. There's no fence, and the front yard is short grass with some low-maintenance shrubs along the house. Unless there's a heck of a lot of house hiding behind it, I'd say it's about the size of our Threadwork suite, maybe a thousand square feet?

"This is my house." He looks less than thrilled.

It's a fact of life that my friends who don't come from money often feel like they have to apologize when they invite me to their apartments or homes. I understand, I think, but I wish they didn't feel like they needed to. It's not exactly normal for someone my age to own a home like mine at all, much less buy it outright. I get that.

I give Micah the same nonjudgmental smile I give them. "Did you renovate it? It looks great. I love the color, and the way you made it feel current—"

He winces. "Don't. This level of cheerfulness from you is spooky."

I press my lips together and swallow. "Right. Sorry. Didn't mean to sound . . ." Condescending? Fake?

He shakes his head. "It's not that. I did exactly what I wanted to do with this place, and I like it." He glances toward the front door, his fingers drumming on the steering wheel. "My mom is home. She can be a lot."

He lives with his mom? I didn't expect that, and I'm not sure what to think about it. Most of the time, it's a red flag. But red flags shouldn't matter when it's someone I'm not dating. "That makes sense. Austin rents are expensive, so saving money is good."

"Don't try to relate to the poor people, Kaitlyn." A smile tugs up one corner of his mouth. "I own this place. I did grow up here, but I bought it three years ago from my uncle."

"Oh. Sorry for assuming." I had definitely sounded condescending. *Saving money is good*. That's what everyone wants to hear a filthy rich trust fund baby say.

"Only my boys come over." He drums his fingers a couple more times and looks at me. "They all know about my mom."

"She can be a lot," I repeat, realizing he means more than a big personality.

"She has bipolar. She doesn't manage it well. If she comes out to the garage, let me handle it."

"Is she having an episode?"

"Do you know much about bipolar?"

"One of my roommates had it. It never caused us any problems, but she had a couple of rough patches."

He nods. "My mom's can get extreme. She's been erratic the last couple of months, but she won't go see her doctor. When I went for a run this morning, she was already awake. That can be a sign she was up all night. One of her triggers for a manic episode is lack of sleep. Or sometimes it's a symptom that she's already in one."

He scrubs his hand over his face, as if he's the one who needs sleep. "She won't do anything to you. But sometimes she gets upset with me. Don't . . ." Head shake, like he's not sure what he wants to say. "Let's see if we can get in and out fairly quickly, and maybe it won't be an issue."

He hits the garage opener and we climb out. I follow him inside, down an aisle between two workbenches with pegboard backs. Tools hang from hooks over one bench. Small bins full of everything from screws to drawer handles line the other.

"Sorry it's crowded," Micah says. "There used to be plenty of room when I started upcycling furniture during college. I get so many commissions now I had to put in more workbenches plus sheds in the back to handle all the salvage my boys bring me."

The garage smells like chemicals and sawdust, but I like it. It deepens the sense that this is Micah's space. "I don't know anything about woodworking, but I have a feeling that for someone who does, walking in here would feel like a kid going to a toy store."

He smiles, a small but real one. "Something like that."

"You said 'your boys.' Is that your store staff?"

"Kind of. It's guys I grew up with around here. We got construction jobs together. Worked them through high school and college when I could. They still do. I started a salvage business, and I subcontract with a few builders and demolition companies. My guys know what to pull from a demo site, and their supervisors don't care what they haul off. I pay my friends by the truckload. Earns them some extra bucks."

"You have sheds, plural? All full of stuff waiting to become something else?"

He points to the back door of the garage. "Three sheds. If I can't find what I need in here, we'll go out there."

"Mind if I look around in here while you do your thing?"

He looks over. "That's fine."

I want to explore the workbench with the assorted bins. I glance through them, most containing pieces of mirror and ceramic. This must be where Micah does his mosaic work.

The picture of the woman on my wall flashes through my mind, and heat washes over my cheeks. This might be the bench where he made her, picking out the curves and dips of her resting body.

Micah is behind the other pegboard. I can't see him, but I hear muted clangs and scrapes.

The door leading from the house opens, and a middle-aged woman in jeans stands on the threshold, plucking at her paint-stained Hillview Academy T-shirt.

"Hey, Ma." Micah keeps his voice neutral.

"It's a mess in here. Who is this? You shouldn't have people over when it's messy."

"This is my client, Kaitlyn," Micah says. "Kaitlyn, this is my mom, Tori. Ma, do you need help with something?"

"Can't I go in my own garage? Is this a business now? Do I need an appointment? Or is this still my house?"

"You can." Micah's tone doesn't change. Still level. "We won't be out here long. I need to find something and head back to work, but you want me to get us some salads on the way home for dinner?"

Her lip curls. "So you can show off how much money you make? No. I'll make a damn ham sandwich."

"That sounds good." He says it like they're having a normal conversation. "Will you make me one?"

"Why? So you can eat out here in the garage like a slob?"

"Good point. No sandwich for me."

"I wasn't offering you one. I don't have time for that. Painting. I need to paint. More orders." She shuts the door hard.

After a moment of silence, I walk around the workbench so I can check on Micah. He's standing with some thin metal rods in his hand, staring at the wall.

"Micah?"

He looks over. "I better show you the options and get you back to the warehouse."

"If you need to take care of her right now . . ."

A shadow crosses his eyes. "No. We need to go to one of the sheds."

My heart hurts for him, but I'm not sure how to make him feel better. "Sounds good. What are we looking for, exactly?"

"Come on." He leads me into the backyard. It's enclosed by a wood privacy fence, and the sheds are the only things back here. The lawn is tidy, but like mine, it's not landscaped. Just plain grass except for a worn dirt path from the sheds to the side gate.

Each of the wooden sheds is about ten by ten, painted a green several shades deeper than the house, with the doors and a few horizontal planks trimmed in black or white. They're flat-topped, with each door offset from the center, each located at a different point along its shed's front plane. The overall effect with lines and balance is . . .

"Why do these give me Mondrian vibes?" I ask.

He looks at me like I cracked a difficult code. "Because you're perceptive."

"You built these," I guess.

He works the combination lock on the middle shed. "I reclaimed the wood from teardowns where they put those condos you pointed out."

"Architect. Sculptor. High-end custom furniture maker. Business mogul. Anything you don't do, Micah?"

"You forgot Batman."

"And Batman."

"Not a mogul though. Small business owner. And I can't keep up with all of it, so we'll see what I give up."

He releases the lock and slides the door aside, reaching in to flip a light. Not a single bare light bulb either. I point to the wire basket enclosing it. "Did you custom-make a cover for a shed light?"

"No." He smirks. "I sketched it out for one of Eva's guys, and he did it."

I follow him into the shed but wait by the door while he heads straight to a corner and comes back with more metal, this time a long silver rod.

"This is a six-foot stud."

"You think highly of yourself."

"Interesting you thought I meant me."

I press my lips together to keep him from winning the smile, and I give him a lazy wave to continue.

"This is twenty-five gauge, which is the cheap stuff, but it'll make it easier to shape."

I cock my head. "Into what?"

"I'll have Eva curve the top three feet into a tube, then wrap these"—he holds up the thinner wires from his work-shop—"around it and fuse it to make it look like rebar."

The wires from the shop look like the metal skewers Joey uses when he and Ava have everyone over to grill. Pineapple and veggie skewers for Ava and meat for the heathens.

"I can picture it. But why do that? Why not use the rebar in the warehouse?"

"Too heavy. I'm thinking we place those vases at either end of the stage and put these inside like stalks. I don't think they'd damage the glass even if they shifted. All bets are off with actual rebar."

I squint at the stud, trying to imagine it. "So you'd make a bouquet of rebar for the vases?"

"Yeah. Eva only needs to weld the visible part, so it won't take too long. Hit it with black paint, and you've got glass vases displaying metal plants."

My eyes widen. "I get it. That will look . . ."

"Good," he finishes.

"Yes. But are you okay with it?"

"I gave you a solution I can live with, and it features Gabriela Juarez's work pretty prominently. If she okays it, it's fine by me."

I want to throw my arms around him and squeeze him out of sheer relief. And to feel his satisfyingly solid torso. That warm, muscly . . .

"Great," I say, so brightly that Micah takes a step back. "Sorry, I'm excited by your idea."

"Then we'll roll with it. Let me grab what I need, and I'll meet you at the truck."

"I can help," I tell him. "I'm stronger than I look."

He eyes my shirtdress of Baltic blue poplin, cinched at the waist with a thin gray belt. When his eyes drop to my high-heeled Mary Janes, he shakes his head. "I'm good."

"You're underestimating me," I tell him.

A trace of his smile appears. "I doubt it. Meet me at my truck."

I shake my head but go, leaning against the door as I wait for him to appear. He comes through the side gate a few minutes later with an armload of studs.

"Want to get the tailgate?"

"Sure, now you need me," I say, walking around to help. "I'm an old-fashioned girl and believe men should open doors, but I'll do it this time."

"There's a button on the taillight."

I hit it and lower the tailgate. When it's loaded and shut, he walks to the passenger side to open the door.

"All right, old-fashioned liar, I've got the door for you."

"Liar? How dare you, sir."

"You're as old-fashioned as I am," he says, shutting the door after me.

I pick up the discussion when he gets in on his side. "I'm old-fashioned in some ways."

He starts the truck. "Like what? You seem like you would definitely buy your own flowers."

I smile. "I would if I wanted some."

"Girl, get those flowers. You don't need a man," he says in a vapid sorority girl voice.

"You're right. Besides flowers, what would I possibly do with a man?"

"You tell me." His tone is somewhere between teasing and serious.

My smile fades. This was not a smart joke to run with. *Nice one, Katie. Just punch the bruise.* "Micah—"

"No to whatever you're about to say. Doesn't need to be dug up. We're good."

Right. Change of subject. "I had no idea you live so close to the warehouse. You grew up here?"

"We moved here in middle school. My uncle bought it and said we could live in it until I was done with school. He didn't charge us rent." He shrugs. "He's bought cars that cost more than our house did at the time, so it wasn't a big deal to him, although he always made it a big deal to us. Told my mom to handle utilities and bills. Told me to handle the yard. And I've been here ever since."

I want to ask so many follow-up questions. *Here in a stuck way? Do you wish you could leave? Why did you buy it?* But that's we're-starting-a-relationship personal, not coworker personal. "How did you get all the way over to Hillview every day? Your cousin?"

"Rode my bike at 6:30 every morning down to Ponca and locked it up behind a tire store. Caught the Metrobus and rode it an hour to a Starbucks on Northland where I met my cousin. Same thing in reverse after school."

Hillview hadn't started until 8:30. "It took you two hours to get to school every morning?" I'm trying and failing not to sound appalled.

"Don't be dramatic," he says. "Kayla liked to be early, so it was more like ninety minutes."

"Micah, that's—"

"Fine," he says. "It was fine. It's why I was tired and moody most days, but I wasn't going to blow a chance like Hillview. And if it makes you feel any better, I got a lot of studying done on the bus."

"Did you like growing up here?"

"Mostly."

His tone doesn't invite me to dive into that answer. Guess that was still too personal. I glance through the window as we turn out of his street, struck again by the mix of houses from dilapidated to renovated to condos. "Looks like this area is changing. Gentrifying, you said?"

"Slowly."

I admit defeat. I don't like being made to talk either, so I'll keep my questions and observations to myself.

As if sensing I've given up, he nods toward a neat white house on the left. "That's Mrs. Horne, the one who made the cover on the footstool you like. You know Ty at the jobsite? His mom." He points to another house, red brick with an aluminum screen door. It looks like it hasn't been updated since before I was born. "My buddy Arturo lives there with his grandma. We have plans to fix up the outside, but he works too many hours. Me too right now."

"Sorry," I say. "We're keeping you busy."

"Worth it if I make the right connections."

"For more art commissions?"

"Architecture clients, ideally. Even one or two could end up spreading the word enough to keep me busy."

"Is that your main focus? Architecture? You said something would have to give."

His forehead furrows. "Yeah. I'd like to move Arturo into running the salvage side full-time. Maybe bring on an apprentice for the furniture making."

A stop sign appears, and he obeys it, pointing at another house. "That's Mrs. Perez. She runs a tailoring business out of her garage. Quinceañeras and formal stuff like that. Once I was over here hanging out with her son, Marco, and I saw Charlotte Cameron leaving after an appointment."

"Charlotte from Hillview?"

He nods. "She was getting a prom dress fixed or something. When she saw me sitting on the sofa playing Xbox with Marco, she looked at me like . . ."

"Like what?"

He pulls through the intersection. "Let's go see what Eva thinks about this arts-and-crafts assignment we're bringing her."

He doesn't say anything for the last couple of minutes back to the warehouse, but I'm beginning to understand how much he leaves unsaid in those silences.

Chapter Twenty-Four
Kaitlyn

WE GET THE CHANDELIER from Gabriela Juarez.

Gabriela approved the concept, and Eva said she could make the pieces for the vases in a couple of hours.

That did not create any breathing space for me. Thursday and Friday, none of my contact attempts panned out. No messages or emails returned beyond one autoreply. Three assistants who wouldn't put me through to their bosses.

No new auction items.

At Madison's house on Sunday for family dinner, I smile big—crocodile big—when she asks me how it's going. I rave so hard over the chandelier commission that they forget to ask about any other new items. Mom looks delighted, Dad nods his approval—which is close to a standing ovation from him—and the pit in my stomach widens, a bottomless hole my worry keeps pouring into.

Talk turns to the entertainment for the gala, and Mom gushes over how Sara Elizabeth's personal assistant is the sweetest thing. Then she moves on to our gowns and crowing about how she'd *told* Madison she would lose her baby weight just like *that*, because hadn't Mom done that herself after each of us?

When dinner ends, Harper announces through the baby monitor clipped to Oliver's waistband that it's her turn to eat, so I make my excuses and leave before I can get drawn into a chatty goodbye with Mom.

Instead of studying when I get home, I sit down to review my contact list for the auction. Again. I go over every contact I can think of with even the slightest connection to me or anyone in our family or the company.

I push my memory harder to come up with more names, more connections, no matter how obscure. I don't have any pride left. I will beg in the most professional way possible to get their donations. If professional doesn't work, I'll try pathetic.

I go through my sorority's Instagram, every roommate I've ever had, anyone I knew in college with any kind of connection at all. They all go on my list. I go back further, to high school, and . . .

Drake Braverman.

His family owns a few car dealerships. They're loaded. I see him every now and then, mainly at a wedding or two in the last couple of years. I always smile. He doesn't seem to register that I'm being ironic.

I will start with Drake Braverman in the morning.

No, I'll start now. I grab my phone and search Instagram, finding his account. It's mostly him posing in front of different exotic cars they're selling, always leaning on the hood, feet crossed at the ankles, hands resting on his lap, one hand gripping the other wrist in a pose that shows off a different flashy watch.

I follow and message him.

Hey, Drake. Long time, no talk.

I go up to wash my face and put a pitch together in my head. I'm going to get an appointment with him, and I'm going to close the deal.

He answers as I'm standing in my closet, choosing an outfit for the morning.

> Lol, if you mean you never talk to me, then yeah. Long time. What's good, Kaitlyn Armstrong?

> Wheeling and dealing, which is your specialty, isn't it?

> You know it. You looking to get into something new?

> Definitely looking to hit you up for something. If I call your office tomorrow, will you take it?

> Gotta hear this. Call after lunch. My assistant will put you through.

He signs off with a laugh-cry emoji, and I choose a suit and set it on a hook, ready for the morning. Then I put myself to bed wearing a grim smile, because I will absolutely be making a donation happen. A big-ticket item.

I understand Drake Braverman. And I'm going to get what I need.

·♥·♥·♥·♥·♥·

Yes.

Yes yes yes yes yes.

It is Monday after lunch, and I just hung up with Drake Braverman.

It isn't a big win; Drake didn't say yes to a donation on the spot. But he did agree to meet Thursday for drinks, so it's a win.

I take a minute to savor it. I'm going to bring him a pair of gorgeous Copperhead boots and a pitch he can't refuse.

Micah's words keep running through my head. *He's bought cars that cost more than our house did at the time.* That's what he said about his uncle.

It applies to the Bravermans too. The Bravermans take vacations that cost more than the sports cars they sell.

We're doing this to create opportunities for people who don't have the luxury of even cheap vacations, much less a car. I can't say I know how it feels. But I know how I feel when I see it in Bangladesh.

I have to make this happen. I'm going to Drake with a big ask, swinging like I expect a homerun.

"Suz," I say, popping my head out the door. "Call up to Raj for a pair of men's Thorntons in size twelve, gray alligator, please?" It's always better to guess bigger than smaller on a man's boot size when you're asking for a favor.

Raj's whole job is PR, and that includes letting the Armstrongs request boots whenever we want them. Hmmm. Maybe we should create a design exclusively for people who do big charitable favors like this? Call it . . . platinum certified or something elite, and a pair will be one of those *if you know, you know* kind of status symbols? Wealthy people love owning things money can't buy.

I walk out to Suz's desk. "Actually, tell Raj I'm a genius and put a meeting on the books with him later this week."

"Got it."

"I'm going to be practicing a pitch for the rest of the afternoon, so hold any calls unless they sound like they want to give us money."

I don't get any more meetings over the next two days, and Thursday tries to knock me down all day before I'm supposed to meet with Drake for drinks. Raj calls to tell me that we're out of any boots over size ten in the building, but he'll have more in next week.

I gamble that it will be better to show up with a pair in hand and a promise to exchange them, so I tell Raj to send down the tens.

I spill salad on my blouse at lunch, leaving a grease spot on the blush pink silk, right over my boob.

Two more assistants decline meetings on behalf of their bosses.

By 4:00, my nerves are stretched thin, and I evacuate my office before anything else can go wrong and head home to change. A silver lining, maybe? I can choose something more suited for drinks.

I pull out a simple blue-gray Natori shift in my closet. It's the color of my eyes, and I always feel confident when I wear it. It's sleeveless with a V-neck. It's less structured than what I usually wear, made of silk that skims my hips, and the hem floats right above my knee. It looks perfectly professional with a blazer, but when the jacket comes off, the cut emphasizes my favorite features: my strong arms and strong legs.

I want that message coming across to Drake tonight. Strength, strength, strength.

I choose four-inch stiletto heels with a pointy toe. They mean business. It's the perfect balance.

No sooner do I change dresses than my phone goes off. If this is Drake canceling . . .

> Stuff for the vases done. Pic doesn't really capture it. Have time to swing by?

> Tomorrow is better. Would that work?

> Not here again until Monday.

I can't say no when he did all this as a massive favor. I glance at the time. The warehouse is by the freeway. If I head over now, I can make it to meet Drake at the hotel bar with a decent cushion, especially if I valet to save time.

> Be there in twenty.

I grab a handbag that will fit my iPad so I can show Drake what the Marigold Institute does, slick on a power lipstick—a NARS red—and head out for some light project supervision followed by world domination.

Chapter Twenty-Five

Kaitlyn

ONLY MICAH'S TRUCK IS in the warehouse parking lot when I pull in, and it gives me a moment of pause. He isn't trying one of his non-date dates, is he?

I remember how closed off he'd been at his house last week. Definitely not a fake date.

I climb out of my car and walk in. Micah is sitting at the table by the door, sketching something, and he looks up as the door snicks open.

"Hey." He sets down his pencil and stands. "You look nice."

I glance down. "I have a meeting. I look more official with my blazer. I left it in the car." I'd thought it would be warm in the warehouse, but it's nearly as cool as the early evening air, which is hovering down near sixty.

"Do you want to grab it?"

"It's okay. I can't stay long."

"Right." His smile doesn't change. "Let's go look."

I set my bag down and reach for a hard hat, negative four million percent thrilled about messing up my hair.

"Don't worry about it," he says. "Since no one is working on anything right now, nothing can fall on you."

I thunk it back on the table and fall in step with Micah as he walks to the stage zone. Again, there's a feeling of teleporting to a different place when we cross beneath the tmarigolds.

"We're still right on schedule," Micah says. "The extra time on these studs came out of the planned overage, so we're also still on budget."

"That's great." It's inadequate and formal. I want to ask him how he feels about the progress, if it's matching what he pictured. I'd caught a glimpse of his sketch on the table. It looked architectural. Was he doing work for the firm while he waited for me? Is it hard balancing all this with his work for the firm?

I keep the questions to myself. I need boundaries, and I have a time constraint. I can't get lost in Micah. A conversation with him, I mean.

He stops and points. "That's the gist."

He—or someone—has taken a rectangular cardboard box and cut it down to roughly the height of the Juarez vase. He's also spraypainted it red like the vase and stuck in the mock rebar to give a sense of the scale and scope.

"Is this piece called 'Industrial Arts and Crafts'?"

He smiles. "It's called 'I worked through my lunch break to figure this out, but it should work.'"

I take a few steps back. "Is that roughly where you see it sitting in relation to the stage?" When he nods, I try to picture the other elements. "It sounded way too basic when you explained your idea. I was trying to figure out how to tell you to try harder on the last-minute favor I begged for without upsetting the talent."

"The talent." His hands are in his pockets—he's in dark gray joggers today—and he rocks a couple of times, like he's considering this label. It forces me to consider his quads and wonder if I can ban joggers that force me to consider his quads on the jobsite. "The talent's reaction depends on how you feel now that you've seen it."

"The talent never misses," I say. "In fact, I'm annoyed that this solution is going to make Gabriela Juarez's vases look better than they deserve based on her inconveniencing you."

He comes to stand beside me, facing his cardboard vase. "Awww, Katie. It's good to know you care. But it's fine. I respect the hustle, and it was good of her to accept a commission when she isn't sure who will end up winning it."

Evergreen and citrus drift toward me. My pulse speeds up, and I need distance.

I walk a few steps away, like I want a different angle on this crappy box. "I care about everything for this gala. I eat, sleep, and breathe this gala. And if a glass artist makes things harder for our sculptor, I care about that too." There. Perfect tone of exasperation but keeping it light. Keeping it on the event.

"How do you feel about your sculptor making things harder for himself with an idea that would be awesome for the gala?"

I turn to look at him. "Tell me."

"Better to show you. Up to the loft?"

"I have a meeting soon." I glance down at my watch.

"A meeting," he repeats.

"Yeah. Sometimes it's over desks, sometimes over golf, and some-times over cocktails. Or so Madi tells me. This is my first time doing a pitch this way, but if alcohol is involved, I like my odds."

"I need to figure out how to get more golf meetings."

"Can you explain your idea in ten minutes or less?" That still leaves me a cushion for meeting Drake.

"Yep. Let's go."

He turns and heads for the stairs but stops at the foot of them, looking down at my shoes. I feel the path of his glance down my legs like a touch.

"We're taking the elevator." He punches the button and the door rumbles open.

My spiked heels have zero desire to argue.

He waves me in. "Ladies first."

I walk past him, wishing there was a reason to brush against him, glad there's enough room that I don't have one. *Boundaries.*

The elevator *is* small, though, since it's only used for loft accessi-bility, not freight. It's half the size of a regular elevator and shrinks more when Micah steps in and presses the button to take us up. He's not even close enough for me to sense his body heat, but he's still filling every inch of this elevator, his sneaky citrus and evergreen scent tickling my nose.

"So what's this idea?" I ask.

"Wait a few seconds, Katie. You can do it. I have faith in you."

"It's your ten minutes we're burning, but fine."

The elevator bumps to a stop and we cross the landing it shares with the stairs to the loft.

"What am I looking for?" I ask, scanning the warehouse. It's interesting to see the sculpture from this aerial view, but I could have done that another day.

"Gala means red carpet," Micah says.

"Right. Already rented."

"It will come in through there." He points to the roll-up door closest to the foot entrance for trucks to park during loading and unloading.

"Right. Floral arch?" Twenty thousand red Kashmiri gada, to be exact. It's a lush variety of marigold, and since it felt only right that we use the beloved Bangladeshi flower, it also made sense to have them made of silk by Bangladeshi workers so they could benefit. We could keep the flowers sustainable by reusing them in future galas.

The plan is to roll up the bay door and build the floral arch for the guests to enter through, all part of the luxe Threadwork Discovery Gala Presented by Armstrong Industries experience.

"I was looking at photos from previous Met Galas, and something kept jumping out at me. The grand staircase. Women choose gowns specifically for the way they will photograph on that staircase. It got me thinking: what if instead of walking straight through the arch, we built a staircase?"

My eyes follow his pointing finger to the bay door. "Why would a single-level event need stairs?"

"Think of it like a bridge. They climb the stairs on one side, walk down the other."

"I don't get it. Stairs to nowhere? Explain like I'm five. But also in less than five minutes." Staircases and red carpets don't mean much without the auction items, and I need to go land a big one. One that will finally give me some momentum.

"You're doing a temporary tunnel from the parking lot to the entrance, right?"

"Yes. You can rent anything, including event tunnels."

"Props to whoever dreamed up that niche. But the point of having guests come through it is to distract them from the reality that they're walking into a warehouse. They enter from the parking lot, walk twenty yards through this tunnel, and step into Event Land?"

"Basically. There will be soft lighting and flower arrangements all through the tunnel."

"And everyone waits inside it until it's their turn to walk out and pose in front of the Threadwork branding, do the step-and-repeat for the press, show off their gowns. Then they walk into Discovery?"

This is not new information. He's known the plan since the first time Madison walked the space with him. "Micah, I really need to—"

"Anticlimactic."

I pause, mouth open. Anticlimactic? "Sorry, should we ask each guest to give us a walkout song and make it a production?"

"Deepen the illusion. Make every part of the experience from the second they step into the tent tunnel reinforce the feeling they're leaving behind the familiar. Like Disneyland. Every ride starts from the second you get in the line. If you're going on the Jungle Boat, you're weaving through a dock front."

I'm starting to get it. "Paint me a word picture about the stairs."

"The step and repeat will end where the stairs begin. The steps will be long and fairly shallow, and the rise will level out as it passes through the marigold arch. Those are fifteen feet high. If we figure the guests will all be under seven feet tall—"

"Unless Angel Clarke wears heels," I joke, naming the center for the Dallas WNBA team who will be coming.

He grins. "I stand by my estimate. Even in heels, Angel Clarke wouldn't hit it. We'd build the stairs eight feet high. Guests finish red carpet photos and move to the stairs. Spoiler: also red carpeted."

"Genius." My tone is dry.

He gives me a serious nod. "I've been saying. At the stairs, the ladies are ready to climb, then they stop halfway up."

It clicks. "They pose showing the back of the dress."

"Yeah. It's a whole production with the Met Gala stairs, but photographers and guests and celebrity blog stalkers are all happy. Then through the arch and down the staircase on this side."

He traces something in the air with his fingers, maybe the shape of the staircase he imagines. "Then they get to make a dramatic entrance for everyone below to see and admire their dress. Like every movie with a ball. Ever, I think?"

"Is that another hobby genre for you?"

"Only when there's a zombie crossover."

"Zombie balls have the top-of-the-stairs moment? I'd watch that."

"I'd watch it with you." His eyes drop to my lips like he's back in the memory of our other zombie movie experience.

Boundaries.

My smile fades. "A grand staircase sounds like a several-grand project. I'm open to the idea, but I'll need to know more." I look down at my watch again. If I'm not on the road in the next five minutes, I'll be late. "Could we meet Monday?"

"Don't need to. I'll explain while I walk you out." He holds open the loft door for me. "This will be a cheap build. Plywood painted black. Red carpet makes it look high-end. Any guesses what the handrails will be made from?" His eyes sparkle as we reach the elevator and he pushes the button.

I step inside. "Rebar."

He follows me in. "Rebar."

"It's on theme," I say, sending the elevator down.

"With labor and materials, I could get this done for about two thousand."

"That's it? Two thousand? That's—"

A hard jolt knocks me off-balance. I stumble forward, catching myself with my hands against the elevator door.

Micah's hand flies out to grip my elbow and steady me. "You okay?"

"Yeah, fine." I push back hair that slipped into my face. "You?"

He releases my elbow. "Fine."

"What happened?"

He crouches to study the elevator panel. I scan the top of the door and the ceiling, not that I'd recognize a problem if I saw it.

"Not electrical," he says. "These light up when I push them, and the overhead light is on, obviously. Has to be mechanical."

"Can you fix it?"

He looks over his shoulder. "Can I fix an elevator?"

"It's not an insane question. You're good with your—never mind." I break off when I realize finishing the sentence will only set me up. "Does it have one of those emergency call things?"

"All elevators have them," he says. "It's the law."

"So push it!"

He stands and gives me a look of concern. "Are you okay? You sound . . ."

"What? Stressed that if we don't get out of here in the next three minutes, I'll be late for my meeting?"

"Right. Just call and explain. No one will hold this against you."

We have the same realization. My dress does not have pockets. My phone is in my purse, which I left on the table when I came in.

"Oh," he says.

I do not panic. Not ever. I'm not about to start now. "Can I use your phone?"

Micah leans against the wall and crosses his arms over his chest. "As soon as I get it from the table."

Still not panicking, but I feel a rising urge to scream. "We are stuck in an elevator in an empty warehouse with no way to let anyone know?"

He crouches by the panel again. "I'll push the emergency call button."

We wait. Several seconds tick by.

"Should we hear anything?" I ask.

He doesn't answer, only presses the button again.

I count to thirty Mississippi. "Is this a silent thing? Is it triggering an alert somewhere, letting them know to send a SWAT team to get us out?"

"Elevator SWAT," he repeats. "Not sure that's a thing."

The mellow way he says it puts my teeth on edge. The calmer he gets, the higher my frustration climbs. "Can you pry open the doors?"

His laugh dies when he realizes I'm not being funny. "For real?"

"Yes, for real! I'm late." I try, but my nails are just long enough that I can't slip my fingertips into the crease where the doors meet. I shift, pressing my chest and face against one of the doors, then brace my feet and sort of . . .

"What are you doing?" Micah asks.

"Getting this thing open." I push in the opposite direction as hard as I can, trying to slide it by force of will, maybe, but I'm also holding my breath, which explodes in a whoosh when my forearms give up on a feat of strength they weren't trained for.

"Could you do something?" I snap at Micah while I pull off a shoe then wobble on my bare foot while I yank off the other one.

"I'm thinking."

"That doesn't seem to be getting the door open."

"Your way won't work either. I know enough about elevators to know that."

"It works on TV."

He doesn't comment.

Frustration is building a head of steam so dense I can't believe it's not giving me super strength to yank the doors open. I look at the ceiling. "Can't we go through there? That's how people always do it on—"

"TV?" He shakes his head. "If I can get up there, I still won't be able to pry open the doors, but I guess it's worth figuring out where we are between the floors."

It takes two steps for him to cross to the rear corner beneath the panel. I don't like the frown on his face. He reaches, but he has to go up on his toes to touch. His shirt rides up, exposing his abs, lean and long as he stretches.

I drag my gaze to the ceiling hatch. Nothing happens when he presses, so he works his fingers around the edges.

After a minute, he drops down and points to the center of the hatch. "Locked. Can't do anything without the key."

"This is stupid." I have never sounded less calm, cool, or collected, but I don't care. Why is it so hard to try to do a good thing like make it to a meeting that will give me the momentum I need for this auction? Why do even the things that work out take five extra steps, like Gabriela Juarez's demands?

Helplessness buzzes under my skin, and I'd rather be standing naked on an anthill. At least I could kick it and walk away.

"Could you move over this way?" I ask.

Micah makes the two steps a saunter. "You want to try?"

I bend down and swoop up my shoes. "No. I want to do *this*." I stalk to the corner beneath the hatch (it takes me three steps) and jump, shoe in hand, trying to swat at it. I don't even get close, which only makes me angrier.

"This escape room sucks!" I yell, throwing my shoe at the hatch as hard as I can. It bounces off with a dull thump and falls to the floor. I have never been so disappointed in a Louboutin, and I don't care at all that it's scuffed now.

"What are you—" Micah starts to ask, but I slice him with a death look so fast that he presses his lips together.

"I'm not trying to open it. I'm *punishing* it." I throw my other shoe. The heel hits, making a slightly louder noise before it falls. I scoop them back up, ready to chuck them again, when Micah steps in front of me, squatting slightly, arms out in the universal sign for "piggyback ride."

"If you want to get the point across, you probably need to smack the snot out of it."

I climb on and he straightens. I take a half-dozen serious whacks before I drop the shoes and press his shoulders.

He lets me down. "Did it help?"

I go sit in the control panel corner. "No. But thanks for the lift." I rest my head against the wall and close my eyes, listening to the rustle as he sits down too. "How are we going to get out of here?"

"Might have to wait until morning, when the crew comes in."

My eyes fly open. "What? No. What if I have to . . ." Pee. Just thinking it makes me need to go. "I hydrate. A lot."

"Uh . . ." He looks blank and scratches his chin. "Think dry thoughts?"

"Pray you don't see my potty dance." He makes me want to throw a shoe again. Not at him. But he makes me want to throw a shoe. I try calming breaths.

After a minute he says, "If my mom notices I'm not home in the next hour, she'll text. Then call. When I don't answer, she'll get mad or worried. Probably both. Most likely she'll walk down to Ty's house because she knows he's working on this job with me. Maybe, if she's upset enough, Ty will volunteer to drive over here to make her feel better. He'll see our cars, and then our odds are good."

"How likely is all of that?"

"If I change my routine on my mom, I always let her know. I can count on her to escalate the situation."

How many times has this played out in different ways in their life? The underlying tiredness as he said "escalate" suggests he's probably quit counting.

"How is your mom?" I ask.

He only shrugs.

Tell me more, I want to say. But why should he be willing to do that when I made it clear I don't have time to hear his stories, now or even months from now.

The irony of the situation hits me. I closed a door on Micah so I could focus on work, but all the time I put in over the last two days to prep for this meeting with Drake is wasted because I'm with Micah again.

Being right doesn't give me a warm, fuzzy feeling. I shiver, the cold of the elevator getting to me.

Micah crawls over to sit beside me. "Wish I had a jacket to give you."

"It's okay. Unless you meant to strand us here, in which case your planning could use some work."

"I'll make a note."

"Add something about happening to have chocolate with you next time you incapacitate the elevator."

"Brilliant. No wonder Madison chose you to replace her."

The tiny flickers of humor I'd been finding wink out.

"Whoa, what just happened?"

I don't know what he sees in my face, but I *feel* bleak. "Madison chose wrong."

"That doesn't sound like Madison. She doesn't miss a step."

"Madison's only misstep was believing in me. The rest of them are mine."

He absorbs that for a moment. "I watched you work for four years in high school. I would have no problem trusting you to handle anything important."

I snort. "Seems like you and Madison have both forgotten that I choke in the clutch."

"Is this about your meeting tonight?"

"That's only the latest in a chain of failures."

"Tell me." It's an invitation.

"I'd rather eat dirt than list all my failures for you."

"Okay. I like quiet." He settles against the wall and closes his eyes. I close mine too.

After about a minute, he whispers, "Are you thinking about pee?"

"DAGNABBIT, Micah." My eyes fly open.

"I'm just saying, since that and failure are on your mind, and you don't want to talk about failure . . ."

"I don't want to talk about anything."

He nods. I close my eyes again and try to think dry thoughts.

Soon he starts humming, but it's muted, and he can follow a melody, even if he doesn't stick with any of them for longer than a verse. "Umbrella" by Rihanna. "Fire and Rain" by an oldies singer.

When it turns into "Water Under the Bridge" by Adele, I whip my head to glare at him.

He smiles. "You know how to make it stop."

"Beat you with my shoe?"

He hums "Riptide."

"Stop."

He hums louder.

"Fine, Micah! Fine. Everything for the gala is going perfectly, except for the part I'm in charge of. I'm supposed to lock down all the big auction items that will bring in the cash, and I can't."

"I need context. Is this a Kaitlyn Armstrong fail where you are upset with an A-?"

"F, Micah. This is an F. I have tried and tried, and I—" My voice catches. I swallow and force myself to say it. "I can't."

"You locked down the Juarez chandelier. That's impressive."

I pull my legs up, tuck my dress, and settle my forehead on my knees. "We'll show a small profit. The entertainment is amazing. Everyone will be blown away by the food and venue. We'll probably clear enough to cover a year of expanded classes at Marigold. But when it's time for the auction, everyone is going to realize how bad I whiffed this. Only they won't know it's me. They'll see that *Threadwork* whiffed it. But my parents will know. And Madison will know. And everyone will pity and judge them for not being able to pull off what the other major organizations around here do, and they'll have to share the humiliation, even though none of that is their fault."

"The meeting you're missing, it would have changed all that?"

I shake my head. "I convinced myself it would. That somehow, this time, I would have the right words when I've never had them before." I hug my legs more tightly to my chest. "Whatever it is that makes people fall all over themselves to say yes to Madison, I don't have it."

He rests a hand on my back, below my shoulder blade, well above my waist. It's not a touch that's asking for anything. It's a touch that says *I'm here.*

"Based on six months of working with Madison, I can tell you exactly what she has that you don't."

Just what every girl wants to hear. "Can't wait."

"She has no respect for boundaries."

I consider that for a second before turning my head enough to study him out of one eye.

"Tell me it's not true," he says. "That woman will charge in and flatten all objections if she wants something."

My mouth twitches. "It's true."

"There are pluses to Madison trespassing through any marked fence she wants to. And there are pluses to you always being mindful of them. You can compare the differences, but you can't assign either philosophy a higher value."

"You can in dollars. Because Madison would have gotten every auction item she needed. She'd be turning people away. Like no, sorry, we can't accept your offer of a Super Bowl suite catered by Carmen Berzatto. Ask again next year."

"Maybe the problem is trying to do it her way?"

I shrug. I've already explained the problem: not being Madison.

He withdraws his hand. I want it back.

"Walk me through it," he says. "Tell me what happens when you get a no. How does the meeting go?"

"Most of the time, I can't even get a meeting. I'm trying to set up calls and appointments with people I know by name or reputation, and Threadwork doesn't mean anything to them. I can't even get in the room to explain the mission. Sometimes 'Armstrong' means something. Our last name is the only reason I've gotten the few donations we have."

"So you need connections. I kind of thought your family was one of the most connected in Austin."

"My parents are. And it's mainly their generation controlling the wallets and making philanthropy decisions."

"So . . . why not have your parents do the asking?"

"Because it's not *their* job. It's mine."

"But they would help?"

"Yes, but . . ."

"I don't get it," he says. It's a confession, not an accusation. "It seems simple. What am I missing? There has to be a very good reason you're not asking them."

Perceptive. Always perceptive.

"All right, Micah." I straighten my legs and sit back against the elevator wall. "Let me tell you the rest of the story of graduation."

Senior Year, Ten Days Before Graduation

Kaitlyn

I STARE AT MRS. Gaspard, not understanding. "I'm salutatorian?"

"It's a remarkable achievement anywhere, Kaitlyn, but especially at Hillview. These are the only two named class ranks. You outperformed everyone."

"Except Micah Croft." It was that calculus test. How could everything have come down to one test? "Four years of work and none of it matters because I failed a test the day after breaking my nose?"

"You didn't fail it, Kaitlyn. You got a C on a test in a college-level calculus class. That's nothing to be ashamed of."

"How can you even be sure about the ranks?" I ask. "Things could change after finals next week."

Mrs. Gaspard gives a small sigh and rests her arms on the desk, meeting my eyes with sympathetic ones. If she's expecting tears, she'll be disappointed. My nose has only had four days to heal. The swelling is coming down, but crying would be so painful with the pressure and the mucus . . .

"You would have to get at least a ninety-seven on the final and Micah would need to get below a sixty-three for that to happen."

"I can get an A!"

"I know. But do you think Micah would get anything less?" Her voice is gentle but firm.

I slump against my chair. Of course he won't. But we wouldn't even be having this conversation if he had listened to me last week about calling my mom. She still would have dragged me to the doctor when she saw my nose, but I could have kept it from her until *after* that test.

"I'm telling you now because I wanted to give you time to adjust to the idea," Mrs. Gaspard says. "I know your expectations for yourself. I know you don't see salutatorian as the brilliant achievement that it is. But I . . ." She sighs again. "I hoped I'd find a way to help you see it anyway."

Am I supposed to reassure her now? *No, Mrs. Gaspard, you did a great job. It's not your fault that everything I've worked for crumbled around me exactly when I would have no time left to fix it.* It isn't her fault. I don't blame her. But I'm not in the mood to cheer her up. I have a different, much bigger conversation ahead of me.

I stand and hitch my school bag over my shoulder. It has a draft of the graduation speech I won't be needing tucked inside it. "Thank you for letting me know."

Mrs. Gaspard stands too. "Kaitlyn, is there anything—"

"I'm fine, Mrs. Gaspard. I need to go."

Her forehead furrows, but she nods.

Micah is sitting in the reception area when I walk out, earbuds in, staring at his outstretched legs. I know who he's waiting for and what she's about to tell him.

He glances up, and when he sees me, he plucks his earbuds out and stands. "Kaitlyn, how is your—"

"It's fine." I keep my eyes straight ahead, like I'm on my way to another very important meeting. "Congratulations," I say as I leave the office.

"For what?"

I don't answer, but I hear Mrs. Gaspard call his name. He'll know soon enough.

And far too soon, I have to tell my parents that after holding the top spot for ninety-nine percent of high school, I lost it at the last minute. My stomach already hurts from imagining their reaction, and a headache is starting, making the dull throb around my nose feel like it's extending all the way up to my scalp.

I don't even know how to bring it up with them, but it comes out over dinner.

"How was school, sweetie?" Mom asks.

"I'm not valedictorian."

Dad sets down his forkful of roast chicken. "What are you talking about?"

"I'm salutatorian."

"When did this happen?" His eyebrows bunch and his cheeks turn ruddy.

"I found out today. It's because I got a bad grade on my last calculus test."

Mom has stopped eating too, her hand resting against her sternum in a loose fist, clutching for pearls she isn't wearing. "The graduation announcements went out. They say you're valedictorian."

I stare at my plate. I know. She ordered a hundred of them. Many of those recipients will be at the ceremony next week to see their own kids or grandkids graduate. My name will still appear in the program. Just not in the spot advertised.

Dad throws down his napkin, dinner half-eaten. "Fantastic. Now all of our so-called friends can call me a liar about this too." He pushes away from the table, not bothering to look at me.

"Gordon, please," Mom says, but he storms out. She sighs. "That group filed another lawsuit against him this morning."

I nod, my throat too tight to say anything.

"We really did not need this kind of negative publicity. There is no circumstance in which we can afford to look as if we're telling people one thing when the truth is another."

I look up, thinking I've missed a step. "My graduation announcement is publicity?"

"Isn't it? You've just handed ammunition to everyone in our personal circle who wants to take a shot at us."

With that, she pushes her plate away and leaves the table too.

I am left bleeding out.

Chapter Twenty-Six
Micah

Kaitlyn finishes her story, not looking at me. "Some wounds don't heal."

At some point during her story, I drew my legs up too. My wrists rest on my knees, and I rotate one, flexing and curling the fingers. I watch them as I say, "I have a couple of those. I get it."

"It was bad enough to see the look on his face when I told him I wasn't valedictorian," she says. "But he was right. There were Hillview parents who made a point of saying things to him after the ceremony. 'Beautiful announcements, but I thought Kaitlyn was the valedictorian.' Thrilled to rub it in his face. I had to stand there and watch him take it, pretending like he wasn't bothered, forcing himself to make a joke about how 'calculus got the upper hand at the finish line.'"

"Kaitlyn, you didn't fail." I stop flexing my hand to rest it on her knee and give it a gentle squeeze. "I beat you."

She whips her head to glare at me, but she wants to smile. She almost does. "Because you broke my nose."

"That pole broke your nose when you walked into it because you were so into me."

"I hate you."

I lean my head against the wall and give her knee another light squeeze. "I don't think you do." Maybe this would be easier if she did. Maybe I would be less hungry for her. For the smiles I win from her. For the way she lets me in enough to pull me deeper before she shuts me out again.

"Why do you call me Katie sometimes and Kaitlyn other times?" she asks after a couple of minutes.

I open my eyes. "I do?"

She nods.

"Not sure. I do know I will always think of high school you as Kaitlyn. Do you have a preference?"

"I prefer if you refer to me as Ms. Armstrong."

"Brat."

"Only when I don't get what I want."

I smile. "I don't think that's true. I think you just described your sister."

"The one who gave you forty thousand dollars to do that sculpture? Your benefactor? That brat?"

"Tell me I'm wrong."

She flashes a grin. "You're not wrong. She can be a brat. But somehow she makes you not mind."

"Must be a sister thing." This is the most "difficult" Kaitlyn has ever been, and I still don't mind being trapped in this elevator with her.

"I'm sorry about my meltdown." She gestures to our accommodations. "This isn't your fault."

"It's okay. I understand it better now. But for what it's worth, if you tell your family about the auction, I'll bet all they see is how hard the job is if you can't pull it off. Not that you failed."

"Not the Armstrong MO, but points for assuming healthy family dynamics. Do you want to take a turn? You can have a meltdown if you want."

"I don't melt down. Want a confession inst—?"

"Yes."

"Ha. Don't get excited. It's nothing interesting."

"Confess. I'm tired of sitting outside of my turtle shell by myself."

I sort of regret opening this door, but she's right; can't make her sit in here with only her confession between us. "My confession is that sometimes I'm too comfortable with meltdowns."

She purses her lips like she's thinking. "Because of your mom?"

"Yeah. I don't have bipolar, but in a way, when you're the kid of someone who has it, you can kind of get . . . addicted to the mania? Maybe addicted isn't the right word." I pick at a piece of lint on my joggers. I may have some of this stuff figured out now, but I don't have much practice explaining it. "More like if that's what feels normal to you from someone else, you start looking for it. Remember when I mentioned my college girlfriend?"

"The one I hate?"

I shoot her a glance. "You're very hateful in general today."

"Not sorry."

"This one sounds like jealousy."

"Wishful thinking."

"Uh huh." She's jealous, and I like it. "If you are, don't be. We were together two years, and it should have ended after six months. She wasn't bipolar, but definitely a *big feelings, big expression of those feelings* type. I thought that was how it was supposed to be when you love someone. Huge fights. Drama. Shows the feelings are deep. But my roommate was a psych major, and he made me listen to a podcast about codependency. Turns out thinking something is only real if it's constant drama is codependent."

She winces. "I didn't mean to trigger anything for you. Are you okay?"

"No, that's not what I was—" I break off with a short laugh. "I was trying to say I'm okay with your big feelings, that's all."

She stares at me, her eyes big and soft.

"Don't look at me like that."

"Like what?"

"It's giving 'kiss me.'" I became an expert on that look on Halloween.

"I don't want you to kiss me." When my glance flicks to the goosebumps on her arms, she folds them.

I pat my lap. "Come here, friend."

"You're not listening, Micah."

"That's exactly what I'm trying to do. But you're cold, you've got goosebumps, and I can warm you up and not stare at you. Win-win." I make my legs into a vee. "Come sit here so I can listen without staring at your lips."

She hesitates before she gives a small shiver and scoots closer. "Only because I'm cold."

I situate her in front of me, then wrap her in my arms and wait for her to relax.

After a few seconds, the starch goes out of her spine, and she gives me her full weight and a small sniff. "You're a good jacket."

"Happy to help." I answer with a gentle squeeze of my arms. "Speaking of which . . ."

The starch is back. "Is this going to be a lecture on why I need to ask my family?"

I run my thumbs up and down her bare upper arms, hoping it calms her. "No. It's me telling you I understand why you won't."

"What do you mean?"

"I've been lucky my whole life that people have always been willing to help me. Maybe they felt for me because of my mom. But the help was always there, and I always took it. I didn't know what else to do. But not all help is equal."

"Meaning . . ."

"My uncle and his family, they helped us so much financially. The house, my tuition. I'm grateful. But we don't have a close relationship, and we never will. He holds it over us all the time. Him. My aunt. My cousins. They don't want us to pay it back. They want the high they get every time they think about what good people they are for doing it. But they're not my real family. Real family is different."

She frowns. "What do you mean, your real family?"

"Chosen family."

"Your neighborhood?"

"They gave when they had less to give, and stuff that means more than money. Time. Care."

"That's how Madison's friends are. When she and I started working on our relationship, they scooped me up like I'd been there all along." She nestles against me. "It really means something. To be chosen."

"If your family is like my uncle, I get why you don't say anything." Does she realize she leaned into me when she talked about being chosen? I'm not dumb enough to point it out.

Quiet falls between us, and I listen to the distant noises from the elevator shaft, small ones, like when a house settles at night.

"My neighborhood is part of the reason I couldn't ask you to prom," I tell her. "I was broke. But I also babysat for my neighbor, Jeremy, every weekend. His wife left him, and he could earn more if he worked swing shifts, but he had a hard time finding childcare. So I watched his two kids. He paid me what he could afford, but he also taught me a lot of stuff. How to fix stuff in our house. I had to patch a lot of drywall."

"Your mom?" Her voice is soft.

Her hair brushes my chin when I nod. "He taught me woodworking. Stripping and repainting. One time, I found a nightstand waiting for garbage pickup and refurbished it. Made twenty dollars. My first sale. I went over and gave him half. He shoved it back and said it was a babysitting bonus."

"I'm imagining borderline emo high school Micah working on that discarded nightstand the way you did schoolwork."

I smile. "How did I do schoolwork?"

"Patient. Thorough. Meticulous. Had to be the same when you fixed that nightstand."

"Probably, yeah."

"It's easy to picture you bringing that money to him. You were a great kid."

"I was raised by a great neighborhood."

"Sounds like it."

The thing about chosen family is they will also choose the people you bring them. "Katie, if Thanksgiving is going to be that stressful, come to ours. A few families on the street get together. It's low-key.

Paper plates. No one asking you for a gala report. You're welcome at our table, friend."

I rest my chin on her head and feel her tiny sigh.

"It sounds nice. Our Thanksgiving is fancy. China. Silverware. Linen napkins. Our nice clothes. Stuffy. Armstrong stuff is always high-key. But it will have one thing yours won't."

"What's that?"

"My baby niece."

"I withdraw my bid."

"Other than that, I'm dreading it."

"I can be your wingman." After her description of the dinner after our class ranks changed, I don't want her to face down her parents alone. "I'll back you up if they give you a hard time about the auction."

Starch again. She straightens, creating a gap that makes my chest cold where she'd been resting.

"I'm not telling them."

"Are you that scared?"

She moves away, standing to stretch, and doesn't answer.

"Kaitlyn."

"I'm not scared of my family."

"I meant scared of asking them for help."

"I don't want to talk about this anymore."

"Fine." It's not fine, but I know this look. I've been locked out. I cross my ankles and choose to stay loose. "What's worse? Failing or asking for their help?"

"I don't have the bandwidth to sit and dissect my failures while I'm actively failing with Drake Braverman right now." She shoves her hands through her hair, and it's only the second time besides zombie night that I've seen it anything less than sleek.

Drake Braverman. I take her in again, noting the details. A dress, a lot different than the suits I see her in for work. It's so pretty on her. She looks strong—she *is* strong—but also soft in a way she never dresses around me. I don't like it.

It's not my place to not like it, but I can't help the words that come out of my mouth. "This was all for Drake Braverman? Got it."

She gives me the look my question deserves—mild disgust that quickly turns to cool distance—and doesn't bother responding. Just sits in the opposite corner, leans back, and closes her eyes.

I wish she would yell. The silence is harder. But that's an old impulse. My mom's silence always scared me more than her angry manic phases. At least when she was yelling, I knew she was still *there*.

This silence from Kaitlyn, it feels weaponized.

I keep my own silence, forcing myself to focus on all my non-gala work. The add-on unit I'm working on for a Round Rock home. A fireplace mantel I want to build out of tile recovered from the Western restaurant renovation. A chair I need to repair in my dining room.

An hour later, we're still sitting in silence when Ty's voice breaks it, calling my name in the distance.

Thirty minutes later, the Austin Fire Department has liberated us, and when we finally make it to our cars, Kaitlyn and I haven't spoken.

"Bye, Kaitlyn. Sorry about the elevator thing."

She gives me a single nod and drives away without another word.

Chapter Twenty-Seven
Kaitlyn

AGAINST ALL ODDS, WHEN I get home at almost 9:00 and call Drake to explain getting trapped in an elevator, he laughs and agrees to another meeting.

"Come by the Ford dealership first thing in the morning," he says. "After that, I take off for Thanksgiving with my parents in Vail."

"I'll bring apology pastries," I promise before we hang up.

I'm too keyed up to study, so I try to relax before bed by watching *Real Housewives* for an hour. Madison has the worst taste in television, and like any addict, she has dragged me into the mind rot with her. But even the loud spray tans of New Jersey can't keep my mind from flashing back to the night with Micah.

Every look. Every touch. Every time I caught the scent of citrus and evergreen.

The judgment on his face when I said I wouldn't tell my family.

We've only had a couple of years of figuring out how to show up for each other for real. Should I be able to trust my own family not to be disappointed in me over the auction? Yes. But they should be able to trust me to deliver on my part of this job.

I pass a restless night, sleeping in uneasy fits between racing thoughts about the way I spoke to Micah in the elevator and what I'll say to Drake in the morning.

When I arrive at the dealership ten minutes early with coffee and pastries, I've hidden the stress and sleeplessness beneath perfectly applied makeup, a Chanel pink-and-gray plaid dress, and Oxfords with a three-inch heel. It says professional, feminine, and expensive. It says *Give me what I'm asking for.*

The receptionist sends me up to the second floor. I take the stairs.

Drake Braverman looks at ease behind his enormous walnut desk when I pause in his doorway. He comes around to greet me, a smile on his face.

I brace for the hello hug he offers. He keeps it friendly and short before escorting me to a chair and retaking his seat.

"Bold of you to drive up in an Audi we didn't sell you," he says, leaning back and smoothing his tie.

"You know what I drive?"

"One of my guys called up when you parked," he says. "Have to know what you're in so we can figure out what to convince you to get next."

I smile at him. "What are you going to try to convince me to get?"

"Pfft. Nothing. That's a beautiful car. Drive it until it doesn't speak to your soul anymore."

That makes me laugh. "It really does speak to my soul. I bought it this summer as a present to myself for finishing law school."

"Hey, congrats," he says. "I'd say it's a big deal, but I bet you did it without breaking a sweat."

"It's a huge deal, and I'll take all the credit, thank you." That makes him laugh. "I'm glad you want to talk cars, because that's what brings me in."

"Right. You have a foundation, you said?"

"Yes. Madison has been interested in issues of fair trade and impact entrepreneurship for several years. Two years ago, she finished her MBA by starting a company in Bangladesh that does microfinancing. It will be profitable by the end of next year."

"Impressive," he says. "Good for her."

He means it, and I pause to give him another smile. It's good to remember that most of us do grow up.

"Because we've had a unique long-term perspective from our place inside the Bangladesh economy, she also founded a nonprofit organization dedicated to help Bangladeshi garment workers who want to change or advance in their careers."

This is where potential donors smile or give encouraging nods, or say something like "That's great. Love to hear it." Drake's eyes narrow in a speculative way, but his expression doesn't otherwise offer any clues about what he's thinking.

"I'd love to show you how Threadwork does our work." I reach into my bag for my iPad and hold it up, an unspoken question. When he nods, I set it on the desk, moving through the slide deck in five perfectly paced minutes.

"Any questions so far?" I ask as I close the iPad.

"Just one. What do you need from me?"

Again, it's hard to tell what he's thinking. His tone is pleasant but neutral.

"We're hosting our first annual New Year's gala, a high fashion luxury experience." I explain the highlights of the night, concluding, "It sold out months ago. But we anticipate raising an additional two million dollars during our live auction with the help of our generous guests." I draw two tickets from my handbag. "For the generous donors who help us round out our auction offerings, we would be honored to also have you as our guests with our compliments."

His eyes shift from the tickets to me. "What kind of donation are you hoping for?"

"You know this crowd. They'd love to win a public auction by overpaying for a luxury car, generously donated by your family." I summon the smile I've been practicing, one I've borrowed from Madison and injected with as much of her shamelessness as I can fake. "Maybe an extra Porsche you have lying around?"

Drake smiles back. "Respect for the big ask, Kaitlyn. But I have to say no."

My smile doesn't dim by a single watt. "It's a good thing we'd be happy taking something like a Mustang. There will be parents in our crowd planning to send their first kids off to college next fall who would love to know the money they spent on that college car went to a good cause."

I expect him to laugh, but he doesn't. His smile fades, and he's already shaking his head. *No. Don't say no,* I will him with my mind. But the word is already coming out of his mouth.

"We can't do that," he says. "We're committed to philanthropy, but we've also committed our funds for the year. If we were to go beyond that, it would have to be the right cause, and I don't think this is it."

I don't want to feel the disappointment trying to engulf me, so I don't. I push it away with *my* smile, the Kaitlyn Armstrong special. Serene, graceful, slightly enigmatic. "I'm sorry to hear that, but I understand philanthropic priorities. I appreciate you making the time to see me, even after an elevator made me ghost you last night."

His smile is back, and he stands, signaling the end of our meeting. "I'm sorry I couldn't give you the answer you wanted, but I'm not sorry I got to see you again, Kaitlyn. Glad you're doing well. I'll walk you out."

A Texas gentleman. He had to grow up some to get there, but that's what he is, through and through. He leads me through the outer office, but as he reaches for the glass door to the hall, I remember something.

"Oh, I almost forgot. I had a pair of Copperhead alligator boots in gray for you last night, but I forgot to bring them with me this morning. I'll make sure to send them over."

He smiles and makes a big show of looking down at his feet. I follow his gaze to his black Copperhead Thorntons. "Come on, Kaitlyn. You didn't think I was going to meet with an Armstrong in anything but my best boots, did you?"

I shake my head, laughing despite my disappointment. "You're a good egg, Drake. Have a great time in Vail."

"Will do."

My smile stays painted on until the door to the stairwell closes behind me. I replay the meeting as I take the two flights down, but when I reach the bottom, I pause.

I'd given him my best presentation so far. Impassioned but professional. Results-focused so he could see where his donation would go. It's clear he has a good opinion of me. I suspect we'd be friends if we made more of an effort to cross paths.

That pitch should have worked, and I believe Drake will be honest about why it didn't.

I march back up the stairs. Drake is pulling on his suit coat when I tap on his open door, and he looks at me in surprise as he tugs the sleeves down. "Hey."

"Can I ask why you said no? I'm not trying to change your mind. I've done everything I can to make this a compelling proposal, and I need to know what I'm missing. I'm hoping you'll tell me."

He gives a single nod, like he gets it. "Threadwork Discovery Gala, presented by Armstrong Industries."

"You don't like the name?"

"I don't love the cause. I respect the hell out of you and Madison trying to make up for the damage the company did. I understand why you'd feel like you need the company to sponsor the fundraiser. A lot of people would say it's a smart PR move."

"But not you?"

He shrugs. "I don't know why Gordon himself isn't doing more to clean up a mess he made, and I'm not interested in trying to improve his image. I admire the work your foundation is doing, but when it comes to our charitable giving, we've already got partnerships with local causes. We're Austin strong. We bleed burnt orange, run on Torchy's Tacos, and give back in our community."

"I can't be mad at that." But in some ways, it's the worst answer he could give, because his concern is fundamental, not something I can fix with a tweak to the slide deck. "Thanks for being honest."

"No problem. I'll walk you all the way out this time, since I'm leaving too."

"Is it okay if we take the stairs?"

He laughs and gestures for me to lead the way.

Chapter Twenty-Eight
Kaitlyn

DRAKE HANDED ME THE answer I need and don't want. This cause is too distant to the people we're asking to donate.

I brood over it. Obsess over it.

We can depend on the gala guests to throw big money at whatever we put in front of them. The impulse to flex in front of peers will kick in. But we have a massive supply problem, and I don't know if it's solvable. As much as I care about Threadwork and the people in Dhaka it helps, Drake's critique is fair.

That afternoon, Micah texts.

How did the meeting go?

No to the auction

Tell your family

I think about it. Long and hard. About the looks on their faces. About the stress this will put on Madison. About how Madison's stress will weigh on Oliver. Maybe even Harper.

I think about something else all day too. Micah's words. That maybe the task was never possible. More than anything else, I think about how even knowing how big my failure is, Micah still has faith in me. Not that I can do it, but that if I can't do it, it can't be done.

That is more faith than anyone has ever had in me.

The full weight of it hits me. Micah's faith in me is complete *despite* my failures. He was there for me last night. He wants to be there for me today, tomorrow, the day after that. He told me that. He's *shown* me that. And I said *Thanks but no thanks, gotta study*.

I am an idiot.

I am the world's *biggest* idiot.

I check the time. It's almost 4:00. I grab my purse from my desk drawer and almost run out of the office. "Headed out! Everyone else should go too! See you Monday."

The office door closes on the sound of three cheers.

I get in the car and curse every extra minute the holiday weekend traffic slows me in getting to the warehouse, but when I arrive, a few vehicles are still in the parking lot, including Micah's truck.

Inside, it's much noisier than I'm used to. The high whine of a saw and the pounding of several hammers cover the sound of the door opening and closing behind me. I don't see Micah anywhere, but the guy running the saw spots me and turns it off. He's standing on the other side of the beginnings of the staircase, and he looks down and says something with a nod in my direction.

Micah rises next to him, and suddenly there is six-feet-plus of sexy architect staring at me across the warehouse. He's wearing a Santa hat, and that's when I register the rest of the changes. Sometime today, they've made a rebar Christmas tree in the middle of the floor, hung with empty soda cans, wood scraps, and a few paper snowflakes.

I put on a hard hat and walk toward Micah. He says something to the guy on the saw, who nods and goes back to work. He swaps his Santa hat for a hard hat and walks to meet me by the Christmas tree.

"Hey," he says. "Surprise inspection?"

I can barely hear him over the saw and point to the supervisor loft. He turns and I follow him to the corner with the elevator. He pauses and mouths, "It's fixed."

I smile and press the call button. The door slides open. We step in and the noise outside drops by half when they shut. We don't say anything as it makes its short trip, but when the doors start to slide open, I push the Door Close button.

"Hey," I say at normal volume. "I liked the Santa hat."

"Hey. OSHA violation." He knocks his hard hat. "Can't let the client see that. Speaking of which, I didn't expect to see you today."

My stomach behaves like we're doing an elevator speed run, float and sink, heavy and light. He's in a white tee and camo carpenter pants, but they're soft-looking, like flannel. It is insanely hot. Him. In the outfit. It's making the elevator warm. Or maybe just me.

"Didn't expect to be here today," I say, "but I probably should have. Probably should have been here even sooner. Days ago. Weeks ago."

He cocks his head, waiting for me to explain.

"About an hour ago, I realized I've been an idiot. I would have been here sooner, but traffic is bad. I came to tell you . . ." I pause to take a deep breath. Why am I nervous? He already said he wants this. "I was wrong on Halloween. We should date."

Surprise crosses Micah's face. Maybe I should have set up a whole scene? Hinted at this conversation before inviting him to dinner at my house? Pointed to *Zombie Lake* on the TV screen and waggled my eyebrows?

Why is he taking so long to answer? I rub my sweaty palms down my gray suit pants. "Micah?"

He rubs the back of his neck, still eyeing me. "I don't think so."

He says it the way I talk to Daisy Buchanan when she's accidentally done something naughty, like tangle herself in my sweater. *No, Daisy.* Gentle but firm.

"No?" I hear my heartbeat in my ears. *Hello to you, cortisol, the rejection hormone.*

"Too much whiplash," he says. "We get close, you withdraw and say no dating. Last night, we get close, you withdraw, and I get the silent treatment in a dead elevator for almost an hour. Today you're here saying 'no, let's do this'?" He shakes his head. "Red flag."

"I'm not a red flag." It's the most insulting thing anyone has ever said to me. I take a step back in the small space. "I've never been a red flag. I am the queen of spotting and rejecting other people's red flags. I am a green flag. I'm such a green flag, they should slap a star on my forehead and sing 'O Christmas Tree.'"

His eyebrows go up. "Who is 'they'?"

"The freaking elves."

"Believes in elves. Noted. That's another red flag."

"Elf yourself, Micah." The last time I felt this self-conscious, there was a light post involved.

His lips twitch, but none of this is funny.

"Whatever," I say. "A relationship sounds great as long as I'm perfectly calm and pulled together. One elevator meltdown, and it changes everything. Got it."

"I'm not going to say yes to this just because you're in a mood, Katie. I'm ready to say yes when you're sure you want a relationship."

"I came over here because I realized that you are the one person who already knows I've failed, and it doesn't matter to you. Doesn't that make you my person?" I press the first floor button. "If that's not me knowing what I want, then I don't know what is."

"So you're here because I make you feel good." The elevator stops. He leans over and sends us back up. "I'm happy to do that, but I want to be wanted when everything else in your life is good too."

"Wants to be wanted, does not want to be needed. Sounds healthy." The salt in my tone is unhealthy.

The elevator opens, but since the construction noise has died down, we ignore it.

He waves out toward the warehouse. "I will be everything you need in here. I got you."

The doors rumble shut, but the elevator stays put.

"Here," he gestures between us, "I want to be wanted *and* needed. Needed because I'm wanted. I'm ready when you are, but not before."

I stare at him, my frustration growing. "If me standing here saying I'm ready isn't enough, how am I supposed to prove it?"

He shakes his head. "I don't know. You'll know when you know."

I clench my jaw hard enough to snap rebar. We're talking in circles. *I want you. No, you need me, and I want you to need and want me. I just said I want you. I need proof. What proof? I don't know.*

I reach for the button to send us down again, but the elevator starts the descent on its own. Apparently, *it* knows its own mind. Good job, elevator.

The doors open to Ty. "Quitting time, boss. We good?"

Micah nods. "Go. See you Monday."

"My mom said to tell Tori she better be bringing pecan pie to Thanksgiving."

"Best on the block," Micah says.

"Best on the block," Ty repeats, turning to signal the other guys to go.

I snatch off my hard hat, irritated I've been riding up and down in an elevator asking Micah to be my man while wearing it. Why does this man always see me at my worst?

I walk out to the warehouse and cut beneath the sculpture, wanting the fastest route to the exit. Micah calls my name, but I don't look back. I leave the hard hat where I found it and head to my car, the other guys already pulling out onto the highway.

"Wait." Micah's hand closes around my wrist, the lightest hold.

I tug and he lets go.

He slides his hands into his pockets. His hair is a mess, sweaty and mashed. "Come for a ride around the block?"

"I need to get home." To sulk.

"It's my block. Five minutes. That's it."

"I've seen your block."

"Please?"

Resisting will only make me look childish, so I walk to his truck. He opens the door for me, and a couple of minutes later, we're pulling into his neighborhood. I stay quiet and study the houses in the dusk.

On his street, he slows below the residential speed limit and points to a small gray house. No fence, plain but neat. "That's the Morrises. Their son joined the army when I was thirteen. They let me use their lawnmower to take over the yards he used to cut as long as I did theirs too. From that point on, no matter what, our power never got cut again if my mom forgot to pay because I always had enough saved to cover it."

My jaw softens. But only a little.

He points to a yellow house on the other side of the street. "Mr. Martinez made sure I never had to bike to the bus stop in the rain. He'd wait in front of my house with his pickup truck for me to throw my bike in, and he'd drive me over."

"At 6:30 in the morning?" I ask.

"Every single time it rained."

He points out other houses to me as we roll slowly down the street. One who left new jeans and sneakers on his doorstep every Christmas Eve, but he only knew that because another neighbor told him. One who showed him how to pay the utility bill his mom had ignored and opened a bank account for him that his mom didn't know about so she couldn't clean it out on one of her shopping sprees.

There was the house where the dad had taught him to grill at the same time he taught his own kids.

Here was the house where a retired Sunday School teacher had lived. "At Easter, she'd gather all the kids on the street in her front yard and read them the Easter story from a children's Bible. We all sat still for it too, because afterward, she turned us loose for an egg hunt in the back, and she made sure every egg had a dollar bill in it because Jesus paid for us." He laughs. "That whole thing confused me for a long time."

"She sounds sweet." I can't be sulky anymore.

"She was. When I got older, I'd bring her a potted lily every Easter Sunday until last year when she passed."

We're nearly to his house, when he stops at the red brick house before it. "That's Jeremy's house. His oldest just started community college. She wants to be a teacher. The younger one is a junior. I tutor him sometimes in trig."

I'm struck again by how much was going on with him in high school. "I don't know anyone like you. You go around giving and taking care of people like it's second nature."

"I was taught by the best." He starts driving again, passing his house. "I'll take you back now."

"You're blessed to have grown up on this street. It's rare."

He shakes his head as he turns onto the highway back to the warehouse. "It's not. And you do know people like me. That's what I wanted to show you. *You're* like me, and you have people like me."

He pulls in next to my car. "Didn't you say this is how Madi is? And her friends? That they would do anything for each other? For her? For you?"

"For her, yes."

"You don't think they would do anything for you?"

"I've never needed them to."

"But would they?" he presses.

I climb out of the truck. He cuts the engine and follows me to my car, waiting.

I drum my fingers on the roof. "I know you think the answer is yes, but they all have lives now. Husbands. Careers and babies. I would never ask them to drop any of that for me."

"Would they do it for Madi?"

"Yes." No hesitation. If the term ride-or-die hadn't already existed, they would have invented it.

"And would she do that for them?"

"Yes."

He places his hands on the roof of the car on either side of me, not touching me, but he leans in so that I lean back, flat against the door. "Would Madi do that for you?"

"She has a lot—"

"Kaitlyn. Would Madison do that for you?"

I sigh. "Yes, but *I'm* trying to be that for *her*."

"You *are*. What else would you call putting your life on hold for seven months?"

"It's not that big a deal."

"Liar." It's a soft and sweet word, the way he says it. "Couldn't you have taken the bar in July if you weren't stepping in for your sister?"

"How did you know that?"

"I have lawyer friends. You could have, right? But you pushed it all the way off to the February date to get through this gala."

"So?"

"Would *she* do that for *you*?"

"If I had a baby? Yes. She would run interference so I wouldn't have to worry about anything. And that's what I'm doing for her. Dragging her into the gala problems is *not* running interference."

"You are the most stubborn woman I've ever known." He rubs his hands over his face and gives a muffled groan before he drops them. "Last time I made you mad, you didn't talk to me for eight years, but elf it."

I snort.

"This needs to be said. What would Madi want more? For you to hide this from her, then you both watch it fail, and you're both miserable? Or for you to ask for help, you both watch it succeed, and you celebrate the win together?" He tips my chin up and waits for me to meet his eyes. "You know who Madi is. Let her be that for you. Tag her in."

He drops a kiss on my forehead. Then he opens my door, waits for me to get in, and stands there watching me drive away.

Let her be that for you.

Can I?

I consider the question all weekend. Can I ask Madi to help? Can I go to her and say "I can't make this auction happen"?

It's still not as simple as Micah makes it sound. I see now an underwhelming auction was inevitable and not my fault, and that does ease my guilt. But that also means Madison isn't likely to come up with a solution either. What is the point of tagging her in to deal with an unsolvable problem? If I disrupt her new-mother time, she's only going to spend the next four weeks stressing about falling short of our goals.

But will *she* feel that way?

That's what I grapple with. If I don't tag her in, will she always wonder if she could have turned it around if she'd known?

She hasn't asked for detailed updates because she trusts me.

What does that trust deserve? Peace and protection? Or full transparency?

I know what I want to do for her as her sister. But I know what Madi will want. And they are not the same.

Chapter Twenty-Nine
Kaitlyn

I GET TO THE office on Monday, tired from wrestling with my decision but determined to tell Madison today. I text her after my morning meetings.

I want it over with *today*, but I can at least spend the afternoon figuring out extra fundraising opportunities for next year to offset where the gala will fall short.

It's late afternoon when Suz pokes her head in my door. "You busy?"

I look up from the reservation site for my parents' country club. I'm searching for open dates to do a charity golf tournament and cross-checking the weather records for the lowest likelihood of rain.

"I'd love a break."

She disappears for a second then comes in carrying a plate of cookies. She sets them down in front of me, and I gasp. Even through the red cellophane I can see they're gorgeous.

She hands me a card. "These were just dropped off for you."

I open the card.

Hey, Katie-Kat,

I know you're dreading Thanksgiving no matter what you decide. I know your mind is always on New Year's Eve and the gala. But the best holiday of the year comes in between, and I don't want you to miss it. It might surprise you to know that I elf myself regularly, and not only do I believe in Christmas music before December, it's already streaming in my truck this week. And on my morning run. And at the office. And on the jobsite.

These cookies are made by my neighbor, Mr. Nairz, who makes them every year at Christmas and Easter. You can't buy them even though he'd make a killing if he sold them. He'll only give them away to people he chooses. He's had a soft spot for me ever since I helped him build a three-foot-tall gingerbread house to win their family competition a few years ago, so I sweet—pun intended—talked him into making some for you.

Thoroughly Elfed,
Micah

"They're from Micah," I say.

"I want to see them. Unwrap it," Suz demands.

I do, and we ooh and aah. I'm still studying them, amazed, when she announces Khôi and Aisha need to see them too and goes off to get them. There are six, all done in royal icing, from a Tiffany-blue snowflake with a lacy pattern to a Christmas tree hung with finely painted ornaments.

"Thank that man," Aisha says. "I worked in a bakery during college, and those would not be cheap."

"His neighbor makes them and won't sell them. He only gives them away," I say.

"Thank that man," she repeats.

I pull out my phone.

> The cookies are beautiful. Thank you.

> You're welcome. You have to eat them. They taste better than they look.

> I can't eat art!

> It's Mr. Nairz's rule, and he'll ask me how you liked them.

> This feels wrong.

> Taste one. Then it will feel wrong not to eat it.

"He says we have to eat them. It's a rule." I set my phone down to all of them smirking. "Why are you looking at me like that?"

"You and Micah," says Suz.

"Are colleagues," I say.

"You dress nicer on the days you know you're going to see him," Khôi says.

"I dress nice all the time."

"Yeah, but you do it up extra," Aisha says. "And put on lip gloss. Haven't seen you do that for other *colleagues*."

"All of you get out."

"I'll leave when you give me a cookie," Suz says.

I hand them each one, giving Suz a Christmas stocking "embroidered" with snowflakes. "I hope your real one is full of coal."

She takes it from me and follows Khôi and Aisha, still smirking. A second later, an inappropriate moan rolls down the hall, but I don't scold her because I just took a bite of the Christmas tree, and I understand. They're not sugar cookies, they're shortbread made by angels, obviously, because they are divine.

I send Micah a gif of the Grinch eating roast beast.

He responds with a gif of the Grinch's heart growing.

I smile through the last two hours in the office. Before I leave, I cover the last two cookies with the cellophane. I'm leaving them to enjoy tomorrow, because with my coming conversation with Madison looming, they'll be my only bright spot in the day.

By midmorning Tuesday, I realize not even divine cookies can save the day.

I blink at Suz, who is standing in my office doorway, biting her thumbnail and watching me.

"Maheen is not coming?" I repeat.

Suz stops chewing at her thumb. "Not today. Her assistant is on the plane with the dresses, but there was some issue with Maheen's travel documents. They wouldn't let her fly out today."

"Okay." I rest my hands on my desk, palms flat. "Okay, okay, okay." I pat the desk with each word. "Okay. Okay."

"Remember the dresses are coming," Suz says. "Her assistant wouldn't check them, so they can't get lost on any of the layovers."

"Okay."

"Are you glitching?"

"Thinking." I stop patting the desk. "Call Doug Cutler at the consulate in Dhaka. See if you can find out what the problem is and if there's anything we can do to expedite it."

"On it."

"When does that plane get in?"

She checks her phone. "It lands at 11:23 AM tomorrow."

"Call Couture Alterations in Bee Cave and see if Vania can fit me in at 1:00." She's the only one we let do our alterations short of the designers themselves.

Suz nods and disappears.

I text Madison to tell her that work is holding me up, but I expect first dibs on the baby on Thursday. I'm not mentioning the Maheen situation until I understand the potential outcomes. Bad enough I have to tell Madison about the auction.

Suz is back a few minutes later. "Vania is booked until Christmas. I reminded the owner the Armstrongs are VIPs, but she said it's Bee Cave so everyone is VIP, and it's our gala that's keeping her so busy. Talk about irony . . . "

It's almost funny. Almost.

I only nod. "Keep me posted on the consulate."

She darts out again, and I press the heels of my hands into my eyes. What am I supposed to do? This was the whole point of having Maheen coming to Austin this early. We'd have four weeks for fittings and alterations, Madison's dress being of most concern since Maheen went two sizes up when she designed the gown to accommodate any baby weight. We'd all counted on plenty of time for adjustments.

This is a potential disaster. It would be easy enough to find other gowns, but the chairs of the Discovery Gala cannot show up wearing established designers.

Those cookies are now emergency cookies, and I pick out the snowflake, biting into it, chewing slowly with my head propped in my hand, elbow on my desk. I admire the lacy pattern again, amazed by the talent of Micah's neighbor. Who would've thought there would be so much talent in one—

Oh.

Oh oh oh.

I reach for my phone.

There might be one possibility ...

He sends the number. Her name is Lidia Perez, and I dial it as soon as I get it.

Ten minutes later, I have an appointment for the next day at 1:00. She'd insisted she didn't have time because she was preparing for their large family Thanksgiving, but I told her I'd pay her what I paid Vania if she could fit me in. When I named the amount, she said she'd see me at 1:00 and hung up like she was afraid I would change my mind.

No chance, because if we can't get Maheen here, this may be the only shot we've got.

Wednesday is *wild*. Aisha fetches Maheen's assistant, Aleina, from the airport and brings her straight to the office. She's a few years older than me, dressed in a travel-friendly teal jersey tunic and wide leg pants. We apologize profusely for rushing her into work instead of giving her time to recuperate. She assures us she slept on the plane and apologizes profusely for Maheen not yet being here.

Then we're on our way to see Lidia Perez in Suz's borrowed Subaru since my car isn't made to handle a passenger with luggage.

When I knock on the Perezes' front door, a girl around eighteen answers it.

"Hi, I'm here for a possible fitting with Lidia?"

She smiles. "I'm her daughter, Isa. Follow me."

She leads us through their small, neat house to the garage, which opens off the kitchen, which I almost don't escape. It smells incredible, a large pot simmering on the stove, rich smells of roasting peppers coming from the oven. I pause for a deep, appreciative whiff.

Isa grins. "We've been cooking for days. Got the whole family coming tomorrow."

"Thanks for working me in," I say. "I know it's not ideal timing."

"No problem," she says, letting us into the garage.

"Oh my gosh, this is adorable." They've turned it into a tailoring shop complete with a changing screen for clients, a three-way mirror, and a seating area with two armchairs, an accent table, and a minifridge with bottled water. Everything is decorated in a muted turquoise.

The work area is neatly stocked with all the tools a dressmaker could need, and two sparkling quinceañera dresses hang on a rack near the worktable.

A short woman in her fifties with graying hair, thick glasses, and a measuring tape around her neck smiles at us.

"You are Micah's friend?" she asks with a light Spanish accent.

"I am. I'm Kaitlyn and this is Aleina, who I'm going to make sit down and have some water right this second."

Aleina has politely declined to let me carry the garment bag both times I've offered, but something about the shop has set her at ease, and she hands it to Isa.

"Aleina, do you know the expression MVP? Most valuable player?" I ask as she settles into an armchair.

"Of course. Mirajul Islam is our MVP in our Premiere League."

"You're our MVP for coming here straight from the airport."

Aleina smiles. "No one tell Mirajul Islam."

"Soccer?" Mrs. Perez asks, her expression brightening.

"Yes."

"Then we have much to talk about," she says, grinning, which makes Aleina laugh. "Isa, get out the dress and see what we're working with."

"The red one, please," Aleina tells her.

As Isa opens the garment bag, I explain the situation with Maheen and how we've ended up here with Aleina and three dresses.

"I'm going to be very honest with you, Mrs. Perez," I say.

"Lidia is fine."

I nod. "Miss Lidia, Micah spoke highly of you, but Micah isn't in the garment industry. We are. We desperately need this work done, but it has to be done right. I'm hoping you're as good as the woman who usually does our couture alterations. Aleina is here to protect Maheen's vision. There will be Facetime calls and too many cooks in the kitchen. This is an audition. I'm sorry to make you prove yourself, but . . ."

Miss Lidia looks at her daughter. "What do you think, Isa? Can we do this?"

Isa winks.

Miss Lidia turns back to us. "I could tell you not to worry, but I'll show you instead."

I spot a flash of crimson, and then Isa turns, holding my gown against her. Everyone's eyes are on me as I study it for several seconds. There is no beading, no lace work, no frills. The color is the shade of the silk marigolds we're decorating with.

I turn to Aleina, who watches me without expression.

"It's breathtaking," I say.

She smiles. "Maheen said you would see what most can't when looking at it on a hanger."

"Change and let's see what we're working with," Miss Lidia says.

I take it behind the screen and slip into it quickly. I wore a strapless bra, and as I step into the dress and slide it up, I already know Maheen has made a dress to die for from the way it feels on my body. I step back into my heels and emerge from behind the screen.

Isa gasps and Miss Lidia smiles.

Aleina only says, "Yes."

I move to the three-way mirror and take my own deep breath. Maheen is a genius. The dress drapes from my left shoulder, leaving that arm bare, to curve around my waist and flow to the floor as it wraps behind me to my left hip. It creates almost an overdress effect, with the top draping piece opening all the way to my hip to show the column of red gown beneath it. It is both highly structured and incredibly fluid, sewn from fine crepe, the draping so effortless that only a master could do it.

Lidia attaches a pin cushion to her wrist and looks at Aleina, pointing to a spot under my bust and near my right hip.

Aleina smiles, her first truly relaxed smile since we've met. "Yes, that's right."

After an hour of gentle nudges and pinning by Isa and Miss Lidia, I hold my arms out and examine the results. "Should we call Maheen?"

Aleina shakes her head. "No, she will be happy. But I will send her a picture."

I pose so she can snap it, then Miss Lidia holds out a hand to help me down from the stool.

"Thank you," I say. "Your eye is impeccable. Until we know how Maheen's travel status resolves, it would mean the world if we could keep you on retainer. I'll pay you for this fitting, then bring in my mother and sister to meet you on Friday. I'll model my dress for them, and with Aleina and Maheen's approval, they'll be very relieved to know that you can handle their fittings too."

Isa and her mom exchange glances. "We're charging you a premium for working this in," Isa says.

"That's just good business." I smile and look around the shop. "You're incredibly talented. Have you ever wanted to open in a commercial space, maybe hire additional seamstresses?"

"Commercial leases are too expensive," Miss Lidia says. "I like working out of my home."

"And you?" I ask Isa. "You're very talented too. Are you considering fashion school?"

She blushes. "No, it's too expensive. I'm taking classes at the community college right now, but I learn everything from my mom or watching YouTube tutorials."

Miss Lidia pats her daughter's back. "She designed her own formals."

"Mom . . ."

Aleina stifles a yawn, and I hand Miss Lidia a credit card. "Thank you again for working us in. I need to get Aleina to her Airbnb so she can rest."

"Do you have Thanksgiving plans tomorrow?" Miss Lidia asks Aleina.

Aleina shakes her head. "This is a big holiday here, correct?"

I would have invited her to join our Thanksgiving, but while they have improved over the last few years, they're not what I would call "fun." We'd planned to give Maheen and Aleina a cellphone and an unlimited Lyft budget, plus a list of places they might like to go, using the long weekend to rest or explore before diving into work on Monday.

"It is," Miss Lidia says. "Come join ours. There is so much food, so much loud family—"

"—and kids. Way too many kids. *Primos*. Cousins," Isa explains. "Five hundred, it feels like. But also tamales. My mom's are the best. Please come."

Aleina laughs. "This sounds very much like Eid-ul-Fitr. If it's not any trouble . . ."

"You must come," Miss Lidia says with such finality that I find myself nodding too.

"I'll get it all arranged for you," I tell Aleina. "But for now, I promise we'll get you some sleep after I make one more quick stop."

Aleina has no objection to leaving the dresses with Lidia, which is the surest sign I could ask for that we've placed them in the right hands.

I drive two streets over, and when I spot Micah's truck in his driveway, I breathe out a sigh of relief. After everything going wrong, maybe the tide of bad luck is turning. Aleina assures me she is content to wait in the car, away from the unfriendly nip in the late November air.

I knock, once again needing to dry my sweaty palms on my slacks.

Micah's mom answers the door and frowns, but I think it's surprise, not displeasure. I hope.

"Hi, Ms. Croft."

"Tori," she says. "You here for Micah?"

"Both of you, actually." This is a risk. Maybe I should have checked with Micah to see if this would be okay, but I hope he takes this as a sign that I'm fine with his mom. Fine enough to subject her to mine.

"Micah," she calls, stepping to the side. I'm not sure it's an invitation, so I stay where I am.

He appears from a hallway and stops, surprised. "Katie. Hey. Everything okay?"

"I wondered if you and Tori would want to come over for Thanksgiving tomorrow."

He hesitates, exchanging looks with his mom, but I can only see her profile, so I can't read the look.

"At your place?" he asks.

"My parents' place," I say. "You'll know at least half of us. Madison, Oliver, and Harper will be there." I smile at Tori. "Harper's my niece. She's two months old."

"We do a neighborhood thing," Tori says.

I can't tell if it's a yes or no. "My mom does a formal spread, and we eat at 6:00."

Tori rolls her eyes. "My parents did that too. Rest of Texas eats at 2:00 so we're done in time for the Cowboys game. Where do your parents live?"

"Waterfront."

She scoffs. "No, thanks. I'll take card tables and Dixie plates in the yard right here, thank you."

I steel myself against the embarrassment rejection always brings, but she's not done.

"You should go," she tells Micah. "I'll be fine."

He looks from her to me and back again, his forehead wrinkling. "You sure?"

"Yeah. You'll have plenty of time to say hey to the neighbors before you go, and I'll watch the game with Cindy." When he still hesitates, she sighs. "Truly, kid. Going might set me off, but staying here, I'll be fine." She turns back to me. "Thank you for the invitation though."

"You're welcome," I tell her. "Micah, I could really use a wingman tomorrow."

His eyes soften and he nods. "I'll be there."

As I walk back to the car, I smile. He'll be there. Of course he'll be there. It's Micah.

And Micah always shows up.

Chapter Thirty

Kaitlyn

We decide Micah should meet me at my house, and when he rings the doorbell, I open it wearing a tight smile and Lela Rose silk pants in a hand-painted floral motif with a cashmere sweater. The colors are muted mauves and creams, tasteful for a family dinner. A semiformal family dinner.

I nearly swallow my tongue when I see Micah. He's in a three-button brown suede blazer over charcoal slacks and a thin forest green sweater.

"You look good," I say. He looks *perfect*.

"Can't embarrass my client," he tells me. "Who's driving?"

I reach for my purse and pull out my keys. "Can you handle the Audi?"

He grins. "Grandson of the Croft racing empire? I'll be fine."

He greets Daisy with scritches before I lead him to the garage and hit the automatic opener. He holds my door for me, settles into the driver's seat, and starts the engine. A slow smile curls over his mouth as he feels the purr and thrum.

I get it. Usually, starting the engine sends the same vibrations up my legs and back, but this time Micah's smile does.

He backs out smoothly, and once we're on the road toward my parents' place, he glances over at me, his expression serious.

"Wingman," he says. "That means you're telling them about the auction?"

"I am."

"You nervous?"

I pluck at my pants, trying to make the crease . . . creasier. "I have a plan, and I'm trying to be optimistic. I *am* optimistic." But it sounds more like a question.

"What's my role here? Bodyguard energy? Snoop Dogg at the Olympics hype?"

"You play gifted architect and honored dinner guest, and if my dad tries to intimidate you, give him that blank look like you already forgot he's talking."

"I don't do that," he says with a trace of amusement.

"It was your defining look in high school."

"Gifted architect, huh?"

I smile. "I'm not telling you anything new."

He shrugs. "Nice to hear it. Now, how do you turn the radio on? Majic 95.5 is already doing Christmas songs."

"Come on. At least wait until tomorrow."

"Driver's rules. Radio, Katie."

I groan but put it on, and we spend the rest of the drive with him humming along softly while I tell him about who he'll meet at dinner and what to expect.

My parents live in a gated community because of course they do. The guard lets us in and we drive another mile to get to their street. Their house is . . . ridiculous, honestly. It's fifteen thousand square feet, and it was too much space even when all four of us lived here. Madison and Oliver's car is already in the driveway, and I'm glad the six-car garage is closed. Micah doesn't need to know they have a Bentley, a Rolls, and matching Mercedes.

Micah parks and makes no comment about any of it.

"Here we go," I say. I lead him into the house and follow the sound of conversation to the living room.

"Katie!" Madison cries as I walk in. "And Micah!"

After Dad has handed Micah a drink and introductions have been made, Marta, my parents' long-time housekeeper, comes in and tells Mom, "Dinner is served."

We all rise and trail after my parents to the formal dining table set with gleaming crystal and china. We take our places with Micah between me and Madison, and then Marta and her grown daughter begin serving, setting fully plated Thanksgiving meals in front of each of us. Dad offers a Thanksgiving toast, and the feasting begins.

"Who cooks all this?" Micah asks after trying the turkey.

"Mom has it catered. It's good," I say. "Maybe not neighborhood potluck good."

"Nothing ever is," he says. "This is a different kind of delicious. Thanks for inviting me."

Inevitably, Madison asks how the gala plans are going.

"I'd like to hear too," Mom says, ears perking up across the table.

"The venue looks incredible," I say. "To be expected when you have the most talented architect in town. Madison chose well."

"Tell us about your work, Micah," Mom says, the consummate hostess. "What drew you to architecture?"

I breathe a sigh of relief as the conversation moves on. I'll tackle the auction when everyone is in a post-feast stupor.

Eventually, pie is served, plates are cleared, and Harper begins to fuss in her carrier strapped to Oliver's chest, signaling it's time for everyone to move.

Back we go into the living room for after-dinner drinks, and as everyone settles onto furniture and a lull falls over the room, Micah shoots me a curious look.

I clear my throat. "If I could have your attention, please."

All heads turn to me. Madison's eyes dart between me and Micah.

"I told you that Micah has done a brilliant job with the art installation, proving Madison's idea was genius. The venue will have everyone talking in the best way. But we do have a problem."

Madison straightens. "What problem?"

"The auction," I say. "Donations are far below what we had hoped. I've done everything I know how to do, started asking some questions, and found the problem, and I may have the solution."

"What do you mean donations are far below?" Mom asks. "Have you tried—"

"Mom," I say, holding up my hand. "Very probably yes. I will explain why they've been hard to get and how I think we'll fix that, but I'm going to ask you to trust me for one more day. I'd like to *show* rather than tell you."

I stand, feeling like I need the extra authority. "Let me explain what we have first." I list off the auction items, and they nod at each of them. It's not until I hit the end of the short list that concern crosses their faces.

"That's it?" Mom asks.

"Yes."

"Care to explain this 'problem' you're talking about?" Dad asks. His tone has an edge that warns he's about to lose his temper. That won't mean yelling. It will mean cutting sarcasm and get worse from there.

I knew this would happen, and I draw a deep breath, prepping myself not to retreat.

"No, Dad." That's all Madison says.

Oliver is standing beside her, gently bouncing Harper, but he stops and rests his hand on Madison's shoulder, squaring his own and settling a level stare at my dad. At the same time, Micah slides to the edge of the sofa cushion and perches beside me. He crosses his arms, fixing my dad with the exact same look. It's a warning. *Don't.*

The silence is growing tense, and I should break it, but I can't. For the first time since the auction shortage turned critical, I want to cry. But they're tears of gratitude. Three people are stepping up—not to protect me but to *back* me.

While I try to level out my sudden weepiness, Mom clears her throat.

"Regardless of why this happened, I was just thinking about Margaret Lim. She owns that antiques shop in New Orleans," she says, "and she mentioned this fabulous wall paneling she brought straight over from a castle in France. Well, not straight over. Some Hollywood producer brought it over for his mansion in the 1930s, just lifted it straight off that castle wall and put it in his study, I believe. Anyway, Margaret bought it at his estate sale about three years ago, but she can't get any nibbles on it. Everyone wants to do tacky farmhouse or Swedish college student."

"Why are we talking about Margaret's panels?" I ask patiently.

"Because I can think of at least three showoffs who would try to outbid each other in an effort to buy some class if you presented those panels right, and I do believe Margaret will let us take them off her hands for cost at this point."

Oliver rounds his eyes. "Castle walls, Katie-Kat. We need them."

"You hush, Oliver," Mom says. "You know you have some fancy Oklahoma horse people who would love slapping them up in their house."

"No, ma'am," he says. "You're thinking Virginia horse people," which makes my dad chuckle.

I can't believe my parents are taking this so well, but Madison isn't finding anything about this funny. Faint stress lines show around her eyes. "Why is this the first time we're hearing about this?"

"Because I thought it would kill me to see the look you have on your face right now," I tell her. "I was terrified of letting you down until Micah pointed out that not telling you was worse."

"He's right," she says. "I needed to know. Who have you approached, what did you ask for, and why did they say no?"

I go to her, kneeling down and resting my hands on her knees. "Madi, do you believe that up to this point, I have done everything I can and given it the best I have?" It's the scariest question of all.

She leans over and hugs my head, which is very Madi, but gently, not full of exuberance, which isn't Madi at all. "Of course I believe that. I love you."

I believe her, but I also know she still thinks I missed something, thinks she would have found a way to fill the auction already. She believes this, but she's hugging me and loving me anyway. This is how it is now. I can practically feel her shifting this burden to herself, taking it from me without withdrawing an ounce of her support.

But this is not how it will go.

"Love you too. Let me up," I tell her. "I'm not done yet."

She straightens, stress still showing around her eyes even though she smiles at me.

I squeeze her knees. "The second I accepted that I had to tell you, the universe did its thing and the answers started coming. I'm asking you to trust me a little longer. Can you do that?"

"Yes." She shifts in her chair, like she's fighting to keep some words in, but Madison being Madison, they burst out anyway. "But am I allowed to ask how long?"

I grin and stand, going back to my spot beside Micah to address everyone. "I know it's going to be hard, but I'm going to ask you all to resist calling your friends to start asking for donations. *Especially* you, Mom. I want you and Madison to meet me at the warehouse tomorrow at 10:00, and I'll show you how we're going to turn things around. Will you promise not to call in any favors before that?"

"Yes, but Margaret—"

"Please, Mom."

She looks troubled, but she nods. "No calls until I hear your plan."

"Madison," I say, meeting her eyes. "I've thought it through and put the pieces in place, and I'm ready to show you. Will you promise to consider it long and hard before you react?"

"I promise," she says. No hesitation, and it eases the clenched feeling I've carried around in my chest since Drake's words truly sunk in. "But I can't promise I'll stay on the sidelines after tomorrow."

"Understood." I shoot Oliver a glance as he nestles Harper against his chest and sways. "Sorry, Oliver."

He smiles. "It's fine. It wouldn't be the worst thing for her to have a little less free time."

"Does she keep making projects for you?" I ask.

Madison glares at him. "What? You have to agree that the downstairs bathroom needed a glow up."

Oliver clears his throat and smiles at me, saying nothing.

"Tomorrow at 10:00?" I repeat. Madison and Mom both confirm. "Good. Then I have a few things to work on tonight, so I'm going to rescue Micah here from all your nosiness, and I'll see you in the morning."

Micah stands and Dad sets his drink down to walk us out.

"Don't worry about it, Dad. We'll see ourselves out." We wave and leave.

"You did great," Micah says when the front door is closed behind us. "You didn't even need me there."

"Maybe not, but I wanted you there."

He draws me into a hug, and we stand there for a long time. I'm not even thinking anything, just drawing calm from his warmth and the quiet.

"How are you feeling?" he asks after a while.

"Okay," I say, stepping back. "Like actually okay." I hold out my hands for my keys. "I stuck with water all night, so I'm driving. And controlling the radio."

He rolls his eyes but hands them over. When I start the car and "It's the Most Wonderful Time of the Year" plays from the speakers, I leave it, and I don't miss Micah's smile.

Chapter Thirty-One

Kaitlyn

I'M ALREADY WAITING BY my car when my mom pulls into the warehouse.

She climbs out of her Mercedes. "Good morning, cagey youngest child. I want to see inside."

She gives me a hug. It's the kind of polite social hug we give friends and acquaintances, short and light, but I do know she means it.

"Not yet," I say. "I have something else to show you first. Look, there's Madison."

My sister pulls in with her silver Cayenne. I gesture for her to roll down the window. "Stay in the car. Mom and I will join you. We're going on a field trip."

Mom raises her eyebrows. "As if this warehouse weren't field trip enough."

"Mom," I say, a note of warning.

She sighs. "All right. Shotgun. That's how you call it, right? For the front seat?"

"Yes, Mom," I say, grinning. It's such an out-of-character thing for her to say. And when I settle into the backseat beside Harper, I grin again. "Ha, I win."

Mom glances back and scowls. "Ohhh, you."

"We're going about a mile down the road, Madison. Take a left out of the parking lot. We're headed to Montopolis, girls."

"That's certainly a change of scenery," Mom says. Madison and I both ignore her judgy tone.

A few minutes later, we're parking in front of Lidia Perez's house. "Here's the other part I didn't tell you yesterday. Maheen Sultana has a visa issue and didn't make it here with the dresses."

"We need to call Doug—"

"He's already working on it, Madi. In the meantime, her assistant Aleina made it without a problem. When I tried to book with Vania for a fitting, I was informed there was no way for us to get in."

"Did you talk to—"

"Yes, Mom. The owner said our gala has them tied up. But I'd heard about Lidia through Micah, and she agreed to work me in on short notice. Aleina and I came over Wednesday and did a fitting. Aleina supervised, and she's pleased. She feels Maheen would be comfortable with Lidia's skills. Now I want you to see for yourselves. If Maheen's documents don't clear in time, we will still have beautiful gowns. Are you ready?"

"I suppose," Mom says in a tone that couldn't be more doubtful.

Madison rubs her forehead like she's fighting off a headache. "Let's go see."

A few minutes later, Mom and Madison are settled in the armchairs with Harper sleeping in her baby seat at Madi's feet. Aleina, it turns out, has been adopted since Thanksgiving and informed she will be staying in the Perez guest room until Maheen is in town, so she's in the shop to supervise as well. I slip around the screen to put on the waiting dress, and when I walk out, Madison gasps and Mom's eyebrows go up.

I step up on the stool in front of the three-way mirror, and I'm even more taken with the dress now that it's tucked and pinned for the perfect fit.

"It's incredible," Madi breathes.

"You're a goddess," Mom declares. "Maheen is a genius."

Aleina inclines her head in appreciation. "She will be pleased to hear you feel this way. Mrs. Perez is very talented too. She understands the fabric and the body."

Mom gets up to inspect more closely, eyeing the pin placement, rounding me slowly. "It's excellent work."

Miss Lidia nods, a courteous smile on her face, but the verdict doesn't surprise her.

"Would you like to see your gowns?" I ask.

"Yes," Madison cries, and it startles Harper into a squeak. "Oh, sorry, baby, Mama has you. Let's see Grandma's first." But as Madison loosens the straps on Harper's carrier, Isa appears and crouches beside the baby seat.

"I'll handle it," Isa says. "Enjoy the dresses. I have two thousand baby cousins."

Madison looks at me for reassurance.

"I don't know. Wednesday, she told us five hundred."

Aleina smiles. "After meeting them yesterday, I believe today's count is correct."

Madison gives Isa a nod, and they both turn their attention to Aleina, who goes to the garment bag and pulls out Mom's dress.

Mom gasps and Madi and I ooh as she brings it to us, holding it up for us to examine. It's plain black crepe in a gentle trumpet silhouette, sleeveless with a boat neckline. Instead of sleeves, a sheer black floor-length cape is attached at the shoulders, dripping with sequins and beading that spill down, gradually becoming sparser as they near the floor.

"Beautiful," Mom says. "It may need minor adjustments, but the size looks right. This is a good silhouette for me. Tell Maheen it's lovely."

"Nailed it. Me next," Madison says.

Aleina fetches the final dress. When she turns and walks toward us, our jaws drop. It is a fuchsia cloud, hard to take in all at once beyond the hundreds of layers of tulle. I don't have a sense of the shape or anything else because of the sheer volume of intense pink.

"It will require some fluffing," Aleina says, causing Madison's eyes to widen. "I had to twist this and bring it in a vacuum-shrink tube?" She says this as if she isn't sure her explanation is making sense. We both nod. "This is what Maheen is most interested in. Your feelings about it."

"I'll be honest," Madison says, her eyes sparkling, "I'm not entirely sure what I'm looking at, but I love it anyway. Can I try it on?"

"You may need some help with this one," Aleina says, "if you do not mind if I assist?"

"Come on, friend. Let's do this," Madison says.

She disappears behind the screen while Mom and I entertain Harper. A few minutes later, Madison steps out and Isa squeals then claps her hand over her mouth, but she only said what we're all feeling.

It's what the dress deserves. Madison hurries to the stool in front of the three-way mirror, turns one way then the other, and grins. "Nailed it again."

"Not in a million years would I have thought I would like this, but it's perfect, honey," Mom says.

"I agree. Perfection," I say.

The dress falls to her knees in the front and to the floor in the back. It's made of so many layers of tulle that it's opaque, but the netting is so light that it floats around her in tiers. The haltered bodice plunges nearly to Madison's navel, showing off her nursing-maximized cleavage to advantage by emphasizing her shape, but the only skin showing is the one-inch strip all the way down until the skirt begins.

"Maheen wanted to give you something generous that would adjust to any figure concerns you had after recovering from birth, but—"

"Your body is rocking," Isa pronounces.

"Thank you," Madison says. "I'm told it's a first-baby thing, and I might get away with it one more time, but luck runs out on baby three."

"Amen," Miss Lidia says with a smile.

"The tulle is meant to hide"—Aleina gestures toward her lower abdomen—"and we can close the plunge higher if you prefer."

"No!" five other women say at once.

Madison starts laughing. "It's very loose, but beyond that, I don't want to change a thing."

Maheen designed for each of us so differently and so brilliantly. "Maheen may be your greatest discovery ever, Madison."

"And I believe Miss Lidia may be yours," Madison says.

"I'll second that," Mom adds.

"This one is going to take a few fittings," Aleina says. "If at all possible, Maheen would like to handle this one herself. If not, she is very confident to let Mrs. Perez do it."

"Well, you've solved the missing designer problem perfectly," Madison says. She steps down from the stool to stand in front of me. "It makes me even more curious to hear what you're planning for the auction."

"Then get changed, slacker," I tell her. "You're holding up the next part of the field trip."

My phone vibrates as we're walking to Madison's car.

> Why do I see your car at the warehouse but not you?

> We'll be there soon.

"We're going to drive around a couple of blocks," I tell Madison when we're settled in the car. "I want to show you some things."

And for the next fifteen minutes, I take them on a tour of the homes where all the talented people Micah knows live, making Madison idle in front of different houses as I lean between their seats to show them pictures on my phone of what the occupant of the house makes. Mrs. Horne's weaving. Jeremy's furniture. They gasp out loud when I show them Mr. Nairz's cookies.

When we reach the storage units by the neighborhood exit, I have Madison park so we can talk.

"That was a cool field trip," she says, "but tell me what this has to do with the auction."

"Let me tell y'all what Drake Braverman told me about why they won't donate," I begin. "They aren't connected enough to our goals. I asked him point-blank what it would take for them to open their wallets, and he said they're more invested in local causes, things that strengthen the communities here. I thought about how Micah pieced together knowledge and resources from people in this neighborhood to get where he is now. But it was meeting Isa and Lidia that made it all click. I'm going to send you both a proposal. Look it over really quick."

When their phones buzz, they each open the document and scan the information.

"Those are the bullet points," I say, "but I spent all day yesterday before dinner running the numbers, and I can back them up with a comprehensive breakdown."

Madison looks up. "You want to turn the warehouse into a community center?"

"Basically," I say. "It would be for teenagers and adults to use as a makerspace. They'd have free access to equipment and materials. Someone like Isa could explore design without having to save up to buy fabric that's too expensive to take a risk on. She could play and create and find her voice without the price tag hanging over everything. There are so many Micahs and Isas right here." I wave out toward the neighborhood. "This wouldn't be job training like we're doing in Dhaka. This would be about nurturing talent that can't afford to develop after the bills are paid."

Mom scans the numbers again. "You think if Madison announces this as a new part of the Threadwork mission, we'll get more donations?"

"I do. We won't have a lot of time. It will take all of us asking everyone we know. It's a huge new commitment for Threadwork. But—"

"But it's good," Madison says. "Not just because of the donations. This makes sense, Kaitlyn. It feels right for Threadwork."

"Yeah?" So many intense feelings are trying to bust out of me that it's the only thing I can say. Relief that she sees it. Pride that I thought of it. Excitement about this new possibility.

"I've spent so much time looking backward at the wrongs Dad did—"

"You know he's been trying to fix them," Mom says, always quick to defend him.

"I know. He's doing better. But my point is that I've spent so long looking backward at one place and one problem. I love the idea of providing an opportunity for people to be creative when they wouldn't otherwise have the resources."

She twists more fully in her seat to meet my eyes. "You're confident on your projections?"

"Yes. This will work, and"—I take a deep breath here—"I'll need to tell Dad this, but . . . I'd like to stay at Threadwork full-time as an inside director when you're back from maternity. However you need me, but I have ideas. Director of impact and strategy?"

Madison frowns, and I rush to convince her, because I want it *so* badly. "I'll do whatever I need to, but you're going to need another full-time big picture thinker."

"But director?" she asks.

"Coordinator? The title doesn't matter as much as the work."

She shakes her head. "I'm thinking vice president. Vice president of vision? We'll spitball."

"So yes?"

"Yes!"

I throw myself at the back of her seat, wrapping it and her in a hug that makes her laugh and choke at the same time. "I promise to run with this makerspace. It won't be your problem at all."

She unhooks my stranglehold, still smiling. "I'm the last person you need to convince that you're the woman for the job."

"And you're okay with folding this initiative into the gala's fundraising goals?"

"It's brilliant at every level," she says. "Let's do this. Mom? What do you think?"

I turn to her, bracing for her verdict. Sometimes I think Mom is more of an Armstrong than any of us even though she married in. "Mom, I know you—"

"Just a minute, Kaitlyn." She presses the backs of her hands to her cheeks, and I wonder if we're about to be subjected to one of her sudden-onset illnesses. Then she settles them in her lap. "This will definitely make it easier to secure some excellent donations. I'll start making calls today, starting with Margaret and the castle panels."

Madison and I both wait for her to address the bigger issue. The second of the Armstrong heirs is choosing not to join the family business. This has been my biggest worry. I don't want to let my parents down again, but I've had a series of lightbulb moments over the last several days, and this is the second brightest: I want to help build what Madison is growing, not become another piston in the powerful Armstrong machine.

Mom takes a deep breath and sighs. "I'm disappointed. Your father will be disappointed. But not in *you*, Kaitlyn. Disappointed about letting go of the future we imagined."

I want her to say that it's fine, this is a noble thing I'm choosing, and they're cheering me on. But I wouldn't believe her if she did. I wish that she was the kind of mother who would be all in on anything I decide to do, but getting hung up on the fact that she isn't would doom me to constant disappointment. She gave me what she's capable of, and it's enough right now.

Not for Madison, apparently. She gives Mom a warning stare. "We will dig into *that* later. Right now, we deal with the auction." She looks at me again. "If I start making calls today to schedule a board vote for a makerspace on Monday, will you be ready?"

"Yes. I'll have a comprehensive proposal. This center can be a reality in less than a year." Madison and I know our board well. If we have the numbers, they'll say yes.

Harper makes a couple of nursing noises from her baby seat next to me and gives a small grunt.

"She wants to eat," Madison says.

"Drive back to the warehouse," I tell her. "You can nurse her there."

Madison takes us back to the warehouse while Harper fusses. "Micah's here," she notes, spotting his truck.

I ignore the cajoling note in her tone that says *tell us what's going on there.* "Good timing. He can show you the changes himself."

We park, Madison gets Harper out, and I lead the three most important women in my life to the door. "I'd ask if you're ready for this, but there's no way you can prepare." Then I open the door.

Christmas music spills out. Madison and Mom step in.

And they gasp.

Chapter Thirty-Two
Micah

WHEN I SPOT KAITLYN and the others, I'm working down near the stage. I stop the music and make my way over.

Mrs. Armstrong doesn't notice me, but even though her voice is faint as her eyes travel over the rebar, I hear her say, "I had no idea."

Madison is silent as she stares up at the canopy of massive marigolds. Her face wears the wonder I felt when I saw the Basìlica de la Sagrada Famìlia in Barcelona on an architecture tour my senior year of college.

I've seen people look pleased or charmed by things I've designed, but I've never seen someone look like this, and I'm fiercely proud again that Madison chose my proposal.

"This is incredible," Mrs. Armstrong says, trying to look everywhere at once. "I know I'm in a warehouse. Concrete floors. Windowless walls. Hideous lighting. But it feels like . . ."

Kaitlyn smiles as I reach them. "You've left my mom speechless."

I stay quiet so her mom and Madison have their experience in silence. And it *is* silence. I have no crew in here today. I came in on my own to work on a side project.

Kaitlyn squints at the unfinished project on the other side of the warehouse, a wire cage partially filled with Styrofoam packing peanuts. Her eyes come back to me and the bits of white fluff sticking all over my gray thermal and black jeans.

She looks at me longer than she needs to in order to figure out what the white stuff is. Her eyes trace my shoulders and thighs like I'm letting these clothes live their best life.

When she catches herself staring, she darts a look back to my project. "Micah, are you building a snowman?"

"Yes."

"Are you supposed to have today off?" she asks.

"Yes. And I'm spending it building a snowman."

Harper lets out an angry wail.

"She needs to eat," Madison says.

I point to the supervisor's loft and the table and folding chair beside the door at the same time. "You can sit either of these places or one of the front offices if you want."

"Here and now is always better," she says as Mrs. Armstrong takes the baby.

Madison settles into the chair and begins to unbutton her blouse. Mrs. Armstrong hurries to stand in front of her and gives me a polite smile. "She's going to nurse."

"It's a working mammary, Mom," Madison says, "not the nuclear codes. Micah will be fine."

"This is one of those generational things, so you'll have to humor me," Mrs. Armstrong says.

I know I'm supposed to be on Madison's side here, but I'm still not used to my friends' wives nursing wherever and whenever. Kaitlyn glances at me to see how I'm taking this, and whatever she sees on my face makes her bite back a smile and take pity on me.

"Micah, why don't you give us an update?"

I nod and turn, conveniently placing Madison and Harper behind me as Mrs. Armstrong hands off her squalling grandchild. There's a baby grunt followed by smacking sounds.

"Go ahead, Micah. I'm listening," Madison says.

"Right. So, the entrance will be through there." I point to the closed bay door to our right. "Guests will leave the step-and-repeat, go up the stairs for another photo op, then descend the grand staircase on this side." I point to the unfinished stairs. "They'll look more impressive in a month. Then guests enter the installation . . ."

I continue pointing to different elements, showing them where the dinner tables and stage will be, the lighting rig, and other practical considerations.

"Could I walk through it?" Mrs. Armstrong asks when I finish.

"Of course." I lead her farther into the steel canopy, answering questions.

When she thinks we're out of earshot, Madison asks Katie, "What's going on with you and Micah?"

Kaitlyn's voice is lower, but I'm too focused on her answer to miss it. "We figured out how to work together."

"Right. I've never invited a coworker to family Thanksgiving. Neither have you. In fact, you've never invited anyone to Thanksgiving. So talk."

If Mrs. Armstrong can make out what they're saying, she gives no indication, and I take a few hurried steps over to point at one of the welded joints of a leaf to explain how the welders did it.

Mrs. Armstrong has several questions and twice that many opinions as we move through the canopy, stopping often to touch something and say, "My goodness."

When we reach the edge where the canopy curls outward to accommodate the stage, she turns to study the whole thing.

"Madison wouldn't listen to me when I tried to make her see reason about holding this at the Four Seasons or Austin Proper, and I'm so very glad. It's stunning."

"Thank you," I say, knowing she probably doesn't pay compliments lightly.

"You're a talented young man."

"I appreciate that." I don't need to hear it from her to know it's true, but for Madison and Kaitlyn's sakes, I'm relieved that she's pleased.

"Let's go check with my girls. Madison may be ready to take Harper home."

I nod and give a polite *go ahead* gesture.

"—blown away," Madison is saying as we reach them. "I can't believe what you've done with it."

"That's all you and Micah," Kaitlyn says, smiling at me.

"You're the battlefield general making it happen," Madison says. "You don't get to downplay your work on my watch."

As we reach them, Madison pulls a burp cloth from her diaper bag and sets Harper on her knee, patting her back. Harper gives an enormous burp that makes me laugh. "How did that sound come out of her?"

"She's a marvel of engineering," Madison says, "just like this installation."

"You can't compare Micah's art to a baby burp," Kaitlyn scolds.

"I'm honored," I say, still grinning. Maybe guys never outgrow burps being funny.

"And I'm thrilled," Madison says. "This is beyond what I even dreamed. Thank you for taking this project."

"Thank you for choosing me to do it," I answer. *For so many reasons.*

"There's only one thing missing," Madison adds, scanning the warehouse.

Kaitlyn looks as surprised as I am to hear we've missed something, especially since we've added to her vision.

"There," Madison says, pointing at the wall opposite the bay door. "The Marigold Austin sign should go there."

I wrinkle my forehead. "The what?"

Madison doesn't answer, standing instead. "Harper has had enough to hold her over until I can nurse her properly in front of a *Selling Sunset* marathon. See you Monday," she tells Kaitlyn. Then with a wink at her mom, she hands Mrs. Armstrong the diaper bag. "We have some big-ticket phone calls to make." They disappear through the exit, leaving Kaitlyn and me alone.

"Did she say Marigold Austin?" I ask.

"She did. It was your idea," she says.

"Pretty sure I never said those two words together."

"Maybe you had an assist from Drake Braverman."

"Now I'm really confused."

She tilts her head and smiles. "Come on. Let's build a snowman and I'll tell you about it."

A half hour later, the snowman is headless, and I am speechless. I stand in front of Frosty, listening, while Kaitlyn leans her arms on the snowman's empty wire head—we ran out of packing peanuts—and finishes her explanation.

"And that is how, between you introducing me to the talent in your neighborhood and Drake explaining what it would take for them to donate, Marigold Austin happened."

My own head feels empty as I try to wrap my mind around what she's explaining. "This is a done deal?"

"I'll need to pull a proposal together by Monday afternoon for a board meeting, but they'll go for it."

I run my hands through my hair, staring at this magical woman. "I'm blown away."

"I have something else to tell you."

"Not sure I can absorb anymore but hit me."

She grimaces and straightens. Wipes her hands down the front of her dark tan velvet pants. Clears her throat. "I'm . . . ready."

"You're ready?" Did I forget something we're supposed to do?

"For us. I'm ready." Her eyes meet mine.

I go still for a second as I read her expression, her blue eyes shiny with hope, her teeth gnawing at her bottom lip like she's expecting another rejection.

"You're ready for us," I repeat. My heart rate kicks up.

She nods. "The next month is going to be wild handling the final details for this gala, and I've suddenly given myself the massive job of creating Marigold Austin. There will be nothing normal about my schedule, but if you can find some of your legendary patience, I'd much rather balance all of that with you than balance any of it without you."

I was prepared to wait as long as it took for her to say these words, but I was afraid it would take months—at least until February and the bar exam—before she would say and mean them. But it's now. I smile as it sinks in. It's happening right now.

This seems to give her more courage. "It doesn't feel at all like balance without you, Micah."

"You're ready." I slide the snowman away with my foot. I glance from it to her. "There's nothing between us."

"Only literally?"

I cross my arms, knowing it accentuates my chest. This wonder of a woman deserves a reward, and when her eyes drop straight to my pecs, my smile stretches into a full grin. "In every sense. Just one question, Katie-Kat. What took you so long?"

We reach for each other, and I pull her so tightly against me that we may as well be welded. I duck to kiss her, no gentle hello this time. I've been starved for her, and she kisses me back as if she's been just as hungry for me.

Eventually, she pulls slightly away. I murmur an objection. "We have lost time to make up for."

"Yes. I don't know how much will be enough, but there's not a measurement I can think of that will cover it."

"Not time, not quantity, not intensity." I kiss her where commas would fall between each phrase.

She presses another full, soft kiss against my lips. "I agree. I only needed to catch my breath."

I brush a kiss against the corner of her mouth. "I prefer to take it away."

"You've been doing that since ninth grade."

I press my forehead against hers, almost disbelieving she's finally confessing. "Call it payback."

She leans back enough to look into my eyes. "This feels impossible."

"It feels inevitable," I counter.

"Impossible the way magic is impossible."

"Inevitable the way physics is inevitable."

"I beat you in physics," she reminds me, smiling.

"Then you should understand the inevitability even better than I do, Katie."

She smooths her thumbs over my lips, swollen from kissing her, and I pull her to me to double down.

"Words like that, the good work you're doing here"—she traces my mouth—"must always be rewarded. And who, after all, is more generous than the head of a nonprofit?" She pulls away only long enough to turn the Christmas music back on, and then she's in my arms, applying herself to rewarding me with her legendary diligence.

Truly.

Legendary.

Chapter Thirty-Three

Kaitlyn

MONDAY MORNING, I WALK into the office humming "Frosty, the Snowman," and Suz, who has never heard me hum, pauses in the process of booting up her computer.

"Good Thanksgiving?" she asks.

I stop in front of her desk. "Micah is my boyfriend now. Madison made me spill my guts on it all this weekend, and I swear, if you try to make me do the same thing, I will spend your Christmas bonus on cat toys for Daisy."

Suz grins. "*Almost* worth it." She mimes zipping her lips.

I set my things at my desk, but I'm out of the suite and in the elevator without stopping. I spent the weekend hanging out with Micah in his woodshop while he made ornaments out of polished tile, and I worked on the proposal for the board, luxuriating in my spreadsheets and running numbers.

Also, there were many kissing breaks.

I hit the button for the executive floor, smiling as I replay all those kisses. It's like neither of us can quite believe we got to this point. We can do this, explore every taste, touch, and sound. Micah makes really good sounds.

I'm checked out, thinking about them, when the elevator chime brings me back to reality. Dad's receptionist waves me into his office. I'm here to cross the final hurdle.

He looks up when I walk in, and I glance around, noting how little it has changed since the first time I came here when I was little. Dark wood and leather, and if the furniture has been replaced, it's with similar pieces. But there are new pictures of Harper Ivy Mae behind his desk, and I smile at the discovery that Dad is one of those grandfathers—grandpas—who wants everyone who enters his office to see his grandbaby.

"Kaitlyn," he says, as I take a seat.

"Did Mom tell you?" I ask.

He leans back, elbows on his armrests, fingers steepled. "I want to hear it from you."

"When Madison comes back from maternity leave, I want to stay at Threadwork."

"That's your prerogative." His tone is even. Detached.

"I know that. But Dad, I want your blessing."

He's a handsome man. Strong chin, dark hair turning silver at the temples. But the lines around his eyes don't look like laugh lines, and that strong chin looks more unyielding than rugged.

"Why?" he asks. "Withholding it won't change your mind."

"No," I admit. "But only because I know it so well now."

"You're really going to put aside three years of law school to run a charity?"

"Help run a charity," I say, "and no, of course not. I'll still take the bar. You know nonprofits have as much or more regulatory oversight than other companies. We won't need to hire outside counsel to keep us compliant."

"Or you could do that here, where your salary would make your law school classmates green."

"Dad, this is that thing you do that upsets Madison. Where you use money to control us instead of saying how you feel."

He drops his hands to the armrests and curls his fingers around them. "Why does my blessing matter?"

"Because I'll never forget the look on your face the last time I disappointed you. Salutatorian," I add when his eyebrows draw together like he's confused. His forehead smooths. "I've been chasing perfection ever since, always wanting to get everything right so you'll keep giving me those head nods."

"Head nods?" He looks mildly exasperated now.

"Yes. The ones that say 'good job' without words."

"You didn't seem worried about upsetting me when you started taking Madison's side on everything."

"Because Madison was right," I told him. "You know that. I would have chosen different methods, but she was right about the facts all along."

He says nothing. It's a massive concession.

"This isn't about Madison though. It's about me and you. It's about different ways of approaching past wrongs. I could keep us on track as the compliance officer. Or I can trust that you've changed and don't need your daughter watching you like a hawk. I can do this thing I've found a passion for. Move past atonement for past wrongs and into growth and change."

He's quiet for a long time, keeping eye contact with me. He's said before that it's an intimidation tactic he uses in business negotiations, so I stay still and resist the urge to defend or plead.

Finally, he sighs. "You have my blessing."

"Thank you. I also need you to give us the gala warehouse for Threadwork's expanded mission."

At last, a smile creases his face. "You're as bad as your sister."

I smile back. "Thank you. So we can have the warehouse?"

"You can have the warehouse. Get out of here and let me work."

He doesn't get up to hug me. I don't even think about rounding his desk to hug him. But his smile lingers as I walk out of the office, still there when I turn to wave at the office door. He answers with a shooing motion, but the smile stays.

When I get down to Threadwork, Suz settles the phone on its cradle and looks up as I walk in. "Your dad just called. He says salutatorian was about him, not you, and you've never disappointed him a day in his life." Her eyes are wide as she delivers this, given that most of her communication is with Dad's secretary, taking her terse orders or impatient requests.

I press my lips together because they want to tremble, and nobody has time for a weepy breakdown on board meeting day. I walk to my office, truly ready to write our new chapter this afternoon.

Chapter Thirty-Four

Kaitlyn

THE SECOND THE THREADWORK board votes unanimously to approve Marigold Austin, the madness begins. No phone is left unrung, no contact left uncontacted, and no friend or acquaintance considered too unconnected to hit up for ideas.

The donations pour in, and some come from the most surprising places. Sami offers up the opportunity to sing live with her and Pixie Luna the night of the gala, the winner getting to perform an Ella Fitzgerald classic with them. "Trust me," she says, "there's a frustrated singer out there who will cough up big bucks to take their shot in front of some of the industry execs in the crowd."

Madison's former boss, the owner of the nightclub where she worked, has a soft spot for her, and he and his wife offer to host a couple at their Norwegian fishing cottage, which happens to come with a view of the aurora borealis over the Norwegian Sea.

Micah hits up his uncle to donate a Formula One experience for the next American Grand Prix, with full access to the Croft team garage, drivers, and race engineers. Mom calls to complain about this one because Dad plans to bid on it, which means it's a much bigger deal than I grasped. Mom's objection is that it's "unbearably loud."

Mom's antiques friend comes through with the castle panels plus an offer to take a winning bidder on an antiques excursion through Spain. Mom says not to be too impressed. "She'll make a nice commission on whatever the winner buys on that trip."

We end up with a Patek Philippe watch donated by an actor from Austin who was recently named their spokesperson. A poker night with the UT head coaching staff. A round of golf with Jordan Spieth.

And then there is me. I go looking for redemption and the donation I most want to land: I convince Drake Braverman to take one more meeting with me.

This time we meet at the warehouse. I reintroduce him to Micah, let him take in the full impact of Micah's installation, and then I explain the vision for Marigold Austin.

When Drake leaves, he's committed to donating a Ford Mustang Shelby GT500, which I know—because I like cars—will be snapped up by a parent sending a kid to UT in the fall. Especially when we reveal that the leather interior of the white car is embossed with a gorgeous UT logo.

In the midst of it all, I spend every free second I have with Micah, and since there are few of those, I spend work time with him too. I use the supervisor loft as an office when he's onsite at the warehouse. Other times, we're at his woodshop while he works on a piece. He's made a nook for me, creating desk space and bringing in a chaise so I can curl up to study.

It's not enough to satisfy either of us, but we're both satisfied that we're spending all the time we can together. I know it won't always be this way, but it feels like it as we charge through the first half of December, trying to secure the additional donations we'll need to open Marigold Austin without dipping into the funds for the Marigold Dhaka expansion. Aisha is holding our print spot for the gala programs until the last possible minute, but the printer will need our final auction booklet by the sixteenth to complete it by New Year's.

Maheen's documents clear two weeks after Thanksgiving, and when she arrives in Austin, Aleina is so thoroughly enmeshed in the Perez household that she insists they can't complete the dresses without the help of Lidia and Isa. Maheen, after summoning me for a fitting, agrees. I wish I could be there for Mom and Madi's final fittings, but there's no time.

My biggest fear—that Madison will have to give up time with Harper—doesn't materialize. She promises she's found a good work/life balance, but it's not until I call Oliver to get a true read on the situation that I believe it.

"Trust me." He laughs. "We're all much happier when Madi has a few hours of work to keep her busy. It's the outlet she needed."

By the time we get to Micah's make-or-break date for the installation—a very inauspicious Friday the thirteenth—I'm not sure I have it in me to sprint to my own deadline for the auction items the following Monday. But there's also not a choice.

When Micah finishes at the warehouse on Friday afternoon, we stand together in the center of the installation and look around. Every last bit is in place for the event team to take over the following week, bringing in all the trimmings to make the space lush.

"You did it," I say, resting my head on his shoulder. Not only is it comfortable there, I'm almost too tired to hold it up on my own. "You're amazing."

He presses a kiss to my forehead. "Care to join me for a wild night of celebrating with some takeout in front of your TV?"

"Best offer I've had in weeks."

He winces. "I gotta step it up."

I pat his chest. "If only I had time to let you. We can breathe—"

"Next year," he says with me. It's our joke since the new year is just over two weeks away.

"Come on," he says. "I'll walk you out, change my clothes, and meet you at your place with something we can eat straight out of the container."

"You had me at food."

When Micah walks into my house a half hour after I get home, Daisy, who has already eaten and therefore feels magnanimous, decides to get up to her wicked flirting with my boyfriend, rubbing up against him and winding around his legs.

"She thinks you're her Gatsby," I say, eyeing the shameless Daisy Buchanan. "I think she's trying to shame me for my outfit." I'd changed into butter-soft yoga pants and a UT sweatshirt as soon as I got home.

"There isn't much I wouldn't do to earn her attention, I admit it," he says.

"I'll banish her if I'm not fed."

"You mean shut her in your room that's bigger than my house?"

"Yes."

"Then come eat, woman. And never apologize for yoga pants." He waggles his eyebrows.

"I like that you think my yoga pants are sexy, but please never waggle your eyebrows at me again. It's giving creepy old guy at the country club."

I can't be bothered to pull out a chair, so I climb atop the starling table, sit cross-legged, and dive into the pad thai he hands me.

"I thought we were going to eat on your sofa and let the TV rot our brains," he says.

"Not yet." I snap up a shrimp with my chopsticks. "Protein first. Then talk."

He joins me on the table and we eat in quiet. When the last shrimp is gone, I feel rested and fed enough to talk.

"So, architect boyfriend, you're done with the biggest part of your job." I say. "How does it feel?"

"Good," he says. "The firm will slow down now until after the New Year too, which is good because I need to be at Remix more."

"'Tis the season," I say.

"'Tis the season," he agrees. "But you don't get any kind of break at all. How are you holding up?"

"In the next two weeks, minus Christmas Day, I have meetings with the event planners, the caterers, the media company doing the hype videos for the auction items, the florist, photographer . . ." I trail off. "I can't even remember now without my planner."

"Madison owes you big-time."

"She so does."

"Do you think she would give you Harper?"

I consider this. "It's worth asking."

The ease of being in my own house with Micah has worked its magic on my tired body. "No studying tonight. We're going to watch a movie and not talk about work, unless it's to tell each other how amazing we are at our jobs."

"I back this plan."

"I was thinking we could watch a classic."

"*It's a Wonderful Life*?" he guesses.

I roll my eyes. "*Friday the 13th*, of course."

He sets his chopsticks down and gives me a look. "You can just say you want to make out, you know."

That is how he ends up with noodles in his hair.

We end up watching a *Happy Days* marathon instead. Micah wakes me up around midnight to tell me he's taking off before he's too tired to drive. I walk him to the door, extract a deep and bone-melting kiss as punishment for leaving, and don't even bother dragging myself upstairs to bed. I sleep on the sofa until Daisy sits on my chest at kibble o'clock. Her stomach tells perfect time.

Maybe it's the change of location to the sofa, but I wake up brimming with energy and an excellent idea.

> Play hooky at the store and come over here.

> Have to take care of a few things, but I could be there by lunch?

> Deal. But the second you come through the door, work doesn't exist. Or bar exams. Or galas.

> Deal

I set my phone down and jump up to put my plan into motion.

Chapter Thirty-Five
Micah

IT'S ALMOST 1:00 BEFORE I make it over to Kaitlyn's, but as I shut the door behind me, I call out, "I'm here, and nothing outside of this house exists."

"Kitchen," she calls back.

Elf starts playing as I pull off my coat in the entryway.

She smiles at my bright red sweater with snowflakes on the chest and jeans. "Don't go to Target. You'll get mobbed."

I pull her in for a kiss then let her go to glance at the TV. "Is this an elaborate setup so you can tell me to elf myself again?"

"It would be if I'd thought of it. Do you not like this movie?"

"Only broken people hate *Elf*." I rub my hands together. "It's freezing outside, by the way." It's in the low fifties, but in Austin, that's close enough.

"Poor baby." She slides her arms around me. "Does it make you feel any better to know we're going to be toasty inside while we're completely irresponsible today?"

"Weirdly, yes. It warms my heart."

Her eyes twinkle. "What do you get when you ask a valedictorian and salutatorian to relax?"

"I don't know. What?"

"A cutthroat cookie-decorating competition, duh."

"You, the lawyer, would like to compete against me, the visionary artist, in aesthetic feats? Bring it."

She turns on the oven and pulls a covered bowl from the fridge. "I could not talk Mr. Nairz out of his shortbread recipe, but he gave me this." She removes the foil with a flourish. "Dough for two dozen cookies!"

"No way. Seriously?" She must have made a good impression on Mr. Nairz.

"Picked it up this morning," she confirms.

"So we eat half the dough and bake half, right?"

"Obviously."

She sets shopping bags on the counter and pulls out more stuff. Baking sheets, cookie cutters, icing bags, and an apron she ties on. It's like one of those photo backdrops with a painted picture but you supply the head. This apron has a woman with Kardashian proportions in a sexy Mrs. Claus dress, but with Kaitlyn's grinning face above it.

I burst out laughing when I read the tattoo on "her" cleavage. "Top of the naughty list, huh? Promises, promises."

"Don't worry, you have one too."

I put on an apron announcing I have "resting Grinch face." I frown at her.

She sticks her tongue out at me. "It's funny because it's true."

For the next two hours, we roll out the dough, shape and bake our cookies, watch the part of *Elf* where Buddy exposes Santa as a fraud, take the barely burnt cookies out to cool while we mix our frosting, and then we get down to real business.

She had chosen a snowflake cookie cutter, saying it would be easy to fancy up with lines and dots "to make them elegant." I chose the square gift box cutout.

Now as she stares down at our results, her face says she realizes she miscalculated. Badly. She has six snowflakes that go from uneven glops and streaks on the first one to something that looks like it could have been done by a highly competent fifth grader by the last one. I have an artfully arranged stack of six brightly wrapped gifts in paper with intricate patterns.

She stares from mine to hers.

I shrug. "Mr. Nairz taught me some stuff."

She narrows her eyes. "It only matters what our objective judge, *my sister*, thinks."

I smirk while she snaps pictures and texts them to Madison.

Without knowing who did what, which cookies are better?

Harper cried when I showed her the snowflakes, so Micah wins.

"That was rigged," Kaitlyn complains.

I drop a kiss on her nose. "I still like you even though you suck at cookie decorating."

"Fine. I forgive you for being good at frosting."

I scoop her up and carry her over to the sofa to settle her on my lap. "Thank you for this whole day. What happens when you fail the bar exam because you didn't study today?"

She pinches my side. "It won't be funny if that happens."

"It won't happen."

She sighs. "I hope not. But now I have a confession."

I tug at the bib of her apron above her "cleavage." "I know this isn't your real body."

"A real confession."

Her voice is serious. I don't want to change the light mood, but I always want her to be able to talk to me. "All right. Hit me."

"I know Christmas is a big deal to you, but I'll be working like crazy right up until Christmas Day. I'm trying to cram all the Christmas in today because I won't have time." She drops her head against my chest. "I'm getting so tired of saying I won't have time."

"I know. Front-row seat, remember?" I smooth her hair, still not tired of being able to touch it whenever I want. I'll never be tired of it. "Are you going to be okay if all this work . . . doesn't work? What if something falls apart with the gala? Like no one comes or no one bids?"

She bolts upright. "Do you know something I don't?"

"No." I settle her back against my chest. "Everything will be amazing. But I'm wondering how you'll feel if it's not."

She's quiet for a beat. "It will be embarrassing. But I'm handling every detail that can be handled, and at some point, that's enough."

"What about how embarrassment is worse than death for you?"

"I never said that."

I smile against her hair. "I know you."

She runs her finger over the snowflakes knit across my chest. "The last two weeks have taught me that the only way to get kicked out of my family is cheering for anyone besides Texas. This whole gala could fail, and I guess they'll still keep me. Madison ambushed me at the office the other day and did amateur therapy again. Something about how I'm worthy of love?"

I tighten my hold. "You are." Is this it? Is this when I put into words what I've been feeling since Thanksgiving? No, *recognizing* since Thanksgiving. I've been feeling this for longer than that.

Love. *Say it.* Because this can't just be me.

I open my mouth. "Thank you, Kaitlyn." Not the three words I meant to say. But I don't want to send her running scared again by dropping the other three big words on her too soon. "I love that you did this. The dough. The Christmas movie. It's the most thoughtful thing anyone has ever done for me."

"Except for Mr. Martinez and the bike in the rain."

"Second most thoughtful thing anyone has ever done for me," I amend. "Thank you for making time you didn't have. But I am responsible for my own Christmas spirit, and now I'm taking responsibility for your Christmas spirit. Leave it to me, okay? I would never let it get lost in the shuffle."

"Micah . . . I don't want to butt into things that aren't my business, but I also want everything about you to be my business. So your mom . . . will she be okay with the holidays? They're intense for anyone. If you need to be around for her more, I support that."

"She's okay." I love that she cares this much. I wish I had a sign that would tell me when she's ready to hear how deep my feelings run. "Christmas season kind of stabilizes her, believe it or not. That's when she does the most business, and it's good for her. The last day she can ship an order and have it arrive by Christmas is the twentieth. Then she crashes. It's not usually a depressive episode. More like unwinding?"

She nuzzles against my chest. "I'm glad. What's Christmas usually like for you?"

"Low-key. We go to my uncle's on Christmas Eve, which isn't our favorite. But it's fine. My aunt says, 'Tori, how's your little Etsy shop doing?' My mom says something like, 'Almost good enough to afford fillers like yours,' and we eat and exchange gifts and there's awkwardness but no drama."

"Team Tori," Kaitlyn says, "even if she kind of hates me."

"She doesn't hate you. She's embarrassed because you met her on a bad day, but she was okay when you came over to invite us to Thanksgiving."

"True," she says. "But she still avoids me."

Mom doesn't come out of her bedroom where she makes her peg dolls if she knows Kaitlyn is over. "She's asked about you a few times. I go at her pace. Does that bother you?"

"No. I want her to be comfortable with me." She tilts her head up to press a kiss where she can reach, which is under my chin. "Now, you were saying you're going to elf yourself?"

"No, I said I would be in charge of Christmas spirit. Think of it as being your Christmas concierge. That's a rich person thing, right? Using concierges for everything?"

"Totally. I have seven on speed dial." She gives an enormous yawn that she tries and fails completely to keep behind her hand. "The last three weeks are hitting me all at once. Can you take over starting now?"

I shift her to the side, pull the throw blanket off the sofa behind us, and tuck it around her. Then I pick up the remote. "On it. We begin with Hallmark. Today's movie is called *Christmasland*."

"You know that without looking?"

I don't answer.

She tucks her feet under my thigh and wiggles her toes. "You're a zombie movie expert and a Hallmark Christmas movie expert?"

"Let's go with enthusiast."

"Micah? Do you have the whole movie lineup memorized?"

"Only for the seventeen that looked interesting," I grumble.

And even though it takes her a full five minutes to stop laughing, we do finally watch it.

Chapter Thirty-Six

Kaitlyn

FOR THE NEXT TEN days, Micah makes sure each one has Christmas in it. One day it's walking into the office to find an enormous poinsettia threatening the health and well-being of our waiting area furniture. On another day, he shows up at my house with a twelve-foot Douglas fir tied to his truck and proceeds to decorate it while I study on the sofa. He covers it in white lights and hangs it with his handmade ornaments. I've never loved a Christmas tree more.

Mostly, Micah focuses on small things. Making peppermint hot cocoa for us to sip while we're in his workshop one night. Bringing Daisy Buchanan a felt mouse wearing a Santa hat.

Work *never* stops, but it's mostly management. Signing off on a proof of the auction guide. Requesting changes to the video the media company produced.

My hardest job is figuring out what to get Micah for Christmas when I have no time to shop.

When I once again find myself wishing for more time in a day—time to enjoy a full lunch hour, time to plan structured dates with Micah—I realize I know the perfect gift.

He comes over Christmas morning. Christmas Eve was the big event with his mom, Christmas night is the big deal for the Armstrongs. We're going to spend the whole day together until I leave for my parents' place at 5:00.

I've told him I'm in charge of our Christmas since he's had to do all the rest of the work. When he walks in at 9:00 AM dressed in a Christmas sweater as requested, I have a breakfast of stuffed French toast, bacon, and sweet potato hash waiting, along with pomegranate mimosas garnished with sugared cranberries and rosemary.

He grabs his heart. "I have not been a good enough boy to have earned this."

I jump into his arms and kiss him. "Are you kidding? Not only do you deserve this, we should probably give you the Mustang from the auction as a bonus."

"I accept."

"Even if it's just breakfast, no Mustang?"

"Especially because it's *your* breakfast."

We sit across from each other at the starling table, the amber flecks looking festive with the red and gold place settings I chose. He gives his report from Christmas Eve at his uncle's house, and I smile the whole time, even at the parts that aren't funny.

"Are you laughing at me?" he asks, half smiling back as he finishes his story.

"No. I'm ... happy." Getting to spend all day with him, that's the gift.

"Remember you said that when you're enduring it next year," he teases.

My heart gives an extra thump like it does anytime he says things like that. Like mentioning us and next Christmas together in the same sentence.

I didn't think I was someone who needs to hear "I love you." It was nice when my last boyfriend said it. I even said it back. But I *crave* it from Micah.

This is so very, very different.

When breakfast is done, we clear the table and wash our plates, and I smile again at how much I enjoy doing simple things with him.

"What do we do now?" he asks as he dries the last plate. "Watch some football?"

"You want to watch football on Christmas?"

"Those men are giving up time with their families. The least we can do is honor that."

"Are you being serious?"

"Nope."

I pop him with the dish towel, a skill I didn't even know I had. "You're about to go on the naughty list. I guess we aren't doing presents next."

He grabs the dish towel and wraps it behind my back, pulling me in. "Yes to the naughty list." He gives me a kiss that tastes like French toast and pomegranate. "But also yes to presents, please."

I kiss him back. "Or maybe this for the rest of the day."

He drops the dish towel and boosts me up on the counter. "Definitely yes to this."

Eventually, we get to the gifts. I'm beard burned and my lips are swollen, but it's a new tradition we're definitely keeping.

I sit in front of the Christmas tree and Micah settles across from me, two wrapped gifts beside him. Daisy Buchanan makes her appearance, arriving out of nowhere like a Christmas ninja as she pounces into the cradle of Micah's crisscrossed legs.

"Merry Christmas, Daisy," he says. "Maybe we should do your present first?"

She flicks her tail.

"She'll allow it," I interpret for Micah.

"All right, Mrs. Buchanan. I got you this." He unwraps the smaller gift to reveal a cat collar bejeweled with rhinestones, art deco style.

I'm the one who purrs. "Flawless."

"Should I put it on her?" he asks.

"Not if you want to keep your hands."

"I'll let you do it when she's in the mood."

"My turn." I reach for his gift under the tree, sure he can figure out by looking that it's a watch box.

He unwraps it, his eyes widening when he opens it to reveal a classic TAG Heuer, a steel three-hand style with a black face. "This is really nice."

"It's an entry-level watch if that makes you feel better," I say. "It's not expensive enough that you have to call it a timepiece. I chose one they described as 'virtually indestructible' so you can wear it to jobsites if you want. Not that you have to. Actually, this isn't even—"

He leans over to kiss me. "I love it. I know we haven't talked about money, but—"

"We don't need to," I tell him. "Not today. We can discuss whether my millionaire status is weird for you some other time."

He laughs. "Fair enough."

"That's not even the gift," I tell him. "I wanted you to have something to unwrap, but it's more of a symbol."

He pretends to think. "Time is running out? Kill time? A stitch in—"

"It's the present." When he cocks his head, waiting, I explain, "Your present is the present. As in I'm going to be more present."

"Babe, I—" He stops, and we both break out laughing.

"Babe?" I gasp on a giggle.

"That sounded weird, didn't it?"

"Yes, but no one has ever called me babe, and I like it. Keep going."

"Babe"—he pauses for more giggling—"you don't have to make up for how busy you are. You're doing good things. It's one of the things I . . ."

I hold my breath.

"That I admire about you."

Oh, cool.

I take the box from him and slide the watch off. "I'm not apologizing. I know you get it. But I've been thinking more about what I want. What makes me happy. It's changing a few priorities for me next year."

"Oh, yeah?" The lines around his eyes doing their pre-smile activation. "Tell me more."

"The bar exam, for example. I'll still take it in February, but I'm cutting way back on the studying. If I don't pass, I'll try again in July."

"Katie-Kat, you want to spend more time with me?"

"You're not the worst." I squeak as he hauls me into his lap.

"I accept," he says, pressing a kiss against my neck. "We *are* building a relationship. Which brings us to your gift."

He picks it up and sets it in my lap. It's about the size of a Kleenex box, and it's light.

I untie the ribbon and pull off the wrapping paper to reveal a Christmas corsage with red and white roses and gold-edged ribbon. It's very pretty but also confusing. Before I can figure out what to say or possibly ask, Micah is lifting it out of its plastic box.

"I never got to ask you to prom," he says, lifting my wrist to gently slide the corsage over it. "But I have this incredible event next week, and I wondered if you'll be my date to the Threadwork Discovery Gala on New Year's Eve."

I slip out of his lap so I can kneel in front of him and look him in the eye. "Yes."

"Yes to the gala at which I don't expect you to wear this corsage?" he asks, smiling.

I reach out to cup his face, running my thumb over his cheekbone, loving the way the lights on the tree reflect in his brown eyes, giving them a Christmas gold warmth.

"Yes to this." I lean in to kiss him. "This and everything."

Chapter Thirty-Seven

Kaitlyn

I EXIT THE LIMO, allowing my gown to settle around me before I step onto the red carpet leading into the entrance tunnel. Mom and Madison are in the car right behind mine. I press my hand to my stomach to calm my nerves.

It's time.

I'd left the warehouse midafternoon after ensuring everything was set up and ready. Micah had been with me all day, jumping in where needed with everyone from the event planner to the sound guys. But I left to meet Madison at my parents' house to get ready, and Micah went home. He should be waiting for me at the end of this tunnel.

I force myself to take even breaths as I walk through the soft lighting of the tunnel, passing stunning floral arrangements representing the countries of the designers being featured tonight.

I see Micah before he sees me, and my breath catches at the sight of him in formal wear. He's gone with black on black, a single-button suit with long satin lapels over a black band collar shirt. A razor thin line of jet-black beads runs down the placket of the shirt. Coupled with the black-and-gray snakeskin Copperhead boots he's chosen for the evening, there is not a man in the entire state who has this much swag. He's gorgeous and wearing his modern tux as comfortably as he does his joggers.

When he spots me, he freezes.

I step from the tunnel and stand still so he can get the full effect, and he smiles, but his eyes stay intense. Hungry.

"Wow," Madison breathes softly behind me. "Look at him. Look at him looking at you."

I ignore her as Micah and I walk toward each other. He holds out his arm for me to slip my hand through.

"You look incredible," he says. "So beautiful."

"Thank you." I enjoyed consulting with Maheen this summer over color and design. It pleased me to know that I was a credit to her work, but tonight, I'm wearing this for an audience of one. "You're the most handsome man here."

"So far, I'm the only man here."

I give him a small headshake. "It won't change when the rest of them come."

He brushes a soft kiss against my hairline. "Let's go show them how it's done."

The event staff direct us along the red carpet to the step-and-repeat, where we pose several times against the Threadwork backdrop for the pool of photographers. Because the gowns will be from rising designers, several fashion sites have sent correspondents, and some entertainment sites are covering the celebrities on the list.

Where the backdrop ends, the staircase begins, the red carpet rising along the wide-but-shallow steps painted with black lacquer. An event staffer politely holds Micah back and cues me to pause on the fifth step so the photographers can get a shot of my gown's back. Micah is released to escort me the rest of the way.

The stairs crest in a landing bisected by the open bay door, which has been utterly transformed with flowers. The arches spill over with the thousands of red silk marigolds it took a crew of six people three full days to attach. It's extravagant. Transformative. Nearly worthy of the masterpiece it leads to.

Another staffer sends me to pose on the top step for a photographer waiting inside, and Micah escorts me down the grandest part of the staircase. It widens with each step, curving backward at the edges, exactly the staircase a princess would descend in a castle.

We've arrived early so we can greet the other guests, and we move for Madison and Oliver to make their entrance. Madison reaches the bottom of the stairs and rushes over to throw her arms around me, nearly drowning me in fuchsia tulle. "Nobody ever had a better sister!"

"Then you won't have a problem with the job title I've chosen when you come back from maternity leave."

"Anything you want."

"Goddess Divine of Threadwork."

"Done. I'll order the nameplate."

We greet my parents, who come down next, Mom looking regal. Madison's best friends follow in quick succession with their husbands, each looking awestruck by the marigold canopy.

Micah and I go with Sami to check out the stage for Pixie Luna's acoustic set. She nods in satisfaction. "Sounded good at the sound check earlier."

She turns to study the rest of the space. Tall, elegant table centerpieces rest on slim columns, flowers spilling from a crystal vase on top. Gabriela Juarez's glass vases flank the stage. Silk gauze hangs from different points in the sculpture, lit under Micah's direction to create even more visual interest.

"This will be the swankiest gig Pixie Luna has ever played," Sami says, hugging me. "You did so good, Katie-Kat."

"Whoa," Micah says, and I turn to see Sara Elizabeth coming down the stairs in a silver gown, catching and refracting every light aimed at her.

"Pretty cool, huh?" I say.

"I knew she was coming, but it's wild seeing a celebrity in person."

A few minutes after the official event starts, our first guests appear at the top of the stairs, looking delighted by their entrance experience then stunned by the venue. They come at one- to two-minute intervals after that, the space quickly filling. The waiters begin passing hors d'oeuvres, and when a tray of deviled eggs reaches us, I discover the filling has been piped in the shape of marigolds. I take one and smile, mentally increasing the caterer's bonus.

I expected to be in high demand because of currently running Threadwork, and I am. All the Armstrongs are. But it's not long before Micah is drawing more attention than anyone, so many of the jaded millionaires and business barons wanting to meet the architect behind the art installation that has surprised them for the first time in a long time.

When the tables have filled—and the wineglasses too—the deejay fades out the music and announces the host for the evening, bringing up Sara Elizabeth. I exchange a smile with Madi at the next table, because she knows what I know when she hears the thunderous applause: we are going to *smash* our goals.

Sara Elizabeth welcomes everyone, thanks them for their time, and introduces a short video about the work the organization has done in Bangladesh. It's followed by supportive applause, but when it dies down, she announces, "Ladies and gentlemen, this will be an evening full of surprises, and we've reached our first one. Threadwork is thrilled to announce the Marigold Austin Initiative!"

The next video plays, overviewing the plans for this space in the new year, and ends to even more enthusiastic applause, and I smile. Funny that Micah and Drake, two ends of the spectrum, are the reason we found our way to Marigold Austin.

"If you'll direct your attention to the right of the stage," Sara Elizabeth is saying, "you'll notice that like the overcrowded tourist trap called Times Square, we have our New Year's ball. Except it's gorgeous. And as you drink more and spend more throughout the evening"—the audience laughs—"your generous donations will be tallied. It will drop at midnight, but how far depends on whether we meet our goal. If we reach it, that ball will drop all the way down, and we'll ring in the New Year right!" More applause. "Now please enjoy your dinner and be prepared for more entertainment and surprises throughout the evening."

She leaves the stage, the servers bring in plates of spicy sweet bruschetta, and the volume of conversation and laughter rises against the instrumental jazz the deejay keeps low in the background.

Sara Elizabeth takes the stage after the salads are served. "Ladies and gentlemen, we thought we'd make the wait for the incredible roasted duck entree coming your way a little easier by providing you with some dinner music. Fresh from certifying their first platinum album, please welcome Austin's own Pixie Luna!"

Sami and the band take the stage and play their five-song set, four of their own songs plus a haunting cover of Tom Petty's "Wildflowers." They finish to thunderous applause and take several bows, before Sami gestures for quiet.

"Y'all, you probably saw in your programs that someone will have the opportunity to bid for a chance to perform an old holiday classic with me. Well, that time has come!" she says to whoops and whistles. "I hope y'all have been practicing, because we have, and we're ready for you! The bidding starts at ten thousand dollars. Do I hear ten thousand?"

"Wait, wait, wait," says another female voice over the PA system.

Sami blinks, confused, and looks behind her, but the guys in her band look confused too.

"That auction guide said the buy-now price is fifty thousand dollars," the voice continues, "so I'm going to double it to make sure I win."

Micah looks at me, and I look over to Madison, who does not look confused. She looks smug.

A strangled squeak comes from Sami, who is watching someone approach from the perimeter of the tables, and a spotlight lands on the woman.

"Is that . . ." Micah squints. "That's Brandi Carlile."

My mouth drops open. That is Sami's absolute idol. "Oh no."

"Is that bad?" Micah asks.

"Sami is never going to make it through this song," I say. "She's going to die."

Sami is, in fact, standing there looking like a deer in the headlights as Brandi Carlile climbs the few stairs to the stage. She holds out her hand, and says, "Hey, I'm Brandi Carlile, and I'm a huge fan. It's nice to meet you."

When Sami still stands there, staring, saying nothing, Brandi leans over to pick Sami's hand up from her side and shake it.

This finally gets through to Sami, who yells, "Madison Armstrong Locke!" and bursts into tears.

Madison, of course, looks unfazed. Sami's husband is sitting next to Oliver, and both of them look suspiciously unsurprised.

The crowd is going wild, which is saying something for so many middle-aged guests in evening wear, but they are completely won over that a star as big as Sami is starstruck by one of her own heroes.

When Sami pulls herself together, she and Brandi Carlile do a blues-rock version of "What Are You Doing New Year's Eve?" that has couples up and dancing in the spacious aisles between the tables. And when Brandi asks Sami if she wouldn't mind doing Pixie Luna's biggest hit together, I think the guys in the band might pass out too. But they do it and bring everyone to their feet at the end.

The whole night goes like that. One of the highlights is when the designers who accepted our invitation to the gala take the stage and the women go wild. The men might have been quieter on that one, knowing how much the gowns cost them.

The bidding on the auction items is fierce, and I laugh outright when Mom breathes a sigh of relief as Dad loses the bid for the Formula One experience.

Micah says, "When should I tell him I can get him VIP access anyway?"

"Let him suffer for a day or two," I say. "He gets his way too much."

The Gabriela Juarez chandelier commission goes for fifty thousand more than I'd projected, and the Mustang GT500 goes for double its cost when the video reveals the UT interior.

By the time dessert has been served and removed, I am a borderline quivering mess. Intensely overcome with the generosity of the bids, yes. But also focused on the surprise I've been most nervous about this evening. I'm the only one who knows about it, and Micah is the only one who's going to hear about it.

Sara Elizabeth invites everyone to stand and either make use of the dance floor or the conversation nooks that have quietly appeared at the perimeter of the room, and the lounge Micah suggested has materialized around the bar at the back. Waiters kindly invite people at the center tables to find more comfortable seating, and the second a table empties, it disappears from the floor.

In two minutes flat, the vibe of the space has changed again. The lights lower and take on a blue tinge, the deejay switches to dance music and turns it up, and everyone who is young enough, fun enough, or maybe drunk enough switches into club mode.

Madison grabs my forearms and says, "We did it." She leans over to murmur close to my ear so I can hear her above the pulsing bass of the music. "We're at 2.3 million right now."

I, who am not a squealer, squeal while Madison grins. She loops her arm through mine. "It's time to shake our moneymakers because they have clearly done the job."

I boo her stupid joke but she hauls me out to the floor, where I, who am not a dancer, dance. And we laugh, all the worry that has gone into the gala gone, because Madison and I know. We know. We did it. We're ready to let that joy carry us through the last fifteen minutes of this year that is ending so beautifully, into the new year that will start better than any year of my life.

I throw my arms around Micah, and I know the cheesiest smile is beaming out of my face, but I don't care. He laughs, lifting me up to spin me, giving me a kiss as he lowers me, keeping me close.

When the opening notes of Prince's "1999" start playing, the deejay breaks in long enough to announce, "This is the last song before our countdown, so get those donations in to make sure Threadwork can keep changing lives!"

Micah rests his forehead against mine. "It's almost the new year. That's wild. Any New Year's resolutions?"

"One."

"Are you sharing it?"

"You first," I say. "Did you make any?"

"One," he says.

The music fades out, and a spotlight finds Sara Elizabeth on the stage. The screen behind her lights up with a thirty-second clock. "It's time, ladies and gentleman. In a few seconds, we'll begin the countdown to the New Year and find out if your incredible generosity has helped us reach our goal. The ball will start moving at the ten-second mark, and if it makes it all the way down when the countdown is done, we've done it! Is everyone ready?"

There are cheers and shouts from all over the floor.

I turn back to Micah, my eyes meeting his. He holds my gaze, his eyes steady and bright.

"Ten, nine, eight," Sara Elizabeth says, and the crowd picks up the chant.

I take a deep breath.

"Seven, six, five . . ."

I force myself not to squeeze my eyes shut. *Go in with your eyes wide open.*

" . . . four, three, two, one! Happy New Year!" she and everyone else shouts.

Except me. And Micah. Instead, at the exact same time, we each yell, "I love you!"

Then we yell, "I said it first!"

Micah hauls me against him to deliver a kiss I feel all the way to the soles of my feet and in the depth of my soul.

"Katie-Kate-Kaitlyn?" he says, his hands framing my face. "I think we have to call it a tie."

I press a deliriously happy kiss against his lips.

"No, Micah Croft. I think it means we both win."

Epilogue
Micah

You can't be an innocent bystander when you love an Armstrong sister.

If I had ever thought my future involvement with the Threadwork Gala would end with designing a massive rebar marigold art installation, I was re-educated within a week of last year's event. Kaitlyn and Madison took all of five days to recover before the subject of this year's gala had come up over brunch at Madison and Oliver's house. Before I could finish my omelet, I'd been sketching out an idea on a paper towel.

Now we're sitting beneath the fulfillment of that vision on New Year's Eve in yet another venue that the guests can't stop talking about. We have a stunning view of the Blanton Museum of Art—from the top level of the parking garage next to it.

"You and Madison did amazing work," I say quietly by Kaitlyn's ear. I don't want to disrupt the guests listening to the Vitamin String Quartet performing live as we enjoy our soup and salad course.

This year's theme is Glass Ceiling, inspired by Gabriela Juarez's work as a way to talk about the limits women hit in the garment industry in nations where textile manufacturing is a major economic driver.

Kaitlyn's eyes dance as she turns to brush a kiss against my cheek. "Only because we hire the best people."

I designed the plans for this temporary event space, and for the last three weeks, construction crews have been in a mad rush to finish this "top tier" build, the concrete now transformed by temporary flooring and walls, and above all . . .

Above all, an incredible ceiling glints and glows, an abstract sea of glass ribbons, interwoven without ever tangling as they spread in gentle, patternless curves over the event space. Gabriela made the opaque glass tubes in shades from ecru to blush pink, drawing her inspiration from a vintage baby shower invitation she found in a box of old postcards and stationery at a thrift store.

I keep catching guests looking up at it, lost in awe.

Kaitlyn shimmers with happiness. Or is it thousands of glass beads? All the women shimmer with them, their beaded gowns catching and refracting light. Kaitlyn worked with Maheen again, and this dress is the blue of Kaitlyn's eyes, designed and sewn by Maheen, fitted by Lidia Perez, beadwork done over the course of three months by Isa.

The quartet finishes its performance to loud applause, and this year's emcee, Gina Smith- Harden, Austin native but America's morning show sweetheart, takes the stage again. She's already presented a short film overviewing the achievements of Marigold Dhaka and Austin, and she's back to introduce the next performer.

"Arturo Ramirez is a rising star, a young man with an old soul who croons like the greats. Tonight, he'll perform an American standard made popular by Frank Sinatra. But listen closely for a clue to our surprise auction item. Ladies and gentleman, please welcome Arturo Ramirez to perform 'Fly Me to the Moon.'"

Madison, seated at the next table, twists to give Kaitlyn a look that says What are you up to?

Kaitlyn grins at her sister and claps as the singer takes the stage. "Wait until you see what I got for the auction. Madison will never believe it."

"You got a juicy donation and didn't tell me about it?" I ask. Looks like two of us are plotting surprises tonight.

She only grins and turns her attention to the stage as the music plays, and sure enough, Arturo begins singing in a baritone that immediately earns whoops from the audience. He's the heir to the Sinatra/Connick/Bublé crown.

He gets more enthusiastic applause when he finishes. When it dies down, he smiles and says, "Thank you. And now it's my honor to introduce a hero and scholar, astronaut Monique Johnson!"

A tall, slender woman takes the stage, her dark skin stunning against her sparkling white dress. Madison has now turned all the way around, kneeling on her chair and mouthing something at Kaitlyn. I can't make out the words, but Kaitlyn smirks at Madison and nods at the stage.

"Ladies and gentlemen, on behalf of Moonshot" —a gasp from the audience, including me—"I'm here to announce the next item up for bid. You won't find it in your auction guide because our CEO, Michelle Lee, wanted to keep the element of surprise. Tonight, you will be able to bid on a trip to space."

Excited chatter breaks out among the gala guests as a media package plays about the next Moonshot rocket launch. When it finishes and the swelling orchestral music accompanying footage of the view from the last Moonshot mission concludes, the astronaut steps back to the microphone.

"I will tell you from personal experience, this prize is priceless. Good luck, ladies and gentlemen."

Gina Smith-Harden has returned to the stage, and she takes over. "Bidding begins at one million dollars. Do we have a bid for one million?"

A few seconds of low buzz sounds but no hands go up for the bid. Then a server approaches the stage to hand Gina a note. She accepts it, reads it, and smiles. "We have a buy-now offer for two million dollars. Can I get a ruling from our gala chair?"

Madison leaps to her feet and calls, "Yes! Heck, yes!"

The crowd erupts into laughter and applause, and I'm not sure how many of them hear Gina announce that the space trip now belongs to billionaire Rylan Hurley.

Madison races around our table, her gold gown capturing and throwing out brilliant light as she beelines for her sister. Kaitlyn is rising up to meet her, laughing as Madison sweeps her into a hug.

"We've already hit our goal," Madison says.

Kaitlyn nods, probably because Madison is squeezing her too tightly for her to speak, but Kaitlyn doesn't look like she minds one bit.

The rest of the evening goes well, and by the time the night has turned to dancing while we wait for the midnight countdown, they are nearly thirty percent over their fundraising goal. Every now and then, one of the sisters will call something like "Fashion school scholarships!" or "Culinary school in Dhaka!" and the other one will whoop.

I love watching their joy, but in a way, I'm watching it from a distance, more and more of my focus and energy turning toward my next big New Year's Eve move.

I stay on the dance floor with Kaitlyn, Madison, Oliver, and all their friends, but my heart beats harder with every minute we get closer to midnight. When the deejay announces the last song before the countdown, I edge Kaitlyn toward the back of the dance floor where the bar is, telling her I want a drink to toast her with.

The countdown starts, the ball drops, everyone cheers, and we welcome the New Year with a kiss that tastes like champagne and possibility.

I draw her outside of the temporary venue, away from the warmth of the heating lamps and dancing bodies. I've picked the side that overlooks the museum and Gabriela's glass bluebonnet garden.

"You okay?" Kaitlyn asks smiling.

"I'm great, actually." I clear my throat and shrug off my tuxedo jacket. It feels good outside, the air brisk in the mid-fifties, but Kaitlyn chills easily, so I drape it around her shoulders.

"Looking forward to another amazing year," she says. "Thread-work is killing it. We're going to be able to start working on our stretch goals eighteen months early after tonight!"

"Just Threadwork?" I say with a half smile. "Nothing else amazing to look forward to this year?"

She pushes up on tiptoe to press a warm kiss against my lips, her fingers sliding into my hair. "Always you."

"That's how I feel." I swallow hard. I'm not nervous. It's more like . . . I'm overcome? Overwhelmed? I have loved this woman in front of me for so much longer than the year we've been together, and I'm greedy for more. More Kaitlyn. More time. "This was the best year of my life. It doesn't seem like it can get any better, but I know it will, because it happens every time I'm with you. You want to hear a cool math formula?"

She wrinkles her nose and lowers herself from her tiptoes, but she lets her hand slide from the back of my neck down to my chest to rest it against my heart. "Tell me."

"You know what you get if you add enough days together?"

She tilts her head. "No. What do you get?"

"Forever."

Her eyes soften. "Still not long enough."

I slip my hand into my trouser pocket and pull out the small ring box that's been burning a hole in it since I got dressed for the gala. Her eyes widen as I bring it up between us, her free hand moving to cover her mouth. My jacket slips from her shoulders, but she doesn't notice as she looks from the box to me again.

"Micah?" Her voice quavers, hope dancing through it.

"I love you, Katie-Kat Kate Kaitlyn Armstrong. I have for a long time. You make me laugh. You make me think. You make me happy. You make me better."

The hand covering her mouth moves to rest beside the other one on my chest, and she gives me a wobbly smile, her eyes shining up at me. "Jinx," she says.

"You didn't say that."

"Yes, I did. In my heart."

I grin down at this fierce, tender woman, and I'm not sure how my body can even contain my heart for how full it feels. "Kaitlyn

Armstrong, I want to string every day of the rest of our lives together until it becomes forever with you. Will you marry me?"

"Yes." She says it before I even get the last word out.

"You didn't even look at the ring," I say. I'd spent a lot of time working with a jeweler to design just the right one.

"It's perfect," she says, still not looking at it. Her eyes don't leave mine. "But it could be a bread twist, and I wouldn't care. I love you, Micah. How should we start forever?"

I open the ring box and take out the two-carat cushion cut diamond engagement ring I bought with the bonus I earned from designing Deborah Fisk's detached guest house this past spring. Kaitlyn can look at the ring whenever she wants, but I need it on her now, so I know this is happening.

She chose me. She is mine forever now, and I've already been hers at least that long.

I slide the ring on her finger, and she smiles at it, then back at me. I draw her in, drowning in her clear blue eyes.

"I think forever starts like this," I murmur, and I claim a kiss from my fiancée.

When she finally pulls away to draw a shaky breath, she presses her hand to my cheek and brushes her thumb across my lips. "If that's how forever starts, then I'm glad it never ends."

And once again, Kaitlyn Armstrong soon-to-be Croft gets the last word.

Author's Note

As someone who has a clinical diagnosis for a misunderstood disorder (OCD), I wanted to make sure that even though bipolar disorder isn't a key point in the story, it's still represented accurately. I read up about bipolar disorder in several peer-reviewed sources before I wrote Tori Croft's character. Originally, I specified that she has bipolar 1, a more severe form of the disorder, but I quickly discovered most people don't realize that there are three different types of bipolar disorder. I decided not to specify which type her character is living with in order to avoid confusing readers. When I finished my first draft, I asked several people with personal experience to read and give me feedback. These readers were partners or children of people with bipolar disorder or people who themselves live with it. I made adjustments to Tori's character and her dynamic with Micah based on the nuances these readers pointed out. But what I also learned after feedback from nearly a dozen readers' experiences is that bipolar disorder doesn't look the same from person to person. From the way each experiences their manic episodes to how well their disorder is managed by medication, there is no one way bipolar disorder manifests. It is marked by changes in mood, energy, and activity levels, but the specifics of how these changes look and feel vary among people living with it. If you would like to learn more about bipolar disorder, the National Institute of Mental Health (NIMH) website is a solid starting place.

Acknowledgements

I had to call in so much technical advice to tackle this story, and I owe many thanks to those advisors. First, to Sara B. Ajster, who met a near stranger at a cafe to talk architecture and whose particular interests in her field helped shape Micah's strengths. To Joe Tolley for his welding expertise and Holly Papa for her guidance in metalworking and general art knowledge. Thank you to the generous readers who talked to me about their experiences with bipolar disorder. Thank you to the donors who contributed to hurricane relief efforts in North Carolina and helped me name several important characters. Thank you to my writing group for their work in shaping the voice and structure in the early chapters and especially to Brittany Larsen for an early read that gave this couple better grounding. Thank you to the Zoom Crew for the writing sprints, especially RANÉE CLARK and Esther Hatch this time through. Thank you to my special researcher, Karie Crawford, for looking up the most random and seemingly unrelated things. Thank you to the Writer's Room for helping me to "punch up" some of these jokes. Thank you to my editor, Jeanna Stay, for keeping my pages tight. Thank you to my assistants, Cathy, James, Eden, and Hallie, who all handle details that free me up to write. I'm lucky. No thank you to Scooter, who is a mooch and constant distraction. But the biggest thank you of all to my family for their patience and support, followed closely by my gratitude to the community of readers and friends I've found through this writing journey.

About the author

Melanie Bennett Jacobson is an avid reader, amateur cook, and champion shopper. She lives in Southern California with her husband and children, a series of doomed houseplants, and a naughty miniature schnauzer. She holds a Masters in Writing for Children and Young Adults from the Vermont College of Fine Arts. She is a *USA Today* bestseller and a four-time Whitney Award winner for contemporary romance and the author of more than two dozen romantic comedies.

For a free book from the author, please visit
www.melaniejacobson.net